The Girl

a novel by
CATHERINE COOKSON

HEINEMANN : LONDON

William Heinemann Ltd
15 Queen Street, Mayfair, London W1X 8BE

LONDON MELBOURNE TORONTO
JOHANNESBURG AUCKLAND

27997 /
Holmes ⋁
£4.10
9.77

Printed and bound in Great Britain by
Morrison & Gibb Ltd, London and Edinburgh

Contents

❧❧

Author's Note

I must express my thanks to Mrs M. J. Wescott for passing on to me her grandfather's treasured book on Allendale and Whitfield which was written by George Dickinson Junior and published in 1884. Her grandfather was Doctor Arnison who, like his own father, practised in Allendale for many years. This little book has afforded me a wealth of information and inspired the idea for *The Girl*.

I have taken the liberty of using the name Arnison for the doctor in the story, but other names are fictitious, as are the personal events and the village of Elmholm.

PART ONE

❧⁓❧⁓

The Girl 1850

1

From the hills in the early dawn,
Small, thin, mist-wreathed, she came upon him;
Hair sodden to the brow,
Eyes like agates,
Lips apart, tongue flicking at words frozen in her head.
Gliding to his feet,
She caught his hand and said,
"Come help me, mister, or she'll be dead."

They had taken two days to cover the twenty-three miles from Newcastle to Hexham, keeping mostly to the grass verges or the fields that bordered the side of the road in case they should be knocked down by the coaches or the dray carts or, as was more likely, the travellers on horseback who came upon you quicker and without the warning of the coaches or the drays. As for herself, Hannah could have scooted from the road with the agility of a deer, but not her mother, for she, even before they left Newcastle, had been trailing her feet.

This morning they had risen from the stinking straw in a field barn before the sun was up and for the first four miles of their journey they had shivered. The can of boiling water begged from a cottager into which, at her mother's bidding, Hannah had put a handful of raw oatmeal, had helped to thaw them out. But now, having reached Hexham at three o'clock in the afternoon, they were hot, sweating, hungry and thirsty.

Hannah Boyle was quite used to large towns, she had been born in the packed bustling melée of Newcastle riverside, and whenever her mother had visitors and so would push her outside to play she had gone up into the city by herself and looked at the big buildings, and some of them were so big and so grand that they outdid in her imagination the stories told her by one or other of her mother's sailor friends who had seen wondrous places across the sea.

But this town was different. Although she was weary, she gazed about her with interest because she liked what she was seeing. The market square she dubbed in her mind a canny little place, and the shops bonny, and the streets tidy.

But her mother speaking brought her from her scrutiny. "Here, take this," she said, and, handing her two pennies, added, "Go . . . go over to that baker shop across there an' . . . an' see what you get most for it."

"Yes, Ma . . . You'll be all right?"

"Aye, I'll be all right. Go on."

As the child ran across the square Nancy Boyle leaned back against the wall that supported an archway, and she muttered to herself what might have sounded to an outsider like a prayer: "Christ!" she said, "let me make it."

When, of a sudden, she began to cough she brought a rag from her pocket and held it to her mouth; then presently spat into it, clenched the rag in her hand, returned it to her pocket, and once again rested against the wall; all the while her breathing coming in painful gasps.

As she now watched her eight-year-old daughter making her way towards her dodging between a trap, a gentleman on horse-back, and a dray cart, she endeavoured to hold her breath, and when the child reached her side she gazed down at her for a moment before she could say, "I've . . . I've a good mind to skelp your lug for you. I've told you about dodgin' atween carts, haven't I?"

"I'm all right, Ma."

"One of these days . . . you won't be all right when . . . when you're cut in half. . . . What did you get?"

"I asked her for stale bread an' look" – she opened the bag – "there's some cobs, six or more, two with sugar on, an' a big tea-cake. She was nice, the woman. . . . Will we eat them here?"

"No, no. . . . Oh, all right, take one, then let's find a horse trough an' get a drink."

As they walked from the square, Hannah, her mouth full of the last of the bun, asked, "How far is it now, Ma, to this place?"

"Some miles I think from what the woman at the cottage said."

"How many?"

"How do I know? Why the hell do you keep askin' such questions! Aw, I'm sorry. I'm sorry." The woman now shook her dirt-streaked face from side to side, and the child said quickly, "It's all right. It's all right, Ma." Then, as if her last question had not caused her mother to repulse her, she asked, "Will the man . . . will he be nice, Ma?"

"He'd better be." The words were scarcely audible.

They were walking down a street now with fine shops on either side and when they came opposite an inn where two draymen were unloading barrels into a cellar, the woman stopped and enquired of one of the men, "Could you tell me how far Elmholm is from here?"

The man straightened his back, looked her up and down, and then at the child by her side, before replying, "Elmholm? 'Tis some way beyond Allendale."

"Well, how far is that?"

"Oh, all of nine miles I'd say. But Elmholm's a bit further on, another couple of miles. But you might cut it short by going over the hills."

"Which way's that?"

"Well now, go along the road there for about four miles until you come to a little hamlet by the river, follow it along on the flat till you see the hills, then you've got a steep bit of a climb, but the hills 'll bring you down into Elmholm quicker than going Allendale way. There's plenty of tracks to follow an' once you get up there you'll see the hamlets below. You can't miss Elmholm, it's a tidy size."

"Ta, thanks." She nodded at the man, and the man nodded at her; then he watched them walking away, the skirts of both the mother and the daughter trailing the dust on the paving flags. He watched them until they had passed the end of the street and when his mate called to him, "Hie-up! there," he turned to him saying, "Asking the way to Elmholm, she was; I wouldn't like to waste a bet on her makin' it. No, I wouldn't that.". . .

5

How long it took them to walk the four miles and for how long they walked by the river they had no idea, but they were resting yet again when the drover came upon them. "Elmholm?" he said. "Oh well now, you're on the right track but it's time you left the river and took to the hills. Take that sheep track" – he pointed – "an' start climbing."

It was close on five o'clock before they reached the summit of what had appeared to them the last hill because they'd had to take so many rests; and now once again they were sitting down, and the child, standing before her mother, said anxiously as she pointed towards the valley, "Should I run on, Ma, and see if there's any place we could shelter, an' then I'll come back for you?"

"You . . . you stay where you are; I'll . . . I'll be all right in a minute. He said it was just beyond those hills. After this big one."

"But you're dead beat, Ma."

"Don't worry." There was an unusually gentle note in the woman's voice as she put out her hand and gripped her daughter's arm. "I've been worse than this'n I've survived. Only the good die young, they say" – she made an attempt at smiling – "so that leaves me out, don't it?"

Hannah didn't smile back at her mother, and her face was straight as she now reached out with both her arms, saying, "Come on then, Ma, get on your feet an' . . . an' hang on to me 'cos those hills there look steep."

The hills were steep. Nancy Boyle crawled on her hands and knees to the top of what again appeared to be the last of them, then she lay face downwards; and now she didn't attempt to bring the handkerchief to her mouth as the blood ran from it.

When she sat up Hannah wiped her mother's face with what looked like a ragged petticoat, which she had taken from out of the bundle she was carrying; then she said, "Lie still, Ma, 'cos we're nearly there. I can see houses and it'll be easier going now. . . . What's the name of the man, Ma?"

Nancy Boyle didn't answer, but she dragged herself to a sitting position, then hitched herself slowly to the side until her back was resting against a butt of rock.

"I can't go on for a while," she said; "we'll have to stay put until I get me breath."

6

"Aye, Ma. Yes, Ma. An' look; eat this bun with the sugar on. Sugar's good for you."

The woman took the proffered bun and broke a piece off it, which she put into her mouth and chewed on slowly; and when she had finished the bun and half the tea-cake, Hannah, who had hungrily consumed two dry cobs, said brightly, "You'll feel better now, Ma, with something in you."

"Aye . . . aye, I'll feel better soon, but I must sit for a bit."

And they sat for a bit. But it was a long bit, and all the while Hannah sat gazing at her mother. The fact that she was spitting blood did not alarm her unduly, her mother seemed to have always spat blood, well, for a long time, but what was alarming her now was the deepening pallor of her mother's skin and the way her eyes seemed to be sinking into the back of her head.

She shivered and looked up into the sky. The twilight was beginning, and although it would stretch out it would be dark within the next hour or so. They'd have to get down to those houses because she could see no place to shelter them here. It was a wild place; everywhere she looked appeared desolate and wild. Funnily wild, was how she put it to herself. The sky was so high, not like it was in Newcastle just above the roof tops. And there was too much space; everywhere was filled with space. She didn't like it, she wanted to be closed in, hugged around by walls.

She got on to her knees and knelt by her mother's side, saying softly, "Can you make it now, Ma?"

"What?" It was as if the woman were being dragged up out of a deep sleep, for she blinked her eyelids, looked about her, then said, "Oh aye. Oh aye."

They were only half-way down the first hill when they had to go on to their hands and knees and descend for some distance crabwise, and when they reached a kind of ledge that was pitted with boulders and bare of vegetation the woman once again sat her back against a rock, and after a while, her words coming singly on each gasp, she said, "How . . . much . . . further . . . does it look?"

Hannah turned her head from side to side, taking in the scene. Hills and hills. Nothing but hills. Those directly in front of her

7

rolling down into a valley appearing a slaty grey; others, a dull green; and those to each side of her were spreading away into that everlasting distance where they finally met the sky.

She was filled with a feeling of panic as in a bad dream. She felt she was alone and that there was no escaping from this place.

Swinging around, she gazed down on her mother; then dropping to her side, she caught at her hand and, gripping it tightly, brought it to her chest and held it there.

"What is it? What's the matter?" Nancy Boyle was roused from her lethargy. "What did you see? . . . What did you see down there?"

"Nothing, Ma, nothing."

"What d'you mean, nothing?"

"Well, the village must be there, I saw it from the top, but it's still some way down yet."

"Well . . . it . . . won't get any shorter . . . if . . . if we stay here. Give me a hand up."

Hannah helped her mother to her feet and once again they were stumbling and slipping down the steep side of the hill.

After what appeared to them both as a never-ending space of time they eventually reached the last slope. But bordering this slope was a strip of woodland, and in the now fading light the shadows within it appeared jet black, and it was Hannah now who stopped and said, "Have we got to go through there, Ma?"

"Well . . . it's either that or go round it, an' I can't see us doin' that, 'cos . . . 'cos I'm dead beat."

It was the mother now who held out her hand to the child, saying, "Come on; it didn't seem that wide from up there, we'll soon be through it."

But once in the wood with no path to follow, the woman led the way aimlessly between the trees, whose entwined branches, although leafless, shut out the last glimmer of the fading daylight, and she was unaware that instead of walking across the belt of woodland she was traversing its length.

"My God!"

"What is it, Ma?" Hannah was clinging tightly to her mother's arm now.

"Nowt. Nowt."

They were now groping their way from tree to tree and Hannah whispered, "Are we lost, Ma?"

When her mother didn't answer, she shivered and pressed close to her side; then peering about her, her mouth fell open before she cried excitedly, "It's a place, Ma, look!"

Letting go of her mother's arm, she stumbled towards a wooden erection, which turned out to be a three-sided roughly made shelter, its purpose apparently to keep sacks and tools dry from the worst of the weather.

"Look, Ma; we could stay here till the mornin'. There's sacks here an' all. . . . An' look, feel, they're dry."

"Dear God! Dear God!" Nancy Boyle shook her head as she stumbled into the shelter, then bent almost double as a fit of coughing seized her.

"Lie down, Ma. Look, I'll put these three sacks on top of each other and it won't be so hard for your hips."

"No . . . the ground's dry . . . lie down aside me here an' we'll put them over us. Is there any bread left?"

"Aye, two buns, Ma."

"Well, we'd better have them but let's get bedded down first. Then . . . then eat slowly an' it'll last longer. It fills you more when you eat slowly."

Lying close together, the sacks over them, they munched slowly on the buns, but hardly had they swallowed the last mouthful when they both fell into exhausted sleep.

It was the mist that woke her. It was as if the hut was filled with a grey light. The child sat up and coughed. Where was she? What had happened? What was this stuff all about her? When her teeth began to chatter and her whole body shivered she realized it was simply mist, just like the sea fret that used to come off the river and fill their room. She blinked her eyes. The light was breaking; it was daytime again. They could get up and go on now and perhaps find some cottager who would give them a can of hot water. Oh, she was thirsty. She wasn't hungry any more, she was just thirsty, and cold, so cold.

Turning on to her side, she shook her mother, saying, "Ma!

9

Ma! it's mornin'." Three times she shook her before her voice rose to a high cry and she yelled, "D'you hear me, Ma? Ma! wake up. Wake up!"

When her mother groaned she almost fell over her in relief, and she spoke quietly now as she said, "Ma! it's mornin', we can go on."

"Hann . . . nah!"

"Yes, Ma?"

"I can't go on. Go an' . . . an' fetch . . . somebody."

"But . . . but, Ma, where? Where will I fetch them from?"

"That . . . that village. . . . Go on."

When Hannah stumbled to her feet, her limbs were so stiff she almost fell over. She couldn't see her mother's face now because of the mist and she whimpered, "But . . . but I won't be able to see, Ma."

"Go on."

As she stepped from the shelter into the wood she bit tight on her lip, and she stood, not knowing in which direction to move. Then of a sudden the mist in front of her swirled away and there in the distance, not more than ten yards away, was the open hillside.

Picking up her skirts now in both hands, she ran with stumbling gait towards the light, and as she came out of the wood she saw immediately in front of her, across a sloping hillside, a house, a quaint looking house.

As she made to run towards it, it was blocked from her sight by another swirl of mist, but she knew where it was now, and in leaps and bounds she ran through the wet curtain and didn't stop until her feet left the grass and she knew she was walking on paving slabs.

The stamping of horses' hooves and the voice of a man brought her to a stop, but only momentarily, and then she was walking towards where the sounds were coming from.

As she came out of the mist she saw at the end of a long paved yard, which flanked the quaint house, a young man. He was standing amidst a number of horses, tying one to the other, and he stopped in his work and his mouth fell open, while his head poked forward as he peered at the minute figure approaching him.

The young man didn't move or speak until the slight form came near him and put its hand on his arm; then he drew in a long breath, wetted his full lips with his tongue, blinked and said, "God Almighty! who are you?"

"I'm Hannah Boyle. Come, come help me, mister, or she'll be dead . . . me ma."

"Your ma?" He bent his back now until his face was level with hers and he asked quietly, "Where's your ma?"

"In the wood back yonder" – she thumbed over her shoulder – "in a hut. We got lost last night; we slept in the hut."

"An' she's bad?"

"Sorely."

He straightened up, rubbed his hand tightly across his unshaven chin; then taking the rope he was still holding in his hand, he moved towards the stone wall that bounded the yard and, slipping the rope through a ring in the wall, he said, "Wait there, the lot of yous;" then turning to the Galloway pony that was already saddled, he spoke to it as if to a human, saying, "Keep an eye on them, Raker, no tricks," and without further ado strode across the yard, Hannah now hurrying by his side.

"Where you hail from?"

"Newcastle."

"Newcastle? That's a distance. What's brought you this far? Looking for work?"

"No."

He glanced down at her. "What then?"

"I . . . I don't know."

He paused in his step and screwed up his face as he looked down at her. "You don't know?" he said, and moved his head first one way then the other as if to get a better view of her. She didn't look an idiot.

They had almost reached the wood before he spoke again. And now he asked, "What's your ma sick with?"

"The consumption." She made this statement as another might say "a slight cold".

He had stopped dead now. The consumption. You could pick that up. Aw well, he didn't pick things up, so why worry. But what was he going to do with her? Consumptives died. He looked at the child by his side and walked hurriedly on again.

When he reached the hut and bent over the woman lying under the sacks he endorsed in his mind what he had thought a moment earlier. Aye, they died. And if he knew anything it wouldn't be long afore this one kicked the bucket.

"Hello, missis." He talked loudly as if speaking to a deaf person.

"I'm sick."

"Aye, I can see that. Can you stand?"

"Aye . . . aye . . . I . . . don't know."

"Well have a try." He bent down and put his arm under her shoulders while at the same time turning his head to the side. He wasn't superstitious, and he had a theory that if you had to get the smit you got the smit, but at the same time he didn't believe in going out and looking for trouble, and breathing consumptive breath was one way of doing it.

"That's better . . . it's only a little way down to the house. . . . Where you makin' for?"

"The village of . . . of Elmholm."

"Oh aye; well, you haven't very far to go now. . . . You know somebody there?"

He was more than half carrying her and he waited for the answer, but when none came he paused in his stride and said, "I said, do you know somebody there?"

"Aye."

"Well, I know everybody in the village an' for miles around, happen I could bring them up to you."

When again she didn't answer he turned his head and stared at her, and as if becoming aware of his critical scrutiny she said something that brought his dark eyebrows meeting above his long nose. "I want to see their house first," she said.

"Well, what's their name?"

There was a long pause before she answered, "Thornton," and then she added, "I think."

To this he made no response but stumbled on. Thornton, she had said . . . I think. Well now what would the likes of her want with Matthew Thornton? It was well known that he had come from ordinary stock, but not so ordinary as he would have relations the likes of the one he was lugging at the moment. And what would his lady wife say to having guests such as these two sprung on her? Oh! God in heaven! she'd have such a fainting fit she would never recover. Oh, if only he could be there to see it. Thornton, she had said . . . I think. . . . Queer what the tide and the mist washed up.

"That's it, just a little further, we're almost there."

They were now crossing the yard and he added, "You'll have to bed down on straw for you'll never make the ladder up above."

Hannah now followed her mother and the young man through a double doorway into what looked and smelt like a stable. Two sides of the large room was taken up with horse boxes, and against the third wall were stacked bales of hay and full sacks, and on nails above these hung a conglomeration of horse equipment. Near the far end of the room a ladder went up almost vertically to a trap door above.

Hannah now watched the man lower her mother on to some loose straw on a long wooden platform raised about a foot from the uneven stone floor, then pull two brown blankets from off a partition and put them over her before bending down and asking, "Is that better, missis?"

When Nancy Boyle made a small movement with her head, he said, "I've got to be on me way, I've got to deliver a bunch of horses." He nodded at her now. "I'm a horse dealer you see, but . . . but you stay there until you get your legs again. I'll go up above" – he jerked his head towards the ladder – "and bring the old 'un down. He's me grandfather, he'll see to you. He'll make you some crowdy. He's as deaf as a stone but he's still all there up top." He tapped his brow. "Nearly ninety he is." He nodded again as he backed from her and made towards the ladder.

Hannah now climbed on to the platform and knelt beside her mother and smiled widely at her as she whispered, "You'll be all right now, Ma. He's nice, kind, isn't he? Will . . . will the other man be like him?"

"No."

"Oh!". . .

"What the hell! you should be on your way. What d'you say? Sick? Where?"

13

Hannah looked upwards at the two men coming down the ladder, the young one sliding from rung to rung as if his feet were greased, but the older one placing each foot firmly on the rungs and gripping the sides of the ladder as he made his slow descent.

Then he was standing gaping at them, and as Hannah stared at him she nearly laughed as she thought, He looks like a sailor, a funny old sailor.

The old man's head was completely bald except for two tufts of white hair sticking out from behind his ears, but what his head lacked in hair his face made up for, for it was almost covered with a thick white stubble. He had once been a very tall man but even now that he was stooped he still retained the appearance of great height.

When he stood by the side of the platform and looked down first on Hannah, and then on the woman, he appeared fearsome, and he sounded so as he cried in a high thick voice, "Nice bloody kettle of fish this! What's wrong with you, woman?"

When he was pulled around he stared at his grandson as he watched him mouthing words and gesticulating. Then he said, "The consumption?" His head jerked and he gazed down once more at the figure on the straw before emitting the syllable "Huh!" and turning and striding out of the stable and into the yard. But from there his voice came clearly to Hannah as he shouted at his grandson, "What if she snuffs it?"

And the answer, not so loud but still audible, came, saying, "Don't you worry about that. You won't have to bury her, she's got relations in the village . . . Thorntons."

"What d'you say?"

"I said Thorntons."

"Her! That pair related to Thorntons! Bloody joke that is."

"Aye, so thought I; but that's who she's makin' for."

"Thorntons. Huh!" And this was followed by a deep chuckle.

"I'm off then."

Hannah started and looked up at the young man who was now standing by the shallow platform. She hadn't heard him come in.

"I won't be back till late s'afternoon. Stay as long as you want . . . till she manages to get on her legs."

"Ta."

"Eat plenty crowdy; the old 'un 'll fix it for you."

"Ta," she said again.

He stared at her for a long moment, smiled and turned away, and she looked after him until he disappeared through the double doors. Then once again she gazed down on her mother.

Her face was no longer grey but a pink colour; she must be feeling warmer because she was sweating. She wished she felt warm, she was still shivering; and she felt so tired as if she hadn't been to sleep all night.

"Here! get that into you."

She started then blinked while she held her hands out towards the bowl of steaming porridge. She must have dozed off.

"Can she feed hersel?"

"I'll . . . I'll help her."

"She wants propping up. Get her on her elbows and I'll push a sack under her." He now went to the wall, and taking from it a sack of grain, he pulled it on to the platform, then tipped it on to its side so that it fell just below the sick woman's shoulders; then he bawled, "You drink tea?"

"Yes, please." Hannah nodded at him, and he stared at her for a moment before saying, "Aye, you would; you'd be a fool to turn your nose up at tea. . . . Doubt if you've ever tasted it."

He turned away and walked down the length of the room and through an open aperture at the far end, but before disappearing through it he bawled, "Come and fetch it when you've finished that."

Alternately now, Hannah spooned the porridge first into her mother's mouth, then into her own – the old man had only put the one spoon into the bowl – but before the bowl was half empty, Nancy pushed it away from her, saying, "You finish it up."

"You feel better, Ma?"

"Aye. Aye."

"Would you like a drink of tea? The old man said we can have some."

Nancy seemed to consider, then shook her head slowly, saying, "I'm goin' to sleep; I'll be better after a sleep."

"Yes, Ma."

Hannah now almost gulped up the remainder of the porridge.

15

Then rising from the straw, she made her way down the stable and through the aperture; and there she saw the old man sitting near an open kitchen range, which reminded her of the one in the communal bakehouse in Newcastle, only this one wasn't so big. There was a great heat coming from the range, but the old man was sitting quite close to it. He was chewing on a thick slice of bread and pig's fat, and when he opened his mouth she saw he had three teeth in the bottom and one in the top.

"Want some tea?"

"Yes, please."

"How is she?"

"She's asleep."

He had turned from her as he spoke and now he turned again to her and bawled, "I said, how is she?"

"She's asleep." She mouthed the words, then remembering what the young man had done she rested her head on her hand and closed her eyes, and he said quietly now, "Best thing. Best thing in the world, sleep. How old are you?"

"Eight."

"What?"

She could count up to ten on her fingers so she demonstrated, and he repeated "Oh, eight;" then smiled at her, and she smiled back, and as she drank the tea he had poured out for her he went on munching the bread and lard.

Once when he turned and looked at her she was staring round the room. It was like a kitchen, she thought, in that there was a battered delf rack against the wall with a lot of odd pieces of crockery on it, and on the floor in the corner was a frying pan and two kale pots; and along one wall was an old settle with a horse-hair pad on it. She could see the horsehair sticking out in several places. And there was a wooden kitchen table and three straight-backed chairs. But mixed up with everything were straps of leather, and horse traces, horse brasses, and horseshoes. The horseshoes were hanging on nails driven in between the large stones that made up the walls. She had never seen such big stones. The houses in Newcastle were made of bricks, but all along the way here she had seen houses made of stones, but never as big as the stones in this one.

He startled her now by shouting, "Do you like it, me Pele house, me Pele tower?"

She nodded at him.

"Fine house."

She nodded again.

"Stood up to wind and weather, women and wars." He now put his head back and laughed; and when he looked at her again she smiled at him, and after a moment his face became serious and he bent towards her and, his voice a little quieter now, he said, "I was born here, bred here, brought three wives here; reared two sons but they're gone now, dead, the bloody mine; and what have I left? Ned, only Ned. He's a good lad, Ned." He bent further towards her now. "He's like me, chip off the old block, goes his own way, owns no master, nobody'll bond him, no by God! Me, I was the same. But my lads, well they were funny, took after their mothers, no spunk. And the lead got them. I told them it would, but no, they wanted to make money, quick money. And who were they making it for? Bloody old Beaumont. Stick to horse dealing I said. As long as there's mines they'll want mules and Galloways, but no, they had to go smelting. Poison, that's what lead is, poison. Do you know that? Poison."

He now sat back in his chair, reached for the big brown teapot from off the top of the stove, poured himself out a steaming mug of the boiled black tea, took a long drink of the scalding liquid, smacked his lips, then once again bent towards her, where she sat wide-eyed staring at him, and said, "Biggest horse dealer hereabouts in the country me da was; sold the Galloways by the dozen to the mines. They used to bring all the ore out on saddleback at one time; then what did they go and do? Build bloody roads inside an' out an' use carts. Not so many Galloways needed then; but still enough." He now stretched out a grubby hand and patted her knee and, his face wide with laughter, he said, "Cart no bloody good without a horse to pull it, is it?"

She shook her head, smiled and said, "No, no," and was about to add her quota to the conversation by saying, "The horses in Newcastle are three times the size of yours, with big, bushy feet, especially the ones that pull the beer drays;" but she decided very quickly in her mind that she wouldn't be able to imitate horses with bushy feet, so she continued to smile and gaze at him while he went on talking.

"D'you know, I could turn over more money in a day when I was young than both my lads could pick up in a month in the mine. A pound a month each they got down on the nail, the rest was kept for the pays. You don't believe me? It's as true as I'm sittin' here. Subsistence money they called it, and begod! they subsisted poorly on it. Anybody that goes into a lead mine is a bloody fool, their soul's not their own. Look what happened last year when they went on strike. Eighteen weeks they were out, then what? Sacked, over a hundred of them sacked, and more than half of them lost their homes, the very roof over their heads. And what's going to happen to them? They're sailing away to America come next month. That's for you and your mines. The only ones who make anything out of the mines are the owners an' their agents. And Thornton's one of them. . . . Why you goin' down to Thornton's?" On the last question his voice had dropped almost to a normal tone.

"I don't know." When she shook her head as she answered he understood what she was saying and repeated, "You don't know?"

"No."

"Huh! . . . Huh!" He gave two short laughs. "Well hinny, Ned says you walked all the way from Newcastle with your ma and you tell me you don't know why you've done it? Well, all I can say is you're either a stupid little bugger or a clever little bugger an' from the looks of you I don't think you're stupid, so" – he nodded at her – "keep your own counsel, I don't blame you, keep your own counsel. But if you're goin' down there" – he now thumbed towards the opening – "an' to the Thorntons, why it won't be long afore you know what you're after, an' the village an' all."

2

The village of Elmholm was about two and a half miles south of
Allendale. It consisted of forty-five houses. These included the
two short rows of miners' cottages, which were situated behind
the houses on the right hand side of the village green if you were
journeying from Allendale towards Sinderhope. They had been
built some fifty years previously to house the overflow of miners
then employed in the lead mines and smelting mills. They were
low two-roomed stone dwellings with mud floors, except where
flagstones had been laid down; and at first the sanitary habits of
their occupants had been similar to those which prevailed in the
town of Allendale itself; their middens had been in front of their
front doors, to the disdain of the artisans in the village who kept
their middens at the back of their houses, or better still at the
bottom of their gardens. But time had wrought change so that
now not only were all middens to be found behind the cottages
but for most of the year the villagers all lived peaceably together,
except on days such as fair days, or the Friday after the pays. This
was the day on which the miners received their accumulated pay.
Then the rowdiest among them fought, cracked each other's heads,
and beat up their women. The return to normal wouldn't take
place until work started again.

The village proper was shaped like a pear, the road from
Allendale entering it between Ralph Buckman's blacksmith's shop
and Will Rickson's house and builder's yard before dividing to
pass round both sides of the green, joining up again to leave the
village where, like the stalk of the pear, it narrowed between the
wall of the churchyard and Elmholm House.

The cottages and houses making up the village were of various

19

designs and sizes. Ted Loam's was a two-storied dwelling, the ground floor of which he used as a butcher's shop.

Two others that stood apart belonged to Walter Bynge the stonemason and Thomas Wheatley the grain chandler who, although his main business was in Allendale Town, used his ground floor, too, for the sale of flour and pulses in times of necessity.

But most of the inhabitants were either farm labourers or drovers who, however respectable they were during the week, would invariably, like the miners, become mortallious on fair days, at weddings, christenings, funerals, and occasionally on a Saturday night.

There were, of course, the Methodist Chapel and the inn, which seemed to be of equal attraction to the villagers if one could go by the numbers directing their footsteps towards the one place or the other.

But across the road from the cemetery wall were the low iron gates leading to the short drive fronting Elmholm House, which was Matthew Thornton's home.

It could be said that everyone in the village liked Matthew Thornton in some degree but no one in the village could be said to like his wife in any degree. It was common knowledge that Matthew Thornton had come up in the world and this he never denied. Nor did he deny that his people had kept a small huxter shop in Haydon Bridge, and that he owed what education he had to an old retired schoolmaster who came to live near his home and who had taken him under his wing. The schoolmaster had not only taught him to read, write and reckon, but had instilled into him a bit of the Latin language as well. It was the latter that in a way made him feel different, but as he had told himself from the beginning it could be of no help to a man who was going in for engineering. Anyway, as most of the old 'uns repeatedly stated when discussing the family in the inn of an evening, she, that madam, his missis, must have been captivated by the results of his education, which had given him not only a fine speaking voice but a singing one as well, for, as they said, they had to be fair, she was from different stock, being the daughter of a solicitor in Newcastle. And moreover, as everybody knew, from the parrot in the pub to Frank Pearson's pig, wasn't she related to the Beaumonts through her cousin Marion, and wasn't her cousin Marion's husband half cousin to old Beaumont himself. Dig deep enough down and you reach Adam and Eve, they said.

The male habitués of the inn found a lot to laugh at in Mrs Thornton's claim to the gentry, as did the church and chapel frequenters of the village – but not so their wives, for without exception Mrs Anne Thornton's unspoken claim to being the first lady of the community was to say the least aggravating.

Anne Thornton was a tall woman, her fair hair and pale skin emphasising the clearness of her round blue eyes. Her nose was small, her lips full, almost overfull but well shaped. She had neither bust nor hips to speak of, but what she lacked in these parts of her anatomy she rectified by means of padding. Furthermore, she was a good housekeeper, and a good mother to her four children; as to being a good wife, only Matthew Thornton could have given an answer to that question.

Had her two servants been asked their opinion of her, Bella Monkton who acted as cook-general, and Tessie Skipton who was housemaid, handmaiden, and nursemaid rolled into one, would have looked at each other, pressed their lips together, but said nothing in reply. Bella Monkton, at forty, knew she was a lost woman as far as marriage was concerned, and since positions were hard to get unless you had a mind to bond yourself, she would have thought it expedient to keep her opinion of her mistress to herself.

As for Tessie Skipton, Tessie at eleven years old knew from experience that any place was preferable to the workhouse whence she had been delivered by Mr Thornton four years ago, and for whom she stated daily she would work her fingers to the bone. But it wasn't for him she was called upon to work her fingers to the bone but for the missis. And what did she think of her? She wasn't saying. Only to Bella could she express her opinion, and then it would be whispered in the privacy of the attic, which they shared, each with a straw pallet on the floor.

They got on well, did Bella Monkton and Tessie Skipton.

Each found in the other a substitute; the one a daughter, the other a mother, and their association helped to run the house smoothly because between them they carried out the work of four servants.

The only other servant was Dandy Smollett, who also had come from the workhouse. He was fourteen years old and his duties were to see to the garden and attend to the needs of the horse, with which he slept in the stable.

John Thornton, the elder son, was aged twelve. He was already tall; but although he took after his mother in looks, he did not as yet appear to have inherited her character.

The elder girl, Margaret, definitely took after her father in looks. She had a squarish face, light brown hair, grey eyes, and a wide mouth. But she was a highly sensitive child and was given to crying over animals of all kinds.

Robert, aged ten, also took after his father in looks and was already much taller than Margaret. He was of an adventurous spirit and had a strong stubborn personality; qualities, he understood, he had inherited from his grandfather Thornton.

Beatrice, the youngest child and commonly called Betsy, was an exact replica of her mother, in face, in form, and in character, and being but nine years old her pettiness was attributed to her being the baby of the family and, therefore, having been spoilt.

At the moment all the children were at home, John being on holiday from his boarding school in Hexham, and Margaret and Robert on holiday from the day school in Allendale; Betsy did not yet attend school, being considered too delicate, but this didn't mean that she had no lessons. Each day, for an hour in the morning and an hour and a half in the afternoon, her mother read to her from the Bible, taught her the three Rs, how to embroider, and how to perform on the spinet.

And it was at the spinet that Anne Thornton was now seated, with John, Margaret and Betsy around her. Her hands were on the keys, her eyes directed towards the music, but she remained perfectly still; her lids did not blink, nor did her fingers move as she called sharply, "Robert!"

The children by her side fidgeted. Margaret nudged John, who grinned back at her, while Betsy rose on tiptoe in her soft house-shoes and, looking sidewards, craned her neck to its fullest extent as she looked towards the sitting-room window; and then her voice a squeak, she cried, "He's gone out, Mama; he's going down the path."

Anne Thornton rose from the round swivelling piano stool in such a flurry that her wide skirt slapped at her younger daughter, almost overbalancing her; then she was at the window rapping on it sharply. The next moment she had pushed the window up and again she was calling, "Robert!" and the tone was a command.

The boy turned and stared at his mother for a moment; then he tossed his head and swung his shoulders from side to side before reluctantly returning up the path and into the house.

As he crossed the long narrow hall towards the sitting-room door his mother was waiting for him, but before she had time to chastise him he said, "We're on holiday, Mama; it's a lovely day, I want to go on to the hills."

"What you want and what you must do, Robert, are two different things! I've told you before, and if you disobey me once again I shall speak to your father about you."

This threat seemed not to make a very strong impression on the boy who, pushing his hands into his breeches pockets, his head thrust forward and throwing one foot reluctantly before the other, crossed the sitting-room towards his brother and sisters who were all surreptitiously eyeing him.

Anne Thornton had just seated herself on the stool once more, arranged her skirts and lifted her hands to the keys when again she was forced into stillness by the voice of her troublesome son exclaiming, "Oh, not that one! '*How Oft Has The Banshee Cried*'. It calls it a dirge, and it is a dirge."

There was heavy evidence of the struggle for patience in his mother's voice as she replied, again without moving either her hands or her head, "This is one of Mr Thomas Moore's finest songs. What's more, it's the only one in the book that is arranged for four voices and I want you to get it perfect to surprise your father."

"It will."

There was a splutter from John now and a titter from Margaret; then the sounds dying away, the children looked past their mother

23

as she sat still, straight and silent, towards the music on the stand.

There was a long pause before Anne Thornton said, "I'll sing the verse and you each know where to come in, in the chorus. You first Margaret, then you, Robert, and you, John." And now she turned her head and looked full at her second son as she said, "And remember, all of you, this song is to be sung as it says here" – she pointed – "slow and with solemnity."

She now turned to the piano and in a thin, but not unpleasant soprano, she began to sing:

> "How oft has the Banshee cried,
> How oft has death un-tied
> Bright links that Glory wove,
> Sweet bonds en-twin'd by love!"

At this point she lifted her hand up and slapped at the air and Margaret brought in her voice, singing:

> "Peace to each man-ly soul that sleep-eth;
> Rest to each faithful eye that weepeth;
> Long may the fair and brave
> Sigh o'er their eye that weep-eth,
> Long may the fair and brave,
> Sigh o'er the he-ro's grave."

Here their mother again slapped at the air as the signal for John and Robert to come in.

On the voices went, rising and falling in the dirge, to the final words to be sung in unison: "Sigh o'er the hero's grave."

Margaret piped hers; John gave full alto strength to his; even Betsy squeaked: "Hero's grave;" but Robert, determined to bury the hero deep, sang: "Hero's gra . . . a . . . ave."

It was too much for the children; it was too much for their mother. As John, Margaret and Betsy tried to contain their laughter their mother's hands crashed down on the keys with such force that it checked the sound abruptly as if it had been smothered. Swinging about, she caught her troublesome son by the ear, marched him out of the sitting-room, across the hall to the foot of the staircase, and there, shaking his ear until he sought refuge for the side of his head deep in his shoulder, she cried at him, "Go to your room! I shall have your father deal with you when he comes in."

As she thrust him forward he fell against the first step; then putting his hands to his burning ear, he slowly mounted upwards, but stopped just before he reached the landing and turned as his mother cried at him, "I shall see that he forbids you to go to Mr Beaumont's celebrations."

The boy's lips trembled and it looked for a moment as if he might be about to burst into tears; but he jerked his chin upwards, turned his back on his mother, and ran across the landing to his bedroom.

Mrs Thornton now turned and looked towards the sitting-room door where the other three children were standing, and going towards them and in controlled tones, she addressed Margaret, saying, "Bring *The Young Lady's Manual*, Margaret." Then looking at her son, she asked, "What were you thinking of doing, John?"

"Nothing, Mama." He couldn't very well have said, "Take a walk over the hills, Mama," but that is what he would have liked to say.

"Well then, come into the conservatory with us. Margaret has been reading about metals from *The Young Lady's Manual*. Her father will be delighted to know that she takes an interest in ores and such."

She turned now saying, "Oh, there you are, my dear," and held out her hand to take the book from her daughter.

As they crossed the hall in the direction of the conservatory she opened it lovingly and read aloud:

"*A Young Lady's Book; A Manual of Elegant Recreations, Exercises and Pursuits.*"

Smiling, she glanced from one to the other, saying, "Every time I read that I can recall the wonderful pleasure I experienced when my dear mama presented me with this book on my fourteenth birthday."

The two girls, one on each side trotting beside her rustling skirts, looked up at her, but made no comment. Betsy did not say, "Tell us about the party you had on your fourteenth birthday, Mama," because she had heard the tale so many times it had ceased to be exciting, while Margaret wondered why fairy tales never bored you whereas tales about grown-ups did.

When they were all seated amid the potted ferns in the conservatory Margaret began stumbling her way through the discourse on metals. Slowly and in a flat tone, she read words that conveyed no sense to her:

"Is it not singular, that the ores should sometimes be so totally unlike the Metals? Many earthy minerals we see frequently almost in their natural state; but few persons are acquainted with the ores of the Metals most commonly in use, or reflect on the many processes which are necessary to produce from them such articles as we call, from habit, the most simple conven . . . conveniences. What can be less like Copper than those beautiful green specimens, exhibiting con . . . concentric shells of a delicate radiate structure? or that fine light blue one, surpassing the richest velvet, in its soft and silky appearance? The latter is hy . . . drate of Copper; – that is copper combined with water; the green ones . . ."

At this point the laboured soliloquy was happily interrupted by the conservatory door being opened without first being knocked upon, or even having the door knob rattled, and Tessie rushing in most unceremoniously and exclaiming in an awed whisper, "Missis! Ned Ridley be at the front door with two people."

"Ned Ridley at the front door?"

"Aye, missis, with two people."

Anne Thornton had now risen to her feet and, moving slowly towards Tessie, she bent over her as she asked, "What do you mean, two people? Explain yourself, girl."

"Well, missis, like tramps they are . . . worse, mucky, a woman and a child."

Anne Thornton drew herself up, joined her hands at her waist and said, "Tell them all to go to the back door, and ask cook to ask them what their business is."

"Aye, missis."

"John, sit down."

The boy had gone to the end of the conservatory from where,

if he craned his neck hard enough, he could glimpse the steps outside the front door.

When the boy was again seated his mother resumed her own seat but she didn't tell her daughter to continue with her reading; instead, she sat, in fact they all sat, waiting for Tessie's return. And Tessie came back so quickly that no one of them could imagine she had been as far as the front door, but she gave evidence that she had by saying immediately, and in an awed tone now, "He won't budge, missis, Ned . . . Ned Ridley. He says the people have come to see the master."

Anne Thornton rose slowly to her feet and in a characteristic fashion she put her fingertips first under one padded breast, then under the other, adjusted the buckle of the belt at the front of her gown, patted the white lace collar at her neck and finally, after tapping the back of her starched and gofered linen cap, she marched out of the conservatory, across the hall and to the front door.

Tessie, who had closed the door in the face of the visitors, pulled it open again and, hanging on to it, thrust her head round and stared at her mistress.

As Anne Thornton surveyed the three people standing on the step her expression was at its stiffest. She could not conceive what these other two dirty individuals wanted, but that Ned Ridley should dare to come to her front door incensed her; that he should dare to come to her house at all was an outrage. Her past failure to redeem Ned the young boy from his wild ways had been humiliating, but nothing compared to the derision she had suffered when she failed lamentably with Ned the young man. The memory of their last meeting rankled deeply within her. She had gone over the hills the Christmas before last taking John and Robert with her and proffered a gift to him and his disreputable old grandfather, and they had both laughed at her.

"What do you want for this, missis?" the old man had said to her as he unwrapped the piece of belly pork. "'Tis a poor induce- ment," he had added, "to get us on to our knees. Why Methodist's wife brought us a standing pie, and even that couldn't get us through the chapel door."

But the final insult had come from the boy as he escorted them with mock courtesy to the break in the wall that acted as a gate when, bending towards her, a wicked grin on his face, he had whispered, "Now if you had thought of bringing him a bottle of the hard stuff, ma'am, you would have got him to come down and sing on your step; but not hymns exactly." . . . Oh, those Ridleys!

"What do you want?"

"Good-day, ma'am." The young fellow doffed his cap with a sweeping movement, then held it against his jacket with both hands as he said, "I just directed these two folk, they came out of the mist this mornin'. They slept in the open all night, they did, on their way to see you."

There was a look of utter amazement on Anne Thornton's face as she looked from the woman to the girl, then back to the woman, and now she demanded, "Why do you wish to see me?"

The woman gave two short, sharp coughs, swallowed, then answered, "'Tisn't you, but your man I want to see."

"My . . . my husband isn't at home. And please tell me what you consider is your business with him."

Again the woman coughed, but longer this time. When finally she raised her head she looked into the clear, piercing blue eyes and replied, "'Tis my business and his."

For a moment Anne Thornton seemed lost for words, until she looked into the straight and presumably solemn countenance of Ned Ridley, which solemnity was denied by the laughter in his eyes, and to him she said, "Whatever these people want with my husband I'm sure they'll be able to manage without your help, so will you kindly take your leave. And . . . and remember in future there is a back door."

"Oh yes, ma'am, yes, ma'am, I'll remember in future." Ned thrust his cap on to his head, backed two steps away, then, looking at the woman and child, said, "Good luck, missis; good luck, whatever you're after."

Anne Thornton watched him march down the pathway, swing open the iron gate, turn sharply about and close it, then in a mocking gesture give her a salute by touching the peak of his cap.

Oh, that creature! If anyone in this world could upset her it was that boy. Since she had first made his acquaintance, seeing him as a small boy with his bare behind sticking out of his torn knickerbockers, he had annoyed and irritated her; and further meetings had simply resulted in anger and disgust being added to her emotions concerning him.

"I want to see your man."

Her eyes seemed to jump in their sockets from the departing figure of Ned Ridley on to the woman standing below her; and now she demanded again, "What business have you with my husband?"

"That's my affair."

"Who are you?"

"Me name's Nancy Boyle, and this is me daughter, Hannah." The woman now put her fingertips lightly on to the child's shoulder.

Anne Thornton stared at the child before she said, "If you are begging it isn't my husband you want to see, it's me. There are alms given to the needy at the church. . . ."

"'Tisn't no alms I want, missis; 'tis your man I want to see."

"My husband is at work, you can tell me what business you have with him."

The woman stared up into the stiff, pale face for a long moment before saying quietly, "You'll know soon enough; I'll bide me time until he comes in. . . . Come!" She turned the child about and pushed her towards the gate.

Anne Thornton watched them from the doorstep. Her eyes narrowed, her lips slightly apart, she pondered in some alarm the connection between this dirty creature and her husband. Surely she was no relation to him? She knew only too well that he had come from ordinary folk. Hadn't she been trying to live the fact down for years? But still, as lowly as his people were they would surely have scorned any connection with that person and her child.

What could she want with Matthew? She turned and looked at the brass-faced grandfather clock, and as she did so the mechanism made a grating sound, which was followed by the slow striking of the hour.

Four o'clock. It would be another two hours before he arrived home. What if that creature went and sat on the seat on the village green and someone got into conversation with her and she should say she was sitting there waiting for Matthew Thornton! . . . Dear, dear! She should have kept her in the yard. Where had she gone!

In agitation, she turned now and, lifting the front of her skirts, ran across the hall past Tessie, whose face and gaping mouth were expressing utter amazement at seeing her mistress run. And Tessie's mouth sagged even further as she witnessed the speed with which Anne Thornton covered the stairs, and from the number of footsteps she counted across the landing she gauged her mistress had gone into the boys' room, and she thought she knew why.

Robert, too, was amazed at the speed with which his mother crossed the bedroom, and he was almost pushed off the deep window-sill as she bent forward and leant her face against the pane.

From the window she had an unobstructed view of the road leading to the centre of the village but all she could see on the road were the two Bynge girls, Alice and Mary, chatting to Bill Buckman, and indulging in unseemly laughter, too, if the way their heads were wagging was anything to go by. Where was their mother in all this? Everyone knew that Bill Buckman had a wife in Hexham; and it was rumoured he might have a mistress there as well. . . . Oh! why was she bothering about such things? Where were those two creatures?

"Who are you looking for, Mama?" The boy's voice held no resentment at the fact that he was undergoing punishment.

"No one. No one."

"Is it the persons who were at the front door?"

She turned sharply and looked down at her son. Of course he would have seen them come up the path.

"They didn't go through the village, Mama, they went the other way." He pointed. "Over by the cemetery wall and up the hill. Look" – he now jumped on to the sill – "there they are on the knoll."

His mother followed his pointing finger; and yes, there they were, the woman sitting on the knoll, the child standing by her side.

The small hill to the side of the cemetery wall looked down on to the road along which her husband would come riding from the mine. Did the creature know that? It was possible that Ned Ridley could have informed her. What did she want?

What did she want?

She now addressed her son, saying, "Keep watching those persons, Robert, and should they leave the hill call down to me quickly. You understand?"

"Yes, Mama. . . . Why do they want to see Papa, Mama?"

She stopped abruptly on her way to the door but didn't turn round as she answered, "I don't know."

That boy, he must have opened the window and overheard the conversation. But then, so had Tessie, and that meant that Bella would already know, and what Bella knew the village would shortly know.

Oh! what was this about? If only it was six o'clock.

Matthew Thornton, about to mount his horse before leaving the mine top, looked across the ordered chaos to where Joe Robson, an experienced miner, was demonstrating to his son, Peter, the best way to go about buddling. The art lay in the manoeuvring of the rake back and forth over small ore, or smiddum, on the large flagstone which was encased on three sides by a wooden frame and over which flowed a strong current of water.

After watching them for a moment Matthew got astride his horse while shaking his head at himself. Young Peter, although fourteen and sturdy, wasn't strong enough as yet for buddling, but because Joe had asked that the boy be given a try he had complied, for Joe was a good man and, unlike most of his mates, a sober one. Four of his sons were already in the mine engaged in one capacity or another. Two of them, Archie and Hal, both as yet under seventeen years of age, worked on the knockstones on which they crushed the mixed stones by means of buckers, and his youngest son, although only twelve, acted as a hand sieve boy, so once a month on money week when they received their sub-sistence, Joe picked up more than most men in this particular mine. He wished there were more like Joe.

All in all, the past week had proved very good. Mr Byers was very pleased with the results, and being a fair and upright agent, he always showed the men his pleasure. Now if that Mr Sopwith over at Allenheads was as forthright as Mr Byers, Allenheads wouldn't have known that disastrous strike last year.

The bouse they had brought up today was rich, a good twenty per cent of ore in it. It wasn't every day that happened.

He rode round the perimeter of the reservoir and along by the slime pits, then cut across the hill to the cart track, and from there to the road, wide enough here to allow a horse and rider to pass a string of ponies without having to mount the bank.

He was both hungry and dirty and he had a longing to be home and seated at the head of his table looking down on the four bright faces of his children. He was so glad John was home. He'd take him to the mine tomorrow . . . that's if Anne didn't kick up. Well let her, let her; the boy would follow his own bent in the end whether it was law, as she wanted, or lead, as he himself wanted.

He drew his horse to a walk as he rounded the foot of a hill and saw ahead of him the well-known figure of Ned Ridley riding one pony and leading two others, and he was still some yards behind when he called to him cheerfully, saying, "Hello there, Ned; off to the cobbler's again, are you?"

"Oh aye; aye, Mr Thornton." Ned twisted round in the saddle. "As you say, off to the cobbler's again. . . . You don't know anything harder than iron that would serve as shoes, do you?"

"No, I don't Ned." Matthew laughed. "But I could enquire over at the smelting shops for you."

"Aye, you could."

They both laughed together as they rode on.

"How's your grandfather?" asked Matthew after a while. "I haven't seen him down in the town on market days for some time now."

"No, he's gettin' lazy in his old age. I told him I'd kick him in the backside from here to Haydon if he doesn't come and see me knock hell out of Bull Tiffit on Saturday."

"Oh yes . . . yes, you're boxing Tiffit again. It was a draw last time."

"It won't be this; we'll sweat it out on our knees if necessary."

Matthew looked at the profile of the young fellow sitting straight and jaunty on the pony and he said quietly, "It's a daft game after all, Ned; you could be spoilt for life."

"In what way?"

"All ways. Bull Tiffit is a nasty piece of work and I should say he's heavier than you by a couple of stone."

"That's to me benefit, Mr Thornton. I'm like a lintie on me feet to his scooped-back dray horse."

"Why don't you put some of your strength into making regular money and go up to the mine?"

"Aw, Mr Thornton." Ned jerked his chin upwards and laughed. "You're jokin' again. I've always told you you wouldn't get me into your mine. I'll supply you with cuddies, mules or Galloways, even a broken-down racer if you want it, but that's as near as you'll get me to your mine. Not, mind you, that I wouldn't be pleased to work for you; if I had to have a master I wouldn't look further than yourself, an' it's the truth I'm speakin'."

"Thanks, Ned, thanks; that's a compliment for my character I'll cherish." Again they looked at each other and laughed, and now they were within sight of the house and the cemetery, and to the side of it the knoll, and when a few minutes later they passed below it Ned glanced upwards, and he saw the woman and the girl standing looking down on them. Turning his head sharply, he looked at his companion, but Mr Thornton hadn't even glanced in the direction of the knoll, but was looking towards his own gate, and when they came abreast of it he said cheerfully, "Good-bye, Ned, it's been pleasant meeting you."

"An' you, Mr Thornton . . . an' you."

Dandy Smollett was waiting in the yard to take the horse and Matthew spoke sharply to him, saying, "No skimping with the rubbing down tonight mind, Dandy," and the boy, touching his forelock, replied hastily, "No, master. No, master."

As was his habit, he now entered his house by the kitchen, and sitting on the wooden stool just inside the door he unstrapped the buckles of his gaiters, unlaced his boots and took the pair of slippers Tessie handed to him, saying as he looked at them, "It's about time I had a new pair, don't you think?"

Another night, had he made this remark Tessie would have giggled and said, "Eeh! master, there's nowt wrong with them;" but tonight she took no such liberty, only stared at him until he said, "Lost your tongue, Tessie?"

"No, master."

"The cat died?" He was standing up now, taking off his dusty jacket.

When she again made no comment he looked to where Bella was stooped over the oven taking from it a large dripping tin in which was a sizzling joint of lamb, and when she walked to the middle of the room and put it on the table within an arm's length of him, he sniffed and said, "Oh, I've been waiting for that all day, Bella."

"Well, 'tis ready, master, when you are."

He stared at her for a moment. There was no smile on her face, something was wrong. What had the two of them been up to? Likely they had annoyed Anne and had suffered for it. Ah well, he had better go and find out what it was all about.

He went up the kitchen, pulled open the heavy oaken door and entered the hall and saw his wife waiting for him. He knew by the way she stood that she was impatient for his coming, and a thought crossed his mind that he could wish there were certain and proper times when she would be impatient for his coming.

"Come into the sitting-room for a moment."

"I haven't washed yet." Had she forgotten her rule that he must always change his coat and boots in the kitchen and perform his ablutions in the closet adjoining the morning-room?

"Leave it, leave it; I must talk to you."

As he walked slowly past the foot of the stairs his glance was brought sharply upwards by the appearance of his son Robert, his arms spread between the top stanchion of the banister and the wall. He was calling, "Ma-ma! Ma-ma! they are coming down."

It seemed to Matthew that his son's remark, not understandable to himself, had yet a full meaning for his wife, for now her step tripped almost to the point of a run towards the sitting-room, and

34

with his face screwed up in some perplexity he followed her. She closed the door behind him and, facing him, demanded, "Have you any relatives in Haydon Bridge that you haven't told me of?"

"Relatives in Haydon Bridge? You know I haven't."

"What about Hexham?"

"There's no one in Hexham belonging to me. What's this?"

"Well then, there's some need for explanation here. Two hours gone a dirty creature came to the front door, accompanied by a child. That pest, Ned Ridley, brought them." She drew in a short, sharp breath. "The woman wouldn't tell me her business, she said it was with you. You're sure you have no relatives?"

"You know I haven't. The last one was my grannie, and she died in Newcastle these nine years back."

She now let out a long, slow breath, turned from him, walked up the room until she came to the couch and, gripping the back of it, said, "For some reason personal to herself this woman wants to see you. There . . . there, listen!" She swung round and pointed towards the door. "That'll be her again. She's been sitting up on the knoll waiting for you."

"Sitting on the knoll waiting for me? Well, we'll soon get this cleared up." He now tugged at each shirt-sleeve, pulling the cuffs half-way up his forearms; then loosening his string necker-chief, he pulled it off and threw it aside as he marched out of the room and across the hall towards the front door.

Anne Thornton was by his side when he opened the door, and now she didn't look at the woman and child standing on the step, but she looked at her husband. She watched his eyes first narrow, then stretch wide, while at the same time his jaw dropped, leaving his mouth in a gape.

"'Tis me, Matthew, Nancy Boyle. Remember?"

Yes. Yes, he remembered; and the memory struck him dumb. The woman before him, dirty and dishevelled as she was, was Nancy Boyle all right. But not the woman he had once known. And why in the name of God had she to turn up here. God Almighty! How was he going to explain her? How was he going to explain her to Anne? Oh, he'd never be able to explain her to Anne. Never! Never, in this world.

As he stood dumbfounded he could already feel his home life

toppling about his ears, and he knew in this moment that from now until the day he died, he would suffer in one way or another because this woman for some reason, as yet known only to herself, had come walking out of the past.

He had uttered no word and had given no open sign of recognition, but his hand went out involuntarily towards the woman when, overtaken by a fit of coughing, she bent her body from the waist as she spat into a piece of rag, which was red and brown in parts.

"Come in."

"Matthew!" His very name held a reprimand, and he turned on his wife, whispering fiercely, "Well! what shall I do? Have her explain her business on the doorstep?"

When the woman and the child stepped into the hall he said abruptly, "Come this way," and he was about to lead them towards the sitting-room when again his wife called him by name. "Matthew . . . please!" she said; "not in the sitting-room."

"Where then?" His voice was almost a bark.

"The . . . the morning-room."

It was she who now marched forward and led the way, and when they were all in the morning-room with the door closed Matthew pulled a straight-backed wooden chair from under the round table and without looking at the woman said, "Sit down."

Nancy Boyle took the seat, then leant back and looked up at the man she hadn't seen for almost nine years and who seemed to have grown taller and broader and more handsome, and she thought it strange that out of her own anguish she could in this moment spare a tinge of pity for him, until he said stiffly, "What can I do for you?" Then the pity fled and she answered gruffly, "Just one thing you can do for me, you can look after your own, she's yours!" And with this she thrust the child towards him.

Matthew's response was to step back as quickly as if he were being confronted with a double-headed cobra.

Although he heard Anne gasp and knew that she was holding her face in her hands he did not look towards her but stared dazedly down on the child, who in her turn was staring up at him, and all the while her mother was talking, short disjointed sentences broken by her breathing as if she were under the influence of drink. "Newton," she was saying, "doesn't sound all that different from Thornton. . . . I went to the Temperance Hotel. . . . Remember the Temperance Hotel? The old faggot said nobody there . . . never had nobody there the name of Newton. Of course the old bitch wouldn't have let on if she had known you by your right name . . . 'cos she knew what I was after . . . with me belly full. . . . Funny how I found you. Saw you goin' into that office in Grey Street. Fine office with doorman, so I said to him, 'Was that Mr Matthew Newton went in there?' No; you were Mr Matthew Thornton, he said, and you had to do with lead mines . . . them were the offices. I waited an' waited but you didn't come out. . . . Didn't know there was another door. You see, 'cos I knew me time was runnin' out I said to meself, find him; who better to see to her than her father? And so I worked at it from there."

The crash brought him out of the nightmare and he saw the chair that Anne had been holding on to fall sideways on to the floor and her body waver as if she were about to faint. But when he put his arm around her she did not slump against him, in fact the contact seemed to revive her for she thrust his hand from her and staggered to another chair.

"She's had a shock; 'tis natural, I suppose."

He turned and looked at the woman again, this time as if he could kill her; then went towards her and bent down until his face was level with hers, staring into the sunken eyes as he whispered hoarsely, "You have no proof; there were others."

"Aye." Her voice came flat and calm as she replied, "Afore and after; but she's yours. I told you when you last came, an' that made you skedaddle, didn't it?"

He closed his eyes tightly, straightened his back, turned towards the fireplace and, gripping the marble mantelpiece, laid his head on the edge of it and ground his teeth.

In the name of God why had this to happen to him! He had a vivid mental picture of the consequences spreading in all directions away down the years. The village would be agog; the men in the mines. It would be the high spot of market day in Allendale Town, it might even jeopardize his chance of becoming chief

37

agent at the mine. Yet all these outside reactions didn't seem to matter. What did matter, what was hurting him with an indescribable pain was that his home life, as he had known it, would be no more.

He'd had the love and adoration of his four children, and although he hadn't been at the receiving end of the former from his wife for many years now, and she'd never showered the latter on him, nevertheless she had loved him. That it was in a narrow, pious, pinching way, he had no doubt; still she had been, and still was an excellent housekeeper and an excellent mother. Yet if the truth could be sifted through the events of their married life it was she who should face the blame for his present predicament, for from the time Betsy was born she had feigned a weakness which she said prevented her from carrying out her duties as a wife. When the child was six months old, and her own vigour belied any weakness, she openly stated that in future her duty to him would be at intervals compatible with her cycle; which had meant that his body could crave satisfaction for weeks at a stretch without relief.

It was about this time that Mr Byers had given him the pleasant duty of carrying some samples of ore to Mr Beaumont's chief agent, and this in turn led to him making four visits to Newcastle within the following months, sometimes having to wait for results. The visits could cover two to three days, during which he put up at the Temperance Hotel.

On his very first stay in the city he had come across Nancy Boyle by the mere fact of pulling her from the road just in time to save her from being knocked over by an open coach being driven by a drunken young buck to the delight of his accompanying friends.

Nancy, he saw at once, was pretty, and common; but on further acquaintance he found that she was also of a warm nature and very obliging.

When she had first taken him to her room, an attic at the top of a boarding-house behind the warehouses on the riverfront, he found it poor in the extreme but clean, and as she had explained straightaway it suited her because she was scarcely in it, having to work twelve to fourteen hours a day in the basement of a milliner's in the city. He had not enquired into her past life, nor had she probed into his. But he had taken the precaution of giving her a false name, because after all he was a married man with a family, and a churchman into the bargain, and he was well aware that it was due as much to the latter as it was to his wife's efforts that he held the position he did in the lead mine, because Mr Byers, the agent, was a very strong churchman, and a man who loved to hear good singing, especially good hymn singing.

He recalled now the feeling of panic he experienced when he had last met her when, pointing to her stomach, she said bluntly, 'I'm in trouble, you've done it on me. What about it?" And he could even now hear himself repeating his promises that everything would be all right.

But what had he done? He had skittered back to the Temperance Hotel, taken up his bag, and left. He had spent that night at an inn on the other side of the town; the following day, after concluding his business, he had ridden for home as if the devil were after him.

And now standing behind him was the outcome of that episode. . . . Be sure your sins will find you out.

Although he raised his voice in praise to God each Sunday, he had more so of late been privately questioning the whole fabric of the established church, but what he never questioned was the truth that came out of the Old Book. Time and again its truths seemed to have been shown him. Be sure your sins will find you out.

He raised his head slowly when the woman's voice said, "Well, I'll be on me way. I've done what I came to do; me job's done; she's yours to see to now."

He turned towards her, but she was looking at the child and the child at her, and he watched the little girl throw her arms about her mother's waist, crying in a raucous tone, "Aw, Ma! Ma! where you goin'? I'm not stayin' here. Ma! Ma! I want to come with you."

"Listen. Listen, that's the gentleman I've told you about." She pointed towards Matthew. "He'll take care of you 'cos he's your da. Now you be a good lass an' do as you're told an' some day I'll come an' see you. Aye, I'll come an' see you." She was smiling weakly now, and when the child again clung to her she looked towards the lady of the house, who was now sitting like a ramrod, her face as white as lint, her eyes straining from her head, and she said to her, "She's a good bairn, she'll give you no trouble."

On this she pushed her daughter from her, turned and walked slowly out of the room and into the hall, where she saw four children. They all stared at her, their mouths slightly apart, their eyes round as if with wonder. She paused for a moment in front of them and said, "You . . . you've got a new sister. Be kind to her;" then she went to the front door where Tessie was standing, the latch in her hand and, if it were possible, her mouth and her eyes wider than those of the children.

Tessie stood for a moment watching the woman going down the path before she quickly closed the door and turned to where her young masters and mistresses were now all staring towards the morning-room from where the raised voices of their parents were coming.

Margaret looked at John and John at her; then quickly their glances parted. Their parents never quarrelled. Her mother scarcely ever raised her voice. Sometimes, if she woke up late at night, she had heard rumblings from her parents' bedroom, but she imagined they were just discussing the events of the day. But now, her mama was almost screaming.

Anne Thornton wasn't almost screaming, she was screaming; and what she was screaming was, "She's not staying here! Do you hear me? She's not staying here!"

"Be quiet, woman!" Matthew's voice answered her scream with a bawl, and Anne became quiet for a moment as she stared in amazement at this man who wasn't showing an atom of remorse. This vile tragedy had not brought him to his knees, there was no repentance in either his voice or his manner, and he was daring to speak to her, shout at her as he would at some creature like that one who had just departed.

"She's here and she stays. For good or bad she stays." He turned and glanced at the child whose face, now streaked with tears, looked almost as white as her mother's had done.

"Never! I will not have her in my home; you can put her in the House."

Matthew became still as he stared at her, his shoulders slumped.

Then his head wagged slowly and, his voice quiet now but holding more authority than his bawl had done, he said, "Put her in the workhouse? No! No! Never!"

Anne Thornton turned about and glared at the child. Then she did an unprecedented thing. For a moment it brought her down to the ordinary level of the people among whom she lived, for she flung her arms around herself as in an effort to comfort the shocked and distressed being inside and rocked herself deeply backwards and forwards. She only needed to utter a wail and she would have been like one of the Irish miners' wives mourning the death of her man or her child.

As Matthew looked at her he understood in a measure what this had done to her, and it aroused his pity and tempered his manner and brought from him softly a plea. "Anne" – he went towards her – "I did wrong and I'm sorry, but if you'll only forgive me and face up to it we'll weather this together."

"Weather this together!" She had stopped her rocking motion but her hands still hugged her waist and she glared at him and repeated, "Weather this together! How dare you! You are vile, filthy, you are not fit to . . . to –" She pressed her lips tightly together in an effort to stop her tears flowing, and then she ended, gabbling, "And . . . and the church. Think of the church."

"Damn the church! And damn you for that matter, because if there's anybody to blame for her" – he now thrust his hand back at the silent fear-filled face of the child – "it's you! If you had acted as a wife should, I wouldn't have had any need to look further."

"You would blame me for your vileness?"

"Yes. If there's any sin, as you call it, connected with this business it stems from you . . . Aw, God!"

They stood confronting each other like combatants who would know no peace until one or the other was slain. And then she did slay him, for now she brought out through her teeth, "Well! Well then! if I have been wanting in my duty before I shall be doubly wanting in the future for I shall never let you lay a hand on me in my life again."

Time seemed to stand still as they stared at each other.

"We'll see about that." The words came sieved through his lips.

41

"But when you're making such a promise I'd remind you to think of the Scargill household. Yes, yes." He nodded slowly at her now as he saw her face blanch even further. "His wife, I understand, presented him with a similar proposition and what did he do? He brought three young lasses into the Hall as servants. One of them is still there, and his wife is long since dead. What one man can do another can imitate."

Again he felt his pity rising for her when she put her hands to her throat and audibly gulped at her spittle, but he knew that it would be fruitless to show it, and so what he said was, "It is understood that this child stays, and I'm giving you the opportunity to see to her well-being. If you don't I shall take it into my own hands. And you know what that means, your authority as the mistress of the house will be undermined. You have a choice."

He could almost see her weighing up the consequences of his words. He watched her turn slowly now and look at the child. Then her back seeming to stiffen even more, she turned about and went swiftly from the room.

In the hall, the children were standing in a group at the bottom of the stairs, and the little maid was standing near the kitchen door. It was to her that Anne Thornton beckoned, but when Tessie stood before her, she had to open her mouth wide twice before she was able to give her the order. "Take the girl," she said motioning her head slowly backwards, "into the washhouse and see that she bathes. Miss Margaret will bring you some fitting clothes. Burn those she has on now."

"Yes, ma'am." Tessie dipped her knee, then looking towards the child who was standing near the master at the morning-room door, she held out her hand, saying, "Come on. Come on," and Hannah, seeming to recognize one of her own kind, went forward and took the proffered hand.

They were walking across the hall past the children when there came a sharp rap on the front door. Tessie paused and looked towards it, then turning her head over her shoulder, her glance asked her mistress if she should open it. But it was her master who said abruptly, "Go on with your business, Tessie, I'll see to it."

When he opened the door there stood Maudie, the parson's maid, and without any preliminaries she gabbled at him, "The

Reverend, he says will you come on quick 'cos she's dying, the woman. She mentioned you."

Matthew drew in a long shuddering breath, paused for a moment while he looked sideways towards Anne, then fully round to where his four children were staring wide-eyed at him, and lastly at Tessie and the child she was still holding by the hand. And Hannah, quickly taking in the gist of what the maid had said, pulled herself from Tessie and, running towards the door, cried, "I want me ma! I want me ma!"

Matthew catching hold of her thrust her back towards Tessie, saying, "Do what your mistress ordered, bathe her." Then going out, he banged the door closed behind him and hurried down the pathway.

The Reverend Stanley Crewe was a small, thin man. He was no preacher, no real advocate for his calling, and he was tolerated rather than loved by his parishioners, but he was sincere and kind. He was kneeling now by the side of the woman lying on the grass verge that bordered the drive to the vicarage and he looked up at Matthew and shook his head as he said quietly, "I'm afraid she's gone, poor soul. I . . . I sent for you, Matthew, because she mentioned your name and . . . and something about her daughter whom she left with you. I couldn't understand this. I . . . I thought she was rambling until she gave me this." He now picked up from the grass at his side a long thumb-marked envelope and held it up for Matthew to see, saying, "She said she wanted me to keep it until the day her daughter married, as it says on the envelope, see." He now nodded his head. "It's written in a very good hand."

Matthew bent forward and read: " 'Concerning Hannah Boyle. This letter is to be put into the care of a minister of God, or some legal person, and to be given to the above-named on the day that she weds.' "

"It is sealed too." The minister turned the letter over and showed the large blob of red sealing wax. "She seemed very concerned about the letter." He now nodded down towards the still figure on the grass. "She said something about it having been written by . . . the penny lawyer."

Matthew straightened his back. Written by the penny lawyer?

43

These were clerks with a little knowledge of law, who wrote letters for the poor. He looked down at the letter again. Why hadn't she left it with him? But need he ask? People like Nancy knew all about temptation, and would he have been strong enough not to open it? No, it would likely have been one of the first things he did, even if afterwards he didn't destroy it but sealed it again. No, Nancy, poor Nancy had been wise in her own way. But why was he thinking poor Nancy? He should be cursing her. And part of him was, for she had come into his life like a charge of explosive, and with the same devastating effect. He still couldn't visualize the extent of the consequences of her appearance; and not only her appearance, for that after all had been short, but what she had saddled him with . . . the child.

Why had he accepted the fact without thorough probing and questioning that the child was his? Why?

Because the memory of his running away from her that night like a scalded cat had always remained at the back of his mind.

"I'll have to get in touch with the House."

"What!" He brought his attention fully to the parson now.

"She'll have to be buried."

"Oh yes, yes, of course. But . . . but I'll see to it."

"You?" The parson's eyebrows moved slightly up and then he gave a short, self-conscious laugh as he said, "Well, if you knew her. Is she any relation, Matthew?"

Matthew looked down on the still body and the white face that strangely now was recognizable as the Nancy he once knew and he said slowly, "You could say so. In a way you could say so."

3

For days the village had been agog, and the town of Allendale too. But why, some of the dalesmen said, couldn't the Thornton affair have been brought into the open at another time when there was no excitement about, for it had almost overshadowed the great event of April 11th, the day on which young Master Beaumont came into his own. By! that was a day and a half wasn't it; something to be remembered for years ahead. Two hundred workmen from the Allen Smelt Mills following the Allendale Town band to the King's Head, there to feast and drink. They even set off a cannon in the young master's honour, and illuminated the whole town at night, so showing up to even greater beauty the decorations of flowers and evergreens. And this wasn't to mention the bonfires that had blazed on the surrounding hills. In each of the dales the miners and smelters had dined and rejoiced in their own particular way: eight hundred and seventy in East Allendale, five hundred odd in West Allendale. And what about Weardale? Over a thousand there. Nigh on three thousand altogether, including the youngsters, enjoyed Mr Beaumont's hospitality on that day.

And when the cups had been drained many times and the laughter and joking was mounting high, what subject caused the men to splutter into their mugs and the women to cover their mouths with their hands? Why, the affair up at the Thornton house. Not that anything was actually said in front of Matthew himself because Matthew was respected and liked. In fact, the newcomer into Elmholm House had put a feather into his cap. No, it was his wife that the laughter was against, that madam who looked down her nose at honest working people and who almost strained the muscles in her arms grabbing at the fringe of the gentry.

At the same time however, they all agreed they had to hand it to her for sheer bare-faced audacity for endeavouring to palm the youngster off as Matthew's niece. Matthew's niece indeed! Would a man like Matthew Thornton have let his sister die on the road? Moreover, it was known that the only sister he had was far away in Australia. Who did Madam Thornton think she was hoodwinking?

Anyway, the top and the bottom of it was the woman who died in the vicarage drive had once been a young lass whom Matthew had taken down, and when she knew her end was near and there was no one to look after her bairn, what did she do? She made a bee-line for him. It was as simple as that.

Yes, that part was simple, but the life that the bairn was being made to lead wasn't so simple. Young Tessie said that she was made to eat in the kitchen, and she had a bed of sorts up in the back garret; it was all right in the summer up there but it was as cold as charity in the winter. And the child was a canny bairn, Tessie said; her name was Hannah but the mistress always called her *The Girl*.

It would be interesting to see how things worked out, the villagers said. By! yes, it would that.

Hannah had been living her new life for three weeks. At times it seemed that she had always lived here, and she would have liked living here if it hadn't been for two things. First, she missed her ma; and secondly, she didn't like the missis, she was afraid of her. Every time the missis looked at her she thought she was going to hit her. She thought she could like the mister but he didn't speak to her much although he, too, looked at her. But it was in a different way from the missis. And she wholeheartedly liked the children, that is all except Betsy. Betsy was a spiteful bitch. She was like Annie Nesbit who had lived in the room opposite them in Newcastle and who used to stuff black beetles into the keyhole, and they used to crunch when her ma turned the key.

She liked Tessie and Bella; oh aye, she did, they were nice to

46

her, kind. She looked at Bella now standing at the table, her thick arms pounding the dough in a great earthenware dish as she talked to Tessie who was greasing tins at the other end of the table. They were talking about her. They always talked about her. She didn't mind, in fact she liked it. It made her feel. . . . She couldn't explain to herself how it made her feel, except to think that she wasn't lost.

"Damn shame!" Bella pounded the dough with her fist. "She's tret like scum. Why, if she tret me like that I'd walk out, begod! I would." She now leant over the dish towards Tessie and, her voice a whisper, she said, "You said she told them they hadn't got to speak to her?"

"Aye, she did, Bella, unless it was absolutely necessary. That's exactly what she said, absolutely necessary. An' Miss Margaret spoke up, she said something I couldn't catch. An' Master Robert did an' all. But she shouted at them. Eeh!" Tessie now started to giggle. "Do you mind when she used to lecture me for raisin' me voice? Eeh lad! sometimes now her voice sounds like a candyman's trumpet."

They both turned now and looked at Hannah, and she, smiling back at them, said, "I like peelin' taties. Me ma and me used to peel them all day at an inn. Me ma said if they'd been kept together they would have filled a ship's hold, but as quick as we did them they come an' took 'em away." She laughed again, and Tessie laughed with her. But not Bella; Bella shook her head sadly and said, "'Tis true the sayin', one half doesn't know how the other half lives. I can remember the time meself when I was so hungry I could eat a man with the smallpox." Then she continued pounding the dough with increased vigour as if in thankfulness for her privileged lot.

It was as she lifted the dough with a great plop on to the floured board that the kitchen door opened and the mistress entered. She was dressed for outdoors in a pink-sprigged linen gown and a short light fawn alpaca coat, the back of it sticking out like a fan over the bunched skirt of the dress. On her head she wore a small straw bonnet, the front decorated with a number of blue velvet bows. Altogether she looked a lady, a well-dressed lady.

She stood pulling on her short grey silk gloves as she spoke to Bella, saying, "I am going into the town, I am taking Miss Betsy to see Doctor Arnison; her teeth are troubling her."

"Yes, ma'am." Bella dipped her knee just the slightest.

"You have the orders for dinner?"

"Yes, ma'am." Again she dipped her knee.

"I have left your weekly allowance of tea on the dining-room side table. See that you make it last this time, and I forbid you to use the leaves from the house pot, it is nothing but gluttony."

". . . Yes ma'am."

She directed her attention towards the fastening of the last button of her glove as she said, "You will see that *The Girl* does not leave the house."

". . . Yes, ma'am."

Anne Thornton had not looked once in Hannah's direction. She turned about now and, her skirt and petticoats rustling like crumpled parchment, walked with erect carriage out of the kitchen.

Bella gave one final thump to the dough as she exclaimed "*The Girl!* Even the cat's got a name. An' don't use the tea leaves again. Huh! Anyway, what she lets come out of the dining-room pot is so like water bewitched an' tea bedamned you can see through it, an' I hope they pull all that 'un's teeth out . . . little madam that she is."

The children stood in the hall, surrounding Betsy who was on the point of tears as she whimpered, "He'll hurt me. He'll put big pinchers in like the picture in the nursery book."

"Don't be silly!" Robert pushed her none too gently on the shoulder. "They don't use pinchers any more, they strap you down on to a table and Ralphy Buckman comes with his blacksmith's hammer and goes bang! bang! bang!" He demonstrated, flinging his joined hands from one side to the other.

It was as Betsy let out a shrill cry that her mother entered the hall demanding, "What is it? Stop that noise, Betsy! What is the matter?"

"Rob . . . Robert says they are going to knock it out with a hammer and. . . ."

Anne Thornton now put a protective arm around her youngest

child as she looked at Robert and said, "You're a cruel boy. I've warned you about frightening your sister before, haven't I? Now when your father comes. . . ."

She stopped abruptly, and the three elder children stared at her. For years now it had been her usual procedure when they were naughty to threaten them with dire reprimands to come from their father, which frightened them not at all; but during the past weeks she hadn't mentioned their father's name once to them. And so after a pause, during which she moved her lips tightly over one another, she finished, "You will be dealt with."

She pushed the still clinging Betsy from her, saying sharply, "Stop snivelling! Dry your face and straighten your bonnet." Then looking down at the child's feet, she said, "Your shoes haven't been polished."

"Tessie said she had done them, Mama."

Anne Thornton now clicked her tongue and gave a small jerk to her head; then looking at the other children, she said, "Behave until I return. You, John, better continue with your studies as you're returning to school tomorrow, and you don't want to be unprepared. . . . And you, Margaret, will read the chapter in the *Young Lady's Book* on escrutoire. Your handwriting leaves a lot to be desired." She smiled thinly at her daughter now as she added, "Remember the heading:

For careless scrawls ye boast of no pretence;
Fair Russell wrote, as well as spoke, with sense.

"And you, Robert." She now drew in a long breath. "If I remember rightly you were discussing with your father some time ago the work of Mr Forster, the book he wrote on 'Strata'. You will read the part that deals solely with the lead mines, and I will hear you when I return. And" – she now stabbed her finger at him – "don't for a moment think you'll be able to hoodwink me because I have informed myself to some lengths on that particular part. . . . Come, Betsy." She pushed her daughter before her, went through the door that John was holding wide for her, then out on to the garden path; and the three children stood and watched her until she had passed through the gate and disappeared behind the hedge.

49

After slowly closing the door, John turned and looked at the other two, but as he was about to speak Robert checked him with, "It's all right for you, you're going to school tomorrow."

John made no reply but he lifted his head as if the prospects were pleasing, and when Margaret said "Escrutoire!" in a voice that was deep with disdain, he laughed and repeated "Escrutoire."

"Tell you what." Robert leant towards him. "Let's go and see Hannah."

Both John and Margaret exchanged glances before Margaret, her voice now a whisper, said. "She didn't say that we couldn't see her, only that we hadn't to converse with her unless it was absolutely necessary."

As they all turned towards the kitchen John pulled them to a stop saying, now, "Hadn't we better see if they are on their way?"

"Yes, yes, you're right." Robert dived towards the stairs now, the other two following him, and without ceremony they burst into his bedroom and dashed to the window.

It was John who jumped up on the sill. Then after peering over the village and remaining quiet for a moment, he said, "Yes, yes, there they are, they are passing Rickson's yard. Good, come on." He jumped off the sill, and once more they were dashing, down the stairs this time and across the hall. But at the kitchen door they stopped and grinned at each other; then Margaret opening the door, they filed decorously into the kitchen and walked towards the table.

Bella had finished making the bread, and Tessie had just arranged the loaf tins along the fender and covered them with a warm cloth. She turned her bright face towards them exclaiming, "Oh! hello, Miss Margaret."

"Hello, Tessie."

It was as if they hadn't met for a week, but each party knew what the other was about; that is all except Hannah who had stopped peeling the potatoes and was now looking towards the children, who had moved towards the end of the table and were within an arm's length of her.

It was Robert who spoke to her first. His face was straight and his words expressed a feeling that had been troubling him for days. "You all right?" he asked.

"Oh aye, I'm all right."

It was Margaret now who asked, "Is it hard work peeling potatoes?"

"No, no." Hannah shook her head. "I like doin' taties. Don't I, Tessie?"

Tessie now joined the group. Except for her dress and voice she could perhaps have been taken for their sister; and she said, "That's what she says, miss. An' she says she used to peel them all day long where she lived in the big city in Newcastle. Didn't you?"

"Aye." Hannah nodded brightly. "But once I didn't get nowt cos I took too much skin off . . . only some stew." Her eyes were now fixed on John. He was almost a head taller than the rest, and his hair looked all gold. She was faintly reminded of someone she had seen who looked like him, bonny, beautiful. As she stared at him the memory became clearer in her mind. It was in that church she had crept into where the singing was going on. There was a picture in a window and the sun was coming through it. . . . He was bonny was the big one called John. She liked looking at bonny people. Her ma used to say she too was bonny. She missed her ma. She would like to go every day over the road to the corner of the cemetery where her ma was buried, but she could only look towards it on a Sunday when she followed the family to church. She didn't like church; she always wanted to fall asleep, and there was a funny smell in there, musty, like the wet cellar below the house in Newcastle.

"Tell us what you did in Newcastle. Did you go to school?" Margaret was bending down towards her now so that their faces were on a level, and Hannah smiled into the kindly eyes and said, "School? No, no, I never went to school. But I can count, I can count up to ten. Look" – Hannah now lifted up her dirty wet hands and one after another she bent her fingers and thumbs, and when she had finished Margaret slowly straightened up and cast a glance at Robert and then at John.

Staring down into Hannah's upturned face, John was telling himself that she had beautiful eyes. He had never seen anyone

51

with eyes like hers; they held your attention, you wanted to keep looking at them. He had experienced this feeling since first seeing her; he had thought then it was because she was so curiously dirty and ragged, but now he knew it was her eyes that made him want to keep looking at her.

John's fascinated gaze was brought abruptly from Hannah's face by a proposition Bella was making to them. "Wouldn't you like to take the little 'un up into the nursery for a while?" she was saying.

They all turned and stared at her; then again they were looking at each other.

"It'll take the mistress all of two hours to walk there and back into the town, an' then God knows how long she'll be at Doctor Arnison's. She might even have to wait; he could be out, way over the hills or any place, bein' him."

"Let's!" The exclamation was from Robert. Swinging round, he grabbed Hannah's hand and pulled her upwards, and as he did so Tessie cried, "Eeh! Master Robert, wait a tick; let's get the muck off her hands, she'll make you all clarty."

As Tessie wiped Hannah's hands on a rough towel they laughed at each other as if sharing a joke; then Tessie pushed her towards Margaret, and, she now taking Hannah's hand, they all ran out of the kitchen, leaving Bella and Tessie gaping at each other, their faces full of glee.

Sweeping the table with a wet dish-cloth, Bella cried in no small voice, "Eeh! that's done me as good as a rise in pay. It isn't often you can get one over on the missis, is it, lass?" and to this Tessie replied, "No, you're right, Bella, 'tisn't often you can get one over on the missis. No, by gum!"

Hannah had never felt so happy in her life, nor had she laughed so much. John had lifted her on to the rocking horse in the nursery and they had all rocked her backwards and forwards so vigorously that she nearly fell off, which had made them all laugh. Then Margaret had let her nurse her dolls, and Robert actually let her wind up a model of a crane he had made to which a basket was attached; but the most exciting thing of all that happened to

52

her was when John showed her how to close one eye and look through a glass, and there see colours the like of which she had never before imagined.

But all the fun stopped abruptly when Margaret, happening to look at the painted wooden clock on the nursery wall, put her hand to her mouth and exclaimed, "Look at the time! And I've done no reading."

The three stared at each other, then at Hannah, and it was John who spoke to her now, saying quietly, "You'd better go, Hannah, we've got work to do before Mama comes back."

"Oh aye, all right." She backed from them.

"We'll play another time."

She nodded at Margaret now, still backing.

"I'll take you up into the hills one day."

She turned her gaze on Robert and again she said, "Oh aye. Oh aye."

She turned and opened the door, but as she made to go she looked back at them again and said, "Ta," and they glanced quickly at each other and laughed; then in a chorus they answered her, each replying, "Ta!"

She did a little skip now out on to the landing, and pulling the door closed behind her, she stood for a moment listening to their laughter, her face widening into an even broader smile. Then she walked down the narrow stairs and across the landing in the direction of the main staircase. To reach it she had to pass a number of doors, and one being partly open, she slowed her step and moved towards it; then paused a moment before pushing it open a little further.

By! it was a bonny room. There was a bed with a pretty pink cover on it, and the window to the side was framed in lace curtains with frills to them. She could see part of a dressing-table with coloured boxes on it and shiny things. Oh, it was a bonny room.

Gently now she pressed the door still further open, then stood with her hand on the white china knob as she gazed in amazement about her. It was a bedroom, but there were chairs in it and a couch, and pictures on the walls. She had already earlier glimpsed the children's rooms, but they were nothing like this.

Their beds were wooden, this bed was made of brass, shining, golden brass.

On tiptoe now, she went into the room and pushed the door behind her, and in the middle of it she turned a slow circle. Eeh! if her ma had had a room like this she wouldn't have had the cough, would she? And look at all those bonny boxes on the dressing-table. She walked forward and lowered herself on to the seat that was shaped like a cradle without sides, and her hand went out and very gingerly she picked up a blue enamelled box and, raising the lid, stared at the brooches lying on the pink velvet pad. Fancy having all those brooches! One, two, three . . . she counted up to eight.

The next box she picked up held three rings; one with white stones in it, the others red ones. She liked the red ones, they were warm and shiny.

Then there was the box with the beads, strings and strings of beads.

Eeh! she'd love a string of those beads, the blue ones. She'd seen her ma nick beads and things off the shop counters. Hankies too, lace hankies. Oh, her ma had been good at nicking lace hankies. Her ma said that the shop had so many they never missed them, but they had run once when the shopman had tried to grab her ma. By! they had run that time.

There were such a lot of trinkets here she was sure nobody would ever miss one or two bits. She started at the beginning again and opened the box with the brooches in and, having selected one, she put it in the pocket of her frock; then the rings. She liked the red one. She tried it on her finger. It was much too big but her finger would grow. She placed that in her pocket also. And the beads. She would like a string of beads. She would just take one string. . . . Oh! She hadn't noticed that. She moved the strings of beads and disclosed a gold chain with a heart-shaped locket on the end. Aw now, that was pretty, wasn't it? The prettiest of the lot. And the locket had a stone in the middle of it. Oh, she would like that. Oh yes, she would. But she'd better not wear these things, not yet at any rate, she'd better hide them like her ma used to do. Her ma had made a hole in the bed tick where she used to stuff the things, the little things, in among the feathers. . . . Eeh! that locket was bonny. She lifted the chain and tried to get it over her head, but it wasn't big enough. Then she laughed to herself. Of course, there was a catch on it. She had only to open the catch.

She had to fiddle about quite a while before she could undo the clasp on the locket, but eventually she had it opened. Then she put the chain around her neck and in order to fasten the clasp she brought it to the front, slanting her eyes down to it. But she never got as far as closing it, for she heard a great gasp behind her, and she spun round on the seat to see, standing in the doorway, the missis.

. . . Anne Thornton had had a trying morning. The walk to Allendale Town had been hot and dusty; Betsy had been fractious; and Doctor Arnison had kept her waiting an interminable time. He had even seen to Miss Cisson before her, and yet they had both entered his waiting room together. He had even still further delayed her to attend to a farm labourer who had stupidly thrust a pitchfork through his foot. But these indignities had been small compared to the looks that had been levelled on her by the locals of the town. Even Mr Hunting, the grocer, who had always been most deferential towards her, even he'd had a smirk on his face when he served her. In fact, for one awful moment she had thought that he was going to detail his assistant to see to her needs.

Then there was the village. Oh, the village. She would never forget what she had suffered at their hands on the day of Mr Beaumont's celebration. Even those who in the past had dipped their knees to her looked her full in the face and walked straight past her. And it had been the same this morning. And all this had come about through a man's sensuality.

She hated Matthew; deep, deep in her heart she hated him, and she would never forgive him for the disgrace he had brought upon her. And what was adding to the injustice of it all was that he himself wasn't suffering for his wrongdoing; in fact he was being hailed more loudly than before. And she wasn't imagining this. "How goes it, Mr Thornton?" they cried across the street to him. "Fine day, Mr Thornton." "Hope I see you well, Mr Thornton." There was one time during the evening of the festivities when she was so enraged that she had become fearful, for she imagined herself actually striking out at them, felling them right and left with her clenched fists. She had seen them lying in heaps dead and dying from her blows. The image had caused the sweat to pour from her.

. . . And now here was the cause of all her distress daring to enter her bedroom and finger her jewellery.

"Get off that seat, girl!"

Hannah sidled to her feet and, trembling, watched the woman advance towards her. As the locket and chain was being grabbed from her hand the chain seared her palm, then when the hand caught her full across the face she fell sidewards on to the floor, and as she fell the ring and the brooch tumbled from the pocket of her dress almost to Anne Thornton's feet.

"You thief! You horrible dirty little thief!" She stooped and grabbed up the brooch and the ring and stared at them for a moment; then she looked down on the child.

Hannah wasn't crying. Her mother had boxed her ears so often that she considered such a blow not worth worrying about, but although she wasn't crying she was afraid, very much afraid because her mother, after boxing her ears, would usually pull her towards her and hold her tightly, but this woman's face was frightening. She sidled herself back on her hip thinking to escape under the bed, but the hands came down and grabbed her.

"John! Margaret!"

As she called out the children's names she shook Hannah viciously; then pulling her towards the open door she called again, "John! Margaret!"

A moment later the four children appeared on the landing and gazed at their mother in amazement where she stood just within her bedroom holding Hannah by the shoulders.

"Bring me the whip from the rack, John."

"Mama!"

"You heard what I said, bring me the whip."

The boy looked from his mother to the petrified face of the small girl and he shook his head twice before saying, "You mustn't, Mama. You mustn't."

"Do as I say, boy!"

"No, Mama, you mustn't."

"Margaret!"

Margaret's answer to her mother's command was to back silently towards the far wall, there to stand with her palms pressed tightly against it.

Their mother now looked at Robert, and the children could almost see her dismissing him from her mind: If John or Margaret wouldn't obey such an order Robert never would.

"Betsy! go into the hall, stand on a chair and bring the ornamental horsewhip to me."

Betsy stared at her mother for a moment, glanced towards her two brothers; then whimpering, she turned about and ran down the stairs.

In the interval it took for Betsy to return with the whip Anne Thornton explained to her children, between sharp gasps of breath, the reason for her actions. "She was stealing, she had my ring and brooch in her pocket, and she was about to take the locket, my mother's locket that holds a lock of my father's hair. She's wicked and she must be punished. I will not tolerate a thief in this house."

"Papa would not do this."

She turned her blazing gaze on to Robert now.

"Wouldn't he? He has used the whip on you and John before today."

"Only once." Robert's lips were trembling. "And . . . and because we did something bad. We let the dog loose among the sheep and . . . and he had to shoot it; it . . . it was bad."

As Betsy scrambled across the landing now, her arm extended and holding a short-handled whip in her hand, John protested again, "Don't do this, Mama. Please don't do this," and of a sudden Hannah's voice was added to his and she cried, "No, no! don't you whip me, missis. I'll . . . I'll not do it again. Don't you whip me."

It was as if the child's voice inflamed Anne Thornton's anger to madness for, now grabbing the whip from Betsy and swinging Hannah from her feet, she went back into the bedroom, thrusting the door closed with her buttocks, and there she held the child at arm's length while she brought the whip around her feet. But

57

Hannah being agile jumped and the whip's end merely curled round her long skirt, the tip of it only flicking her ankles. But such was the stinging feeling that it incensed her, and now she began to fight, in her turn kicking at Anne Thornton's legs and lurching and clawing at the hand that held the whip.

She was still struggling wildly when she was lifted bodily and thrown on to the bed; then she felt she was being smothered when her dress and petticoats were pulled over her head and her face pressed into the feathered tick.

She had no stockings on, nor did she wear long frilled knickers like Betsy did, or a little habit shirt; all she was wearing were two long petticoats and her dress and pinafore, so when the whip contacted her small bare body she screamed and bounced as if she were on a hot griddle.

Each time Anne Thornton brought the whip down she was striking at a particular villager: Ralph Buckman's two sons, Bill and Stan, who had dared to laugh in her face when she passed the smithy; that little devil of a woman, Daisy Loam, the butcher's wife, who had dared to say to her last week, "What will I be sending you up the day, missis, you'll want a bit extra with one more mouth to feed?" And then Miss Cisson, who that very morning in the doctor's waiting room had dared to ask her if she would be wanting anything cut down for the new little miss; there were miners and their wives who now had the effrontery to approach her without first being bidden; and Susanna Crewe, who was supposed to be her friend, but who aimed to be more pious than her parson husband, daring to suggest to her certain passages in the Bible dealing with forgiveness. . . . And then there was *him, him, him.*

She might easily have flayed the child to death but for John and Robert coming into the room and grabbing hold of her arms.

The boys' faces were chalk white as they stared from their mother to the small, now merely whimpering, partly naked body on the bed, the back showing a mass of criss-cross weals, some oozing little spots of blood. Then a slight thud brought their attention back to their mother again. She had dropped down on to the dressing-table stool, and after a moment she bent her head forward and buried her face into her hands. But when John, now going towards the open door and saying softly to Margaret, who was still standing against the wall, "Go down and tell Bella to come and see to Mama," Anne Thornton pulled herself up from the seat and, her hands massaging her throat as if to force the words out, said, "No, no! I'm all right. Stay where you are."

Margaret stayed where she was, but she turned and looked towards the stairhead where both Bella and Tessie were standing. They had heard what their mistress had said and so they came no further; but they continued to stand there until they saw Master John come out of the room carrying Hannah in his arms, with Robert supporting her feet. They watched them stumble along the landing and into their own room and Miss Margaret and Miss Betsy scamper after them; then they heard the mistress's door close.

Silently they looked at each other for a moment before turning and going slowly down the stairs. It wasn't until they were in the kitchen that Bella said, "Bairns have to be whipped, granted, but there's a difference atween whippin' and flayin'. Anyway, what had she done to be so treated? Wait till the master comes in, I bet there'll be hell to pay. He won't stand for her being flayed, not if I know anything about him."

4

Anne Thornton had made up her mind what course she must follow. She must be the first to tell Matthew what had happened and why it had happened. She had washed herself down to her waist in cold water, she had changed her dress and done her hair; she had made herself go into the kitchen and see that the dinner was under way. One thing she hadn't done was face her children.

She had seen Robert in the back garden. He seemed to be looking for something. He must have gone down the back staircase for she hadn't heard him cross the landing. At one point she had heard them all upstairs in the nursery, their footsteps crossing and recrossing the floor.

Now aiming to keep her own steps firm, she left the sitting-room, crossed the hall, went down the garden path and on to the main road. Here she turned away from the village, walking by the hawthorn hedge that bordered their land, and when she reached the end of it she stood waiting.

Within five minutes Matthew made his appearance and the amazement showed on his face when he saw her standing in the roadway, and before he reached her he called out, "Something wrong? Something happened?"

Dismounting quickly from his horse, he led it forward towards her, asking again, "What is it?"

"I . . . I have something to tell you."

"Don't beat about the bush, woman, has something happened to the children?"

"No, nothing has happened . . . my children."

She watched his face stiffen. "What have you done to the child?" His words were slow and deep.

"That . . . that is what I have come to tell you. I had been to

Doctor Arnison's and on my return I found her in my room. She was stealing my jewellery. I thrashed her."

"You thrashed her?"

He let out a long breath, there was even the suspicion of a smile on his face. For a moment he had thought she was going to say she had killed the child, because he knew that her hate of the poor waif went deep. This, of course, in a way was understandable; he had hoped that the child's natural charm, and time, would erase the feeling.

"Is that all?"

She swallowed deeply. "Yes, that's all," she said.

He moved slowly forward now, walking the horse as he said, "Well, her background must have been pretty rough, and I don't suppose she looks upon stealing as a crime." He turned and looked at her. "Wasn't she just playing with the things?"

"She had them in her pocket, a ring, a brooch and . . . and my mother's locket."

Oh. Oh, her mother's locket. She laid as much stock on that as on the crown jewels. If the child had to steal something it was a pity it had to be that. "Well, I don't suppose it'll be the first thrashing she's had and it won't be the last, she's got to be made to learn the difference between right and wrong. What were you doing at Doctor Arnison's?" He smiled as he asked the question. It seemed as if they were getting back on to the old footing. Perhaps in chastising the child she had also chastised herself for her attitude these last few weeks.

"Betsy's had toothache, quite a lot of late. I . . . I felt it had to be seen to."

"Oh yes; yes, of course, she was crying last night. Did he take it out?"

"No; he said it wasn't bad. He said there was nothing wrong with it. I don't think he knows much about teeth."

"Don't you? Oh well, it's my opinion that he's forgotten more than most doctors know."

They were going up the drive now, but opposite the front door they parted company, she going into the house and Matthew continuing towards the yard where Dandy Smollett was waiting for the horse. There was no grin on the boy's face, and when in silence he led the horse away, Matthew looked after him for a moment before entering the kitchen.

As usual, Bella and Tessie were preparing the dinner. Bella was pounding potatoes in the iron pan with a wooden pestle and her "Good evening, master" had, he thought, a strange inflexion to it.

"Good evening, Bella," he answered. "Everything all right?"

"It depends on what one calls all right, master; what's right to some folk is wrong to others."

After giving her a keen glance he sat down and changed his shoes, took off his coat, then left the kitchen, making note that Tessie hadn't opened her mouth.

He washed himself, then went to the dining-room. As he entered he heard his wife saying to Tessie, who was placing the vegetable dishes on the table, "Did you do as you were bid and tell the children?"

"I did, ma'am, I told them twice."

"What's all this about?" He looked from Tessie's departing figure to his wife, and he watched her neck swell and her lips move over each other before she said, "They did not hold with my chastising *The Girl*."

He stared at her, his face blank now, then turned abruptly and went out. He took the stairs two at a time and when he reached the landing he called "John! Robert!" then went up the attic stairs and thrust open the nursery door, and there in a close group confronting him were John, Margaret, and Robert, but Betsy was running towards him, crying, "Papa! Papa! they wouldn't let me come."

"What's all this about?" He unloosened Betsy's clinging hands and moved towards the others, and again he said, "Come, tell me what this is about." Although he was looking at John it was Robert who answered. "She, Mama, she whipped Hannah."

Matthew now saw the tears spurt from his younger son's eyes and the words came choked from his mouth as he gasped, "She . . . she used the fancy trap whip on her and . . . and she was all weals and bleeding and kept screaming." Now his voice became so choked that he drooped his head and put his hand over his mouth.

Margaret, too, was crying. Only John was dry-eyed and it was to him that Matthew said, "Where is she?"

"I . . . I . . . we . . . we don't know, Papa."

"What do you mean, you don't know?"

It was evident that John, too, was almost in tears, and Matthew shouted at him, "Tell me what you mean, you don't know."

"Well, after . . . after we had carried her from the room into . . . into our bedroom, we washed her back, and Margaret" – he pointed blindly towards his sister – "she . . . she rubbed her with butter, and . . . and it eased her and we left her lying quiet. We . . . we thought she was asleep and . . . and we came up here and . . . and we talked about it because . . . because it was dreadful, Papa. And when we went downstairs again she was gone."

"Gone?"

"Yes, Papa. We went in the garden, and all about, but we couldn't find her."

Matthew now put his hand to his head. She had met him on the road and said she had thrashed the child and he had imagined that by thrashing she had meant spanking. He had pictured her bending the child across her knee, baring her bottom and whacking it. But then he should have known she wouldn't have brought the child in contact with her own body. She had never as much as put a finger near her since the day she had come into the house, and so when she had said she had thrashed the child she had meant just that. She had thrashed her with a horsewhip and in such a way that she had shocked her own children. Was the woman going mad? Yet on the road she had appeared calm enough, calm and contained. But where was the child?

He looked at the children now and said, "Margaret, take Betsy downstairs to the dining-room. John and Robert, you come with me." He turned and made for the door, but stopped and asked, "What time was this, when you last saw her?"

"About . . . about three hours ago, Papa."

Three hours! She could be anywhere, on the moors or fells by now, and if she were left out all night in that state she could be dead by morning because the nights still held frosts. In any case, even a summer's dawn was chilling to the bones in these heights.

There was no sign of his wife as he and the boys passed through the hall, and outside the front door he directed them. "You, John, search round by the vegetable garden and the greenhouse, and you, Robert, make your way down to the stream. I'll go behind the house to the woodland. If you find her, whistle; if you don't, come back here."

In less than fifteen minutes when he returned to the drive the boys were waiting for him and he didn't waste any time in questioning them, but said, "We'll go on the fells; she'd likely go down the back staircase and out of the side door. You both go behind the village in the direction of the town; keep within hailing distance of each other. I'll go by way of the churchyard. Yes, yes" – he nodded to himself – "she might just have gone that way. But whatever distance you go be sure you're back here before the twilight sets in. Understood?"

"Yes, Papa."

"Yes, Papa."

"Off you go then."

Both boys now turned about and ran round the side of the house while he himself strode down the drive, across the road, and into the churchyard, and wending his way between the headstones he came to the mound that as yet bore no stone. But there was no sight of the child lying on top of it. Jumping the wall, he now made for the hills.

Once out of earshot of the village he began to call, softly at first, "Hannah! Hannah!" for there were boulders and small gullies behind or in which she could be hiding.

When he was standing atop of a hill he saw, far across the valley, Ned Ridley leading a string of horses up the steep rise which led to the Pele house, and as he watched him disappear from view behind the tall erection a thought came to him and he put his hand to his chin and slowly rubbed it. That was the only other house she knew; Ned and his old grandfather were the only other people she knew; but could she possibly have made for there? He began his descent at a run, and when finally he came within hailing distance of the house he saw Ned Ridley come round the back of it and stand waiting, as if he were expecting him.

His running came to a stop a few yards from Ned, and he was too short of breath to speak for a moment or even to answer Ned when he said, "Are you looking for somebody?"

"Yes. Yes, Ned, I am."

"I thought you might be."

He stared into the stiff face of the young fellow as he said, "I just got in. I thought it was you I made out over there on the hills an' I wondered why, until a few minutes ago. You know, Mr Thornton, there's two kinds of folk I hate, them as lay man-traps, and women what take whips to flay bairns."

As they stared at each other their jaws reacted in the same way, tensing the muscles of their cheeks.

"Perhaps you'd like to come in and see what your lady wife has done, eh?"

Another time Matthew's retort would have been, "Don't you dare speak to me in that manner, boy!" but now all he could do was to stare at Ned, then follow him around the side of the house past the steep stone steps that led to a door in the first floor and into the stable-room.

It was dim inside and the lantern was already lit. Ned pointed towards where it hung from a hook in the stone wall, its diffused light shining down on Hannah and the old man seated by her side.

At the sight of Matthew, old man Ridley pulled himself to his feet and walked towards him as if he were about to take him on in a fight and, his voice high and cracked, he cried, "Your bloody wife should be hung, mister. If I had her here I'd show her what flayin' was. I'd curl that whip around her belly." He pointed to a long horsewhip that was lying against a stall. "She must be a bloody maniac. Come and have a look at this."

Matthew walked slowly forward until he was standing against the edge of the shallow platform on which the child now lay on a bed of hay. Her eyes were open and she stared at him, not moving until, dropping on to his hunkers his hand went out towards her, and then she shrank from him, and the movement must have caused her pain because her face twisted and she winced.

" 'Tis all right, hinny, 'tis all right." The old man was pulling the horse blanket from off her now, saying as he did so, "I took her clothes off 'cos they were stickin' to parts of her skin. Turn over, hinny. Gently now, gently." As he helped her to turn he unwound the cotton sheet in which she was swathed. And then Matthew saw her back and legs. From above her little waist down to her heels was a mass of blue weals; some had bled quite a bit judging by the blood on the sheet and the dry clots on the skin. A wave of sickness overwhelmed him, not only at the sight of the little flayed body, but because his wife had inflicted this on a child, a small defenceless child.

"What do you think of that?"

He raised his eyes and looked at Ned but said nothing. What could he say? And what was adding to his present agony of mind was the fact that the child had become afraid of him.

"Hannah!" He bent his face down close to hers. "Listen to me, dear. Listen to me. I'm sorry. Do you understand? I'm so very, very sorry this has happened to you. It will never happen again."

He did not turn his head when a deep "Huh!" came from behind him but went on, "I shall see that it will never happen to you again. Nor shall anyone ever raise their hand to you again. Do you understand?"

Hannah gulped in her throat, wiped a piece of hay from her cheek and whispered, "She did it with a whip."

He closed his eyes tightly for a moment, bit hard on his lip, then looking at her again, he said, "I'm going to take you home."

"No, no!" She shrank away from him. "I want to stay here. I like it here; I want to stay here."

"You can't stay here, Hannah. And I promise you, listen to me." He now put his hand on her brow and stroked her hair back. "I promise you, dear, that your life will be different from now on, nobody will harm you again as long as I live. Do you understand?"

"I shouldn't think about movin' her the night."

He glanced up at Ned.

"You can feel her head." Ned nodded down to her. "If I'm any judge she's in a fever."

When he again put his hand on Hannah's head he realized that she was indeed very hot and might even be in a fever. It would do no harm to leave her here for the night. He again bent his face close to her and said, "I'll come back for you in the morning, Hannah, when you're feeling better. But remember, nobody will ever hit you again. Everything is going to be different from now on. That's a promise."

66

Gently he stroked her cheek; then rising to his feet, he left her to the ministrations of the old man, who was once again covering her up; and walking to the door of the stable-room he gazed out into the fast approaching night, and his heart was sick inside him.

"We don't blame you."

He turned and looked at Ned and said harshly, "Well, you should, for she came into the world through me."

"Aw, there speaks the churchman, Mr Thornton, but if every man carried the blame for what he drops on the way there'd be few in these hills walking head high. Things like that happen, 'tis nature, and who's to deny nature when it comes at you. Not me for one, so I blame no man for fathering a bairn, not me."

Matthew turned his head fully and looked at the young fellow. He had heard tales of Ned's exploits, but had taken most of them with a pinch of salt. People made mountains out of molehills and fathoms out of tiddler ponds, yet he had no doubt but that there was a grain of truth in the stories, and the irony of it was a fellow like Ned would get off scot-free with his escapades while he himself, who had slipped up but once, had it brought right home to his hearth, and the consequence of it lay flayed on the hay behind him.

Well, now he knew what he had to do, what in justice he must do. He had never been a violent man, but now he felt violent. He hadn't believed in retribution but now he knew he was going to act as God and deal out retribution. It was as if he had been planning for weeks what he must do this night and what he must do tomorrow. But to begin with he must ask Ned for his silence.

"I want to ask you something, Ned."

"Aye, fire ahead, Mr Thornton."

"Do you think you can keep a closed mouth about what's happened to the child?"

"Keep a closed mouth, me? Well, I've never found it too hard to keep a closed mouth about most things, but why should I keep a closed mouth about this?"

"Because I ask you as a great favour to me."

"But what about t'others, there's bound to be talk from Bella

67

and Tessie, not to mention young Dandy. They must know what went on for she must have squealed like a stuck pig."

"I'll deal with those in turn, as I'll deal with the one who flayed her."

Their eyes as they gazed at each other were deep and dark, then Ned said, "Very well, if it's like that you've got me word I'll say nowt."

"And your grandfather?" Matthew jerked his head backwards.

"Oh, he'll say nowt an' all if I tell him not to, but he'll do it more readily when he knows you're gonna deal out fair punishment. Aye, he'll do it more readily then."

"Thank you, Ned. I'll be back in the morning for her."

"Aye, well, I'll be here; I'm not due over at Allenheads till noon."

Saying no more, Matthew turned abruptly away and walked from the yard down the hill towards the village and his home.

It was almost dark when he reached the house, but the boys were still waiting for him at the gate. He checked their enquiries by saying, "I've found her, she's up at the Pele house with Ned Ridley. She'll stay there until morning."

"Is she all right, Papa?"

He looked at Robert for a moment before answering, "She will be. She will be." Then turning to John, he asked, "Have you had your supper?"

"No, Papa."

"Then I want you to go indoors now and have something to eat, but don't take long over it. Then you must both go to your room. . . . And listen to me." He looked from one to the other. "No matter what you hear you must not leave your room, you understand?"

When they didn't answer he said again, "I said to you, no matter what you hear you must not leave your room. And you will tell the girls this from me too. Do you understand me?"

"Yes . . . yes, Papa."

"Yes, Papa."

They nodded at him.

"Go along then." He watched them go up the drive and into

68

the house; but he remained where he was for quite some time before he, too, approached the house.

He did not enter by the front door but went round the side and so into the kitchen.

Bella was sitting at one side of the fire, Tessie at the other, and Dandy Smollett in between them, and they all rose quickly to their feet as he entered.

It was Bella who asked, "Did you find her, sir?"

"Yes, yes, I found her, Bella. Sit down." With a wave of his hand he motioned them all to their seats. And now looking from one to the other, he asked, "Have you been out into the village since this afternoon?"

They all shook their heads, and again it was Bella who spoke. "No; no one's left the house, sir," she said.

"Has anyone called?"

"No, no, only the coalman, and that was this mornin'; groceries don't come till the morrow."

"So you have told no one what transpired this afternoon?"

There was a pause before Bella said, "No, sir, nobody, nobody."

"Well then" – again he passed his glance over them – "I want your promise that you will never mention what happened this afternoon, or what might happen tonight . . . to anyone. If I find that the business of my house becomes common knowledge in the village then, Bella, I shall dismiss you; and you, too, Tessie. As for you, Dandy, you will go back to the House."

"No, sir, not me, I wouldn't let on. No, sir, not me. I wouldn't do anything that would take me back to the House, sir."

"Well and good. As for you, Bella, and you, Tessie, I think I can even speak for you, can't I?"

"Oh yes, sir." Bella nodded her head slowly, and Tessie followed suit, saying, "Oh aye. Aye, sir, I wouldn't open me mouth."

"Good, good. Now what I want you to do is this. I want you all to go to your beds and remain there until tomorrow morning at the usual time for getting up. No matter what you hear, don't come out of your rooms. You understand that?"

They all stared up at him, their mouths slightly agape, their eyes wide, their faces awe-filled, and again it was Bella who answered, but her voice was merely a whisper as she said, "Aye, sir, we'll stay in our rooms, if that's what you want."

"That's what I want. Now if you're finished for the night I would get away. Good-night. Good-night to you all."

"Good-night, sir." Their voices were merely whispers that followed him from the room.

He now went into the dining-room where the boys were sitting eating some cold pie and he said to them briskly, "Take what you want upstairs."

"Yes, Papa. Yes, Papa." They scrambled to their feet, dragged pieces of pie from the central plate on the table and a square each of cheese from the board, then hurried out of the room, their heads down as if they were escaping after having stolen the food.

He remained in the dining-room until he heard their footsteps above him crossing the landing, then he went out and towards the sitting-room door. This he flung open but didn't enter the room until he saw that it was empty. Walking towards the fireplace, he noticed that the cushions had been arranged in a symmetrical line along the back of the couch, their corners all pointing directly upwards, and also that the fire had been banked down and a guard placed around it, which all spoke of her having retired for the night. Well, that's what he wanted her to have done, retired for the night; in a way it would simplify things.

What time was it? Half past nine o'clock. He would wait a short while.

He was about to lower himself down on the couch when the arrangement of the cushions brought his bent back to a halt. She did not like the room disarranged once she had settled it for the night. Blast the room, and her, to hell's flames! He took his hand and swiped the four cushions into a jumbled heap in the corner of the couch, then fell back with a plop on to the horsehair seat. It seemed in this moment that all his life he had been following a routine, a routine that had an army discipline about it. During the first months of his marriage her housewifery had pleased him; in fact, amongst other things he had looked upon it as one of her accomplishments. But it had begun to irritate him before the first child arrived, although after the arrival of John he had bowed to it again, for he knew only too well that children could disrupt the household. In any case he had had to admit to himself then that he did like his meals on time, and he did like peace in the evenings to work on his mining papers, which work was an absolute necessity if he ever intended to rise to the position of head mining agent.

But here, thirteen years later, he was still as far away from that position as he had been when he first read *Forster's Strata*. He knew it wasn't even likely now he'd ever reach Mr Sopwith's position, or even that of the under agents, William and John Curry at Allenheads. But in this moment he asked himself what did that matter, the only thing that mattered was what he intended to do in the next half-hour, what must be done within the next half-hour, for after that his rage might wane, although this he doubted because it would be a long while before he looked on her face and didn't see it over-patterned by the child's back.

He sat staring into the dull glow of the fire until the clock in the hall chimed ten; then he rose to his feet, walked firmly to the door, went into the hall and took from the rack the riding whip, picked up the lamp from the side table, then went up the stairs.

Placing the lamp on a bracket on the landing wall he turned the wick down, then opened the bedroom door and entered the room.

Her light was turned low. She was lying well down in the bed, her head on the pillow; but she wasn't asleep for her eyes swivelled towards him as he approached the bedside. He saw that, as usual, she had been reading a passage from the good book before settling down, it lay open where she had left it. He picked it up with one hand and screwed up his eyes. She had been reading David's psalm of thanksgiving.

His eyes scanned the page. There were ticks against various numbers but none against Verse 20 which read: "The Lord rewarded me according to my righteousness; according to the cleanness of my hands hath he recompensed me."

He looked down on her now where she had risen on her elbow, her eyes not on the book in his left hand but on the whip in his right hand, and his next words brought her sitting bolt upright in the bed for he read to her from the book: "according to the cleanness of my hands hath he recompensed me." And with a backward sweep of his hand he threw the book across the room and, his voice a growl, he demanded, "Did you read that before or after you flayed the child?"

She was sitting with her back pressed tight against the brass rails of the bed now and her voice had a tremor to it as she replied, "She stole; I told you I chastised her."

"Huh! chastised her! When you said you thrashed her I thought you had aired her backside and given it to her with your hand, but no, no, you used this." He flicked the whip and the thong swished an inch from her face causing her to gasp aloud.

"Yes, that made you jump, didn't it? It didn't even touch you but it made you jump, so what do you think that child felt like when you whipped her almost to death. Aye, almost to death, because if she hadn't gone up to the Ridleys and been attended by the old man she'd have run on to the fells, and the night would have finished her. And then what do you think would have happened when they found out, eh? You would have been for it; it would have been your neck. And I would have seen you go without raising me hand. Do you hear?"

His face was close to hers now and his lips shrank back from his teeth as if he were looking on something repulsive, and his voice indicated as much as he said, "You know what you are, you're a cruel, vindictive bitch of a woman. You're nothing, do you hear? nor ever have been anything else but a bloody upstart. You've been the laughing-stock of the village and the town for years, and it's never got through to you because you imagined you were somebody, somebody different from the common herd. Well, there are women in that village down there, did they get wind of what you've done to that child, they'd spit on you. They'd pelt you with horse muck, they'd rub your nose in it."

"How . . . how dare you sp . . . speak to me in such a fashion. . . ."

"Shut up! And never use those words to me again. How dare I? I'll speak to you any way I like! Now you know what I'm going to do, I'm going to speak to you in your own language, but before I start I'm going to tell you something else because by the time I've finished with you you won't be able to take it in, not clearly. Well, now listen. Tomorrow morning I'm going to give you some rules whereby you and I are going to live together in this house, and you'll obey them or you'll go, the choice will be yours. Now!"

With a quick movement of his hand he ripped the bedclothes right down to the foot of the bed and before she could leap from it he brought the whip around her bare calves; then as she cried out and wreathed on the bed her night-gown exposed her lower thighs and when the whip stung them she let out an ear-piercing scream. Now, his hand on her shoulder, he swung her around as if she had been a sack of coal, and holding her down by the neck, he pulled up her night-dress until it exposed her buttocks and lower back and then he brought the whip down on her for perhaps ten times, and each time it contacted her skin she screamed.

When at last he stood back from her she lay sobbing and moaning, her hands grabbing handfuls of the feather tick. He stood taking in long slow breaths of air, and when he exhaled his stomach seemed to sink in, dragging his shoulders forward. He had to make an effort to turn away from the bed, and when at last he did, his step was slow and heavy.

Out on the landing, he closed his eyes tightly before making for the stairs.

He replaced the whip in the rack before going into the little study adjoining the dining-room. Here he opened a cupboard below the book rack, and from it he took a tray on which stood a bottle half full of whisky, and putting the tray on the desk, he poured out a full glass of the liquor. After drinking deep from it he sat down at the desk and drooped his head forward on to his folded arms.

The following morning, before sending Dandy Smollett on the horse to the mine to tell Mr Byers that he would be a little late, he caught hold of his leg and, looking up at him, said, "You remember what we talked about last night, Dandy?" and the boy remarked, "Aye, master."

"Good; then go on your way."

This done, he went into the kitchen where Bella and Tessie looked at him silently, but their eyes speaking volumes, and to Tessie he said, "Make the bed up in the spare room, Tessie; I'll be

73

using that for the time being. Then I want you to take the pallet from the little room and put it in the boxroom next to it. I'll see about getting a single bed as soon as possible. That room is to be for my daughter . . . Hannah. You understand?" He looked from her to Bella, and they both nodded their heads, and together they said, "Yes, master."

"One thing more." He was now addressing Bella. "She won't be helping you in the kitchen here again."

There was a pause as he and Bella stared at each other. Then with native boldness, Bella answered, "As I see it that's how it should be, master."

"Then we both see it the same way, Bella. I'll be bringing her down from Ridley's shortly, she might need some attention. I'd be grateful if you'd see to her."

"I'll do all I can for her, master; and Tessie here an' all, we like the bairn."

"Thank you." He nodded from one to the other, then went out, with Bella calling after him, "Won't you have no breakfast, master?" and he answered, "Not until I get back."

The mist was still thick as he mounted the fell, and although the path led upwards, the higher he went the more dense the mist became; and when it seemed to seep through to his skin and made him shiver he thought again of what would have happened to the child if she had been left out all night, and in her condition.

When he pushed open the door of the stable-room both Ned Ridley and his grandfather turned from the platform and looked towards him, and from the looks on their faces he thought for a moment that the child must have died.

"She's in a fever." Ned had risen to his feet. "She's had a bad night."

Matthew bent over the hay and looked down on Hannah. She was awake and he said to her softly, "How are you feeling, my dear?"

"I'm sore, mister."

"You'll feel better tomorrow."

"I'm sweatin'."

He put his hand on her head and when it came away wet he looked across at Ned, but it was the old man who said, "She's

74

full of the fever; you cannot take her down there like this."

Matthew bit on his lip for a moment, thinking, then said, "Will I bring the doctor up?"

"What's he say?" The old man turned to Ned, and Ned mouthing loudly as he gesticulated, cried at him, "He says will he fetch the doctor?"

Old Ridley now turned his head sharply and confronted Matthew again, saying, "Doctor! What could he do I haven't done? Cured more complaints than he's ever heard of, me. I've given her a dose of ipecacuanha, that'll clear her bowels, cool her down. An' she's had a few drops of laudanum an' all."

"Laudanum?" Matthew's eyebrows moved upwards, and as much from his expression as from the mouthing of the word the old man gauged Matthew's questioning and repeated, "Aye, laudanum. She wanted somethin' to settle her nerves after that lot. But you're not takin' her down there the day unless you want to polish her off altogether."

Matthew now turned and looked at Ned and he said quietly, "It's very good of you both to take the trouble."

"Oh, trouble!" Ned shrugged his shoulders. "We do it for dogs, horses, an' strays; an' I think you could number her in the last lot."

"She's no stray, Ned."

"No? Well, you could have hoodwinked me, Mr Thornton. Aye, you could have that, you could have hoodwinked me, 'cos mind I'm only repeatin' what I've heard, but strays have always got to work for their livin', earn their bite so to speak. Of course, as I've said, you can only go by what you hear. But if one only goes by half of it I would say that in her case she's worked for her keep."

Ned's eyes had never left Matthew's face. Nor had Matthew's lids blinked once. Under other circumstances such bold talk would have made him want to lash out at the fellow, at least with his tongue for he could never hope to beat him with his fists, not Ned Ridley; but he had learned over the years that young Ned could be stung by the tongue and it carried more effect than a blow. Yet on this occasion he did not retaliate in the only way left open to him; instead, his voice slow, his tone steady, he said,

"She is my daughter and in future she'll be known as such."

"I'm glad to hear it, Mr Thornton. Aye, I am that. But, of course, you're speakin' for yourself; do you think you'll get others to act in the same way to her?"

There was a long moment before Matthew replied, "Yes, others will act in the same way towards her or else they'll have to answer to me."

Ned said nothing to this, and Matthew turned and looked at Hannah again. The old man was wiping the sweat from her brow with a cold wet rag, and he bent down to her and, taking her chin gently in his hand, he brought her face to the side until she was looking at him, and quietly and firmly he said, "I'll be back later to take you home, either tonight or tomorrow, depending on how you feel. I've got a room ready for you, it's next to mine. You'll be sleeping near me, you understand?"

She made the slightest movement with her head; her eyes, unblinking, stared up into his.

"Everything from now on is going to be different, you are going to be happy. Yes, yes" – he stroked her cheek gently – "you're going to be happy."

Straightening up, he turned and walked from the platform and Ned went with him as far as the door, where they stood silently side by side looking out into the morning.

The mist was still thick and shrouding everything. There was a blanket on all the sounds outside, yet behind him there was clatter and snufflings and warm activity. He hadn't noticed before that all the stalls were full. There must be eight to ten horses in there; perhaps there hadn't been a time since this place was built that there had never been horses stabled on the ground floor.

He glanced now towards the sharp-featured, tousled dark-haired, thick-shouldered youth at his side. Young Ned looked the spit of his father, and his bone formation was recognizable in his grandfather's face. The Ridleys had a name going right back for centuries, and not one to be proud of, for only in latter years had they become established as bona fide horse-dealers. One of them during the last century had definitely been hanged for horse stealing, two had been transported, and old Ridley himself back there had done time, being lucky to get off lightly with a stretch. It was only the fact that now and again he had picked up a good horse for Lord Buckly that had saved his neck.

All the Ridley men had been characters: outspoken, independent men, but a hard drinking, hard fighting, quarrelsome breed, especially on fair and festival days. . . . Yet who but they would have looked after the child back there without going down to the village and spreading the news of what had happened to her. And in the present circumstances it was doubly commendable that Ned should keep quiet about this affair, for he knew well enough that the young fellow had no liking or even respect for Anne, for she looked upon him as scum and never failed to hide her opinion of him when they met.

"I'm takin' two ponies into Hexham the day." Ned jerked his head backwards. "It's a private deal so it may be close on evenin' afore I get back, but she'll be all right with the old 'un, never fear. He's brought me through fever more than once. He's good at that kind of thing and he knows herbs an' such."

"I'll pop over at dinner-time."

"Aye, you could do that if it will ease your mind, but as I said she'll be all right with him. An' he loves wee 'uns."

Matthew stepped from the doorway into the mist, then turned and said briefly, "Thanks."

As briefly Ned answered, "You're welcome," and on this they parted. . . .

The mist had lifted by the time he reached the house. There was a pink glow over the yard. He looked towards the stable. Dandy had not returned. As he went towards the kitchen the door opened and Tessie, looking towards him, said, "Oh, master, you're wet."

"The mist's thick on the hills."

" 'Tis very wettin'."

"Your breakfast's all ready for you in the dining-room, master."

He turned to Bella, saying, "Thanks," then asked, "Are the children astir yet?"

"No, I haven't heard them, master."

He did not put the same question about their mistress, and now without changing his boots or taking off his coat he walked up the kitchen, out into the hall, and from there into the dining-room; and the new procedure was not lost on either Bella or Tessie.

It was Tessie who, with her finger patting her lips, said in awe-filled tones, "Did you see that, Bella? Did you see that? He never took off his coat or boots."

In the dining-room Matthew waited until Tessie brought the porridge in; then he sat down at the table and ladled himself out four spoonfuls from the bowl she was holding. As this was only a third of what he usually took she said, "Is that all you'll be needin' master?" and he answered, "Yes, Tessie, I haven't much appetite this morning. Have you mashed the tea?"

"No, master; the mistress hasn't been down to unlock the caddy."

"Here." He took a key from a ring he brought from his pocket, saying, "I think that'll fit it. And tell Bella to make it doubly strong."

"Aye, master, aye. Oh, yes, aye." She scurried out, amazed at the turn of events. . . .

It was as he was finishing the third cup of tea that the door opened and the children entered. John came in first, then Margaret pushing Beatrice before her; Robert came last and closed the door behind him; then they approached the table but they did not speak.

Putting down his cup, Matthew looked at them and said quietly, "Good-morning, children."

In a chorus they answered, "Good-morning, Papa."

"You return to school today, John?"

"Yes, Papa."

"And you, Robert?"

"Yes, Papa."

"Well, I want to talk to you. I'm . . . I'm glad I have this opportunity before you go. First of all I want you to know that there are going to be changes in the house." He stared at them and they stared at him. "What those changes are going to be I shall tell you in a little while after – " He now took up a napkin from the table and rubbed it hard across his lips before he ended, "I have presented them to your mama, but this much I will say

78

now. Hannah is my daughter, therefore she is your half-sister, and in future you will treat her as you would each other. Now" – he rose from the table – "I want you to get your breakfast and remain in the room until I come back, for then I shall be able to tell you of the changes I referred to."

Not one of them spoke, and he rose from the table, cast a glance over them that touched on a weak smile, then went from the room and up the stairs.

He expected the bedroom door to be locked but it wasn't. He expected her to be lying on the bed face downwards but she wasn't.

She was sitting propped up with pillows, and it was evident that she had been out of bed because the blinds were drawn. The sight of her face caused a momentary pang for it had a bleached, stark look; that she had been weeping profusely was evident from her swollen eyelids, but her expression was as he had expected it. He did not advance towards the bed but stood in the middle of the room and for a moment he found difficulty in speaking. Then when he did, his words came out so formally that he imagined for a moment he could be reading from a legal document. "I have come to inform you, Anne, that there are to be changes in the household; from now on the child will be recognized as my daughter. I've already given instructions that she will have a room to herself on this floor. She will also eat at the table with us and will no longer do any menial work." He paused for a moment as he saw her endeavour to move her body further up the bed. At the same time her mouth opened to speak, and he said, "Wait! I haven't finished. With regard to the children, I have decided to send Margaret and Betsy to the private school in Hexham. Hannah will go with them. They will go as weekly boarders, and you shall have the company of them at week-ends, all . . . or none."

Again her mouth opened.

"As for Robert, he will join John this . . ."

"You can't do this. You won't do this!" Her voice sounded strange; her thin high-faluting twang had disappeared; her words had a grating, ordinary tone about them.

"I thought you would have welcomed the idea. You have always stressed that the teaching responsibilities took up so much of your time that you couldn't practise your own accomplishments, your piano playing, your embroidery and such important things." There was a sneer in his voice as he ended, "Things you called the niceties of life."

"You! You won't do this. Do you hear?" She had brought her back up from the cushions, and the movement had evidently caused her pain because she winced and gulped in her throat before she went on, "I'll take action against you. I'll go to Mr Beaumont, I'll see him personally. You . . . you only got the position through my influence. I'll . . . I'll have it taken away from you. I will! I will!"

"You're welcome to try. Oh yes, you're welcome to try. See Mr Beaumont by all means, and I, too, shall see him. I'll take Hannah with me, and I'll show him her back and legs. The lash marks are so deep she'll carry their shadows until the day she dies. Do; go to Mr Beaumont; but by doing so you'll undo the good work I've already done on your behalf, for I've sworn the three in the kitchen to silence; I have also done the same with Ned Ridley and his grandfather."

She was resting on one elbow, and now her other hand came up and covered her mouth. He nodded at her, saying, "Yes, the Ridleys. You remember I told you last night that but for them you might not have got off with just a whipping. And it's true, only too true."

"Well—" He now lifted the heavy lever watch from his waistcoat pocket and looked at it; then replacing it, he said, "I think that's all I've got to say. Oh, except one more thing, perhaps the most vital. For years now you have done your duty as a wife only under protest and, as you may remember, at long intervals apart, and I bore with you because I enjoyed my family life and wanted peace. I can tell you with truth that I haven't had another woman since I took Nancy Boyle, but now all that will be changed. As you said, you could not in the future bear me to touch you; nor would I for that matter be able to touch you, so I intend at the first opportunity to satisfy my needs elsewhere. I only think it fair to tell you this. But you will still, of course, be mistress of this house and nothing on the surface will apparently have changed, so your face will be saved in the village, and in the town."

80

"You're a fiend, a wicked fiend. You won't do this to me, you can't."

"What is the alternative? Will you allow me in the bed with you tonight?" He now took two quick steps towards her and the lightness of his tone changed to a deep growl as he bent forward and demanded, "Will you? All right, I'll give you an option. I'll come to you tonight and every night when I need you and I don't go for my pleasures elsewhere. What do you say?"

She looked up at him. She was still leaning on her elbow. Her breathing was coming in short gasps and it seemed that she was unable to speak. But then she did, and what she said was, "I hope God strikes you down dead."

He remained in his bent position while they glared at each other; then he swung round and almost at a run went out of the room, across the landing and into the room where he had slept last night and, banging the door behind him, he turned his face towards it and, lifting his joined hands above his head, pressed them tightly against the wood.

As he stood thus it wasn't of Hannah he thought, nor of the future and the liberty he had afforded himself in it, but he thought of last night, and like a spectator he saw himself wielding the whip across her bare flesh and hearing her scream with each downward drive of his arm, and he knew that in flaying her he was merely giving vent to an urge that had lain just below the surface of his mind for years. The fact that Hannah had broken the skin was incidental. He would have done it some time or other, he would have had to, to express his dislike of her, because that is what his feelings towards her consisted of, and had done, he knew, for years past now, dislike, not love or hate, merely dislike. Even whilst loving her he disliked her.

PART TWO

The Girl Growing Up 1858

1

Matthew stepped on to the bare boards that felt cold to his feet, and reached for his linings; and as he pulled them on he looked at the woman lying in the bed.

His rising had turned the bedclothes back off her, and she lay on her side naked to the middle of her thighs, and she scratched one gently as she answered a question of his, saying, "Why should I lie to you, 'tis but a small matter? They didn't kiss or nothin', but 'twas the way they looked at each other, with their hands joined."

"When was this?"

"Oh, 'twas in the summer."

"Had you seen them before, I mean together up on the hills here?"

"Aye, when you come to speak of it, aye."

"With the others or just alone?"

"Just alone, together, walkin' like, laughin'. But why worry your head? They know what they are; being related nothing can come of it. Still –" She turned on to her back, stretched her hands above her head and gripped the brass rails of the bed as she went on, "What am I talkin' about, there's Peg Docherty who lives on the bottoms, she had one by her father an' two by her brother, so they say. Well, they were by somebody 'cos her man was at sea. Folks always look for him comin' back to see which one he'll half murder this time."

"Be quiet, Sally."

The tone of his voice brought her head round sharply and the laughter seeped from her face as she said, "I didn't tell you it to disturb you, Matthew, but I wondered if you knew like."

When he didn't answer but went on buttoning his waistcoat

she got quickly from the bed and pulled on her petticoats and skirt and lastly her bodice; but by the time she was dressed he had his top coat on and his hat in his hand, and when she came to him and stood before him he said, as always, "Thanks, Sally," and she, as always, shook her head from side to side, saying " 'Tis nothing. 'Tis nothing."

Time and again he had thought how odd it was that their partings always followed the same pattern. "Thanks, Sally . . . 'Tis nothing. 'Tis nothing."

When his hand went to his pocket she put hers out and touched his arm, saying, "No, not this time. Anyway, I'm hard-pressed to find where to hide it; his eyes are all over the place. And what's the use of it to me if I can't spend it? The only one who enjoys it is me sister. An' by! she does, she looks forward to me goin'," she said laughing.

"You never know, it might come in handy some day; you should keep some by you."

"Well, if that day comes an' I'm ever in need I hope you'll be there."

"I'll be there, Sally."

She now put her hand up and touched his cheek and, leaning her body against him, she said, "Do I make you happy, Matthew?"

"Happier than I've ever been in my life, Sally."

"Well, I've got God to thank for that anyway." She now drew her body away from him and said softly, "It could be another fortnight afore he's off again, but you'll be able to tell by the stones. I'll see to them."

He now pinched her cheek gently, kissed her as gently, nodded at her, then, turning up the collar of his coat, he crossed the small room of the cottage, went through a stone-flagged scullery and out into the dark night.

His horse was tethered in the shelter of some bushes, and he untied him but did not mount him; instead, he led him on to a narrow path that slowly wound its way uphill, then down again. He did not tread warily for he had come to know the path well in the dark, and not until ten minutes later when he approached the coach road did he stop and light the lantern hanging from the pommel, then mount the horse and ride down on to the road.

The night was bitingly cold; there was a smell of snow in the air. The horse's breath floated up like a grey mist through the flickering light. It neighed loudly, telling him that it was both cold and hungry, but instead of spurring it forward into a trot, he kept it at a walking pace; he had a lot to think about before he entered the house. John and Hannah. No! No! the lad couldn't be so mad. Yet he was in the hot years of his youth, and a girl like Hannah was enough to stir any man's blood, let alone when it was flooding the loins for the first time. He must talk to him. But how? What could he say? Well, he could start by talking about Miss Pansy Everton. He had ridden with her at the shoot, and they had followed the dogs at the hare coursing. True, she wasn't the type he would have chosen for his son had he any say in it, but as a daughter-in-law she would certainly please Anne, for although she was of farming stock it was wealthy stock, and unlike most farmers' daughters she hadn't been made during her early days to help out on the farm, but had been sent to school, the same one as Margaret and Hannah had attended. Moreover, being an only child she would likely come into everything when her parents went, and he couldn't but admit that Mulberry Farm was a good inheritance and situated in a beautiful part Riding Mill way. No, John could do much worse financially than marry Miss Pansy Everton, and if all that Sally had implied was true the quicker it came about the better. But the question still remained, how was he going to approach the lad?

The horse neighed again and he himself shivered, and as he did so he felt the soft caress of the first snowflakes falling on his face.

Well, well, he wasn't surprised, it was the middle of November. The country signs had been prophesying a hard winter; some folks were saying it would be a repeat of '53. There had since been no snowstorm such as that winter had provided, yet while it had caused the death of a young stonemason up on Kilhope Head who was caught out on it, it had been the means of providing himself with body solace over the past five years.

One bitter night he was returning from the mine when he heard a cry for help coming from the direction of the river. It had been thawing for days and the river was running freely, but on this

particular day it had begun to freeze again. Before he reached the
river bank he had guessed what had happened. Someone had
foolishly tried to cross by the stepping stones instead of walking
further up and taking the bridge, and they had undoubtedly
slipped into the river. And the accident must have only just
happened for after a short while in that water no one would be
able to shout as this one was doing.

In the early winter twilight he saw that the victim was a young
woman lying half in and out of the water, she was clutching at one
of the stepping stones.

Cautiously, he made his way towards her and, taking her hands,
jerked her upwards; and when they were on the bank her teeth
were chattering so much that she couldn't even thank him. "Where
are you bound for?" he had asked her.

And still unable to speak she had pointed in the direction of
Sinderhope, then after a moment had stammered, "L . . . Lode
Cottage, Sinderhope way."

Sinderhope was a good two miles further on whichever way
she walked, and he had been through the village time and again
but couldn't remember having seen her.

"Is it far from the village?" he had asked her, and she had
nodded, then said, "A distance."

"Come on." He had taken her by the arm and led her at a run
across the field to where the horse was impatiently stamping on
the road, and hoisting her up into the front of the saddle, he
mounted and put the horse into a quick trot, shouting to her,
"You'll have to tell me the road for it's getting dark."

She told him the road, and when they arrived at the cottage,
seemingly in the midst of nowhere, she was so stiff with the cold
she couldn't help herself down from the horse, and he lifted her
to the ground, then led her towards the door, where she bent down
and took a heavy iron key from under the stone in which was set
a boot scraper. Inside, he saw that the place was small, but clean
and comfortable. From the shape of the house outside he guessed
that all it consisted of were the two rooms downstairs and an
attic under the apex of the roof. Seeing that the fire was banked
down, he took a pair of bellows from the stone wall and blew the
ash into flames; then he turned to her and saw that she was

shivering as if with ague, so much so that she couldn't unfasten the loop of her coat.

As his hands pushed hers aside and undid the buttons he asked, "Your husband, where is he? Is he a mine worker?"

She shook her head, then stammered, "Dr . . . dr . . . drover. He's . . . away to . . . to the market, Newcastle."

"Newcastle?" He nodded at her. "That's some way off, Newcastle." And when she nodded back at him, he said, "You'd better get to bed, I think."

This time she made no attempt to answer him but, her eyes closing, she slumped to the floor.

What he did next was to hurry to the other room, pull the patchwork quilt and a brown blanket from the bed, then proceed to take her wet things from her. She was wearing a rough serge skirt, a striped blouse, two woollen petticoats and a print one; under the blouse she wore a habit shirt, and under that a cotton chemise, but no pantalets. Her black stockings were held up by the simple procedure of twisting the top into a knot then looping it under the rolled down top of the stocking.

She recovered from her faint as he was taking off her chemise, but her hands made no protest, she just lay looking at him as he rolled her first in the blanket and then in the quilt, and when he had finished he stared down at her for a moment before saying, "That feel better?"

"Aye, yes." Her voice was low and conveyed a pleasing sound to his ears, as had the sight of her body to his senses.

He had thrown off his own outer coat, and now he went to it and taking from the back pocket a flask of whisky, the carrying of which being a habit he had acquired over the past two years, he lifted a mug from a wall rack to the side of the fireplace, poured a measure of the whisky into it, then tilting the big iron kettle standing pressed against the low black hob, he filled the mug to the brim. And now, bending over her, he put his hand under her head and raised it, saying, "Drink this."

And without murmur she drank it.

Having poured himself a measure and heated this too, he squatted down by her side, and as he sipped at it he asked, "What's your name?"

"Sally Warrington," she replied.

"I haven't seen you about before, not in the market or any-where."

And to this she had explained, "I seldom go down that way. Bill brings back our needs."

"What time will he be home?"

"He won't be comin' the night," she said; "perhaps the morrow towards evening."

"Oh." After that they had continued to look at each other.

"How old are you?" he had next asked her, and she replied, "Coming twenty-eight."

"No children?" He had glanced about him, and at this she had shaken her head.

"Been long married?"

"Since sixteen."

"Since sixteen," he had repeated. She didn't look much more than sixteen lying there and her body still plump and firm. He'd had a few women over the past three years but they were women who had been used frequently for the same purpose, as he himself used them. They were the dregs of the back streets of Hexham.

He was forty years old and there was great unrest in him; he had known of late an understanding of those men who packed up and went, just went. There one minute, gone the next, men who walked out of the house in the morning and were never seen again.

He had risen to his feet as he said, "I'd better be on my way; you'll be all right then?"

She hadn't answered, only stared up at him.

"You're not afraid to be alone?"

"No." She had moved her head slightly. "I'm used to it. I'm alone most of the time. He goes all over the county drovin'. He brings them down from Scotland one time, the cattle, or takes them up another, or into Hexham or Newcastle, anywhere where there's a good market. There's a number of them, drovers, they like being together, 'tis company."

"Don't you get lonely?"

"Aye. Aye, I get lonely."

She shivered again, and he said quickly, "I'll bring another

90

hap," and when he tucked it round her his face hung over hers and he asked softly, "You'd like me to stay a while?" and she answered simply, "'Twould please me if it would you."

That's how it had begun; and for five years now she had pleased him and he her, and no one knew.

Way back there on the road was a broken gate. It lay drunkenly against the gap in the broad stone walls. On top of the stone wall to the right of the gate were some loose stones. The manner in which these were placed told him whether it was safe for him to turn off further down the road or if it were better that he ride on.

It had all been easy because Anne could no longer question his comings or goings; she had no authority over him any more; she was, in a way, like an unpaid housekeeper carrying out her duties for which she received board and lodgings, and two gowns and two bonnets a year, besides free transport to Hexham whenever she wished to do special shopping. That she spoke to him civilly in company was, he knew, simply because she couldn't bear the real situation between them to be made public either in the village or in the town. Yet he felt in this direction she was deluding herself, for the fact that they had occupied separate rooms for years must have seeped out of the house.

Bella, Tessie, and Dandy, as loyal as they were, wouldn't have been human had they not talked about the situation in the house, particularly when the children were home from school, for then Hannah was allowed to roam free without let or hindrance, while the others came under their mother's strict surveillance with regard to holiday duties of reading and improving their accomplishments.

But now John was twenty and a promising engineer, and Robert, eighteen, had for the past year been working in the mine offices over at Allenheads; they could no longer be treated as schoolboys. Nor could Margaret, a young woman of nineteen, be tied to the house under the pretext of improving herself.

Margaret was of an independent nature and was definitely showing it at the present time by stating openly that she wanted to marry a bank clerk in Hexham. Well, everyone knew what bank clerks earned, hardly enough to keep body and soul together, but as her father he had spoken openly to her saying that if this young man would come and state his case honestly he would give the matter his attention.

Then there was Beatrice. Beatrice, Matthew was afraid, was the least loved of his children, at least by him, for she was too like her mother; in thought, word and deed they were almost a pair. But she, too, had left school last year. And now there remained only Hannah.

In the ordinary course of events Hannah would have left school at the end of the Easter term, but there was no ordinary course of events where Hannah was concerned, and the thought of what she might have to endure, being in the house all day with Anne, had made him arrange that she should stay on for a further year. He understood she was very expert on the pianoforte, and had a good singing voice, but strangely he had never heard her sing in the house, and only once had he seen her perform on the piano.

Anne's treatment of Hannah had to be witnessed to be believed. They could be in the same room together but Anne could act as if the girl weren't there; she appeared as insubstantial as vapour to Anne. He had never known her address Hannah openly; when she was forced to speak of her it would always be to a third party, when she would allude to her as *The Girl*. "Tell *The Girl*," she would say to Tessie, "she must be ready at such-and-such a time." "Tell *The Girl*," she would say to Margaret, "she is not to chatter while walking behind me."

"You are not to go on to the hills with *The Girl*," she had said countless times to Robert, and that strange determined boy had sometimes just stared at her, and at others replied, "Very well Mama," then had run out of the house and caught up with Hannah as she rambled over the fells.

Only once had he seen her lose control. This was when she pushed John to the door and cried at him, "*That Girl* has gone out. Go and tell her she is forbidden to go near the Ridleys'."

How anyone could sustain hate at the pitch his wife had done all these years he was at a loss to understand, especially against someone as warm-hearted as young Hannah, for she was so grateful for the slightest kindness, so outpouring in her gratitude

As Bella had once said to him, "She's the kind that would give you the clothes off her back if she thought it would help you." But he had wondered if she would give the clothes off her back to the woman who had ignored her from the day she had laid the whip across her. What did Hannah think of Anne? He didn't know, but as generous as her nature was, it wasn't possible that she could harbour anything but loathing for the missis, as she still referred to her. And, strangely, she referred to him, too, in the same form; she never addressed him as any other but 'Mister'. But she could induce more feeling, more love into that one word than any of his children could with their 'Dear Papa's'.

What was he to do with Hannah? Well – he turned the horse into the gateway and up the drive – one thing he couldn't do with her, and that was to let her go on thinking there could be anything but brotherly affection between her and John. It was sheer madness on both their parts, more so on his, he being the elder by four years.

There were three horses attached to the household now, and when Matthew entered the yard the neighing from the boxes told him that both John and Robert had already returned home.

A few minutes later he entered the house, as usual through the kitchen, and after changing his boots and coat and washing his hands – he had soon taken up the old routine again, because as he put it to himself, he liked to eat clean – he went straight to the dining-room where the family were already assembled, and he greeted them as one, saying, "Hello, I'm a bit late."

"Are you very cold, Papa?"

He turned to his tall plain daughter and answered her homely smile with, "Frozen inside and out," and he chaffed his hands and walked to the blazing fire. He had not openly addressed Anne, nor she him, but after a moment when he said, "We'll be seated then," he took his place at the head of the table, she at the foot, while John and Robert went to one side and Margaret and Betsy the other.

Betsy, like her mother, had little to say during meals, in fact she didn't utter a word during this one, yet her eyes darted from one speaker to the other as if she were about to contradict them, or at least answer them, but she refrained.

"I'll have to take Prince in to be shoed tomorrow, Papa."

"It's no time since he was down there."

"I know, but he's a kicker. I'm sure he likes to see the sparks flying off the stones."

"You should get Mr Buckman to shoe him himself. Those boys pay no attention to their work."

"Oh, Mama!" Robert jerked his head disdainfully. "They've been at it since they could toddle; if they can't shoe a horse now they never will."

"No one can do their work properly when they're half drunk."

"May I have some more potato, Mama?" John handed his plate to his mother and she helped him; and as he took it from her, again he looked at his father and said, "I shouldn't wonder we'll have snow before the morning."

"We've got it now; it started as I came along."

"I hope we have it at Christmas and it stays hard enough for sleighing." Margaret smiled across the table at her brother. "You remember last year on the knoll when I shot the ditch and scooted across the road?"

As the boys laughed Anne said, "All very exciting, but you don't think that you could break your bones and be crippled for life."

"Aw, nonsense!" Robert waved his hand. "With drifts eight feet high on all sides?"

Matthew bowed his head over his plate and paid attention to his eating. If Anne and he had been living like real man and wife he would immediately have chastised Robert, saying, "Don't speak to your mother in that manner, boy," but he had left the bringing up of the children to her, and how they treated her he felt was the result of her training, or lack of it. Robert was a rebel, and had been difficult to manage since he was a child, and it had always been evident that there was no love lost between him and his mother.

John's approach to her was different. John was pliable, he did everything to keep the peace. His asking for another helping of potatoes a moment ago was an example of it. Margaret on the other hand had a bit of both Robert and John in her make-up.

She wanted peace but not at any price. Margaret would make a stand for what she believed in.

Betsy, on the other hand, was her mother pure and simple. That phrase, he had always considered, was never applicable in the way it was used, and never was it less applicable when applying it to his wife, for Anne was neither pure nor simple, but her impurity was mental rather than physical.

The meal over, he rose from the table, saying, "I'd like a word with you, John."

"Yes, Papa."

That was another thing. He would much rather have been called father, papa coming from the lips of the tall, blond young man seemed misplaced. But very likely he was the only one who thought so, for they were all so used to the title he didn't imagine they gave it a second thought.

In his study, he sat behind his desk, and John sat in the chair opposite him, and they exchanged glances of silent appraisal until Matthew said, "You're twenty. My! my! I can't believe it, it makes me feel an old man."

"Well, you don't look it, Papa; you carry your age very well."

The reply which was meant to be reassuring caused Matthew to lower his head and grin to himself and John added quickly, "What I meant to say was . . ."

"I know what you meant to say, John, but there's no use turning one's back on the fact. I am forty-five this year and once you reach this age it's only a jump to fifty, then a step to sixty, then a stumble to seventy."

"Oh, Papa!"

"It's true . . . it's true, boy, life takes on a gallop once you've reached forty. I suppose it thinks, 'Well, you've done your job, you've married, raised a family, what do you want time for now?' And that brings me to a point, raising a family I mean." He wetted his lips, leant his forearms on the desk, bent his body slightly forward and asked quietly, "Have you got marriage on your mind, John?"

"Marriage, Papa?"

Matthew watched the colour flooding over his son's fair skin;

95

it even seemed to light a flame in his hair, or was that a trick of the lamplight?

"That's what I said. You've heard of it?" He pulled a face at his son.

"Yes, yes, I've heard of it." John now rubbed the knuckles of one hand against the palm of the other, then said slowly, "I . . . I haven't given it much thought."

"No? What about Miss Pansy Everton? You've been seeing quite a bit of her over the past year, haven't you?"

"We've met occasionally."

"Do you like her?"

"Oh yes, yes I like her, she's a very nice girl."

". . . But."

"What? . . . What did you say, Papa?"

"I said but . . . but you hadn't any thought of marriage in your mind when you went courting her?"

"Courting her, Papa! I . . . I never went . . ."

"John. John, you know, and I know, that when a young man goes out of his way to see the same young woman a number of times running, that is a form of courting. And if you want my opinion you could do very much worse than court Miss Pansy Everton. Of course it's up to you in the end. I just thought I'd mention it to see which way the wind was blowing, and to know if one of the family was going to please their mother in their marriage choice, because by the look of it Margaret won't. And I think we all know that Robert will go his own road whether he chooses a barmaid or a baron's daughter. And that only leaves Betsy and Hannah. Betsy, I think, will follow her mother's choice . . . whereas Hannah. Well!" – he moved his head slowly – "I myself will have to look out for Hannah. And I have somebody in mind. He's in quite a good position in the legal world. A bit older than her, but I think that's a good thing."

Matthew felt a wave of pity sweep over him as he looked at his son. His fair skin had become a pasty white now. The grey eyes had darkened, the well shaped lips, more suitable to a woman than a man he had often thought, were dry and were moving over each other as if in search of moisture. He forced himself to say now, "You don't look very pleased at your sister's prospect.

I should have thought you would be happy for her to make such a good match."

"You . . . you must be referring to Mr Walters, Papa. I . . . I don't see it as a good match. He is double her age. Moreover, he has been married before. His wife has but recently died."

"I'm aware of all that, John, but allow me to know what is best in this case for Hannah. I've got no need to tell you what her life would be like if she has to spend it in this house, now have I? The situation should need no explanation. So, for her own happiness the quicker she is married the better, and I won't rest until I see her settled. Anyway, the intention of this little chat was to tell you that I would welcome Miss Everton as a daughter-in-law, and I think you'd be very wise to go ahead before someone else recognizes her value, because she's a very attractive girl."

John made no reply, he just stared at his father for a moment, then without a word of leave-taking he rose, opened the door and went hastily from the room.

Matthew inserted his finger into his high collar and eased it from his neck. Sally was right after all. My God! what a situation? Well, there was one thing now he must see to, and quickly, and that was to get one or other of them married, and the sooner the better.

John at present was his best bet. That supposition about Arthur Walters had been nothing more than wishful thinking based on the few times that the solicitor had met Hannah. The last time was in the summer in the square at Hexham. He and John had been waiting in the trap for Hannah to come out of the haberdasher's, into which shop she and Margaret had gone to buy the ribbons and odds and ends that women buy in haberdashers'. While they waited Walters had passed and stopped for a moment, and as they talked the girls had come out of the shop and he had noted that Arthur Walters's eyes had dwelt on Hannah in warm appraisal.

But then most men looked at Hannah with warm appraisal, so why had his mind selected Walters? Because, he told himself now, Walters would be a very good match for Hannah. He was a fine-set-up young man; and hadn't he asked after Hannah only last week again, and this was another time when John had been present.

Anyway, if it wasn't Walters, it must be somebody and soon. If not, there was going to be trouble, and such trouble that would overshadow all that had gone before. He should, he told himself now, be thankful for one thing. Since Margaret had left school Hannah had only come home at holiday time, so the affair, if affair it was between John and her, couldn't have made all that progress.

Hannah's staying at school was the result of Anne's covert suggestion, and he had complied with it, not because he wanted to please his wife in any way, but because it saved him that weekly trip to Hexham in all weathers to bring her home.

2

"Good-bye, Miss Barrington."

   "Good-bye, Miss Rowntree."

   "Good-bye, Miss Emily."

   "Good-bye, my dear."

   "Good-bye, Hannah."

   "Good-bye, child."

Miss Emily Barrington reached into the coach and tucked the rug around Hannah's knees, saying, "Keep warm, and give our love to Margaret and all the family."

   "I will, Miss Emily, I will. A happy Christmas."

A shout from the driver caused Miss Emily Barrington to step quickly back and allow the inn boy to lift up the step and close the door. Then the coach was off, and Hannah lay back smiling. She smiled at the other five occupants and they smiled at her; then she closed her eyes.

Wasn't it good of them, the two Miss Barringtons and Miss Rowntree, to come and see her off. If it weren't for one thing she could wish she were spending Christmas with them. Oh yes, she would love that, as she had loved every day she had been in their school. She knew that they marvelled at her love of school and her willingness to learn, even though there were some things she couldn't take in, such as higher arithmetic, or the rudiments of biology; nor was she outstanding in French; but she had made up for these deficiencies in embroidery and the pianoforte, and last year she had made great strides under Miss Emily in household management.

Yet not one of her dear teachers guessed that her love for their school had grown out of relief at not having to live continuously in her father's house. Not that she disliked her father. Oh no, far from it. She thought he was a wonderful man. And she thought of him as "Father" even while she addressed him as "Mister". It was the missis, his wife, she couldn't bear to live with, the woman who had never uttered a word to her in years and would have paid more attention to a ghost.

It was during the last two years that she had ceased to fear her, and now very often at times she had to pray that the loss of her fear hadn't been replaced by hate, for only as recently as the summer holidays she had, on one occasion, experienced the awful desire to rush at the woman, grab her by the arms, and yell into her face, "I didn't ask to come into your home! I was brought here. And after all he is my father, and I am his daughter and have the right to be treated as a human being." Yet she knew that if she had been brave enough to carry out her desire, even if she had knocked her down, she would have risen to her feet, straightened her gown, looked through her and walked away without uttering a word.

How could anyone be so cruel? She could have forgiven her the whipping, but not the silence of years. What would happen when in the spring she left the school for good? The thought of having to spend her life under the shadow of that woman was creating nightmares in her sleep. The only escape would be marriage. But she would never marry. No; never, never. There was a great door locking that escape.

Oh, John! John!

When had she first known that she loved him and he her? In the spring when they had walked over the fells together? This time last year when she had slid down the bank into some bushes and he pulled her out and she had lain against him laughing, until his arms had tightened about her and she had looked up into his eyes, and he down into hers? No, no, long before that. She had known for years that she loved him. Even as a child her first thought when coming home at the week-ends had always been, I shall see John.

Not that she wasn't fond of Robert. Oh, she liked Robert very much . . . and Robert was always so good to her. He stood up for her even more than John did. John had never openly stood up for her, never openly defied his mother; but then John was possessed of a gentle nature that hated to hurt anyone, even his mother, although she felt he couldn't help but see her as a wicked woman.

What was going to happen between her and John? She didn't know, she only felt that if he didn't kiss her soon she would die. She dreamed of being kissed by him. That day by the hayrick, he had nearly kissed her, but a woman had appeared on the hill and spoilt it all. But if this snow were to lay and they could go off somewhere together on the sledge, then he might. Yes, he might.

She opened her eyes and looked out of the breath-smeared window. The coach had left the town but from its slow progress she guessed that the horses were finding the going very heavy.

And so must have thought the rest of the passengers, for now they were discussing the possibility of it ever reaching Halt-whistle. A more pessimistic traveller even wanted a bet they'd get no further than Haydon Bridge.

And this particular traveller proved to be right. The coach was over half an hour late when eventually they reached Haydon Bridge, and the carrier cart, which usually met it and took the by-road past Langley and over the crossroads up to Catton and so to Allendale, was not to be seen; likely buried in a drift in some ditch was the verdict. But another opinion was that they'd all be better off in the inn while they waited to see what was to transpire.

The inn parlour was packed, and Hannah sat on the wooden settle near the window, her valise at her feet. When one of the coach travellers offered to bring her a hot toddy she refused politely, saying, "No, thank you; I had a hot drink just before we left. Thank you all the same."

That was the strange thing about her education, and Miss Barrington had spoken to her openly of it, she still retained colloquial terms in her form of speech. On this occasion Miss Barrington would have said, "You thanked them once, my dear, there was no need to repeat it by adding thank you all the same."

It was half an hour later when the coachman came in and said he would take a chance and hope they would reach Bardon Mill, but should they all end up in the river not to blame him.

Warmed inside and out the travellers took their leave, all wishing Hannah a happy Christmas and a quick journey home.

When another fifteen minutes had passed and Hannah was beginning to feel the cold seeping through her brown caped coat, she wished she had accepted the proffered warm drink. She could, she told herself, go to the bar counter, but what would she ask for? Perhaps the innkeeper would advise her.

She placed her valise on the seat behind her, then threaded her way through the throng standing between her and the counter. Once there, she waited until she could attract the barman's attention, and when she had done so she leant slightly towards him and said in a voice little above a whisper, "Could you recommend a hot drink, please?"

"A hot drink, miss? Well, yes, yes. What would you like?"

"I'll . . . I'll leave it to you."

"Oh then" – he smiled broadly – "I'll make up something that will warm the cockles of your heart."

"Thank you. . . . Oh!" The last was a gasp as she was pulled round as a voice said, "In the name of God! what you up to here?"

"Oh, hello Ned. Oh, I am pleased to see you." Her smile was wide. "I'm ordering a drink."

"A drink? What you doing here?" There was no smile on his face.

"Well, I've just told you, Ned." She was laughing at him now. "I've ordered a hot drink."

Ned looked from her to the barman, and the barman nodded at him, then pointed to the glass that was half full of hot water, and at this Ned said, "Go canny."

"Yes. Aye, aye, Ned."

"Tell me, what you doing here?"

"Well, I came by coach from school and I'm waiting for the carrier cart."

"Well, you'll have a long wait."

"Why?" Her face became straight.

"It went into a ditch last night and broke the axle; not only that, it crippled the horse."

"Oh dear! How shall I get to the town?"

"You won't, not by carrier, not the day."

"Oh, but I must get home, Ned, I must, they'll be worrying."

"Well, if there's no carrier cart running they'll know the reason why you can't get back. On the other hand, I can get you home all right if you can sit a horse."

"Oh yes, yes, I can sit a horse. You know I can."

"Half one."

"Half one? What do you mean, Ned?"

"I've only got The Raker with me this trip; you'll be up afront of me."

"Oh." She bit on her lip, then laughed as she said, "Well if the horse can bear it I can."

"There you are, miss, get that down you." She turned and thanked the barman, but when she sipped at the hot toddy she screwed up her face, swallowed deeply, then coughed and spluttered a little. The barman laughed, then looked at Ned as he said, " 'Twasn't strong, Ned. 'Twasn't strong, honest."

"I'll take your word for it." Ned stared at the man for a moment, then added, "But give me a strong one, straight, a double."

"Aye, Ned."

When the barman had pushed the double whisky towards him, Ned lifted it up, took hold of Hannah's arm and guided her towards a seat; but before sitting down she pointed, saying, "I was sitting over there where my valise is."

He now pushed her forward through the customers towards the settle, and as they sat down he said, "Daft thing to do, leave your luggage to take care of itself." Then after a pause he asked, "Do you like it?"

"It's very warming."

"It should be; that's what keeps sailors going at sea."

"Really! Oh!" – she went to spring up – "I forgot to pay the innkeeper for it."

"Sit yourself down, that'll be seen to. . . . Are you hungry?"

"Yes, come to think of it, Ned, I am a bit."

"Would you like a pie? Hot or cold?"

"Oh, a hot one, please."

She watched him going towards the counter again and noticed that some men even made way for him, in fact all seemed to acknowledge him in one way or another, and she thought what a blessing it was she had come upon him.

It was very odd, when she considered, how Ned seemed to turn up at times when she most needed him. Nor was it the first time this thought had entered her head. The morning that she came upon him in the mist was as clear today as it was when it happened, in fact clearer, for then she hadn't been able to see his face distinctly. Was it all of eight and a half years ago? . . . And then again at the time of the thrashing. And there had been other times since then. The day she fell into the quagmire, when she could have drowned because Margaret hadn't the strength to pull her out. Ned had been making his way home, on foot this time, and rolling from side to side. He had been very drunk, but drunk or not he had come right to the end of the bog and almost slipped in himself, yet he had got her out. And he had taken both her and Margaret back to the Pele house where he had taken off her clothes and wrapped her in a blanket and sent Margaret running home to ask Bella, on the quiet, for a clean change.

She had liked his grandfather too. She was so sorry when he died last year. In the holidays she had gone up to the house to tell Ned so, and he had been abrupt with her, almost growling that he didn't want to talk about him. And she knew then that he was missing the old man very much, for now he had to live alone. All he had were his two dogs and the horses. But the horses came and went.

Years ago the missis had forbidden John, Margaret and Robert to go near the Pele house or to speak to Ned Ridley. She had no need to forbid Betsy for Betsy turned her nose up at the smell of the stable-room. But the order hadn't included herself, and so over the years she had spent quite a lot of time talking with Ned Ridley. She liked him, she liked him very much, although according to Betsy he was a very bad man: he not only boxed and ran cock-fights, and had bouts of heavy drinking, but did other unmention-able things that could not be spoken of, things indicated only by deep obeisance of the head. Well, be what he may, she liked him; and she was more than pleased to be sitting with him at this minute.

She watched him now coming towards her. His thick black hair seemed to bounce on his head as he walked, and his deep brown eyes looked bright and merry. He had grown heavier

104

during the past eight years, so that now at twenty-six a little of his litheness had gone. Although he was still slim-waisted and had no paunch he wasn't looked upon as the bare-knuckled battling boy he had been at eighteen. Yet she had heard Robert say that he was boxing better, he was more steady, that now he weighed things up and didn't barge in blindly. Robert liked going to boxing matches, John didn't.

There had been talk of Ned getting married last year to a girl in Sinderhope; then for some reason the wedding was called off. Apparently it had been Ned's fault because the girl's two brothers had waylaid him one night, and although he had beaten them off and left them both bloody, he had not got off scot-free, and it was some months before he could box again.

She could imagine him being very attractive to the girls, for apart from his prowess as a boxer he had a certain appeal about him. She couldn't put a name to it. It wasn't that he was handsome, though he was good looking in a sort of rough way. It was something in his eyes, she supposed, the way they would look at one, sometimes laughing, sometimes scornful, sometimes kind. . . . She was so glad she had met him today.

It was after they had eaten the warm pies and Ned had finished his second double whisky, and had followed this with a whole pint of ale, that he grinned at her and said, "Well, what about it, me ladyship? If we want to reach the castle before dark we must away to our mounts."

She choked on the last mouthful of the pie and he, getting to his feet, said, "Go on, go on, that's it, choke yourself." And with this he thumped her on the back, which caused her to laugh all the more.

As they left the inn the innkeeper himself called after them, "Bye, Ned. Take it slowly."

"Aye, Sandy. Aye, I'll let her go her own gait."

Out in the yard, he strapped Hannah's valise to the saddle; then putting his arms under her oxters, he cried, "Hie-up there!" and with a great lift swung her on to the horse. The next minute he was seated behind her. His arms about her, he pulled on the reins, and the animal turned and walked out of the yard and on to the snow-packed road.

"It's a good job she's got a broad back. You all right?"

"Yes, Ned."

"Like it?"

"Yes, yes, I do."

"Good. Get up there, Raker." He flapped the reins, and the horse quickened its stride but didn't trot. And so they went along at this pace, saying nothing for quite some way until Ned said abruptly, "You'll be leaving that school next year, won't you?"

"Yes, Ned, in the spring."

"What you gona do?"

"I . . . I don't know, Ned."

There was another pause before he said, "You'll likely get married."

"Oh." She gave a small laugh. "I don't think so."

"You don't think so? What you talkin' about? Of course you'll get married, a girl like you."

When she made no reply to this he roughly demanded, "What's up with you, don't you ever think about gettin' married? 'Tis natural, especially with someone who's got what you've got. . . . You know you're bonny, don't you?"

"It's nice of you to say so, Ned." Her voice was low, her tone subdued.

'Aw, don't come coy, 'tisn't like you. You damn well know you're more than bonny, you're beautiful. You're the beautifulest thing in these hills, you know that. You know it fine well."

"Aw no, I don't, Ned." She bristled slightly within his hold.

"Well, if you don't, you damn well should do. Haven't you got a mirror in that house, or in the school? And anyway, good looking or not, the best thing you could do would be to marry. What's gona happen to you when the rest go? You lookin' forward to being left with her?"

"No, Ned, no, I'm not."

"I should damn well say not. There should be a law against people like her, they should be put down, drowned when young, like kittens in a pail. The very sight of that woman makes me bile rise. You know what?"

"No, Ned."

"I'll tell you somethin', 'cos she won't." He laughed now. "I always spit when I pass her. I do it on purpose, I just spit into the gutter. I hawk deep in me throat an' I spit."

"Oh! Ned, you shouldn't."

"Why shouldn't I? She's a bad woman that, Hannah, bad. An' dangerous. You know she's got a funny smell comes off her? I know about smells an' women. I think the devil must smell like she does."

Again she said, "Oh! Ned."

He went on now as if talking to himself. "It maddens me when I consider that the likes of she look down on me, it does. She used to put it round even when I was a lad that I was bad. If she hadn't been so badly liked people would've believed her. You don't believe that I'm a bad man, do you, Hannah?" He now bent his head down to hers, and when the smell of the spirits from his breath wafted over her she wasn't offended by it, but she laughed gently and said, "You a bad man? Of course not, Ned. To me you're a fine man. Always have been."

"Of course I'm a fine man." He was yelling now as if to an audience, and when of a sudden he burst into song she leant her head back against him and shook with laughter, while he sang:

> "I am what I am,
> Look at me do,
> For I am, believe it or not,
> I am you.
> Neither good nor bad,
> Nor middling to best,
> We are, you and me,
> Like all the rest."

And now he yelled even louder, "All join in the chorus!" Then he was singing again:

> "God help you,
> God help me,
> God help us all;
> We were all quite decent
> Afore the fall."

107

When he finished they rocked together with laughter until they nearly slipped from the saddle.

Her face wet, she cried at him, "Oh! Ned, you are funny."

"Now I'm funny."

"Yes, you are; you're the funniest man I know. And" – she turned her face half towards him – "the nicest."

Their gaze linked and held, hers open, frank with gratitude in its depths, his a mixture of hardness and sadness with desperate frustration in its depths.

"Sit straight," he said, "or you'll be out of the saddle."

"Oh, I'm sorry, Ned."

As the journey passed, she began to wonder if she had said anything to offend him because all his jollity seemed to disappear, and when she spoke to him he merely grunted.

When at last they reached the gate and he had lifted her down and unstrapped the valise she looked into his face and said quietly, "Thank you, Ned. Every now and again in my life I find I have got to say 'Thank you, Ned.'"

When he made no comment but stood staring at her, she asked quietly, "Have I said something to offend you?"

"Offend me?" His voice was high. "Now what could you say to offend me? Perhaps you haven't noticed, I'm half tight."

"Oh." She laughed now, then said, "No, I hadn't noticed; perhaps because I was the same; that was a very strong drink."

"Aye, it was that; but it would have been stronger if I hadn't come in at the time."

"You think so?"

"Sure of it." He grinned at her.

"Well, that bears out what I say, Ned, you always turn up at the right time in my life."

"Aye well." He turned from her and gathered the reins in his hand as he said, "I hope you noticed I brought you home the back way so to speak, for wouldn't the old wives' tongues have wagged to see you mounted afore me, and me three sheets in the wind, eh? An' you'd better not let madam know either or she'll have you cleansed as if you had the plague." He stared at her for a moment before he added, "I hope you have a good Christmas."

"And you too, Ned. But perhaps I'll see you before then. We'll be on the hills sledging if the snow holds."

"Aye, you might, you might that." He mounted the horse, turned it about, then touched his forehead with his index finger by way of salute and rode off.

She watched him for a moment as he made the horse mount the slippery bank that led to the road that ran along by the cemetery wall, and she had a strong desire to shout after him, "I'll come up to see you on Christmas Day," because on Christmas Day he'd be alone and no one should be alone on Christmas Day. But she didn't shout after him, she turned in at the gate and went quickly up the snow-packed drive, and with each crunching step her heart began to race the faster, because within a matter of minutes now she'd look into John's face, and he would take her hand and the pressure of his fingers would tell her what his own heart was feeling.

3

"What is wrong, Margaret?"

Both Hannah and Margaret were looking down at the icy path as they picked their way towards the village square, and Margaret after a moment, only answered half of Hannah's question when she replied, "It's Mama; she's forbidden me to even mention Mr Hathaway, but I've told her that if I don't marry him I shan't marry anyone. He came all the way here yesterday and Mama wouldn't see him. He couldn't go on to the mine to see Papa because he had to get back, he had only a day's leave and the transport is so uncertain."

"Is that why you walked all the way into Allendale yesterday? I was upset because she wouldn't let me accompany you. Oh! Margaret." She caught hold of Margaret's arm. "Why didn't you tell me?"

"What good would it have done? And Mama forbade me to speak of it, and I couldn't have a word with Papa last evening because he was so late in coming home."

"Everyone seems at sixes and sevens."

"Yes, they do, don't they?"

They exchanged glances.

"Margaret."

"Yes, Hannah?"

"John. Is . . . is he not very well?"

"In health, yes, but perhaps you didn't know." Now Margaret's voice dropped to a muttered whisper and she seemed to give all her attention to where she was placing her feet as she went on, "There's talk of him marrying Miss Everton. You remember Miss Everton, you must remember her, she was at school, but in a higher class. She is, I think, twenty-one now, but you saw her at the hill race in the summer?"

Hannah made no reply. She, too, was paying attention to where she was placing her feet, and Margaret went on, "She's a very nice girl although high-spirited. Anyway, Mama is all for it, and Papa, too, I understand. Robert says that Papa is very much for it. Oh! be careful." She put out her hand and clutched at Hannah's cloak. "It's so terribly slippery. Are you all right?"

There was a long pause before Hannah replied, "Yes; it's . . . it's the ice."

"You are very fond of John, aren't you, Hannah?"

Again there was a pause before Hannah said, "Yes, Margaret, I'm very fond of John."

"Well, that's as it should be, he is your brother; at least your half-brother, you are of the same father."

Their glances furtive now as if shame were being revealed between them, they turned from each other and neither of them spoke again until they reached their destination, which was Fred Loam's butcher's shop.

They scraped the caked ice from the insteps of their boots before mounting the two steps into the room with its sawdust-strewn floor, on which stood a small counter and a butcher's block.

Fred Loam, who had inherited the business at his father's death two years ago, stood behind the block. He was of medium height but looked taller because of his breadth. His shoulders were broad, almost making his back appear humped, and his hands, too, were large, and like the beef he was cutting, his face was of a ruddy hue, but its expression was pleasant. He was a pleasant young man altogether.

There was only one other customer in the shop and after Fred finished serving her he turned to the girls, saying brightly, "Oh, there you are, and 'tis pleased I am to see you both. By! Hannah, aye, I can hardly believe it; you're grown nigh on a foot since the last time I saw you."

"Well, not quite a foot, Fred, perhaps three inches."

"Aw well, a foot or three inches, you grow bonnier."

When Hannah lowered her glance and made no reply Fred

turned to Margaret and, adopting now a polite business attitude, he asked, "And what can I do for you this mornin', Miss Margaret?"

The distinction that Margaret was being addressed as "Miss" and that the prefix had been omitted in Hannah's case was not remarkable, it had always been this way. Mrs Anne Thornton had always spoken of her family as Master John and Master Robert, Miss Margaret and Miss Betsy, but it was a well-known fact that she in no way acknowledged Matthew Thornton's bastard, so the villagers did not take it upon themselves to elevate the child to the same standard as her half-sisters. When small, they had called her Young Hannah, now she was simply addressed by her christian name.

Margaret answered the young butcher, saying, "Mother would like a chine of beef and a leg of pork, please."

"Will that be all? She's not having a fowl?"

"We had one sent."

"Oh!"

It was evident to Margaret that the news didn't please Mr Fred Loam and she added quickly, "It was a gift from my mother's cousin."

"Oh, a gift was it? Oh, well then, I hope it turns out to be tender. But as they say, don't look a gift horse in the mouth." He laughed at Margaret, then turned his attention to Hannah again, saying, "You won't be goin' back to school after this then, I suppose?"

"Yes, until Easter."

"By! they'll have you so learned that you won't look the side we're on shortly."

"Oh, I don't think that 'll ever happen, Fred." She made herself smile at him and add, "As you yourself would say, there's more brains in a sheep's head than in mine."

"That I wouldn't. That I wouldn't." He sounded indignant. "Not when talkin' of you, I wouldn't. By! no. But the next thing we'll know" – he leant towards her now – "you'll be gettin' wed, eh? Anyone in your eye?"

Hannah was saved from answering by the shop door opening at the same time as Margaret said, "Thank you, Fred. We must be getting along."

"Happy Christmas to you both."

"Happy Christmas, Fred," they both answered, and as they reached the door, he called, "There's the big New Year's dance comin' off in the town, will we be seein' you there?"

"I . . . I don't think so, Fred."

"'Twill be a gay affair, county folk droppin' in. It won't be one of your club feasts; although I hold nowt against them if you want a blow out for nowt once a year. . . . It'll be a proper do."

"I'm sure it will. Good-bye." As Margaret went to close the door, his voice so loud now as though he were on the other side of the square from them, he cried, "What about you, Hannah? I'd like to bet your feet can trip the light fantastic."

Margaret gave Hannah no time to answer for she pulled the door closed so sharply that they could hear the bell still jangling when they were someway down the street.

"He takes too much on himself does Fred Loam."

Hannah cast a glance towards Margaret. For a moment she had sounded just like her mother, and she answered quietly, "He means no harm."

"I don't know, his manner is much too free towards you. Pity his mother hadn't kept him in hand in the same way that she did his father, and everyone else for that matter who comes across her path."

Hannah made no reply to this, although she thought it was good to know that Fred stood up to his mother. Mrs Loam was a little vixen. She wasn't five foot high but she had been known to bray her big husband around the upstairs rooms with a stick the morning after a drinking bout. Her antics had caused much secret laughter from time to time in the village, usually around the festive season, for she apparently had her own way of dealing with her husband when he came home the worst for drink. She would undress him, put him to bed, then withhold his clothes the next morning until she had lathered into him. But no villager had yet been brave enough to laugh in her face, for she could use her tongue as well as her hands. In a way Hannah felt sorry for Fred, as she had done for his father, for his father had always had a kind word for her, and even as a child he had told her how bonny she was.

"I'll be glad to leave the village."

"What did you say, Margaret?"

"You are scatter-brained this morning, Hannah. I said, I shall be glad to leave the village."

"I thought you loved the hills and all the country around."

"I do, but the hills don't make the village; it is the people that make the village and they are so narrow in their outlook. They think and act differently altogether from those who inhabit the larger towns. They cling to their old customs. Look at what happens on hiring days in Allendale, with those travelling auctioneers, and the maids openly strolling about the town waiting to be picked by the young men. It's almost feudal. And they still have the fiddlers in the inns and dancing well into the night. Oh, and so many customs that could be well done without."

"But I thought you liked dancing, Margaret." Hannah was showing open astonishment at Margaret's attitude, which up to now she had considered so liberal.

"I do; but there is dancing and dancing and modes of conduct here that are so different from those in the town. You must have realised that yourself. Hexham is a different world. Don't you think so?"

"Yes, I suppose so; but only because of the buildings, I . . . I didn't find the people all that different. There are good and bad, nice and nasty, there too. You remember Miss Ormaston. She was a horrible creature. She was cruel to some of the girls and they were so afraid of her they daren't say anything. Then there was Brown, you remember Brown, the gardener who beat his wife so much he was taken to the Port House to answer a charge. I think people are the same all over, Margaret, some good, some bad, but most of them middling. As for customs, I like the old customs. . . . "

"Well! Huh!" Margaret gave a gentle laugh now and, her manner reverting to its usual pleasantness, she said, "We are spouting wisdom this morning, aren't we? But I suppose you're right. It's only that . . . well – " Her voice dropped to a mutter as she ended, "my heart's in the town. He's so different from anyone I've ever met. I suppose that's why I want to be there, I long to be there, and I view everything there in a different light."

"I'm sorry, Margaret."

Hannah now linked her arm in Margaret's, then said wistfully, "Remember Miss Barrington? At the beginning of every term she would start her English lesson with, 'Never think in clichés'; but I think some clichés are very true and apply to life, such as: The path of true love never runs smoothly."

"Yes, you're quite right." Margaret nodded at her and smiled. "One thing I must say in truth, Hannah, and that is, when I do leave home for the town I shall miss you very much."

"And I you, Margaret, because – " She paused and her lids shaded her eyes as she said, "Above all you have been a comfort to me since I came into your home."

It was the first time that Hannah had alluded to herself and her position in the family and now the words "your home" embodied all her feelings with regard to the years she had spent in Elmholm House, for it had never been her home.

Silently Margaret gripped at the gloved fingers that were lying on her arm and together they went up the drive and into the house.

Christmas came and went without a great deal of jollity, and the New Year too was much the same. During the holidays they had spent a number of evenings playing card games but although on such occasions Anne Thornton was generally out of the room, the atmosphere between all of them was strained. Hannah hadn't had one minute alone with John, and as the time drew near for her return to school she had to face up to the fact that he was deliberately avoiding her.

It was the fourth day of the New Year. The men had all returned to work. Margaret was sitting at the writing table in the sitting-room penning a letter, while Betsy and her mother sat on a couch opposite the fire stitching at embroidery.

Hannah never went into the sitting-room when the missis and Betsy were there if she could help it.

Today she had been in the kitchen talking to Bella and Tessie for a long while. She liked talking to them, she felt at home in the kitchen. But she couldn't stay there for ever, so now she was sitting huddled up under the quilt in her room, and the cold was adding to her feeling of misery.

There was still a lot of daylight left that had to be filled and the sun was shining. She didn't want to read. She could wrap up and go out for a walk. Yes, that's what she would do. And perhaps she could call in the Pele house and see Ned. She had promised to go over during the holidays but she hadn't as yet done so, for she hadn't wanted to move away from the presence of John, not even for a moment.

She had no need to tell anyone she was going for a walk, she had come and gone on her own for years, and so, having put on a woollen jacket over her dress and a cape over that, she donned her close fitting bonnet and picked up the new fur muff the mister had bought her at Christmas, and went quietly down the back stairs, along the passage and out into the yard.

She gave Dandy Smollett a greeting as she passed the stables and he called after her, "Nice to see the sun, Miss Hannah," to which she answered, "Yes, Dandy." Then she went out through the gates, crossed the road and climbed the stile by the cemetery wall, then dropped into snow that almost reached her knees.

It was evident that no one had been this way for days for the path was almost obliterated, she was able to pick it out only by the lower level of snow on it compared with that on the banks.

As she struggled on she told herself that she had been stupid to come this way, she should have taken the main road for there the wind had cleared most of the snow into drifts leaving great patches of bare ground, still very slippery in parts but much easier to get over than the drifts.

When she reached higher ground she dusted the snow from her skirts and cloak and stood for a moment looking about her. The hills all around were bathed in a pale pink light that merged here and there into rose and mauve, which in turn faded away into lilac, to fall behind the horizon of the far hills in a soft downy grey.

The world was beautiful. She wished she were happy enough to enjoy it. What was to become of her? She was beginning to be worried more and more about her future. If only she were clever like Margaret and could teach. Yet she had no desire to inform. She could be a nursemaid. Yes, she supposed she could be a nursemaid. Yet she had no experience of little children, she herself having been the youngest in the household.

She walked on, slithering at times and once sliding on to her buttocks, where she sat for a moment laughing before getting up and going on again. Then there was Ned's house before her seeming to be rearing up out of the snow-covered hill on which it was perched.

She liked Ned's house, especially the rooms upstairs. These were full of curious things, all having been made by Ned's father, or his grandfather, or his great-grandfather: chairs, tables, cupboards, delf rack, pipe rack, even a wooden bed. Oh, the wooden bed was a fine piece of work. Instead of knobs at each corner it had birds carved from the wood. And everything was kept so clean. She was always astonished by the cleanliness of the upstairs rooms compared with the jumble in the kitchen behind the stable room, and the mass of oddments that littered the corners and hung from the walls of the stable-room itself.

She entered the gateless gap between the walls, crossed the yard, then knocked on the big oak door; but as she did so her eyes travelled to the lock. The chain was through the loop and fastened to the lock itself.

She knew a keen sense of disappointment and an emptiness as if she had suddenly been deserted by everybody in the world. She went round the side of the house and up the slope towards the narrow belt of woodland, the sight of which always brought back the distant memory into the present, and she could see herself again, running shivering through the mist towards the house and the figure of the man with the horses.

She skirted the woodland, and went walking towards the far hills, but when she came to the foot of them, she didn't attempt to climb them for in parts they were shining like sheets of silver, which meant ice, so she turned to the left and kept to the level ground which she knew would lead her to the road.

It was about half an hour later as she walked along the top of the bank, and again in deep snow, looking for an easy access down to the road that she saw the horseman coming out of the distance, and her heart gave a sudden jerk, then began to race.

John had seen and recognized her too, from a distance, and

when he came level with her, where she was standing still and straight above him on the bank, he drew the horse to a stop and looked at her for a moment before asking, "What you doing out here?"

"Just taking a walk. I . . . I was looking for a place to get down."

He said nothing more but dismounted: then leaving the horse he looked to right and left before pointing and saying, "I think there's a place along there." And he walked back along the road while she walked along the top of the bank, and when they came to the dip in the bank he stood on what would have been the grass verge and held out his hands towards her.

Leaning forward, she gripped them, and when he said "Jump!" she jumped, and he caught her, and as he had done once before he held her close, but not for as long as he had done on that other occasion. Then they were standing apart gazing at each other.

"You have been avoiding me, John."

"No, I haven't. I haven't." He shook his head quickly.

"Yes, you have. Don't bother to deny it."

He now drooped his head deep on his chest and she watched his jaw bones moving in and out before he said, "It's got to be this way, Hannah."

"Yes, yes, I know, but . . . but you needn't have avoided me."

"I thought it was best."

"You . . . you are going to be married?"

His head slowly came up and he looked at her, his eyes full of sadness as he said, "I suppose so."

"Miss Everton?"

He made an almost imperceivable movement with his hands which he was holding gripped in front of him. It was as if he were attempting to unlock them.

"I . . . I hope you'll be very happy, John."

"Oh, Hannah!" There were almost tears in his eyes now. "If only things had been different, we . . . we could have come together. Yes, yes, we would. I would have run off with you, taken you away from the house and mother, taken you away to the ends of the earth."

It sounded all very fanciful but it acted like a great warm

poultice on her heart. She put out her hand to him and he clutched at it; then she said softly, "I'm . . . I'm glad you told me, John, for I, too, would have gone with you to the ends of the earth, or followed you there. But as it is it can't be."

"No" – he shook his head – "it can't be, Hannah. But we have one comfort, we'll both have something to remember until the day we die. I shall never forget you, Hannah."

"Nor me you, John."

He let go her hand, took in a deep breath, and stepped back from her, saying, "I . . . I must be on my way."

"Where are you going?" Her voice was a cracked tearful whisper now, and he said, "Back to the mine. I've been over to Allenheads with a message for Mr Sopwith. Good-bye, my dear Hannah."

"Good-bye, John." Their eyes held for a moment longer; then he turned abruptly and hurried back to where the horse was chaffing at its bit and pawing the ground with impatience. She stood where she was until he had ridden out of sight; then, the tears raining down her face, her head bent, she walked the two miles home at a snail's pace, and with every step she took she repeated and savoured every word he had said, because she felt she must imprint them on her memory for they would have to last her a lifetime.

That same evening Matthew arranged that he should be alone with his wife, as he did at times when there was something he was to demand of her that would brook no opposition and he had no wish to belittle her further before the family. He had sent Tessie with a message to ask her mistress to join him in the dining-room. He was standing when she entered and he did not ask her to be seated but came to the point straightaway. "I would like you to know," he said, "that I intend to take Margaret and Hannah to a ball in Hexham, which is to be held a week on Friday. John and Miss Everton will likely attend too. I am hoping Margaret's suitor will be there so that I can take stock of him. It will also afford me the opportunity of ascertaining the correct nature of Mr Arthur Walters's feelings towards Hannah. As you know he is a solicitor of good standing in his early thirties; he lost his wife last year; I feel it is his aim to replace her as soon as possible."

Anne Thornton stared at this man whom she hated with an intensity that was second only to the feeling that she had for *The Girl*, and now he was telling her he proposed to arrange a marriage for his bastard with a solicitor while his own daughter must be satisfied with a poor bank clerk, because all bank clerks were poor and would always remain so.

The unfairness of the situation, the injustice of it, was past understanding. There were times when she didn't think she could bear living under the same roof with this man for one minute longer, yet she calmed herself at such moments telling herself that her day would come. If God was just her day would come, and deep inside herself she believed firmly that it would. God in His justice and His mercy would not let the wicked conquer.

For eight years now she had lived under the pressure of a great insult; a personal indignity. Her husband, the man who should have protected her from jibes and ridicule, had exposed her to these things, not only from the villagers but from the townsfolk. No doubt they relished each new amour of his, for that he had carried out his threat to satisfy his lust elsewhere she had not the slightest doubt; but no one had as yet dared to hint to her who the recipients were.

When abroad, she held her head high and spoke only when it was necessary to give orders to shopkeepers. There were times she felt so lonely that she became desperate. She had only one friend in the world, and she was the parson's wife, Susanna Crewe. Not all her children even were true to her. Betsy yes; Betsy was the only one who really loved her. And John, yes; John esteemed her. But Robert and Margaret, no. About their affections she had never misled herself; they were too like their father to appreciate her. This being so, she should not in Margaret's case have worried about her choice of a suitor, and she wouldn't have, except that he was placing *That Girl* above his legal flesh and blood.

"They should have new gowns. It's short notice, but I suppose they could get something ready-made in Hexham?"

"And the money, where is the money coming from?" Her voice was thin and cold, her lips hardly moving as she spoke, the words coming like pressed steel from between her teeth. "You informed me last month that the house expenditure must be cut."

"I'm aware of that; and I was right to inform you when I saw an order for French preserves from the dairy shop in Hexham."

"It was to be a gift at Christmas for Miss Everton, I told you."

"Well, and as I told you, you could get something more substantial than a box of foreign sugared fruits for sixteen shillings. I understood you were making embroidery as a Christmas gift for her."

Her full lips began to tremble as her face became suffused with a dark passion. Then turning her head slightly to the side, but with her eyes still riveted on him, she said, "I can't stand much more of this treatment; I'm warning you."

"Warning me? What of?"

"You will pay for your cruelty to me."

"Cruelty? That's a strange accusation coming from your mouth, you to accuse someone else of an emotion that you are past mistress of!"

"You are responsible for any cruelty I have perpetrated."

"No, no, Anne. No, no; I haven't got that on my conscience. I can pin-point your acts of cruelty since the first year we were together, and towards me. Sadistic, I think, is the correct term for your attitude. Yes, sadistic. Remember the darning needle you drove into my hand . . . by accident? Why did you need to have a darning needle on the bedside table? Oh, I know it had dropped from your work basket, but even so why did you need to use it on me? I lost a lot of blood that night; it went through a vein. Look' – he extended his hand – 'see, it left that little spot. If ever my conscience pricks me for what I've done to you, I just need to lift my hand and look at that."

She was actually talking through partially clenched teeth as she cried low at him, "What chance had a woman to retain a vestige of dignity when dealing with a man like you? An animal would have had more control."

"Oh my God!" He lowered his head and, swinging it from side to side, he laughed mirthlessly, saying as he did so, "It's no good! It's no good! Oh, I wish to God you had married some men that I know of. Oh, I do, I do." He was staring at her now, the smile still on his face. "Still, you married me. Looking back, I didn't pick you, you picked me. As you once said, to make something out of me; and let's give credit where it's due, you did; you got me to buy this fine house; you got me to work from dawn on Monday morning till sunset on Saturday night. Oh yes, you made something out of me. And now" – the smile slid from his face – "you are enjoying the results of your efforts. Well" – he turned from her now – "I see no further need for discussion. I've told you of my plans, and don't attempt to interfere with them because it will be fruitless."

After he had gone, closing the door none too gently behind him, she stood for a moment with her eyes closed, and her hands joined together in the hollow of her neck pressed so tightly on the bow of her bodice that the button behind it dug into her flesh, until she felt she was almost choking; and as she stood thus she prayed again, "Oh God, act justly and let me see my day with him."

4

None of Matthew's plans worked out as he had hoped. John and Miss Everton had not attended the ball, Miss Everton having already accepted an invitation for them both for that particular evening. Then Robert had only been induced to attend under pressure, because Robert didn't like dancing. But these were minor irritations; what were of a graver nature were, first, Margaret's suitor had not put in an appearance, and secondly his plan to ensure Hannah's future was doomed at the outset, for the first person they should see at the ball was Mr Arthur Walters, and he was accompanied by a young lady whom he introduced proudly as his fiancée.

If it had been at all possible Matthew would have bundled them all back into the hired coach that was to take them to their hotel for the night, but the coach would not return until half-past eleven. So for most of the evening he had to sit it out, for he himself was no dancer. He danced only with Margaret who had no names on her card and had to depend upon him and Robert, one being as club-footed as the other. But to Margaret it didn't much matter who partnered her, for her misery was deep.

Hannah on the other hand had five names on her card, which was exceedingly good seeing that most of the men were escorting their own partners.

As Matthew watched her being whirled around the ballroom, he thought she was by far the best-looking young woman in the room. And what was strange to him was, she did look a young woman; not yet seventeen she looked all of nineteen. He felt proud of her; guiltily he felt more proud of her than he did of Margaret. And that shouldn't be.

He had no doubt but that his wife was wallowing in satisfaction over the failure of his plans. Although he had said nothing to her – nor, he was sure, had Margaret – her divining sense was such that she would have known immediately that all had not gone right on the evening. . . .

As the weeks wore on, Matthew became troubled about many things. He was troubled about John, about Margaret, about Hannah. Oh aye, about Hannah.

Then there was the ever increasing worry about money. Three horses in the stable now to be fed and shod. It was true that both John and Robert subscribed towards their maintenance, but it made little difference to the overall expense. As children grew into adults they naturally ate more, and their clothes cost more. Then their school fees over the years had been a drain.

The way things stood at present there was a possibility he might have to take out a mortgage on the house. Of course it was no disgrace, but he had always prided himself on keeping clear of debt of any kind.

He needed comfort. He hoped the stones were in the right direction when he passed them this morning so that he could go over to Sally's tonight. It was only a week since he had last seen her, but oh, he needed her more than once a week, if only to lie against her and be soothed. . . .

As he rode out on this March morning the dawn was just lifting and the whole landscape as far as he could see was painted in silver. There had been a slight sprinkling of snow during the night and it had frozen, and now as the light became stronger the shimmering whiteness hurt his eyes, while at the same time he thought, The whole world looks pure, unsullied, as if it has just been born.

Along the road he passed several small groups of miners and all hailed him cheerfully.

"Grand morning, Mr Thornton."

"Yes, Joe, grand, really grand." Joe Robson was a good man, a God-fearing man, not in a chapel or a church sense, but in the right sense, commonsense and loyalty. Yet the eldest of his six children was along the line at the present moment doing six months for beating up a policeman in Hexham.

124

He came upon another group trudging along, the vapour from their nostrils sailing before them like a cloud. "Mornin', Mr Thornton. Snifter, ain't it?"

"Yes, Bill, 'tis a snifter all right, but bonny."

"You can keep your bonniness, Mr Thornton, an' send me home to me fire an' me bed."

As Matthew laughed at Jack Heslop's remark, Bill Nicholson cried at his mate, "You don't want your fire in your bed, man, you want your wife." The joined laughter rang over the hills and followed Matthew along the road, and he repeated to himself, "You don't want your fire in your bed, man, you want your wife."

As the bend in the road brought him in sight of the broken gate where the stones lay, he saw two of his workmen walking away from the wall and up the hill. He recognized one as Frank Pearman, the other at first he could not distinguish, until the man turned round and looked down the hill towards him, when he saw that it was Tom Shields. He shook his head slightly to himself. They were a pair those two, prank players, like young lads. Only yesterday he had to pull them up. They were working on the new inlet and the richness of it had gone to their heads.

A few weeks ago, as was usual when breaking new ground, the men had formed their partnerships; some of four, some six, some eight, but these two stuck together, deciding as always to go it by themselves.

They had all agreed on the price per bing, and the veins they had struck weren't too bad at all, with more than ten per cent ore after the vein stone, soils and spars had been taken out of the bouse. As things went it was really very good for from the old veins they had been getting only five per cent ore. But these two, Tom Shields and Frank Pearman had started gabbing about who got the lion's share. Although in the main they were jokers, they could be agitators, and agitators today were fools with short memories. They should think back to '49 and the results of that strike. But there'd always be men like Shields and Pearman, half clowns, half knaves. . . . But why were they taking that road? Of course, it would cut off nearly a mile on an ordinary day, but to get over those hills this morning it would be two steps forward and one step back. Had they got a still some way over there? He wouldn't be surprised at anything those two would get up to.

He came opposite the stones and he smiled softly as he saw the direction in which they were pointing. Good Sally. Dear Sally. Comforting Sally. She must have been down early this morning in the dark or late last night.

The day seemed long and tiresome. John, getting his practice in on a surveying job with the head agent and chief engineer from Allenheads, had stopped on his way past and had a hurried word with him, beginning abruptly with, "I don't seem to be able to talk to you in the house, Papa, so I'd better tell you that Pansy has consented to marry me and we shall announce our engagement at Eastertime."

"Good. Good." He had put out his hand and gripped his son's arm. "I'm happy for you; she'll make you a good wife. What do her parents say?"

"They seemed pleased."

"Well, they should" – he had smiled broadly now – "they're getting a fine, handsome fellow for a son-in-law and one who is going to rise in the world, if I know anything."

John had smiled, not unpleased with his father's flattery, then said, "I must be off," but as he turned away Matthew had asked quietly, "Does your mother know?"

"I mean to tell her tonight."

"She'll be pleased."

They had looked straight at each other before John, his face solemn, moved his head once, saying, "Yes, I think she will."

Whilst standing looking after his son until he should disappear from view, Matthew had thought that once engaged John would soon go, for it wouldn't be a three to five year engagement with her. And Margaret too could go at any time, out of compassion for her suitor if not out of love, his daughter being consumed with both. Apparently the young man hadn't turned up at the ball simply because he couldn't afford the dress for such an occasion. Shortly after the miserable night she had received a letter that should have reached her before she was due to leave for Hexham, explaining his reason for not attending her. He seemed forthright if nothing else, this poor bank clerk.

Then Hannah would follow. Somebody was bound soon to snatch Hannah up; the only question that troubled his mind was, who?

All this pointed to the prospect of him being left in the house with only Betsy and her. And what of the day when even Betsy would be persuaded to leave her? What would happen then? He had not taken Robert into account, for he wouldn't be a bit surprised if one morning there was a note from Robert saying he had gone to sea, or joined an expedition of some kind or another.

As he rode away from the mine in the gathering dusk, calling out good-nights here and there, he thought how wonderful it would be, how easy and how uncomplicated life would be if he were going home to Sally, even to that little cottage where the fire was always bright and the kitchen table scrubbed white, and the stone floor kept so clean that, as she so often said herself, you could eat your meat off it.

Before reaching the stone wall he had turned up a bridle path and into the hills. He always made sure before leaving the road that there was no one coming towards him or following on behind.

As he neared the cottage he always experienced a stir of excitement in his stomach. Tonight it was intensified by the lamplight shining from the window.

He put the horse into the lean-to shelter that was supported by a stone wall, unrolled a blanket from the saddle and put it over him, patted him twice on the rump, then went towards the light.

Lifting the latch of the door he went in calling softly, "Sally!" Then again "Sally!"

Then he saw her. She was standing near the open doorway leading into the little bedroom; her fingers were spread across her mouth, and as she stared at him and muttered, "Oh my God!" she was pushed aside and a man came into the room. He was of medium height, but heavily built. His hair was cut short and stood up from his scalp as if each strand were a piece of wire. And his moustache looked as stiff. After staring at Matthew he turned and looked at his wife; then walking slowly towards Matthew he said, "Aye, aye! And what can I do for you, mister?"

"I . . . I was just passing. My . . . my wife asked me to call in and see if . . . if Mrs Warrington –" He inclined towards Sally as he swallowed a dobble of spittle, then went on, "If . . . if she could come and give her a hand." Some part of his mind was registering amazement at the ease with which he was adapting to the situation, until the man spoke again.

"Give her a hand? Your wife sent you to come and ask me wife to give her a hand?" The man stared at Matthew through narrowed lids and, his lower jaw thrust out now, he said, "You come into my bloody house without a knock or by your leave, you call my wife Sally as if 'twasn't the first time, an' as far as I know, mister, me wife's never been out helpin' anyone, top, middlin' or low. I married a woman who would be here when I got back, not one to be a skivvy, so now" – his voice rose to a bawl – "who the bloody hell do you think you're hoodwinkin'? What's been goin' on here?" He jerked his head and glanced back at Sally, where she was standing with her two hands gripping the front of her blouse. Then his voice almost reaching an hysterical scream, he cried, "Bugger me eyes! I see it all now. Aye, aye! I see it all now. You bitch you! You've had little to give me 'cos you were empty. By God! I'll murder you for this, I will."

As Matthew was about to speak, Sally, pulling herself together, yelled in her turn at her husband, crying, "What you on about Bill Warrington, with your mucky mind? The truth is Mr Thornton saved me from drowning once. I didn't tell you 'cos you wouldn't have been interested. And over the years he's looked in once or twice, that's all. An' you speak to him like that."

The man now stared at her, not knowing whether to believe her or not, and she went on, "You should be ashamed of yourself. We have few callers here, God knows, and when anybody comes you insult them. An' a man like Mr Thornton an' all!" She now turned to Matthew and said, "I'm sorry, Mr Thornton. Go on your way now, an' don't look us up again, not after this reception."

Looking at her, and picking up the signal from her sad, frightened gaze, Matthew said, "Yes, I'll be on my way. I am sorry I intruded. Good-bye, Sally."

In the emotion of the moment she forgot her little bit of play acting and, her voice low now, she said, "Good-bye, Matthew."

As the door closed behind Matthew, Bill Warrington turned on her. He didn't yell now but he seemed to blow the words through the straggled hairs of his moustache, saying, "Matthew! Good-bye, Matthew! You loose, lying bitch! . . . Come to ask you to go and help his wife? I know what he come to ask you for. I was right."

Before she could speak or protest in any way, his fists shot out, first his right and then his left, full into her face.

He did not even stoop over her when she fell but, picking up the poker from the fireplace, he went to the door and, pulling it open, he ran out into the night and towards where he could hear the jingle of harness and the snorting of the horse.

The first time Matthew regained consciousness he thought he was dead and had dropped into the bowels of hell, except that hell, as he understood it, was a place of warmth, and wherever he was there was certainly no warmth, for his body was so numb he could scarcely feel it; in fact, at first he thought that his head had been separated from his body. He had no idea where he was and that the sound of horses' hooves on the ground somewhere above him were part of the shivering nightmare.

The second time he came to himself he opened his eyes and saw the stars shining brightly in the black sky. And now he put his hands out and groped about him; but when he went to raise his body the agony in his head was so intense that he fell back and lay still.

He had to make a number of efforts before he was finally able to turn on to his hands and knees, and when by clutching at the earth to the side of him he was able to stand swaying on his feet, he could make out the road level with his chin. He had been lying in a ditch.

He did not know how long he stood supporting himself and staring blankly at the frozen black earth before his eyes, but it was some time before he could gather enough strength to pull himself up on to the road. But once there he found that without support he was unable to stand.

On his hands and knees again, he peered about him. He guessed he was on the coach road, but on which part of it and how far from home he was he had no idea; nor did he know which direction he should take to get there.

It was as he knelt thus that the sound of horses' hooves came to him again, and when he went to shout "Help!" and there merely issued from his throat a croak, he experienced a sharp shivering fear.

He seemed to be in a direct line with the oncoming animal and he raised one hand as if to protect himself, and again he attempted to shout, but the effort was too much for him and he fell on to his side.

Then it seemed to him that in the next minute he was being hoisted to his feet, and he heard Robert's voice and that of Fred Loam exclaiming over him, Robert saying, "Papa! Papa! Oh! thank God," and Fred using stronger language, his voice loud, as he cried, "What a bloody mess! He's been done over. Hold the lamp up, Mr Robert. This is the second do of late. There was that one down near Catton last week, but there they took the horse, 'cos that's what they were after. . . . He can't sit; we'll just have to put him over the saddle." . . .

When Matthew next came to himself he was warm, in fact hot, sweating. He did not open his eyes immediately but lay feeling safe, knowing that he was in bed, but also aware that his head ached with such an intensity that he felt he couldn't bear it and begged to drop off into unconsciousness again.

"Papa, are you awake?"

With an effort he lifted his lids and peered at Margaret.

"How are you feeling, Papa?"

He made no reply but moved one dry lip over the other, and when he felt the spout of the feeding cup he sucked at it. Then after a moment he asked faintly, "Time? What time is it?"

"Eleven o'clock . . . in the morning. Oh, Papa –" she bent over him, tears running down her face – "I'm so glad . . . that . . . that you are home. Oh, lie still, don't move." She put her hand on his shoulder. "Doctor Arnison will be in shortly again." She sat down now by the side of the bed and held his hand. "We were so worried when Bob came galloping back on his own; everyone was worried, all the villagers. The men went out . . . and the miners too, they think so highly of you, Papa." Her tears choked her voice, and he patted her fingers gently; then after a moment he asked, "Where . . . where did they find me?"

"On the main road, near the creek. You must have been lying in the ditch because John and Mr Wheatley had been along that way twice earlier in the night."

"In the night?"

"Yes" – she nodded at him – "it was on two o'clock this morning when they came across you."

Two o'clock. His mind was working slowly. How long had he been lying in the ditch? She said it was near the creek, but why was he lying in the ditch near the creek?

Slowly a picture began to form in his mind, and he saw Sally standing in the doorway with the man behind her. But he had left the cottage unharmed? The picture became clearer. He had his foot in the stirrup when he felt the man behind him; he hadn't time to turn, He could remember nothing after that except the sound of the horses' hooves and the sudden fear that he was going to be trampled on.

But why was he at home, Bill Warrington? Sally had never made a mistake in all the years they had been together. She had timed her husband's comings and goings accurately, and he had read her signs accurately. The sign yesterday morning had said all was clear. Behind his closed lids he saw the wall again and the arrangement of the stones. Then another picture was interposed on the wall and he saw the figures of the two miners climbing the hill, the slippery hill, the road that would take them much longer to get to the mine than would their usual route. Who were they, those two? His mind began to grope through the muzziness of his thoughts. He knew them, he had been thinking about them as he watched them disappear. Yes. Yes, of course, Shields and Pearman, the jokers, the vindictive jokers. Did they realize what they were doing? Had they thought of what the consequences might be? Did they imagine for a moment that Bill Warrington would touch his forelock and say, "Carry on, sir. Take your pleasure." Why did people act so? Why? Why? Damn silly question; need he ask? They were getting their own back because he had warned them about their agitating. And another thing, they must have known about him and Sally. Good God! and he'd thought he'd been so clever all these years.

His head was buzzing; he was very hot; his body seemed on fire and his head twice, three times its size, so big that he imagined it was spreading over the pillows. . . .

His next lucid thought was, just wait till he got back, he would sort those two out. By God! he would, if it was the last thing he did.

I could have died. I could have died. I could have died. Why did he keep saying that? He was very hot, and so thirsty, and his head ached.

I could have died. I could have died. I could have died. The lamp was lit, it was night time. Where had the day gone?

"Am I dying, John?"

"No, Papa, no, of course not. You've caught a chill."

Day and night seemed all mixed up. It was no sooner daylight than they lit the lamp again. But his head no longer ached; he just felt very hot and his throat was sore and it was difficult to breathe. But he was glad that his head was better, for that pain had been dreadful.

"Do you think I'll pull round, Robert?"

"Yes, yes, of course, you will, Papa. Of course. You must pull round, Papa. Oh, you must."

"Hello, Hannah."

. . . "Hello, mister."

"Now, now, Hannah, don't . . . don't cry."

"All right, I won't if you promise not to talk."

"Doesn't . . . doesn't matter, Hannah, if I talk or not, makes no difference now. What time is it?"

"Three o'clock."

"In the morning?"

"Yes, in the morning."

"Where is everyone?"

"John and Margaret have just gone downstairs to make a drink. Robert is resting in my room." She nodded towards the communicating door.

"My . . . my wife?"

". . . The missis is resting in her room. She . . . she is very tired."

"Very tired. Very tired . . . Hannah."

"Yes, mister?"

"Hannah, say father. . . ."

. . . "Father."

"Now, now, dear, don't . . . don't cry. You know something? I'm . . . I'm feeling much better, stronger."

She couldn't speak for a moment; then her voice almost of a like croak to his, she said, "Oh . . . oh, that's wonderful."

"Will . . . will you do something for me, Hannah?"

"Yes, mister . . . father, anything, anything."

He made a movement as if to turn on his side but the effort seemed too much and he lay gasping for a moment before going on, "Will . . . will you take a message to a woman, a friend of mine? She is called Sally, Sally Warrington. She lives in Lode Cottage. You know . . . that way . . . between the creek . . . and the mine. . . . In . . . in the bottom of the wardrobe" – he lifted his hand slightly from the coverlet in the direction of the big Dutch cupboard taking up almost one wall of the room – "under . . . underneath the end board you'll . . . you'll find a bag. Twenty . . . twenty sovereigns . . . in it. I want you to take them . . . to her. It . . . it might help her . . . to get away, and . . . ."

A bout of coughing racked his chest and cut off his words, but lifting his hand now well up above the coverlet he stabbed his finger towards the wardrobe again, and Hannah went hastily to it, opened the door, thrust the hanging clothes to one side, then stooping down, she groped at the boards. But they all seemed nailed fast until her fingers slipped over the edge of the last one. Pulling the single board away from its resting place, she bent sidewards and felt underneath it until her fingers came in contact with a small leather bag.

Back at the bedside once more, she extended her hand holding the bag towards him, and he nodded at her, saying very slowly now, "Hide it until . . . you . . . you find an opportunity to go over. Tell her I . . . I thought of her. You'll . . . you'll do this for me, Hannah?"

"Yes, yes, of course. Anything, anything."

"She was a good friend to me . . . you understand what I mean?"

She stared down at him for a moment before she nodded slowly. Yes, she understood what he meant. The woman had been the kind of friend to him that her mother had once been. She didn't blame him. No, no, not at all, she didn't blame him. Having a wife such as the missis, he would have to find comfort of some sort.

When she heard the sound of footsteps on the stairs she slipped the bag down the front of her bodice and it fell between her breasts.

When John and Margaret entered the room she moved aside, and John, after looking at his father for a moment, turned swiftly to Margaret and whispered, "Go and bring Mama."

As Margaret hurried from the room Hannah went to the other side of the bed, and bending over Matthew, she gathered his limp hand between both her own and, bringing it to her face, she rubbed it gently against her cheek. She could not see him because her face was awash, nor could he see her because he had closed his eyes; but he was still breathing.

She was standing well back near the dressing table when Anne Thornton entered the room followed by Margaret and Robert. She did not wait to see the parting between the husband and wife but went quickly out and into her own room.

The mister was dying. Her father was dying. The man who had wrecked his marriage, and even his family life, by harbouring her was dying. She owed him a debt that she could never repay. For years now she had wanted to repay it in love but she'd had to restrain herself, not only because of his wife but because of his

134

younger daughter. The others would have understood and accepted the affection she had longed to show.

She lit the candle on the small table, then sat down on the edge of the bed. She supposed she should pray but she couldn't, she could find no words with which to communicate her sorrow with the God who ruled life and death.

She sat for a long while perfectly still, how long she didn't know, she only knew that she was aware of the moment of his passing, and she turned now and fell on to the bed and smothered her weeping in the pillow.

It was some long time later when she pulled herself upright and, staring before her, whispered to herself, "Oh! Mister. Mister. What will happen to me now, now you are gone?"

PART THREE

The Girl Married 1859

1

"Mama."

"Yes, dear?"

"I saw her talking to Fred Loam again; they were standing openly in the square. That must be the third time this week."

Anne Thornton slowly lowered the small embroidery frame on to her black-draped knees and after sticking the needle in the canvas she raised her hands, which were partly encased in hand-done fine black-thread mittens, and laying them one on top of the other on her chest she sat silently looking at her daughter.

They were both encased in black from head to foot. Betsy's black cap was a replica of her mother's, the mittens also; only her dress was slightly different.

Anne Thornton's voice was low as she asked now, "Did you bring up with Margaret the subject of what transpired at the ball?"

"Yes, I did, Mama, but you know Margaret, she accused me bitterly of talking of balls, and Papa so recently gone."

Anne Thornton turned her head slowly and looked through the gloom of the room towards the window where the blind was still half drawn, and the fingers of one hand began to tap the other rhythmically. She knew that things had not gone according to her husband's plan on the night of the ball. But she didn't know whether his disappointment was because Margaret's suitor had failed to materialize – this was all she could get out of Robert – or Mr Walters's interest in *The Girl* had for some reason flagged. What was troubling her though was the possibility that the solicitor, hearing of her husband's death, might turn up on the doorstep and ask for the hand of that creature. They might have been meeting during her last term at school; how was she to know!

That her husband's flyblow should ever attain the position of a solicitor's wife in the town of Hexham, while her own daughter might, if she herself did not put a stop to it, become the wife of a mere clerk was unthinkable. The idea wasn't to be borne.

She rose abruptly to her feet now, upsetting the frame, and when it fell to the floor Betsy stooped quickly and picked it up. Then they were standing face to face.

"I want you to go down to the shop and . . . and say to Mr Loam that I wish to see him. Should he enquire why, say it is a private matter."

"Yes, Mama." Betsy's face was bright.

"Go at once; you'll likely catch him before he goes off to Allendale for a killing, it being Monday."

"Yes, Mama."

Anne Thornton watched her daughter almost scurrying from the room. She knew that Betsy would be as glad to see the back of *The Girl* as she was. But glad was an inadequate word to express her feelings, for she didn't want to see the back of *The Girl* altogether, she wanted to be in a place of observation from where she could witness her humiliation, and what she had in mind now would go a long way towards bringing this about.

Fred Loam, she considered, was an ignorant, gormless young man, and his wife, whoever she should be, wouldn't have only him to deal with but his mother also. . . . Oh, his mother! If ever there was a vixen in this world it was Mrs Loam; and she had it in her heart to pity anyone doomed to become her daughter-in-law . . . that is with the exception of one person.

She had a mental picture of the enjoyment she would derive from observing the suffering of *The Girl* under the domination of that coarse, loud-mouthed little tartar, not to mention what she would endure, literally, under Fred Loam's hands.

How she hated that girl, for it was she who had ruined her life, it was she who had bred in her a devastating hate for her husband; and hate him she had, right until the end when, with his eyes open, he had looked at her as he drew his last breath. She hoped, she prayed, that his Maker was dealing justly with him at this moment. That being so, she could see him being made to suffer for a long, long time, as she had suffered for years. Dear, dear Lord, and how she had suffered lying in that room alone, deprived of the companionship that a wife should expect from a husband; companionship that had nothing to do with the demands of the body.

She imagined now that before *The Girl* had come on the scene a strong mental and spiritual companionship had existed between them. She told herself from time to time that they might have had slight differences of opinion now and again about certain things, but that was all; otherwise all had been harmony for those first thirteen years of her marriage.

But now he was gone, and if she had hated him in life she hated him more now, for he had left them penniless. He had left no will, at least none that could be found. Anyway, he had nothing to leave except the house, and by rights that should have gone to John; but John in his generosity had said he would pass it on to her legally, for when he was married he would live in his wife's home, at least for a time. The farmhouse was large and his future in-laws had shown a preference for him to live with them.

So she had the house; but how was she to keep it up? Last week she had heard from Mr Beaumont to the effect that he was allowing her a pension of a guinea a week; which she considered a very mean gesture. How was she to exist once John and Robert had left home? She wished it was Robert who was marrying, then she could have been sure of John saying, "Don't worry, Mother, I will support you;" but not so Robert. She and Robert had never seen eye to eye; in fact, there was a dislike in her for him, and she was sure he reciprocated the feeling.

But first things first; she must get that *Girl* out of this house. If it wasn't for the outcry that would have been raised against her by her sons and Margaret she would have turned her into the street on the day of the funeral.

Her feelings now drove her from the room and into the kitchen. She still put no check on *The Girl's* movements but she wanted to know where she was, and when she returned from one of her rambles she usually entered the house by way of the kitchen.

The kitchen was empty except for Bella, and she passed her

141

without a word, which wasn't at all unusual, went through into the yard and towards the stable as if she were looking for Dandy. Then as she was about to enter the kitchen again, she saw Betsy hurrying towards the front door.

Betsy, catching sight of her mother, came into the yard and as they met, she whispered excitedly, "I just caught him going out. He's coming, Mama; he should be here any minute."

Anne Thornton gave two small coughs, looked back towards the kitchen door, then walked on to the drive, saying softly, "Wait on the step for him, then bring him straight into the sitting-room."

"Yes, Mama."

It seemed that she had hardly composed herself in a chair with her back to the light, arranged her skirts, and taken up her embroidery frame, before the sitting-room door opened and Betsy entered, saying in a stage whisper, "Mr Loam to see you, Mama."

"Come in, Fred."

"Good-day to you, ma'am."

"Good-day, Fred."

He was standing awkwardly in the middle of the room, his cap in his hand, and she did not ask him to be seated but, adding another stitch to the embroidery, she kept her eyes on it as she said, "May I ask you a personal question, Fred?"

"A personal question, ma'am? Ask me what you likes an' I'll answer."

"Have you ever thought of getting married?"

His silence brought her head up to see him gaping at her, and when she realized how he had taken her question she felt inclined to spring up, crying, "How dare you! To think I should suggest such a thing to you of all people, you must be mad!" Instead, she said stiffly and quickly, "I wondered if you had any idea in that direction concerning my" – how could she describe *The Girl*? She found the word that was non-committal "my ward?"

"You . . . you mean Hannah, missis?"

She saw his shoulders sink downwards as he spoke.

"Yes."

"You mean thoughts of marryin' her?"

"Yes."

"Aye, begod! Well –" He was now turning his cap around rapidly between his hands while his head swung from one side to the other and the beam on his face seemed to spread down into his thick neck; then his head becoming still, he looked at her and asked, "You'd allow it?"

"Yes, I would allow it."

"My! Well! . . . Well, if I've got your go-ahead. Eeh! mind, I'll tell you this, missis. I've thought about it, an' not once or twice either, but I never dreamed. Well, I thought you'd have other ideas for her. Even as things stood an' you didn't care a . . ." He broke off abruptly and his head drooped once more, to be brought up with startling suddenness as she said, "You have my permission to marry her as soon as you think fit. You need not consider any disrespect to her father. There are to be changes made in the house and her marriage will be the first of them."

"Have you spoken to her? Does she know?"

She looked directly at him as she replied, "She will do what she is told and be grateful."

His face was solemn now as he said, "Well, all I can say is thanks, missis, an' I only hope she sees it like you said."

"Good-day, Fred. I shall leave the rest to you."

"Thanks, ma'am." He stood a moment longer before turning about and walking straight and steadily from the room.

2

It was a lovely day, a day for walking. The sun was bright but not warm; there was a pale mauve light resting on all the hilltops, but when you looked up into the sky your eyes were lost in a never-ending whiteness through which you could see right to where the stars were.

Twice within the past three weeks she had set out intending to deliver the mister's last message to the woman in the cottage. The first time, she took the wrong road and wandered about for hours and only just managed to get home before dark. The second time, she was caught in a hail-storm. But today, she was on the right road.

Yesterday she asked Ned where the cottage lay, and after describing just where she must leave the main road in order to reach it, he had asked, "Why do *you* want to go to Sally Warrington's?" And she had been evasive, saying, "No reason." Then under his stare she had muttered, "I . . . I have a message for her. You . . . you won't say anything, will you, Ned?" and his reply had been characteristic: "Say anything? What's it got to do with me?"

And now she could see the cottage, and there was a woman outside, a bucket in her hand; and she had seen her, too, and was waiting for her coming.

Hannah stopped by the gate in the wall, and the woman stood beyond it, and they looked at each other.

"Are you Mrs Warrington?"

"Aye, yes, I am."

"May I have a word with you?"

Hannah noticed that the woman seemed to weigh up in her

144

mind whether or not to reply; and then she said abruptly, "Come in."

Hannah followed her into the cottage, and when the woman pointed to a seat and herself took one opposite, she tried not to look at her face, for it was so discoloured. Not only were there purple hues around the eyes but the top lip showed a scar where a cut had been, and one side of her face looked bigger than the other.

"What did you want to say to me?"

"I have a message for you from . . . from my father."

It was the first time she had said those words aloud and she gave a little shiver as if she had received a cold douche.

The woman's head was bent and she didn't speak for some time; then, her voice scarcely above a whisper, she said, "What did he say?"

"He . . . he said I had to give you this." She now opened her cloak, put her hand down the front of her bodice, and brought out the small leather bag, which she handed to the woman.

Sally looked at it for a long moment before taking it, saying, "What is it?"

"It's . . . it's money. He thought you would need it. It . . . it might help you to get away, he said."

"Oh my God!" Sally dropped the bag into her lap, then covered her distorted face with her hands, and when she began to cry the sound filled the room and her choked words spilt from her bruised lips. " 'Twas my fault. 'Twas my fault. But he should swing. He should, he should. 'Twas murder, but who's to prove it. He was far away in Hexham next morning. He's got those who'll swear to it. But he did this 'fore he left. Twice he went at me." As she touched her streaming face gently with her fingers Hannah rose from the chair and went towards her and, putting her arm around the woman's shoulders, she said, "Don't. Please don't cry like that." Yet she herself was crying now unrestrainedly, as she had not cried since the time Matthew had died.

By way of comfort she said quietly, "He . . . he cared for you; he had great concern for you. There are twenty sovereigns in the bag. It . . . I think it was all he had of ready money. He did not leave any."

Sally gulped in her throat, then muttered, "He left no money?"

"No, only what was due to him in his wage. But he . . . he wanted you to have this; he seemed anxious that you should get away."

"Oh. An' God, how right he was! Oh, lass, the thought's never left me head but to get away, nobody knows, but I had nothin'. Your father was always generous, but at times I wouldn't take it 'cos I was feared he, me husband, would find it. So when I went into Newcastle twice a year at the hirings an' then the cattle shows I . . . I went to me sister Lizzie's an' give her what I'd got 'cos she's got a big family and is hard pushed. She would have taken me in now but I wouldn't go empty-handed. But now, oh this, this!" She hugged the bag to her; then, shaking her head, she said, "He was a good man, a wonderful man, an' I'll say it without shame, I loved him, I did." She stood up now and gently wiped her face, then said, "Can I get you a cup of something, soup or milk?"

"No thanks; I'll . . . I'll be on my way. May I ask if you'll be going to your sister's now?"

"Aye, lass, I'll go." Sally's voice was deep now and held a strong note of bitterness. "Aye, I'll go. An' you know somethin'? I'll go this very day 'cos he's away over the border and won't be back for two days. Once there, I can lose meself in the city. Me sister Lizzie 'll fix it. And I've got enough now to pay me way till I get work. I can be away afore dark for I've got little belonging to me except what I stand up in an' a change of shift and a frock an' coat. The lot wouldn't make a decent bundle. Aye, lass, I'll go this day. An' thank you, thank you for comin' and bringin' me his message." She shook her head at this point, saying, "I've got one regret, an' that is I couldn't have been with him at the end, for I can say this to you, she'd be no comfort to him, not from what I've heard. But afore you go" – she put out her hand – "tell me what you gona do with yourself?"

"I wish I knew. I would like to get some sort of situation but I'm not qualified for anything. I'm . . . I'm not like Margaret, that's my half-sister, she's very clever. My accomplishments are more homely, so to speak." She smiled wanly.

"Well, lass, to my mind they'll stand you in better stead than all your fancy learnin'. But never fear, you'll marry, you're so bonny. You'll be grabbed up afore you know where you are. I only hope you get a good man, a kind one, like your da was. Good-bye, lass." She held out her hand, and Hannah took it, then turned quickly away.

Out on the hills again, Hannah made her way slowly down towards the main road. She could understand the mister liking that woman, she was nice, kindly, and before her face was scarred she must have appeared bonny. She was glad she would be going away. As she said, she could lose herself in the city. She recalled the city. She had lost herself many times there, having strayed only a short way from the waterfront. She'd love to go back to Newcastle just to walk through its streets again. If only she knew someone there like the woman did, someone to go to who'd shelter her.

There was a fear rising in her as to what would really become of her. The woman had said she'd be married, she'd be snapped up, but she didn't want to be snapped up, she didn't want to be married. There was only one man who filled the picture of her husband, and because she couldn't have him she told herself with girlish vehemence that she would never marry anyone.

But the question remained, what was she to do? because even if she wanted to, she doubted whether she'd be allowed to live in the house much longer. There was something brewing, an undercurrent; she could feel it.

She was descending the hill above the road when she caught sight of Ned, and her heart lifted. She picked up her skirts and ran down to the wall, then on to the road where he had drawn his lead pony to a stop.

Looking down at her, he said, "Well, been for one of your strolls?"

"Yes, Ned."

He looked away over her head now towards the hills and said in an offhand tone, "To Lode Cottage?"

"Yes, to Lode Cottage."

"What would you be doin' there if it's not impidence to ask?"

She stared up at him, then said quietly, "I was taking a message."

"Oh aye." He nodded at her; then again he said, "Oh aye, it all fits in."

"What does?"

"Well, there's a rumour goin' about that your da wasn't set on by any mad Scot from across the border, or hill highwayman, or horse thief; but 'tis only a rumour."

She blinked at him, then asked, "Where are you off to now?"

"Oh, a long trip this time down into Westmoreland, a house atween Hilton and Coupland, a private deal." He grinned now. "I like private deals, they generally do you well. Kip for the night with plenty to eat and drink."

"Will you be away long?"

"Oh, it all depends if I pick up another lot of them on the way back." He nodded towards the four ponies behind him. "You never know where a blister might light in this business; you don't always get them on the seat of your pants." He smacked his buttock with the flat of his hand.

She made no reply to his joke, but, her face straight, she looked up at him and only just stopped herself from saying, "Hurry back" because that would have been silly; yet somehow when she knew he was in the Pele house she never felt entirely friendless, it was like having a big brother up there to run to.

His tone sounded flat now as he asked, "How's things back there?"

"Oh–" She swallowed, then said, "About . . . about the same."

"What are you thinkin' of doing?"

She shook her head and looked down towards her feet before she replied, "I don't know, Ned, I wish I did, I'm all at sea."

"Can you swim?"

Her head jerked up. "What? . . . What do you mean, can I swim?"

"Just what I said, can you swim?"

"No."

"Well, if you're all at sea and you can't swim you won't survive long will you?" The corners of his mouth were turned upwards, but there was no answering smile on her face and her voice was matchingly stiff when she said, "I don't find it funny, Ned."

She started visibly when, suddenly bending low down towards her until he was almost out of the saddle, he growled at her, "Then you should do something about it. People who can't swim clutch at straws, whereas if they opened their bloody eyes wide enough and stretched out their arms, they would see a plank to their hand. You're not a bairn any longer, you're a young woman. And you know something? You're as dangerous as damp dynamite in a mine. . . . You are. You are that. An' if you don't open your eyes and see what's under your nose one of these days you'll sink, an' *Ned* won't be there to haul you out. . . . Get up there! Get up! Damn you, get up!"

She stood with her mouth open watching the string of ponies trotting down the road and listening to him bawling at the top of his voice "Put a move on! Pick your feet up, damn you! Get on with you!"

What had she done? Why had he turned on her like that? Saying that she was as dangerous as dynamite in a mine. She looked about her as if the hills would give her an answer. Ned and she had always been good friends, he had been like a relative to her. Why had he turned on her like that? All that talk about swimming and sinking and grabbing at straws. She could understand now why some people didn't like him if he went for them like that. After all, she had done nothing to upset him. She remembered him being rude to her once before, practically ordering her out of the Pele house. It was around the time when he was going to marry, then didn't. Perhaps he was having trouble in that way again. But that was no reason why he should turn on her like that. Yet men didn't need a reason to be rude. Robert was very rude at times, John never. Oh! John. John.

John hardly spoke to her these days, and when he looked at her it was in a shamefaced way.

She turned now and walked briskly along the road in the direction of the place she still thought of as home.

It was the following morning. Betsy went to Hannah with a message to say that she was to take an order to the butcher's and she had to go alone and immediately.

As she took the slip of paper from Betsy's hand, Hannah looked at her but said nothing. She liked Betsy as little as Betsy liked her. Going into the hall, she collected her bonnet and short coat from the cloakroom, then went out upon her errand.

When she entered the butcher's shop there were no customers present, and Fred turned from the block, chopper in hand, and, his face spreading into a broad grin, he said, "Why! hello."

"Hello, Fred. I . . . I've brought the order."

"Oh aye." He took the paper from her; then going to a door at the side of the shop, he pulled it open and, looking up the steep stairs which led from it, he called, "Ma! Ma! will you come down here a minute?"

During the time that Fred waited for his mother to descend the stairs he kept his eyes on Hannah, grinning all the while; then when Mrs Loam came into the shop he said, "She's come," and inclining his head towards Hannah he said, "Take over for a minute, will you?"

The tight-bodiced, tight-lipped little woman looked squarely at Hannah, then walked to the counter where she turned and said, "Well, get upstairs if you're goin'."

Hannah looked behind her wondering for a moment if Mrs Loam was speaking to someone else; then pointing to herself, she asked, "You mean me, Mrs Loam?"

"Well, I'm not talkin' to meself, lass."

"Come upstairs a minute, Hannah, will you?" Fred's voice was low and persuasive now, and Hannah, looking at him enquiringly, asked simply, "Why?"

"Didn't she say anything to you?" Fred now moved towards her. "The missis?"

"What about?"

"Aw, God in heaven!" As his head wagged frantically his mother cried harshly, "Either tell her here or tell her upstairs, but get it over."

"Come along of me a minute, Hannah." The young fellow now held out his hand towards her, but Hannah didn't take it, yet she walked past him and for the first time mounted the stairs to the rooms above the shop.

She stood for a moment gazing about her at the cold, stiff orderliness of what was evidently a kitchen-cum-sitting-room then she started as she felt her hand gripped in Fred's two beefy ones and, his face close to her, heard him saying, "Don't you know? Didn't she tell you?"

"Tell me what?" Hannah went to withdraw her hand, but he held on to it.

"Well—" He straightened his shoulders now, took a small step back from her while still retaining hold of her hand, and ended, "She gave me leave to court you."

"*She what!*" She almost jumped from his hold. "You! to court me?"

"Aye, that's what I said, court you." His face was straight now. "An' it shouldn't come as so much of a surprise to you. I've talked to you a lot lately an' you haven't offsided me; pleased you seemed like to stop an' chat."

"Only . . . only because you helped to find Father. I . . . I was grateful."

"Aye well, I didn't take it just like that. Anyroad, she says it's all right an' you're not spoken elsewhere, an' me ma's agreeable an' all, so everything's plain sailin'."

"Oh no, it isn't. No, it isn't." She was backing from him now towards the door. "You are under a misapprehension. I . . . I cannot marry you."

"Why not?" His bulky body became stiff now, his manner aggressive, and again he demanded, "Why not? Not good enough you think? Let me tell you I've got more put by than most in this village, I'm a warm man, an' me wife 'll want for nowt."

Hannah took a deep breath, then closed her eyes for a moment before lowering her head and saying, "Oh, Fred, I'm sorry. I'm . . . I'm sure you're very worthy, and . . . and I thank you for the compliment you have paid me." And now she smiled weakly. "It's the first proposal I've ever received and . . . and I do thank you. But I'm sorry, Fred."

"Are you going to tell her that?"

"Yes, yes, I am." Her reply was made in firm tones.

"Well, I wouldn't like to be there when you say your piece, cos let me tell you, Hannah, she means to get rid of you, an' if it isn't to me it'll be to somebody else. An' although I say it meself, you could look further an' fare worse. Aye, you could that."

"I know that, Fred. I do, I know that."

"You don't dislike me, do you?"

"Oh no, Fred, I don't dislike you."

"Well then, why not let's give it a try? Look" – he stepped towards her – "think on it. Go on back and think on it. I'll wait till the morrow and then I'll take your yes or nay for final. But . . . but afore you go I'll tell you this, Hannah. I care for you and I'd be a good husband to you if you're a good wife to me. Of course I know there's me ma, and she's hard to stomach at times, but I know how to handle her and I'll see she doesn't interfere. What do you say? Leave it till the morrow mornin'?"

She moved her head in denial; then, her only wish being to escape, she said, "All right then, Fred, we'll . . . we'll leave it til tomorrow morning."

"That's a good lass." As he made to come nearer she turned and, opening the door, went on to the small stairhead and ran down the dark stairs so quickly that she almost fell down the last three steps.

There were still no customers in the shop and Mrs Loan stopped her sanding of the block and, resting both hands on the long scrubbing brush, turned her head and demanded, "Well?"

Hannah gave her no answer, she merely paused a moment looked at the little woman, then ran out of the shop.

Minutes later she was in the sitting-room actually shouting at the stiff figure who had risen from the couch and was now standing with her back to her. "You can't do this! You can't make me marry him! You have no hold over me. You can't make me do anything. Do you hear?"

When Anne Thornton turned about and walked slowly down the room towards the door, Hannah stepped aside expecting that the woman would at last confront her and speak to her openly but she watched in amazement the figure sweep past her, pull open the door and go out.

Hannah now stumbled up the room. She had a hand under each oxter and her body was bent forward as if in pain, and she groaned to herself, "She's wicked. She's wicked. She can't do this. I'll leave the house, I'll go away." . . . But where? . . . Ned She'd go and tell Ned. Ned would advise her, tell her what to do tell her what rights she had, because this was her father's house although he was dead she was still his daughter.

It was only as she made for the door once more that she realized that Ned would now be far away on his journey over the hills. But there was Margaret. She would tell Margaret. Margaret was sensible, much older than her years; Margaret would know what she would do. Margaret had gone into Allendale earlier; she would go and meet her.

She was in the hall on the way to the door when Betsy came from the office towards her and, standing in front of her, she said calmly, "Mama says that if you don't comply and accept Mr Loam's offer, then you must leave the house immediately as she cannot afford to support you any longer."

Hannah's answer to this was to bend forward, clench her teeth for a moment, then say slowly, "You horrible, horrible creature you! You spiteful, mean individual! I don't know what is going to happen to me, but this I do know, you'll end your days just like her" – she thrust out her arm and pointed towards the study door – "lonely, alone, hated." On this she turned and rushed out on to the drive; then on to the road and through the village; and her passing caused heads to turn, not only to see her running, with both hands holding up the front of her skirt, but also because she had no covering at all on her head, neither lace nor starched cap, shawl, hat, nor bonnet. To some of the older residents it appeared as if they were seeing her running naked through their village.

She was approaching Allendale when she met up with Margaret and she fell upon her, gasping and crying, "Oh, Margaret! Margaret!"

"What is it? What's the matter? What is it, dear? Come and sit down."

Margaret led her to a broken stone wall at the side of the road and, pressing her down on to it, she sat by her side and, taking her hands, she asked again, "What's happened?"

"She's . . . she's arranged I should marry Fred, Fred Loam. Oh, Margaret! Margaret."

"Oh no!"

"Yes, yes, Margaret. It's cruel, isn't it? It's cruel."

When Margaret gave her no answer, Hannah insisted, "It is. Don't you think it is? It is."

"Yes, yes. It's cruel, and she intends it to be cruel. Oh, I know

153

Mama, she intends it to be cruel. But, Hannah, Hannah my dear, it . . . it might turn out to be your salvation."

"What do you mean, Margaret, my salvation? To marry a man like Fred Loam?"

"Oh, I know he is far beneath you, and is really of low intelligence and without education, but . . ."

"Oh, I don't mean that. It's got nothing to do with education as I see it, it's . . . it's just Fred himself, what he looks like, how he talks, how he acts."

"Well, that's what I'm meaning. These things are all part of a man's education."

Hannah now swung her head as she said flatly, "Education! There's Ned Ridley, he's had no education but he's got more brains than most people in the village put together."

"Yes, well, Ned's a bit of an exception. He's highly intelligent and he could have made something of himself if he had cared, I'm sure of that. But . . . but we have a point here, Hannah." She now caught hold of her arm. "You could likely make something of Fred."

"Oh no! No! . . . Look, Margaret, in my desperation I thought of something as I came to meet you. If I could get back to school, Miss Barrington would help me. I'm sure she would."

When Margaret slowly lowered her eyes and bit on her lip Hannah muttered, "No, you think not?" Then Margaret, her eyes still cast down, said, "There is something I must tell you, Hannah, I'm leaving home tomorrow morning, I . . . I meant to leave you a letter. I'm going back to school." She now raised her eyes and looked straight at Hannah. "They're going to give me my board and room in exchange for looking after the smaller children and helping generally. But . . . but what I didn't know about the Barringtons, in fact no one knew about them, is that they are very poor and they just manage to exist. Miss Emily told me privately that during the holidays when there's no income they live very meagrely, and they spend their time renovating all the linen and the household goods. They even dismiss the gardener during those weeks and do the work themselves, so you see I . . . I couldn't ask them to take you, it would be an imposition. I . . . I couldn't do it, Hannah.'

Hannah slid quietly off the wall but she didn't move away from it, she stood with her buttocks pressed against it and her hands gripping the jagged stone edge. After a moment she asked quietly, "Are you going to be married?"

"Yes, as soon as Mr Hathaway can find an apartment suitable to his income."

"Does anyone know? John or Robert?"

"No, no; only Miss Pearce in the town, you know who keeps the sweetshop. She's in sympathy with me, and what I didn't know until recently she is a distant relative of Miss Rowntree. For the past three weeks, ever since Father died, I've been taking a few of my belongings, and putting extra clothes on my person and leaving them with her. Tomorrow morning I shall be gone before Mama is about; I'm catching the first carrier cart into Hexham."

"What will you do if . . . if your mother should come after you?"

Margaret gave a small mirthless laugh, saying, "Oh, Mama won't come after me, Mama cares for only one of her family, and that's Betsy; perhaps a little for John. But in John's case I think it is more pride than love."

Margaret now lowered herself to her feet and she, too, stood with her back to the wall, but she didn't grip it; instead, she threw one arm wide as she exclaimed, "I'll be glad to see the last of this; hills, hills, hills, wherever you go you are hemmed in by hills, some of them tortured by the mines, others desecrated by residue and muck. Having been born here, I should love the place, I suppose, and there's no getting away from it it is beautiful in parts if you like harsh grandeur, but it holds little appeal for me. I prefer people, even in the narrow confines of the city, but you" – she turned now and looked at Hannah – "you love the hills, don't you?"

"What? Oh yes, I suppose so." Hannah's answer was flat. "They were some place to escape to from the house, I felt free when I walked them." Now she turned and looked at Margaret as she ended, "Have you any idea what my life has been like in your home, Margaret?"

"Yes, Hannah, to a small extent; but not being you yourself, I couldn't experience your hurt to the full."

"I hate your mother, do you know that?"

"Yes, I know that."

"At one time I was only afraid of her, and the thought of hating her was like an assumption, something forbidden me. Even up to a year ago I hid this feeling from myself, but now I want to shout it, bawl it into her face. There have been times of late when I've wanted to strike her, as if by doing so I could make her address me, speak to me openly. To her I'm a thing, *The Girl*. She's never called me anything but *The Girl*. As if I weren't there, as if she were speaking of someone who was dead. Oh, I do hate her, Margaret. I do, I do!"

"Then that is all the more reason why you should get away from her. There are likely other men who would offer you marriage but at present only Fred has come forward, and if you don't comply she might be as good as her word and turn you out, and no one could stop her. Robert might try; but I'm sorry to say as much as you care for John, Hannah, I doubt if he would oppose her. What you haven't recognized yet in John is that he is weak."

Margaret turned away as she said this, adding, "Come!" and walked slowly up the road. Then after a moment she said, "That's why he is attracted to Miss Everton because she is a strong character. . . . And he is very attracted to her, Hannah." She now turned her head and nodded at Hannah. "You must face up to this fact and not mourn in your heart for something you imagine you have lost."

They walked on in silence for some way now as if they were enjoying a stroll in the April sunshine.

Presently Margaret said, "It is strange that in the main women are always stronger than men, yet they have to be subordinate to them. They cannot claim any of the man's rights, they are chattels; and yet in most cases happy to be chattels. I suppose love helps. In my own case I know I am of a stronger character than Mr Hathaway, yet I will become subordinate to him. You see, I have asked myself would I rather be like Miss Barrington, Miss Emily and Miss Rowntree? I don't think so. . . . "

"I would!"

The vehemence with which Hannah made this statement startled Margaret. "Oh, don't shake your head like that, Margaret.

I would change places with any one of them at this moment. I don't want to marry . . . I don't want to marry anyone, and I mean it. I know within a little what marriage means. Miss Emily made it clear to me in her going-away talk. She likely said the same to you. There is a personal element that can be highly distasteful, and before marriage, she said, you've got to ask yourself whether you could submit to it. Well, I don't feel I can; not with Fred Loam, or any one else for that matter."

"Then what do you intend to do?" Margaret had stopped and they were facing each other. "You could never live on your own in a town, you would be eaten up. A girl who looks like you, whether you wanted to or not, you would fall prey to men and end up like your mother. There! I've said it. I'm sorry but it's true. Please don't be hurt." She put out her hand and gripped Hannah's arm. "And let me say this; Miss Emily is a maiden lady and maiden ladies don't know all that much about the intimacies of marriage. How can they? And look about you and see the men and women who are happily joined together with a family around them. I am sure there is nothing to be afraid of. It . . . well, what Miss Emily never emphasized was that it's all a part of nature. . . . Accept Fred's offer, Hannah. At least you'd be safe and well housed and cared for if you marry him. But if you don't, then I don't dare to think what will happen to you, because let me say this finally, such are my mother's feelings towards you that she will brave any opposition that might arise against her in the village, she'll even put forward a statement that will make her actions appear justified, and the statement will be that you are trying to seduce your half-brother, because let me tell you I am sure she is aware to some extent of your feelings for John. . . . Marry Fred, Hannah, if only to save the name that you have held respectable so far, marry him."

3

They said in the village that they had never known a marriage happen so soon after the asking, unless it was where the bride wanted to bamboozle the months of the calendar in an effort to shorten her pregnancy.

Some said that couldn't be so in this case; but others said, time would tell, if not, why the rush?

Well, said the wise ones, didn't everybody know the feeling that had existed in that house since young Hannah was dumped on them years ago? And now that the master was gone that stiff-necked martinet had everything her own way, and it was evident she wanted to get rid of the lass.

But why pang her off on to Fred Loam? for all were agreed that Fred was no catch for a lass who looked like Hannah, and educated into the bargain. And then there was Fred's mother. Oh aye, there was Fred's mother.

Fred's mother now stood in the front pew, and to her side stood her sister and two distant relatives, while behind her, filling four rows, were neighbours and the tradesmen of the village.

On the other side of the aisle were Mrs Anne Thornton and her daughter Beatrice, and behind them Bella and Tessie and Dandy Smollett; but the rest of the pews were empty. Although it was high summer the church felt cold and smelt of damp. It smelt of damp at any time but the rain over the past four days seemed to have seeped through the thick stone walls until now even the pews felt wet.

The Reverend Stanley Crewe's muttering voice had seemed to those present to skip over the service, but to Hannah each of his words appeared to be long-drawn-out, weighty, pressing her down, while at the same time sounding unreal.

"I pronounce that they be Man and Wife together."

Hannah, already half turned towards Fred, stood rigid, but he, with a grin on his face, bent towards her and planted a wet kiss to the side of her lips. Her reaction to it was as if she had been stung for she started and turned about, there to see Robert, who'd had the unenviable task of giving her away, looking at her with a sort of warning glance, and she drew in a deep breath and gasped as if she had just checked herself from flight.

Only last night Robert had said to her he thought the whole thing was a crying shame, and if it wasn't for the situation of their birth he would, more than gladly he had emphasized, marry her himself.

She had cried over Robert's concern, yet she hadn't cried when John, standing in the hall, the least private place in the house, had wished her happiness and said he hoped she understood that it would be impossible for him to attend the ceremony as since his father's decease he was working over at the old mine, and she had made herself reply, while looking at him straight in the eyes, that she understood perfectly. And strangely she did. But what she understood more than anything else was that Margaret was right; John, although big and handsome and manly looking, was a weak man. Yet weak or not, she told herself that she would gladly give up her entire life if she could be compensated with just a day of his love.

She was in the vestry now signing the register and she was about to write Hannah Thornton when the Reverend Crewe's voice said gently, "Write your own name, Hannah."

She glanced at him for a moment, then wrote Boyle.

There was talk all around her, there was even laughter, when a voice above the rest cried, "You're gona be drowned on your weddin' night, Fred, I can see you havin' to swim to bed." The laughter became louder.

She felt dizzy, faint. She looked for a moment into the eyes of her new mother-in-law. They were unsmiling, coldly pale blue, like the colour of the marbles the boys played with in the lanes. Some of these though were warmed with pink stripes, but there was no glint of warmth in the eyes of the undersized little woman.

Then she looked at the woman standing far back, the woman

who should have been a mother to her, and her eyes were smiling now, gleaming as if with triumph.

She heard The Reverend Crewe say, "I would like to speak to you, Hannah, for a moment in private, and Fred too. Come this way."

Fred had his arm around her waist, and she submitted to it, for there was nothing she could do about it. They were following the parson into a small room that led off the vestry. It too smelt musty. Two of the walls were lined with racks holding boxes and books. All the books were thick tomes.

She was married, she was no longer Hannah Boyle or Hannah Thornton, she was Mrs Loam . . . Loam, it was of the soil; she wished she were under it, right under the soil at this moment, dead, without breath, without feeling, without fear. Oh yes, without fear, for there was a great fear on her now, and it was centred around Fred's big red hands.

She watched the minister take a key and unlock the door of a wall cabinet and from its shelf lift out an envelope. Then as he moved towards her holding the envelope in both hands he smiled his weak, watery but kindly smile, as he said, "This is for you, Hannah. It was put into my care by your mother on the day she unfortunately died. It was her request that it should be given to you on your wedding-day. I kept it until after the ceremony because I felt it would afford you both pleasure and comfort on this particular day."

Her lips slightly apart she gazed at the minister for a moment before extending her hand, then she took the long envelope and looked at it and her lips moved as she read the words to herself. "Concerning Hannah Boyle. This letter is to be put into the care of a minister of God, or some legal person, and to be given to the above-named on the day she weds."

She glanced now at Fred who was gazing at her with a look on his face that showed definite pride of possession.

"Aren't you going to open it, my dear?" The minister was now handing her a paper knife which she took from him and slowly slit open the envelope. Then taking out the long sheet of paper that was doubled in three and had inside it a yellowed printed form, she looked from one to the other before she began to read

I, Harold Penhurst Wright, solicitor's clerk, do pen this last will of Nancy Boyle in her own words as she so dictates them to me.

Dated this Seventh day of February in the year 1850.

I know that I'm not long for the top so want to do what is best for my child. If she is left alone here she will go to the bad and be used in a whore shop, as young as she is, or put in the House. One or t'other is bad. I was at my wits' end when I saw Mr Matthew Thornton in the city. Hadn't seen him since that time I told him I was carrying a bairn. I thought it no harm if he believed it his'n 'cos I was hard put to live but he went off that night and I never clapped eyes on him again until last week in the city. 'Twas then I made it my business to find out who he really was and where he abided. So what I mean to do is to go to him and put her in his charge, but at the same time I would like her to know that she isn't a bastard for she was got by the man I married, who went to sea and didn't come back, but I didn't know he wasn't coming back at the time, I just thought he was on his two-year trip.

I want my daughter to have this letter on her weddin' day along with her birth certificate so as her husband can't cast it up to her she's from the wrong side of the blanket. I hope she marries a decent man and is happy.

Signed by Mrs Nancy Boyle with her cross.

The seventh day of February 1850.

"No! No! No!"

She was waving the letter first at the minister and then at Fred; then almost pushing it into the minister's face, she cried, "You should have given it to me this morning. I should have had it this morning. I shouldn't have been married then. It says . . . it says he wasn't my father, the mister, Mr Thornton. He wasn't! He wasn't! . . ."

She was tossing her head now from side to side, and when Fred caught hold of her arm in a rough grip crying, "Stop your yelling! What's the matter with you? What does it say?"

She tore herself from him and again she waved the letter in his face; and now she said distinctly and slowly while thrusting her face towards his, "I am not Mr Thornton's daughter. That's what it says, I had a proper father, I mean this" – she was now holding up the birth certificate – "and I would never have married you had I known. I wouldn't! I wouldn't!"

"Hannah! Hannah! hush, you are married. Hush! you mustn't say that."

The little minister was almost knocked on to his back. It was only Fred's outstretched arm that caught him, and even he staggered back against the bookcase as Hannah rushed for the door, pulled it open, and sped on to the grass between the grave-stones, and away past the laughing crowd who were taking shelter in the church porch.

Before she reached the cemetery wall the thin white dress she wore was clinging to her like a bit of wet paper. She had worn a hood and cloak on the short journey from the house to the church, but had left the cloak at the back of the church before going up the aisle on Robert's arm.

When she clambered over the wall her leather shoes sank into mud and she almost fell on her face as she pulled them out one after the other. When her feet found hard ground again she tore like the wind in the direction of the hills and the short cut to the mine.

She had only one thought in her mind, and she was possessed by it, she must see John, she must tell him. It didn't make any difference now, she knew, but she must tell him. It hadn't been wrong, she knew in her heart it hadn't been wrong to love him. And they could have been married. They could. They could.

The wind was driving the rain in slanting sheets across the hills and it also brought to her the distant sound of voices and running feet. They were coming after her. Well, they didn't know where she was going; no one would think of her going to the mine. They might think she would go to Ned's. She would never go to Ned's again. He had passed her twice of late and never looked the side she was on. The first time she had gone to speak to him he had turned his head away and spat into the road, just as he said he did when he passed the missis. . . . The missis, that fiend of a woman, the missis. Had she known about this? No, no, she couldn't have; she would have turned her out sooner had she realized that her husband had been made use of, that all her suffering had been caused through a lie. And that the woman had suffered was true. Oh yes, she had suffered. It was because she had been aware of this, even as a child, that she hadn't allowed herself to hate the woman, until recently.

She had a stitch in her side; she must stop. Where was she? She stood bent double gasping; her hair had come loose from its pins and strands of it were straggling over her face. She pushed it from her eyes and peered this way and that way through the rain. She was at the end of the old by-road that wound among the web hills. No one used this way very much now since the new road had been made. It was tortuous in dry weather, it was a real danger in wet; there were potholes that would take you up to the waist in water. But what did it matter, it cut the distance to the mine by almost a mile. Another half-hour at the most and she'd be there.

She had been cold a short while back but now she was warm. Even though she was wet to the skin she was warm. She must look a dreadful sight, but again what did it matter? John would understand. . . . But if he wasn't at the mine?

He was bound to be at the mine, he said he'd be there, that's why he couldn't come to the wedding.

On the top of a hill she paused for breath again. To one side of her the land fell away in rain-swept layers like floating land-locked islands. The hills themselves seemed to be moving, rising and falling in waves of black and silver mist.

She must be nearing the mine now. Stumbling and gasping, she made her way up a slope to the top of a hill, and there before her on the other side she saw it, the mine, as she had never seen it before. Perhaps it was because she was seeing it through the rain but it appeared as if a number of small huts had been thrown haphazardly at the hill, and there had stuck. On the level area were expanses of slaty water, but all the hill below right down to the valley was covered with dead matter; the whole place looked dead as if it had been laid bare by a plague.

Was this how Margaret saw the hills?

What was the matter with her? What did it matter if the mines destroyed all the hills? What matter how they looked; it was how John would look when he knew.

There were men pushing wooden bogies coming out of the hole in the hillside. They appeared like gnomes popping up out of the earth; they had hessian sacks over their heads, the points sticking upwards yet drooping at the top like fools' caps. There were young boys shovelling muck; there were men riddling stones. They all stopped what they were doing and gaped at her, and one of them, his mouth wide open, licked the rain from his lips before calling to her, "What 'tis, miss?"

He came towards her. "You lost or summat?"

"Mr Thornton. I . . . I want to see Mr Thornton, Mr John Thornton."

"Oh aye, aye." The man wiped the rain from his eyes. "Oh, I see who you are now. But by! lass, you're in a state. And wet to the skin. Where's your cloak?"

"I want to see Mr Thornton."

"All right, lass, all right. Ower yonder, that place there." He pointed to a long, low shed-like structure with a door in the middle and two windows on each side, and she turned from him without even a thank you and ran, wending her way between obstacles of stacks, of props, and bogies, and mounds of earth, unaware of the men here and there straightening their backs, wiping the rain from their eyes and peering at her, then looking at each other.

She did not knock on the door but thrust it wide open, and the sight of her startled the three men around the table. Two were sitting at it and one was bending over it. They had been examining drawings on a large sheet of stiff paper and now they stared at her open-mouthed as if they were seeing an apparition; there was still evidence that her gown was white but it was bespattered with mud and clinging to her body here and there as tight as skin, and her hair had fallen about her making her appear like someone wild.

164

"Hannah! in the name of God what's . . . what's the matter with you?"

"Oh John! John!" She came towards him, but there was the distance of the table between them and the presence of the other two men, and it was to one of these John looked and said, "I'm . . . I'm sorry, sir. This . . . this is my sister, my . . . my . . ."

"No, no, I'm not!"

"*What!* . . . What's the matter with you? I thought. . . ."

The two men rose from the table, the elder of them saying, "We'll go; you deal with your family matter, John. It's all right. It's all right." He raised his hand to silence something that John was about to say, then he stared at Hannah for a moment before taking up his hard hat from a nail on the wall and a coat that was hanging near by it, and he donned them both and went out followed by the other man who wore neither hat nor overcoat.

"Have you gone mad, Hannah? What do you mean by coming here? I . . . I thought you were being ma . . ."

"I know, I know I shouldn't have come, but . . . but I had to tell you. John – " She came slowly round the table, hanging on to the edge for support, until she was standing close to him and she looked into his face now as she said between gasps, "We . . . we are not related. They . . . I mean the Reverend Crewe, he . . . he gave me a letter. It was to say that your father . . . your father hadn't fathered me. It's all in the letter here." She put her hand down the front of her dress and pulled out the sodden envelope and proffered it to him. But he did not take it, he even shrank from her, saying now, "It's no good, Hannah, I'm . . . I'm promised. It's all arranged. You should have married Fred, it would have been the best thing . . . I'm sorry, I'm sorry."

She stared at him blankly for some seconds, then she closed her eyes tightly and blinked. It was as if she were rousing herself from a deep sleep. It was right what Margaret had said, he was a weak man, but she had told herself that, weak or not, she would have given her life for one day of love from him. But now she knew that even if she had come to him last month and told him what she had just told him, he wouldn't have given her that day of love.

"I am married, I was married before I saw the letter."

She watched his whole face change, the furrow smooth out

from between his brows, his cheeks drop, his lips fall together; her words, she thought, had acted on him like a hot iron over wet linen; she felt she could smell his relief.

Slowly she dragged her eyes from his face and walked towards the door, and when he said softly, "Hannah," she looked at him over her shoulder and said, "I thought I would just come and tell you."

She was outside now. The rain was coming straight down, it was like a weight on her head. She passed between the obstacles once more; she passed by the men pushing the bogies now towards the mouth of the mine; and the man who had spoken to her before stopped and called, "You see him, miss?"

And she stopped and answered, "Yes, thank you."

When she found she was actually smiling at the man she thought, I'm going mad; people don't smile under these circumstances. I must be going mad. . . .

Before she had left the precincts of the mine she was running again, but she wasn't taking the same road back, for she had turned in the opposite direction from that by which she had come.

After a while she stopped running and just walked steadily but aimlessly forward. She had no idea where she was going, nor did she care. Vaguely, she knew that if she stayed out in the wet long enough, perhaps all night, she'd get pneumonia and die, as the mister had done. It was odd to think he wasn't her father. In a way now she was sorry. What would have happened had he lived and found out? He wouldn't have held it against her. Oh no, not he. Why couldn't John have taken after his father? John. John. The relief on his face when she said she was married, she would feel the pain of that for evermore.

Married! She was married! There'd be a commotion in the village. Fred would be searching for her. Married? One didn't feel any different being married, at least not yet. It was what happened in bed that made the difference. Miss Emily had suggested that a woman could never be the same after that experience. Until that conversation with Miss Emily she had actually thought

166

that babies came by kissing. It was something to do with the tongue in your mouth, that's why it had been very wrong to allow a man to kiss you, except on the cheek, until you were actually married. She had been shocked and very worried the day she had seen Dandy kissing Tessie on the mouth. That was about two years ago. She had waited for news of the baby coming and had wondered in her naivety if the missis would attend her or the midwife be brought in from Allendale Town.

Yesterday, she had been a girl, today she felt a woman, and yet so far she was married in name only. And that's how it would remain for she'd never go back down there to Fred Loam's house. Never! Never!

What time was it? She was married at two o'clock. It would have taken her almost an hour to get to the mine; and how long had she been walking since then? She didn't know. An hour? Two hours? Would she reach some sort of habitation before dark? She didn't know where she was; the rain was coming down even heavier now, and she couldn't see the outline of the hills. Well, what did it matter? But she was cold, she was shivering. She must lie down in some place and rest. But where? If she sat down here she might never get up again, she could die. Well, isn't that what she wanted? No, no; she only wanted to get away from the village and everyone in it, away from Fred.

When some time later the belt of trees loomed up before her, it was as if nine years had rolled back and she was leading her mother into the darkness of the wood.

She stopped and leant against the bole of a tree. She must have walked for hours in a huge circle, and she was now within a few minutes' walk of the Pele house and Ned. She would go to Ned. . . . But wait; Ned wouldn't speak to her. But she needn't go to the house, she needn't see him. There was the shippon at the end of the yard. It was full of old bits of machinery, the overspill from the horse room; if she could get in there she could hide and rest till morning.

She went slowly through the wood now, her steps dragging. She made sure there was no one in the yard before she entered it, and keeping close the the wooden wall of the shippon she made for the door, pushed it open, then went in.

. . . "What the hell have we here?" The voice was thick and guttural.

She was staring at Ned who was holding a lantern above his head while his other arm supported a number of pieces of old harness.

"What the hell do you want? Now look here! Get the blazes out of it."

He came lunging towards her, almost tripping over the debris on the floor, and when he stood within an arm's length from her the lantern showing up his face told her he was drunk.

The light also revealed to his befuddled mind the terrible state she was in, and his head swaying on his shoulders, he looked her up and down. Twice he went to speak but closed his mouth again before, his tone a little quieter but still a growl, he said, "They're lookin' for you. They've been round here twice. You know that?"

She didn't speak, she simply stared at him.

"God! look at you." He took a step back from her now and for a moment she thought he was going to fall backwards, the lantern with him; but she did not start or put out her hand to stay him for it was as much as she could do to support herself now against the wooden door to stop herself from sliding down to the ground.

"Why the bloody hell do you come to me, eh! You're trouble. You know that? That's what you are, trouble. Ever since I first clapped eyes on you you've brought me trouble. An' you know what?" He now stepped towards her again. "You're a bloody ungrateful sod."

Still she didn't speak or move. He, too, became silent; but then barking at her again, he yelled, "Ger out of here an' into the house!" and lunging forward again, he gripped her by the shoulder, swung her round, pushed her out of the door and into the yard and, staggering, followed her into the stable-room.

The familiar smell, the warmth, the jumbled comfort, the clanking of the ponies in the stalls, the whole atmosphere was too much and, dropping down on to the platform where she had lain once before and where he and the old man had attended her, she bent her body double and sobbed aloud.

And all the while he stood over her yelling at her. "Bloody cryin' 'll do you some good now; you were married, they said, and skedaddled. By God! if I was him I'd murder you when I caught you, if you did that to me. . . . He's a bloody numskull, we all know that, but no man deserves to be deserted at the altar. 'Tis the woman who's deserted at the altar. . . . Stop that bloody cryin' an' tell me" – he gripped her by the shoulder and pulled her upright – "why make for me, eh? Come on, tell me, why make for me? You overlooked me, didn't you? You were in a tight corner but it wasn't so bloody tight as you were goin' to stoop an' take Ned Ridley."

She was gasping; her mouth was open, her eyes wide as she stared at him.

"You've tormented me since you were a bairn, you know that? From you come into that yard" – he threw his arm back and pointed towards the door and nearly fell sideways as he did so – "all those years gone, from that very mornin' you had me under your thumb. You know what I did? I wrote a bloody piece of poetry about you comin' at me that morning. That's something you didn't know, I write bits of poetry, boxes upstairs, full of 'em. I write 'em and forget 'em. But not that bit, no. Like the bloody fool I am, I used to say it to myself when I saw you." He stopped and they stared at each other, she gasping as if fighting for air, and he, his hands on his knees, his face level with hers, swaying slightly.

"Ah, to hell! What's the use." He turned from her now, saying, "You want a drink an' something hot inside you, and some dry togs on you, or it's a bloody corpse the groom 'll be pickin' up."

She watched him go towards the back kitchen. She heard the clanging of the kettle and the rattle of the tin mugs, and as she listened a voice was speaking in her head. The tone was incredulous and almost touching on laughter. She could have married Ned. Ned had wanted her. All this time Ned had wanted her. That's why he wouldn't speak to her when he came back and heard she was going to marry Fred Loam. Why hadn't he said? But if he had, would it have made any difference? She had loved John. . . . Somewhere in her mind she recognized she had thought, had loved, not did love.

"Drink that." He pushed the mug between her trembling hands; then moving some distance from her, he slumped down on

to a bale of hay and for a moment he dropped his head into his
hands and shook it. Then looking at her again, he said slowly,
"Of all the times I could have taken you an' didn't. The times
you've been in here an' tempted me silly. She's only sixteen I said.
Then a few months ago what did I say to meself? She's seventeen
now, so what about it? No, no, I said; hold your hand, man, an'
there'll come a day when she'll turn to you. That bitch of a witch
down there 'll do summat to her an' she'll run. An' when he died
I said to meself, Now show your hand, I said, do the thing
properly. Go down to that bitch an' say, 'I could buy and sell you
where money's concerned.' An' I could." He was nodding widely
at her now. "There's money stacked round here that would make
your eyebrows rise. Me great-great-grandad didn't swing for
nowt, he left his token behind a brick in the wall." He threw out
his arm again in a dramatic gesture. "Then me great-granda died
and he left his token an' all. Then the old 'un died recently, and
by! what was his token? If I'd the old bugger here this minute I'd
token him, I would that! Me father, he left nowt, miners never
leave nowt, so I could say to her, 'Missis, I could buy you out of
house an' home,' or, 'I could build on to that place up there an'
make it into a small mansion for her,' but I didn't get the chance,
did I? You up and bloody well took a gormless nowt like Fred,
an' him having a mother like he has. My God! you'll go through
it with her. An' you know what I say? I say, serve you damn well
right 'cos you haven't got the sense you were born with."

He now dragged himself to his feet; then his voice flat, he went
on, "Aw well, it's finished, I've learned me lesson. It's the only
bloody fool thing I've done in me life, but never again. An' to
think I didn't get married 'cos of you. Huh!" He threw his head
back now and laughed so loud that he startled the animals; then
ended, "Well, they'll be on their rounds again shortly to pick you
up. That's if you don't drop down dead afore that. . . . Stop
shivering." He turned from her now. "You want something to
put round you, a sack. No, a shawl. I'll get you a shawl; but mind"
– he stabbed his finger towards her – "I want it back – 'twas me
mother's."

She watched him now pulling himself slowly up the ladder to
the room above, and the minute he disappeared through the trap-

door she dropped the mug on to the platform as she struggled to her feet; then she ran to the door and out into the rain again.

They could come but they wouldn't find her; she wouldn't be able to stand the humiliation of being dragged down into the village by a man who would now be beside himself with anger.

She was in the middle of the belt of trees when she heard Ned calling her name. "Hannah! Hannah! Don't be a bloody fool. Hannah! come back I say." His voice coming through the rain-drenched trees sounded as if he were calling through a long tunnel.

It wasn't until she emerged into the open again that she realized the rain had stopped. She didn't attempt to take the hill path this time knowing that she would slip and slide and that Ned would soon catch up with her because he could run like a hare, at least when he was sober.

Away to the left the land sloped to the valley and fields, and away beyond was the beginning of the Buckly Estate. If she could get into there she could lose herself.

When she reached the valley bottom she was gasping for breath and she paused and turned; and there he was bounding drunkenly down the hillside. She ran on again but more slowly now as if she, too, were drunk.

The grassland in the valley gave way to ploughed fields, and the soil stuck to her shoes. Ned wasn't far behind her now and intermittently his voice came at her, just calling her name, "Hannah! Hannah!"

There was the wood ahead. Once in there he'd have a job to find her, and anyway she doubted if he would follow her because Lord Buckly came down hard on trespassers, at least his keepers did. But they wouldn't hurt a woman, so she told herself, because she wouldn't be after the young pheasants.

The stone wall was only about four feet high and her mind registered surprise that its top wasn't fortified in any way with glass chippings or spiked wire, and as she rolled over it Ned's voice came from just yards behind her and his tone was different now and held the sound of a gasping plea. "For God's sake, Hannah, stop! Stop! Not in there. Not there, you bloody fool you. . . ."

She was about ten paces beyond the wall when his next words, screaming high above her head, brought her to a freezing stand-still. "It's trapped! Mantrapped. For God's sake listen to me!"

She was standing stiffly but swaying from one side to the other listening now, and she turned her head towards where he was leaning over the wall gasping, and she watched his slowly raise his hand upwards as he said, "Don't move, just don't move, they could be anywhere, the place is ringed, just keep still."

As she stared at him through the fading light she wondered if this was his kind of a trap, that he was just saying this to get hold of her, but the expression on his face and the fact that he seemed to have sobered up told her that it was no ruse on his part. She watched him climb over the wall, then keep his eyes on the ground as he came towards her. The grass was long and tangled in the open belt of land between the wall and the wood proper. She watched him coming near, planting each foot carefully but still swaying a little.

When he was within an arm's length of her he stopped and, pointing ahead of her, said, "You . . . you would never have got in. Look! it's all wired. But this is where they catch 'em, the fools who try. He's a dirty bugger, Buckly, he takes payment in limb for his birds, an' even for a rabbit. . . . Give me your hand."

As she held out her hand to him, he muttered thickly, "By God! you want to consider yersel lucky."

As she stepped towards him he let out a fearful oath; then pointing to the ground within a yard of her, he growled, "Look at that! That'll tell you just how lucky."

She looked in the direction of his pointing finger but couldn't make out anything except a patch of tangled grass.

He now led her slowly back to the wall; then pushing her roughly against it, he said, "Now you stay put. Don't you dare move. I'm gona make sure that that one catches neither fox, hare, nor some poor bugger's leg."

She stood now gripping the front of her sodden dress in both hands as she watched him pick up a broken branch cautiously walk back towards the clump of grass, and when he lifted up the stick it was as if he were about to attack a wild beast.

It all seemed to come about from the force he put into the blow, for as he brought the stick down on the trap his feet left the ground and he stumbled forward; then as the unearthly scream re-echoed through the trees she screwed up her eyes tight and covered her face with her hands. But the next moment she was running towards him where he was lying on his side, his legs now thrashing the ground, his left arm extended, its hand spread and running red with blood.

"Oh Ned! Ned! Ned! Ned!" She was tugging fruitlessly at the iron teeth that were clamping the side of his hand.

He was on his knees now, his body contorted, his face turned into that of a gargoyle. When she saw what he was aiming to do, she got her two hands on one side of the trap while his was on the other, and when the teeth came apart his mangled hand fell away and he rolled on to his side and tucked his hand under his oxter while the toes of his boots beat into the earth.

She was kneeling beside him holding him as she moaned and cried, "Oh Ned! Ned! I'm sorry. Oh, what have I done? Oh Ned! Ned! Come on, get up; you must get home."

As if he were obeying her he stumbled to his feet. His hand still held tightly under his oxter, he staggered to the wall and rolled over it; then, his body almost double, his chin tucked tightly into his chest, he started the journey home.

When he swayed and she thought he would fall she put both arms about him and held him; otherwise, she held on to his right arm. But not once did he speak to her, nor did he utter any sound at all now.

Twice on the journey he stopped and dropped on to his knees to rest, but he didn't take his hand from his oxter. . . .

It was dark when they reached the yard and, once inside the stable-room, he spoke for the first time. Looking towards the lantern that was still burning he muttered, "Fetch it," then he went on into the kitchen.

Quickly, carrying the light, she followed him. Then she watched him go to a bucket of water that was standing near the wall and, kneeling before it, slowly ease his hand from his oxter and plunge it into the bucket.

When he lifted it out again and she saw his two fingers dangling as if by threads she felt she was about to faint away.

He stared at his hand for a moment before plunging it back again and muttering, "A sheet. Get a sheet."

She looked about her wildly, "Where? Where?"

"Upstairs, in the drawer. Take . . . take the lantern."

She didn't know how she got up the steep stairs to the room above, and half-way up she trod on the front of her dress and only in time saved herself from falling to the ground, lantern and all.

In the room, she pulled open three drawers before finding the sheets. They were flannelette. She pulled two out and hurried down the ladder again, and when she entered the kitchen she found him now sitting with his back to the wall, his feet straight out but his hand still in the bucket.

"Tear it into strips."

It was tough material and wouldn't rip like linen and when he screamed at her "Cut it! Take a knife," it almost fell from her cold trembling hands.

When she had at last torn off two strips he said, his tone quiet again, "Fold one up and make it into a pad."

After she had done this, he signalled to her to put it on the floor by the side of the bucket, then swiftly he lifted up his hand and placed it on the pad of sheeting; then putting the mangled fingers into place he folded the sheeting over them before saying to her, "Now wrap it up as tight as you can," but before she even had time to begin the bandaging the pad was soaked red.

When at last the bandaging was done he said to her, "Tear the rest up; I'll likely need them afore the night's out."

"Will . . . will I fetch Doctor Arnison?"

"No, there's not much use now; I'll go down to him in the mornin'."

"Oh, Ned. Oh, I'm sorry, I am. . . ."

"Shut up!"

"I just want to say . . ."

"Shut up, will you! Do you hear? Shut up! else I'll kill you."

She stared down at him. His face was white, a dirty pasty white, but his eyes were burning, blazing black in his head.

When he pulled himself up from the floor he went to the rack where the crockery was kept and, picking up a bottle that was still a quarter full of whisky, he filled a tin mug almost to the

174

brim with it. He held it in his hand for a moment as he looked at her and said, "I'm going to kip down on the straw, I'll leave you to fend for yourself," and with that he walked past her where she was standing at the open doorway to the stable and she watched him walk down its almost dim length to where the hay was stacked. She saw him lower himself on to the bales, drink deep from the cup, then lie back.

She stood thus looking in his direction for almost five minutes before she turned and, sitting down by the wooden table, she lowered her head on to her folded arms and groaned to herself, "Dear Lord! Dear Lord! what have I done this day?"

It was in the middle of the night when she heard him groaning. She had lit another two lanterns before wrapping herself in the horse blankets and lying on the platform further along the wall from where the bales of straw were. She realized that she must have fallen asleep and that the night had turned very cold because even in here with the thick walls keeping in the body heat from the horses she was shivering; yet there was sweat between her breasts and on her brow.

Half dazed, she got up and staggered towards him and, kneeling by his side, she said softly, "Can I get you anything, Ned? A drink?"

When he didn't answer she realized that he was asleep, and so she went back to the platform and lay down again. But it was some long time before she fell into a doze because she was so cold.

She was dragged from a deep nightmarish sleep by someone gripping her shoulder and calling her name, and she sat bolt upright and stared blinking through the morning light at Ned.

"Get up, will you?"

"Oh, Ned!" She was on her feet, her hands out supporting him, even while she found it difficult to stand herself. "You're ill. Look, lie down, lie down here." She turned him about and he dropped on to the platform. Then she gave a small gasp as she looked at his arm. The sleeve was rolled up and his forearm looked scarlet and twice its normal size.

He blinked at her, wetted his lips and said slowly, "I . . . I can't go down; can . . . can you get somebody?"

"Yes, yes, Ned; I'll . . . I'll go to the town, I'll get Doctor Arnison."

"Get me . . . a drink first . . . will you? Tea . . . anything."

"Yes, Ned." But as she went to hurry away her legs almost gave way beneath her. She was acting like someone drunk. What was the matter with her?

She blew up the banked-down fire with the bellows, put the kettle on, and when it boiled she mashed the tea; then she poured out a mug full, put in three spoonfuls of sugar and took it to him. It was scalding but he drank it almost at once, then lay back.

She went into the kitchen again, and as she poured herself out a mug of tea she told herself that she felt ill; that she didn't know how she was going to get to the town, it was all of three miles away, that's if she gave the village a wide berth, and she must give the village a wide berth. But she must go; his hand was infected, his arm was infected. It was dreadful, a dreadful thing to happen to him, and she was to blame. She wished she was dead. . . . Oh! how she wished she was dead.

She pulled herself to her feet, went into the stable-room and, going to Ned, bent over him and said, "I'm away then, Ned, I'll be as quick as I can." This time she did manage to stop herself from adding yet again, "I'm sorry, Ned. I'm sorry."

He merely nodded at her, then turned his head away; and she went out into the morning light, into the clear bright sunlight, and for the first time since she had woken she looked down at herself. She was filthy. She put her hands to her hair. It was hanging about her shoulders in matted strands; she must look like a wild woman. But what did it matter? The only thing that mattered at the moment was getting the doctor for Ned.

She was only half-way across the hills to Allendale Town when she told herself that she couldn't go any further. Her head was spinning, she was feeling ill.

When she reached a bridle path she sat on the grass verge and held her head in her hands. Perhaps if she rested for a while she'd be able to go on.

When the voice above her said, "Eeh! Eeh! it's you. By! you're not half in a mess. . . . They're lookin' for you. The whole village's been out lookin' for you," she raised her head and saw a young boy standing above her. It was Peter Wheatley.

"Pe-ter! Pe-ter!" She was finding now it was painful to speak. 'Pe-ter! I must . . . get Doctor Arnison. Ned is ill, Ned Ridley. He . . . he got caught in a trap. Will . . . will you go to the town and fetch him? The doctor . . . the doctor."

"The doctor's not in the town, he's along there, away at the bottom of the road there." The boy pointed. "Mrs Thompson's had a bairn."

"Thompson's? The cottage? Oh." She pulled herself to her feet. "Oh thanks. . . . Thanks, Pe-ter."

She was some yards away from the cottage when she saw the doctor come out of the door and walk towards his horse, and she called "Doc-tor! Oh Doc-tor! Doc-tor! don't go."

Doctor Arnison turned slowly about and looked towards the bedraggled creature that was stumbling towards him, and when she came abreast of him he muttered under his breath, "My God! child, what's happened to you?"

She was hanging on to him now. "Doctor, you must come, it's Ned, Ned Ridley. The trap's taken off his fingers."

"What! Ned, Ned Ridley?"

"Yes, yes, doctor, Ned Ridley. He got his hand caught in a trap, a mantrap."

The doctor now put his hand on her head and said quietly, "You're very hot, child. Where have you been all night? You know there's a hue and cry out for you? Now about Ned. Are you imagining this. . .?"

"No, no, doctor. Come." She tried to pull him. "Ned, he . . . he saved me. I nearly walked into the trap, and he slipped and it took his fingers off."

"Oh no! No!"

"Yes, yes, doctor."

"Get up." He went to help her up on to the horse and she shook her head, saying, "Not through the village. Oh no, doctor, no . . . not yet. I'll go back over the hills."

"You've got to go through the village some time, Hannah,

you've got to go back. From what I hear you are now a married woman."

"Later, doctor, later, I . . . I must go back to Ned now. Please, please."

"Very well."

He watched her stumble away. He didn't know what was really wrong with Ned Ridley and he wouldn't until he saw him, but he knew what was wrong with her. She was in a high fever. He shouldn't have let her go over there alone, yet he could imagine her reception whenever she were to join the Loam household, and she wasn't in any fit state to be badgered. Well anyway, he'd be at the Pele house before she was, that was sure.

He mounted his horse and set it off at a trot. . . .

On her journey back Hannah had to rest four times before she reached the yard again; and when she saw the doctor's horse already there she stood leaning against the wall and her head drooped on to her chest; then after a moment she crossed the yard and went into the stable-room.

The doctor turned from bending over Ned and said abruptly, "Good; come and hold the lantern."

Reluctantly it seemed, she went towards him; it was as if she had to drag her legs after her. She took the lantern from the doctor and as she held it breast high she looked down on Ned, but he was looking at the doctor and, his lips scarcely moving, was muttering, "What do you mean about the arm, not takin' it off?"

"No, not if I can help it . . . and if you're lucky. But if that inflammation goes any further, well – " He paused then added, "First things first. I'll have to get them off and tidy you up." He made a short stab with his forefinger towards the hand lying on the bloodstained bandages. "Got any spirit about?"

"Aye."

"Well, you'd better take a long swig of it, Ned, for I'll have to take the top of your middle one off an' all."

There was a moment's stillness in the stable, broken only by the neighing of one of the horses, and this seemed to convey something to Ned because, closing his eyes, he muttered thickly, "They've never had their feed."

"Aw well, they won't die by losing one meal. Don't worry about them, let's get you tidied up. Where's the whisky?"

"Kitchen . . . cupboard."

The doctor now turned to Hannah and said quietly, "Do you think you can fetch it?"

She made no answer but put down the lantern and went towards the kitchen. There were two bottles of whisky in the cupboard. She took out one, looked at it for a moment, then pulling out the cork, she poured about half an inch into a tin mug, which she raised to her lips and swallowed the contents in one gulp as she had seen Ned do. The next minute she was bending over the table coughing and spluttering and clutching at her chest; but when the spasm was over she straightened up and told herself she felt better, warm in fact all the way down to her waist.

When she reached the doctor's side again he glanced at her and, his lips set in a tight smile, he said knowingly, "You should never gulp at that stuff. Give it here." He took the bottle from her; then more than half filled a tin mug she held out towards him, and when he handed the mug to Ned he said, "No need to tell you the best way to get it down you, is there, Ned?"

Ned made no reply but, rising on his elbow, he gulped at the contents and when he handed the mug back the doctor, in an aside to Hannah, said quietly, "Fill it again; he's going to need it."

It was as she went to do his bidding that the stable-room door was thrust open and Fred Loam stalked in; but he stopped in the middle of the room and stared at the three people on the low platform.

It was the doctor who spoke first and then quite casually, "Glad to see you, Fred; I'm going to need help here."

"Glad to see me, be damned! What's all this about? You!" He was advancing on Hannah now when the doctor took the short step down from the platform and, thrusting out his hand, grabbed Fred by the shoulder, saying sternly, "Whatever your differences they can be settled later; if I don't see to Ned right away it'll be his arm I'll be taking off next. Now I want you to give me a hand."

Fred turned his gaze slowly from the doctor and glared at Hannah, where she was standing now, her back pressed tight against the stone wall at the far side of the platform, and she in turn looked at him.

He was as dishevelled as she was, and he looked wild, half crazy. She stopped herself from whimpering, "I'm sorry;" the time was past for saying such futile words, and sorry wouldn't cover what she had done, both to him and to Ned.

It was her mother to blame. Yes! Yes! it was. She was now shouting in her head at her mother: "You should have kept your mouth shut. I'd have rather been the mister's flyblow. Yes, I would, I would."

It must be the whisky, she thought, that was burning up her body, for even the tangled strands of her hair seemed to be giving off heat, for they lay hot against her face and she pushed them back from each side of her cheeks as she watched Fred standing by Ned's side now looking down at the hand and saying, "How did he get that?"

The doctor made a small movement with his head, then said, "Trap, he got it in a trap. Hannah, bring me a bowl of boiling water, and Fred, bring my bag nearer."

As they went to do the doctor's bidding they had to pass each other, and when Fred glared at her and his lips squared away from his teeth she turned her head away as if warding off a blow.

The doctor rummaged in his bag for a moment; then taking out an implement that looked like a miniature three-sided poker with a wooden handle, he handed it to Fred, saying below his breath, "Go and stick that in the fire. When it's red bring it back quick; the joints are dirty I'll have to cauterize them."

Fred looked at the small instrument in his hand for a moment, then turned and went into the kitchen.

Again Hannah and he had to pass each other and when he came abreast of her he caught her by the shoulder and, bringing his face down to hers, he growled, "You've made a bloody laughing stock of me, haven't you? But by God! you'll pay for it. I promise you that, I'm not to be laughed at. An' where've you been all night? In here with him?"

"Leave go of me." She took her two hands and thrust them

180

against his chest and he let go of her, but he remained standing a pace away. "Leave go of you, you say! You forget who you are. You forget what happened yesterday. You married me, do you remember? You married me. God! I could kill you this minute. I could take a knife and slit you up."

When she closed her eyes and her hands fell flat on the table and she bent over them, he stared at her for a moment and, his voice changed and quiet now, he said brokenly, "You shouldn't have done this to me, Hannah, you shouldn't." Then he went to the fire and thrust the implement with such force between the bars that his fingers were singed and he had to pull the instrument back to save the handle catching alight. . . .

They were all on the platform again. The two mangled fingers and the top of Ned's middle finger were lying on strips of blood-soaked sheets to the side of her. Ned had just finished drinking another half mug of whisky and his face looked like parchment spotted here and there with dark stubble. The doctor, taking the implement from Fred's hand, said, sharply now, "Hold him down by the shoulders."

She watched Fred's great hands gripping Ned's shoulders. When the doctor put the hot instrument to the raw stumps of the fingers it was the smell of burning flesh that made her stomach heave, but it was Ned's piercing scream which seemed to lift her bodily up, then throw her down to the floor, that blotted everything out for the next three days. . . .

"Go down," said the doctor to Fred, "and bring Mother Fletcher up from the village; he can't be left alone for the next few days. And it'll be touch and go whether or not I shall have to move up further; it all depends on the singeing; if it does the trick."

"What about her?" Fred pointed to where Hannah was lying insensible on the straw, and the doctor replied, "Well, as soon as you're back we'll take her down. She's another one that'll need attention for the next few days, or perhaps weeks."

"Why?" The word was an abrupt demand.

"Because, Fred, if my diagnosis is right your wife's got a fever on her, but as yet I can't tell what kind. Once she's in bed and I can examine her then I'll know more."

"A fever?" There was actual fear on Fred's face. Fever could mean cholera, and there had been an outbreak of that along the Tyne.

"Oh, don't get worried, it could just be an ordinary fever caused by exposure, and by the look of her she's certainly been through some exposure."

"It's her own bloody fault."

"Yes, perhaps it is, Fred. But that's your business, for you to sort out; mine is. . . ."

"Aye, take it from me, doctor, an' I will sort it out an' all."

"No doubt you will, Fred, no doubt you will, but now go on, get down and bring Mother Fletcher, because I can't stay here all day, I've got a full list. Ah, and your cart to take Hannah down. Go on now."

It was an hour later when they lifted Hannah into the cart. She had regained consciousness but was gabbling incoherently most of the time, and of his two patients the doctor was more concerned about her at the present moment than he was about Ned. Ned was a tough type; even if later he should have to take his arm off to the elbow, he would survive, but this girl was a different piece of humanity, and although her physical condition was causing him some worry, her mental state was of even more concern to him.

He had only a garbled idea of what had happened since the wedding ceremony. The village gossip had quickly spread to the town and everybody in that small but widespread community had known about it before the light failed. Some of the townsmen had even joined in the hunt for her, looking upon it, he thought, as a bit of a lark, helping a man to hunt his bride on his wedding day. . . .

It was as if the whole village had had word of their coming for there wasn't a door that was closed, except perhaps that of her one time home, thought the doctor; and that was hidden from view anyway behind the trees.

When he pulled his horse to a stop outside the butcher's shop and Fred, having jumped from his seat was walking towards the

oor, the doctor cried at him, "Carry her in, man! She's in no fit
ate to walk."

He watched Fred cast a furtive and angry glance up and down
he street and across the green before coming back to the cart
here he grabbed at Hannah's inert body and, as he would have
arried a dead sheep, pig, or young bullock, he threw her over his
houlder and stamped into the shop, the doctor following him.

"So you've found her?" Mrs Loam, her small body bristling,
arned to the doctor and cried, "Nice how-do-you-do. If I had my
ay she wouldn't get in the door."

"If you'd had your way, Daisy, half the population of the village
nd the town, even, would be under the sod. Out of me way." He
lmost pushed her aside and followed Fred with his burden up the
airs, through the kitchen and into a small bedroom, most of which
as taken up with an iron and brass bed, and when Fred dropped
Iannah's limp body unceremoniously on to it, he cried at him,
Careful! Steady on, man. Have I to keep reminding you, she's a
ck woman?"

"You've to keep remindin' me of nowt, doctor, not even the
ct that I've been made a bloody monkey out of. How would you
el in my place.?"

"I don't know, never having been in such a situation, although
think I would tell myself, the better face I put on the matter the
ss the neighbours would have to laugh about. And now send
our mother in here, she'll be more use than you at this time."

A minute later, Daisy Loam came marching into the room. Her
ands on her hips, her small face grim, her chin thrust out, she
aced the doctor, saying, "If you think that I'm gona nurse that
n, doctor, you're mistaken."

"Daisy" – the doctor now bent down to her – "you and I have
nown each other for a long time, and we've both got our faults.
line is meanness I'm told, because I demand my fee on the spot,
nd in cash instead of eggs, chickens, or a bit of pork, although at
mes I've been known to make exceptions. Your fault, Daisy, is
at your mouth is too big for your body." His voice had risen on
he last words until it was almost a shout, and he ended, "Always
as been and likely always will be. They won't need to dig a grave
or you when you die, they can just double you up and stick you

in your mouth. . . . Now get at that side of the bed and help get those clothes off her."

Like two combatants, they stared at each other. Then, her lip parting from their tight compressed line, she wagged her head and she said, "You don't frighten me none. I'm tellin' you for nowt I'm not havin' her here; she's not respectable."

"Whether you keep her here or not will be yours and your son's business. If you decide to send her back to where she came from, well and good; if you decide to send her into the workhouse hospital, well and good; but before either of those things happen I've got to get her clothes off, examine her, and make her ready as it were, for wherever she's going. And" – his face was close to hers again – "it might be into her coffin, Daisy. Now that would satisfy you, wouldn't it?"

The little woman turned her head slowly now and looked at the bed and the doctor's last words did seem to satisfy her because without further ado she started to undress Hannah. It would be a better description to say that she started to tear the mud-and-blood-stained clothing from her. . . .

It was about twenty minutes later when the doctor went into the kitchen and, looking from the son to the mother, then back to the son again, he said, "She's very ill and she's got little resistance; the next twenty-four hours or so will be the most crucial. She could die, but if she doesn't I'd better warn you she'll need nursing for some weeks ahead. So, Daisy" – he now turned his full attention to Mrs Loam – "I'd see about getting her a place in the workhouse hospital, eh?"

"What d'you mean, workhouse hospital?" Fred was looking from one to the other.

"Well" – the doctor turned to Fred now – "your mother tells me she's not having her here, so you can't just leave her in the street, and I doubt whether she'd be given admittance in the house along the road, so it's nothing but the House hospital."

"The House hospital!" Fred was looking at his mother. "Aye, I think you would an' all, you would send her there. Well, let me tell you, whatever she's done, she's done it to me an' I'll be the one who says if she goes or stays."

"Talkin' big all of a sudden, aren't you?"

The doctor picked up his bag, and as he passed between them he moved one hand as if his action were meant to separate them, then said, "I'll be along later in the day. In the meantime give her all the drink she can take, water, tea, anything."

As no one went to open the stairhead door for him or follow him down the stairs he said loudly, "It's all right, it's all right, I can see myself out."

Not until the shop door clanged closed did Daisy Loam turn on her son. Taking her fist she banged it on the bare kitchen table as she cried at him, "Blasted fool! that's what you are, a laughing stock. The whole countryside's afire. You won't be able to lift your head in the town, and on Hexham Fair day . . . well, the town crier 'll be chantin' it. He was right, the doctor, she should go into the House."

"Shut up!"

"Don't you tell me to shut up." She came at him, her forearm raised. "I'm warnin' you I wouldn't stand any old lip from your father, so I'm not standin' it from you."

"Listen, Ma." He now bent down towards her. "As I see it now, me father was a bloody fool, a soft-headed, frightened, bloody fool. Now this is my house, my shop, my business; all he asked was that I take care of you, an' I'll do that, but I'm goin' to run me own life. . . . Don't you bloody well dare!"

She had picked up a long wooden rolling-pin from the table and had raised it above her head, but his voice stayed her hand, and, his face now almost purple, he went on, "As true as I'm standin' here, I'll fell you to the floor if that as much as flicks me."

The rolling-pin was lowered. She stepped back from him, her lower lip thrust out so much that it exposed where it joined the gums, and her face twisted into a sneer as she cried, "God! to think I should live to see the day. I could spit on you. That anything that came out of me should turn so bloody soft, an' for that 'un in there" – her arm bent at the elbow, she thrust her thumb out stiffly towards the bedroom door – "after all you know about her, after all the whole countryside knows about her. What for did she run from the church after she read that?" She was now stubbing her finger down towards the crumpled rain-smeared paper lying on the table. "She'd heard that she was no relation to

185

them. Well, why didn't she turn to the second one, Robert, and declare her news? Why did she have to run hell for leather over the hills to the mine, to the big, fair-headed ninny? The men that were on shift there had their own ideas why, an' they didn't keep it to themselves, did they? Came through the rain like a wild woman in her bride's frock, mud up to the waist, hair streaming. Some said she looked like a witch. And then she goes gasping into the cabin and shouts at him, 'We're not related.' Pat Sculley was outside and heard the lot. Then apparently getting no satisfaction from that quarter, what did she do? She runs to Ned Ridley; an' she runs to the right bloke, doesn't she? for if ever there was a whoremaster he's one; he's been at it more times than Barney's bull. And tell me this, where did she spend the night? In the Pele house, if all is to be believed. And do you think they would lie with a bale of straw atween them?"

"Be quiet! D'you hear? Be quiet! You've said enough. But let me tell you this, no matter what you've got right you've got the last bit wrong."

"Wrong, have I?"

"Aye, because some time yesterday Ned Ridley got his hand caught in a trap an' I've just this mornin' helped to take his fingers off."

She remained silent for a moment, her body straightened from its aggressive position, and she blinked her eyes, then said, "His hand in a trap?"

"That's what I said, his hand in a trap. An' he's lost three fingers and half the hand, and he's likely to lose the rest of it up to the elbow."

As she turned away now and went towards the fire, he went on. "From the little bit the doctor told me, an' what he got out o' her, Ned saved her from goin' headlong into the trap itself."

"To my mind he should have let her go." She threw a steely glance at him over her shoulder. "However bad he is, he's o' more use in the world than she is. But what's a man with only one hand?"

"By! Ma, you're a bitter pill. And I'll tell you something now when the truth is on the table. 'Tisn't the day or yesterday I've thought it. An' another thing, you've taken me for a softy al these years, an' for peace's sake I've let you wear the trousers, but no more. When I pull them on each day from now on it'll be as the man of the house."

"God Almighty! God Almighty! the new order." She was looking into the fire and her head bobbed forward with each word, and he repeated, "Aye, God Almighty! God Almighty! the new order. An' the first part of it is this, I'll see to her meself, and you see to the shop."

She turned on him now like a little fury, screaming, "Why don't you also tell me if I don't like it I know what I can do?"

His face running sweat, his thick lips pushed outwards, he answered her in kind. "You've said it, so let it stick. She's me wife, an' she's going to be given her place by you and everybody else, or they'll know the reason why."

When he stalked from her out of the room and banged the door behind him she gazed at it for a moment; then her head back, she let out a high, shrilling laugh and, looking up towards the low ceiling, she asked, as if of God, "Did you ever see one of those great big turnips, an' when you opened it up there was nowt inside, all boast, full of wind an' watter? That's my son, wind an' watter."

Fred, standing at the side of the bed looking down on Hannah thrashing from side to side, heard his mother's words, and he bowed his head against them.

He had stood up to her, but could he keep it up? His father hadn't been able to and he had been a strong man; he had bartered his strength for peace. . . . And he, too, liked peace.

PART FOUR

The Woman

1

It was July. The world was bright outside; the hills were blue, green, purple and black and the sky was like a white veil trailing over them.

She had been able to get up out of bed now for three days and to sit by the small square bedroom window. Her chair was low and the sill shut from her gaze the back earth yard, with the dry midden at the bottom and the ditch beyond, in which the residue from the village flowed into the river.

How long had she been in this room? Four and a half weeks if she counted the days, but four and a half lifetimes if she went by the change within her, for not only had her body lost its flesh but her mind had lost something too. Never again would she feel young, never again would she count her age in years, never again would she think as a girl thinks.

At times she was devastated at the change that had taken place in her being, but at others she recognized the inevitableness of it. She had caused so much havoc in one day that had it not wrought a change in her, then she would have questioned whether or not she was human.

She could have accepted her change of environment and quickly adapted to it, but for two things: Fred's mother and Fred's hands.

Fred's mother was an inhuman woman. Apparently she herself wasn't the only one who thought so, for the two villagers who had kindly called to see her had expressed their opinion of Mrs Loam in whispered but emphatic terms. Mrs Wheatley, the chandler's wife, and Mrs Buckman, the blacksmith's wife, had both looked in on her, and she had not underestimated the courage it took for them to brave Mrs Loam, nor the significance of their visit. She liked to think it showed that no matter what she had done she wasn't being condemned by the entire village. Yet at the same time she wondered if they weren't merely taking advantage of the situation to get a sly dig at Mrs Daisy Loam.

"You stick to your guns, lass," the blacksmith's wife had said.

"Stand up to her or she'll wipe her feet on you," the chandler's wife had said.

Stick to your guns . . . stand up to her, it was easier said than done. If only she felt stronger. Doctor Arnison said it would be another month before she felt herself again, and only yesterday she had asked the doctor to tell Fred just that. And he must have done so, for Fred came in and stood by the window here and, looking out of it while speaking to her, he had said, "She won't stand for you bein' in here much longer; she says she wants help, it's her back." He had turned and looked down at her and in a form of appeal had added, "If you could make the push, just to get about the kitchen an' do odd jobs for a start, it would pacify her."

As she looked up at him she had experienced a feeling of pity for him, and all of a sudden the thought came to her that if they were on their own something good might evolve from this union; that was until he pulled a chair to her side, sat down, then, slipping his hand under the blanket, caressed her thigh.

It was strange but when she thought of him she seemed to divorce him from his hands, those big, red, wandering hands that seemed to have a separate life apart from him, how he spoke, how he acted. If they strayed beyond her own hands their touch made her whole body recoil. . . .

That was yesterday; and from something he had said then she had dreaded today. And today was here, and Fred was here, coming into the room to sit beside her again and put his hands on her.

"Grand day outside."

"Yes; yes, it looks lovely. I . . . I wish I was able to walk over the hills." As she made this remark she had a vivid picture of the Pele house and the mangled fingers lying on the bloody sheet. No one had mentioned Ned to her since she had been better, not

192

even the doctor; and every day she meant to bring up the subject, but she felt she couldn't.

"Oh well, it won't be long now, you'll soon be on your feet and trotting about. I . . . I told her" – he thumbed down towards the floor and the shop – "that, come the end of the week, you'd be lendin' a hand."

Sticking his foot out, he deftly hooked it around the supporting rails of the wooden chair and dragged it towards him and sat down by her side.

She hadn't put the blanket round her today, not because she felt too warm, for even with the sun hot outside she still felt the cold; but she had left it off in the hope that its absence might deter his hand from straying; and for a moment it seemed to be having the desired effect. . . . But only for a moment, for, resting his elbows on his knees and clasping his hands between them he leant forward and, seeming to address them, he said, "I'm cramped to bits on that couch out there; I think the time's come for me stretchin' me legs so I'll turn into bed the night."

When he turned his head and looked at her she swallowed deeply, then gave a little gasp, and he brought himself fully round to her now and whispered fiercely, "I've been patient, you can't say I haven't. 'Tisn't everybody that would have waited as long as me. And she's scorned me she has. Me life's been hell on earth lately with one thing an' another, but that most of all. Now you can't say I pushed you; an' don't look at me like that. You're me wife, and there's a time for everything. Anyway' – he got abruptly to his feet – "I can't wait no longer and that's the top and bottom of it, so I'll be in the night." He nodded abruptly at her, then went out.

She leant her head back against the rail of the wooden chair. A time for everything. She turned her eyes towards the window in the direction of where the Pele house lay and a voice rang through her head, crying, "Oh Ned, why weren't you there when I needed you?" But it came back at her, asking now, "Would you have known why you needed him?" She shook her head from side to side. No, perhaps she didn't know then, but she knew now; oh yes, she knew now why she had needed Ned Ridley, why she'd always needed him, as he had apparently needed her, because now

193

her mind was a woman's mind and tonight her body would be turned into a woman's body.

Why were lives planned in such a way? Why were people made in such a way that the thought of one particular being touching you could fill you with revulsion and terror even though he was not bad, not evil.

Life was a strange, complicated thing; she had a strong almost compelling urge to be rid of it.

2

"Now! mistress." Mrs Loam weighed the term with scornful ridicule and she repeated it, "Now! mistress, you've had nigh on three weeks fairy-footin' it around the house, washin' a cup here, dustin' a vase there. Well, the time has come when you've got to earn your title, because I'm not able to carry on both top an' bottom, so in future I'll lay out your duties for you – I wouldn't sit down if I were you 'cos you'll only have to get on your feet again in a minute."

"I'll sit down when I wish, Mrs Loam."

"Will you, begod! Well now, let me tell you, lass." The little woman altered her tone from one of mockery to that of threat as she poked her sharp ferret face towards Hannah and went on, "I can make your life bearable, but only just, or I can make it sheer hell on earth. Now get that into your head straightaway. An' listen to this an' all. Me son could do without you; if you had been lost for ever on those fells, he would have got by as if he had never known you; but me, I'm a horse of another colour, he can't do without me 'cos I've forgot more about butcherin' than he'll learn in his lifetime. He's a dunderhead, he can hardly give a customer the right change for a florin, do you know that? He had the chance like any other village lad, he went to Allendale Town School for nigh on three years, but did he take anything in? Nowt, only air. I run this business . . . *me*! As I did in his father's time. Who went to the market then and still goes to pick the beasts? *me*. If he went on his own they could pang a sack filled with straw on him and he'd buy it for a heifer; but me, they don't pass skin and bones on to me. Monday 'tis the only time he does any butcherin' because then he does the killin'; but any damned fool with a hammer can kill a beast as long as there's a couple to

195

hold it. So now, mistress, you see the position. If there were to be a toss-up atween us, he'd let you go, he'd have to, so we'll start by allottin' out the work, eh?"

Gripping hold of the edge of the table, Hannah drew herself to her feet. She was trembling inwardly, her stomach seemed to be loose within its casing, but she saw to it that her hands did not give her away; and now, looking steadily back and down on her mother-in-law, she said quietly but firmly, "I shall do my share but don't think you can intimidate me, Mrs Loam, because you can't, for if I care to put my mind to it I'll learn about the butchering business. Yes, and go into the market too." Her voice was gathering strength and she nodded her head down at the little woman as she went on, "And I'm sure people would welcome me and help me, and Fred too. You make your son out to be almost an idiot; well let me tell you something, Mrs Loam, if he were a complete idiot, drooling at the mouth, he'd still be a better person than you."

"You brazened young bugger you! Who do you think you're talkin' to?" Mrs Loam's fist shot out.

"You! Mrs Loam, you! And don't you dare push me again." Hannah had staggered back as the little woman dug her in the shoulder. "Let that be the first and last time because should you lift your hand to me again, I'll strike you back . . . with . . . with the first thing I can lay my hands on."

Dear Lord! Dear Lord! what had she sunk to. Fancy her saying that, that she would strike this woman, this old woman, because she was fifty if she was a day. She had a mental picture of her teachers who had coached her in courtesy. Then as if they were indeed present she wiped them away with an imaginary sweep of her arm. What had education to do with the situation she was in. Was she not merely reacting as her inborn nature prompted her. And if she wished to survive and escape this woman's domination she would have to let that nature have rein; that nature that had been bred of two ordinary common people in the roughest quarter of the city of Newcastle.

She now made herself walk away from the table and toward the bedroom; but before she had closed the door behind her the little woman's voice battered on her eardrums, crying, "All right

ne girl! You're the mistress now but listen to what this mistress
las been doin' for years past, but not any more. Monday you
vash, bedding, clothes, slaughter cloths, aprons, the lot; Tuesday
ou scrub out downstairs every bit of wood in the shop, includin'
he floor, that's after you sweep up the old sawdust; Wednesday
ou bake, and you make a batch of pies, an' in between times
ou've done your ironin' an' your cooking; Thursday you prepare
or the week-end's cleaning, you do your brasses and the steel
ire-irons and the bedrooms. Are you listenin'?" She was now
elling through the door. "Friday you finish in here, then you
o down in the yard and clear up the entrails that's gone stinkin'
nd you finish up doin' the netty; pleasant job that, emptying the
uckets; Saturday if you're still on your feet you help in the shop.
\n' that, me girl, is an easy week." Her voice as she finished rose
o the pitch of a scream.

Hannah was now standing at the window, her hands pressed
ard across her mouth, and her eyes were tightly closed as she
ried inside, "I won't be able to stand it, I won't, I won't, I'll
reak." For a moment she had the mental picture of herself
unning through the village back up to the house and flinging
erself at Anne Thornton's feet and begging to be taken in.

She opened her eyes and looked downwards. There were
omen in their backyards on each side of the railed space and
ney were mouthing words to each other across it.

The whole village would know that Mrs Loam was "giving it"
o her. She turned from the window and sat down on the edge of
ne bed. There was silence in the house now, and as she sat there
rose in her a strength born of defiance, and she nodded her head
o her thinking. Margaret had learned to work with her hands,
o rough work with her hands; little Tessie had done rough work
ith her hands all her life, as had Bella. All the women in the
illage did their own housework, washed, baked, cleaned. Was
ne herself stupid? Couldn't she learn? She was gaining strength
very day; all she needed now to accomplish such menial tasks
as strength of will and the determination to show that little
ixen out there that the accomplishments she was so proud of
ould be attained by anyone who had even the mental capacity
ttributed to her son. There was only one snag, she had never

197

done any washing or baking before. Yet she had watched both Bella and Tessie performing the household chores countless times so what she must do was to try and remember the processes by which they achieved clean clothes and new bread.

If she had been able to spend another year in the house she likely would have learned how to cook, because after Margaret left school Bella instructed her in the making of special dishes.

Margaret. She was hurt by Margaret's indifference towards her. She had thought she might come and visit her when she was ill, just once, but all she had done was send her two short notes; the first one said she was so sorry to hear of her illness, she herself was very busy at the school; the second note said she was glad to hear she was recovering, she was still very busy at the school. There was no mention of Mr Hathaway or her forthcoming marriage.

Then there was Robert. He had been to see her only once, but even on that occasion he appeared ill at ease and had seemed glad to go.

And John. John was soon to be married. . . . Did this fact hurt her? Strangely, not at all, which showed how changed she had become, in fact now she was amazed at the person she had once been, the person who had felt she would die without John's love or at least go to her grave a maiden lady. How young she had been, and silly.

It seemed to her at the present time that not only had the mission thrown her off, but the entire family too; yet she had got on so well with all the others; except Betsy of course. Even Bella and Tessie had drifted away from her. They both had a half-day's leave a month; she would have thought that one or other would have popped in to see how she fared.

Well, it would appear that she had to stand on her own feet now and if she wished to survive in this house she had best follow the advice that Miss Emily doled out at the beginning of every term to new and old pupils alike: "There is no time like the present to tackle the difficult task." So she must go down now, right now, to the wash-house, light the fire and initiate herself into the disagreeable task of learning to do a day's washing. . .

She had the pleasure a moment later of seeing her mother-in-law's countenance stretched in surprise when she marched into the kitchen, took up the tinder box from the mantelshelf, some dry sticks from the pan hob to the side of the fireplace, and an old newspaper from a rack in the corner.

Whipping a rough hessian apron from a nail on the door, she laid it on the fender and placed the other articles on it. Then she rolled up her sleeves, gathered up the hessian apron and without casting a glance at the now silent staring little woman, she pulled open the stairhead door and went down the stairs, her back stiff with the knowledge that whatever reaction her first day's work might bring, the attempt at it had silenced her mother-in-law, at least temporarily.

Her back ached, her arms ached, her legs ached, in fact there wasn't a part of her that didn't ache. She had asked herself a number of times this day how little Tessie managed to get through a mountain of washing, and not only get through it but sing as she worked.

She sat at the table now, scarcely able to eat the meal of stewed mutton and solid dumplings that her mother-in-law had thrust before her. She had noted earlier on in the day that when the little woman was doling out her duties she had said nothing about cooking the daily meals, because as she had already found out, Mrs Loam was a glutton where food was concerned, and she would attend to at least the needs of her stomach if to nothing else.

Fred sat opposite her shovelling the food into his mouth as if he had not eaten for a week, and in between his chewing he jerked his head at her, grinned, and for the third time since sitting down at the table he congratulated her in his own way on her efforts. "By! I can't get over it, you gettin' your hand in with a whole day's wash, eh! By! that's somethin', that is for a start."

"God Almighty!" Mrs Loam's spoon clattered into her bowl. "Why don't you pin a medal on her? Every woman in the village washes on a Monday, come hail, sleet or snow, an' I've never heard of their men gapin' and yappin' like open-mouthed cods. . . ."

"Now, Ma, shut it! an' give honour where it's due. . . ."

"Oh my God!" The little woman raised her hands and her eyes to the ceiling; then getting up abruptly from a half-finished meal, she cried, "This's too much for me, I'm away to me bed."

When her bedroom door banged closed, Fred leant across the table and, grinning widely at Hannah, whispered, "Once we're out of the way she'll be back in here stuffin' her kite. Oh, I know her of old."

Hannah made no comment whatever, she was too weary and too tired even to eat. But before she could go to bed there would be the crocks to wash up, and the great basket of linen that she still had to sort, fold and roll up for ironing on the morrow. . . . But even when she went to bed her work wouldn't be finished. Oh no!

No! She shook her head at the mental picture. If he touched her tonight she would scream, she would claw at him, she would fight him. . . . She looked at him. No she wouldn't, she wouldn't have the strength. She would have to do what she had tried to do other nights, lie passive and let it pass over her as if it were all happening to someone else, for she had discovered that this side of marriage wasn't only physical but mental too. If for instance you couldn't obliterate it from your mind altogether you could in the dark imagine it was happening with someone else. . . .

While she washed up the dirty crocks, and scraped the soot from the encrusted bottom of the stew pan, then saw to the linen, Fred sat by the fire, his stockinged feet on the fender, a clay pipe in his mouth, and he talked. He talked about getting the horse shod and a new hub on the cart wheel. He talked reminiscently of his father telling of the great times they had at the Corn Suppers – he pronounced it "kern" – which were now dying out as the farmers were using their land more for grazing. "End of harvest they'd go on till the dawn," he said, "eating, dancing, dressin' up or dressin' down." He laughed. "I was at a couple when I was but a youngster – By! lad, the things that they got up to. Dad never got to one after he married. She had religion bad then." He jerked his head towards the bedroom door and, his voice low, he added, " 'Tis bad enough now but then it was served up with the mornin' crowdy and the supper an' all, seven days a week. Oh, she's better now. You won't believe it, but she is."

Hannah said nothing, she said nothing until he began to talk in detail about the big strong beast he had killed that morning. "By God! hefty he was. Took three of them to hold him while I hammered at him. . . ."

Quickly turning from the table, Hannah cried below her breath, "Please! I don't want to hear about that," and he laughed now and said, "Aye, well, I don't suppose you would, havin' a weak stomach like. But it's got to be done nevertheless." Then after a pause he went on, "I heard somethin' in the town about up there."

Although she had her back to him and she didn't see him jerking his head in the direction of the house at the end of the village, she knew to whom he was referring. "He's to be married come September. Big do an' all I hear. Our Master John's tryin' to ape young Mr Wentworth Beaumont. But I'd say he'll have a job. By! he will that 'cos that was a day to remember. You were at school then." He turned his head towards her. "Funny that, only two years gone an' you were at school. By! but I never forget that day an' the stuff we sold here. What the others must have made at Hexham, Bywell, and in Weardale, God only knows, 'cos there was some meat chewed up in Allendale that day, I can tell you. All the miners had a field day . . . an' his tenants an' all. The bands playin' and the balls at night. The town was illuminated. As to what happened up at Bywell Hall, lordy! they say that was a do. . . .

"Course, about the jollifications at Allenheads, that was a pity that was, but more of a pity for John Sanderson and Isaac Short 'cos they were suffocated by smoke at the mine that very day. Just near the mouth an' all. An' all through some daft buggers throwing their candle ends into a heap afore they left off work. Anyway, the food didn't go wastin', the poor around there got a bellyful. So I've got to laugh to meself when I think of Mr John Thornton tryin' to cap that lot, and him not one penny to rub against the other. In any case it's her father who's standin' the racket; he's always liked to play big, has Farmer Everton. Gentleman farmer he calls hissel'; his wife's even worse."

He twisted round in the chair now, "I bet you what you like you're not invited, 'cos you know why?" He waited for her to make some comment, but when she didn't, he went on, "Well, 'tis plain isn't it, you're married to me, an' they couldn't ask one without t'other, now could they? . . . Bloody snots the lot of them!"

There was silence in the kitchen for a while: then of a sudden he took his feet from the fender, knocked out the doddle from his pipe on the grate and, standing up, he looked at the fire, saying, "No use banking it down 'cos she'll be out." Then turning towards Hannah where she was bending over the table slowly folding a sheet, he touched her arm, saying abruptly, "Leave that and come on."

She remained in the bent position for a moment while the muscles of her stomach tensed; then putting the sheet on the top of the pile of linen, she lifted it from the table and placed it in the basket before, her feet dragging, she followed him into the bedroom.

3

It was the third Friday in September and the day of the cattle show and sheep fair, the Tup Fair, over near Allenheads corn mill. Both Fred and his mother had gone to the fair; as Mrs Loam had said, she had never missed a fair since as far back as you could remember and she wasn't missing the one today, and her son was going to take her . . . or else.

Mrs Loam had been amazed that Fred himself should have wavered about going just because that upstart bitch of a wife of his had said she didn't wish to go. Apparently she didn't like the sight of cattle being pushed about. And she had married a butcher! Dear God! it was laughable.

And now Hannah had the house to herself and it felt strange. Neither of them had need to enquire what she would do with herself in their absence because there was still plenty to be done. Fair or no fair, it was still Friday and there was the kitchen to finish cleaning. Moreover, as always, they opened the shop on a Saturday morning bright and early, and there was fresh sawdust to be put on the floor; and the back yard had to be scraped over and the midden cleaned.

She walked into the bedroom and to the window and looked over the yard, over the middens and the ditch, away to the hills, the clean hills, the hills she hadn't trodden since the day she had stumbled across them back to the Pele house. She had no memory of being brought back over them to this house.

She had now been married over three months, and for almost two months of that time she had been ill; for the remainder she had been learning what hard work was; and she hadn't been, as Bella would have said, across the doors since, except to go through the backyard to the lavatory.

Last week her mother-in-law had demanded to know which church or chapel she was going to attend on a Sunday: Was she for going back to that 'un at the top of the road? or was she going to pray to God in a proper manner? Which meant, Hannah took it, was she going to attend the Primitive Methodist Chapel?

She could smile to herself when she remembered how she turned on her mother-in-law, crying, "Neither the Primitive Methodist, nor the Wesleyan Methodist, nor the Church of England, nor the House of Friends." And she felt she could give herself credit for her stand, for she knew that had been a very bold attitude to take because in the village, as well as in Allendale, you had to belong to one or the other, that is if you were a woman. Men could be indifferent; men attended the religious ceremonies only if it pleased them, and if they didn't it wasn't held against them. But should their wives and children not attend, then the families were known as godless. . . . Moreover, an entire lack of religious choice was very bad for business, if you happened to be in business.

As she stared into the distance she felt her heart beat quicker. She had not been ordered to stay in the house but she knew that even if she had been she would not have obeyed, for of a sudden the hills were calling, the hard rock, heather-padded, rainbow-hued hills.

She went quickly now to the cupboard in which she hung her clothes and having taken down a brown corded dress she held it at arm's length for a moment before tearing off the bibbed coarse apron that almost enveloped her and her stained blouse and skirt. Within a matter of minutes she was ready for outside with a cloak over her dress and her bonnet on.

The shop door was bolted on the inside but the back door was never bolted, nor was the low gate at the bottom of the yard. She went through it, past the midden, jumped the smelling ditch, crossed the piece of open grassland, skirted the tangle of bramble bushes that ran like a hedge for some distance, and within a few minutes she was at the foot of the first rise.

She didn't stop or look back until she reached the top and there she stood drawing in great gulps of air and gazing about her. She had turned her back on the village and a little way in front of her the land sloped into a shallow valley before rising again to another hill; but away to the left it fell into gentle shallows that spread out into fields. Walking on again she went down the slope but now she veered to the right where the ground rose less steeply and the hills were drawn out.

When she next stopped it was to look up at the steep rise on which the Pele house stood; and now without hesitation she made straight for it, not hiding the fact from herself any longer that this was the main reason why she had wished to get out of doors.

She had wanted fresh air, she had wanted to feel the wide barrenness of the hills and the contradictory close enfolding comfort of them; but more than anything else she wanted to speak to Ned, to look at his hand, to find out how he was managing, to see him and to hear him.

She saw him as she was nearing the wall, and he must have seen her, for she watched him stop abruptly in the yard near the door to the Pele, stare towards her for a moment, then turn swiftly and walk back around the side of the house.

Her step slowed, then stopped. He didn't want to see her. But she must speak to him, she must, just this once.

As she passed the stable-room there was no sound of the chink, chatter and stamping of the ponies, which meant that he had completed a sale and hadn't started on gathering another bunch. But if that was the case why hadn't he gone to the fair? There would be ponies there.

She walked around the side of the house, but he wasn't there; then she saw him on the hillside bending over and scraping at something.

Walking very slowly now she approached him, then stopped when she was about three yards from him.

"Hello, Ned."

"What? Oh!" He jerked his head as if in surprise. "'Tis you." He stared at her for a moment, then again bent his back and went on raking at the earth.

"How are you?"

"Me? Never better. How's yourself?"

She made no answer to this but took another two steps towards him. He was holding the rake in his right hand, while with what was left of his other hand he was pushing pieces of stone here and there over the ground.

He didn't stop what he was doing, he didn't straighten his back, he didn't speak. The silence spread round them and even covered the sound of the metal rake tearing at the ground.

"What are you looking for?"

"Looking for?" He screwed his head round and cast his glance up at her. "Gold, lead gold; I'm gona open a mine here."

Her eyes widened, her lips parted, and she said incredulously, "A mine? A lead mine?"

"Aye, why not?" He straightened up now and stared at her.

"No . . . no reason, except. . . ."

"Except what?"

"I . . . I always thought it took a lot of money to open a mine."

"Who says I haven't a lot of money?"

She recalled his bragging about the savings behind the stones in the Pele house.

"And what you haven't got there's always somebody ready to lend it you if you've got the right security. And this is the right security. It's a hill; there's water handy" – he pointed down to the stream – "an' I bet there's veins under here as rich as any hereabouts. You only want to drive an adit into it an' we'll soon see. But anyway I don't need to see, I don't need an adit. I've found plenty of shoad ore on this hill afore now, and it's the real stuff, not float ore. Look." He picked up a piece of stone that looked as if it had been bleached and he said, "That's it, that's where the money lies. I've found pieces of that from the size of peas to pigs' bladders." He was talking rapidly now, the colour on his face deepening as he went on, "And there's not only lead in it" – he kicked the ground with the toe of his boot – "but silver. Aye, silver. Old Beaumont sent a cake weighing over twelve thousand ounces to that exhibition in London in fifty-one, worth over three thousand pounds it was, the one cake. What one can do another can, you've got to start somewhere. An' if I want to open up a mine here I'll open up a mine and no bloody combine of Beaumont's and his lackeys, like Sopwith and the rest, will stop me." He took the rake now and flung it from him, and she

206

watched it circling in the air before it fell somewhere up the hill, then slide down again. "And what the hell do you want comin' here for anyway? Think I've been free from trouble long enough and 'twas about time you brought me some more?"

Her face twitched. She bit on her lip, her head drooped, then she turned about and walked from him; but when he bawled at her, "That's it! walk away. You bring trouble wherever you go, but do you stand to face the consequences? Not you."

. . . "Hello there." They both turned and looked in the same direction. To the side of them, from the path leading round the belt of trees, a woman was approaching. Even from the distance she looked big, and to Hannah she seemed to grow larger as she approached. She had a basket on her arm and a shawl over her head and clogs on her feet.

"Hello there," she said again. "Nice day." She stopped and looked from one to the other, and now Ned spoke to her, saying, "Hello, Nell, how is it?"

"Oh pretty fair, pretty fair. I brought you a bite. I was at me bakin', an' I thought, I know who'd like a pie."

"You thought right, Nell." He had moved towards her and Hannah stood looking at them both. They looked of a like age, or perhaps the woman could be a little older than him, in her early thirties. Her body was straight and sturdy looking, her face big-boned but pleasant. They were talking together now as if she weren't there.

"I thought you might be at the fair, Ned."

"Aw no, Nell, I've other fish to fry. An' I can get drunk without goin' to the fair." They laughed together. "Come in and have a sup tea."

"Aye, I will, Ned, I will."

They walked on now past her; then as if Ned had suddenly remembered her, he said, "There'll be enough for another cup if you want one."

She moved her head slowly and said, "No thank you."

"Please yourself. That's the best way, Nell, isn't it? Please yourself an' then you won't die in the pet."

"You're right there, Ned; you're right there."

"Why weren't you at the fair yourself, Nell?"

"Oh, 'cos I'm more partial to small company, Ned." Their voices faded away.

As she watched them round the corner of the house she had the wild urge to run again as she had done that night in the rain, but the feeling passed as quickly as it had come.

She did not look back towards the stable-room as she went through the yard but she was aware that the doors were closed and with their closing she knew she had to relinquish something, something she'd never had, something she should have had. But now it was gone, shut in behind the doors of the stable-room. From now on she must face up to the fact that she was a married woman, who washed and scrubbed and baked; she was an ordinary village wife who must forget that she had once played the piano, read books, liked poetry, painted a little, and sang.

She walked down the hillside, up and across the other hills, over the ditch, past the midden and into the house once more. She'd had all the fresh air she needed and she felt she never wanted to walk the hills again.

4

She had been married a year and her mother-in-law's new taunt now was that she must be barren because, as she said, give her son his due he was as full-bloodied as any bull he had ever slaughtered, but by the looks of things he had landed himself with a heifer and, work as he might, he wouldn't be able to change her into a cow.

Hannah let the old woman talk. Over the past months she had found silence to be her best weapon; in fact there were times when she felt she had lost the art of talking except in monosyllables, because when Fred talked he only needed a listener; his conversation ranged between the condition of the beasts he slaughtered, the rise or fall in price of the meat, and the gossip that he heard in the market.

She had not even the pleasure of bidding the time of day with the customers for he would not let her serve in the shop; not that she wanted to, because she hated handling the great slabs of wet meat, hated the sight of the blood, the smell of it, the sticky feel of it on her fingers.

Looking back over the year she couldn't believe that she had been but twelve months in this house, for it seemed she had passed her whole existence here. Yet there had been other times when she felt that it was but yesterday she had found herself in these dull rooms, and that if she didn't escape she would go mad. When this feeling came upon her she fostered it because it seemed to bring her alive again, wrench her out of the dullness of each day, the sameness of each day. It had the power to wipe out her apathy. Whenever she felt like this she would tell herself she must break her self-made rule, the only one she had stuck to, and accompany her husband and mother-in-law to the market.

And then something happened that brought her up out of the depths. Tessie came into the shop.

It was a Saturday morning. She was carrying a bucket of slops down the stairs, and such was the situation of the rooms that the staircase door led into a corner of the shop, and the door leading into the back shop was next to it, and so when she made this journey on the days when the shop was open she would for a brief moment see the customers, and this morning she saw Tessie; and Tessie, looking towards her, cried impulsively, "Oh! hello, miss, I mean missis." And with this she turned her face in apology towards Fred and leaning over the counter, whispered, "Could I have a word with her, Fred, do you think?"

"Why, aye, I won't charge your missis for it. Go on." He nodded, and she went hastily into the back shop; and there both she and Hannah stood looking at each other.

"It's a long time since I've seen you, Tessie." Hannah found it difficult to speak.

"Aye, it is, miss." Tessie now walked towards the far door, drawing Hannah with her, and there, straining her face upwards, she whispered, "I've been tryin' to get a word with you for ages." She glanced back towards the shop. "You know she threatened us, Bella and me, that if we spoke to you we'd get the push? She seems mad at times, she seems beside herself." She didn't add, "She's never got over your wedding-day when she found out you'd really no claim on the master," but went on, "For weeks past now I've been comin' down with an order, ever since Miss Betsy caught cold, an' I haven't clapped eyes on you." She reached up and placed her lips now against Hannah's ear. "I've got a message for you."

"A message?"

"Aye, 'tis from Ned Ridley."

The colour swept up over Hannah's face, while at the same time she screwed up her cheeks questioningly, then whispered back, "Ned?"

"Aye; I met him on my half-day. 'Twas a market day in the town an' we got crackin', an' he said if ever I saw you I was to ask you to go up."

"Me?" Hannah now pointed to herself, then whispered, "Go to the Pele house?"

Tessie was nodding. "Aye, that's what he said. An' I had to keep me mouth shut. Well, I did, I didn't even tell Bella, 'cos Bella's tongue wags itself loose at times, an' I thought the way you're placed . . . well, you know what I mean."

Hannah nodded dumbly; then they both started as Fred appeared in the doorway. There was laughter on his face but there was a question in his voice as he said, "Tellin' secrets?"

"No, no, Fred . . . well" – Tessie tossed her head and laughed now – "it'll soon be no secret that Mr Robert's done a bunk."

"Mr Robert done a bunk?" Fred now moved slowly forward, wiping his hands on his apron. "Well, well! When did this happen?"

"Oh." Her head was bobbing up and down. "Eeh! well, I'm not supposed to know or say anythin', but three days ago he went off like that." She snapped her fingers. "Left her a note . . . the missis, sayin' he was going to the Americas, somethin' about his da's cousin. From what I could gather that went on atween the missis and Miss Betsy, Master Robert had been writing to his aunt who was married to a man on a farm. Anyway, off he went, telling them in the letter not to worry, and that he couldn't stick the mine."

"Well, well! Master Robert gone off. There'll soon be nobody there for you to look after, Tessie. Then what'll you do?"

"I'll still have a pair of hands on me, Fred."

"Eeh! you're a cocky monkey, that's what you are Tessie Skipton. Come on, your meat's ready." He half turned, then looked back at them and said, "Have you had your fill of gossip atween you?"

"Aye, yes." Tessie came towards him. "I just wanted to tell miss, I mean missis, that bit about Master Robert, an' the latest about Miss Margaret not getting married after all. By! the missis was cock-a-hoop about that." Tessie turned and nodded towards Hannah. "All the bits in the Bible came out for days: As ye sow so shall ye reap, and what happens to them who don't honour their father an' mother. Oh, we got it morn, noon, an' night."

She laughed now, and Fred with her, and Hannah, picking up

the pail of slops again, went out into the yard and towards
ditch. Margaret not married; what had happened? Poor Margar
she had been so sure of the man, so willing to give up everythi
for him. . . . And Robert going off like that to America. As Fi
said, they were nearly all gone. Of course there was John, l
John was living far over the hills.

But these events weren't what Tessie had come to tell her .
Ned wanted to see her. Why? Why? She raised her head a
looked away over the ditch, over the field, and over the rise, l
she felt no great impulse to rush in the direction of the Pele ho
because she was asking herself again, why? Did he want to p
her in the picture, to tell her that he was marrying that wom
that big woman called Nell; the woman who baked for him, a
had said openly and meaningfully that she preferred the compa
of two to a crowd?

She turned about and not looking where she was going she tr
in some mire and, her face wrinkling in deep distaste, she wip
the mess from her clog on to a clump of grass; then walking alo
the bank to where a rivulet of clean water ran out of a gravel ba
into the stream, she took off the clog and washed it, then rinsed l
bucket in the stream before going further up the bank and layi
it on the gravel bottom until it was half full of water, which wo
go towards filling the wash-house pot for Monday's task.

As she entered the shop Fred was standing idly looking out
the window and he turned to her and said, "They're cutting do
up there all right; one-and-six-worth, that's all she got. I've s
them spend as much as ten shillings a week when he was alive. I
hardly worth while keeping open; it's only the bloody miners w
come in regular, an' then they can't pay up until the end of
month, an' some of them not then, an' they're grumbling like l
at havin' to pay fourpence ha'penny a pound. I'm almost payi
that for it meself."

He shook his head, then banged the chopper into the blc
before saying now and with bitterness, "I could always be sure
the Bynges and Ricksons havin' a collop three times a week, I
there was Mrs Rickson and Flora Bynge in Allendale Town, a
Mrs Wheatley an' all, all buyin' there. They were shamefaced wl
they saw me. I'm all right to be made use of in the winter wl

212

y can't get out of their bloody doors for snow, but in the
nmer they jaunt into the town. Well, I'll . . . I'll remember, I'll
nember." He nodded at her. "And there's that lot along there"
ne motioned his head towards the other end of the village –
ining together to have a mart at Christmas. Hope the next one
y have one of 'em gets felled to the ground instead of the
st."

She closed her eyes for a moment against the picture that the
rt conjured up. It was a custom towards Christmas-time for a
mber of people to join together and buy a fat beast; then the
n, who would be mostly drunk, killed the animal by a slow
cess; some would hold the animal's head whilst another
empted to strike the beast. Should he miss, as happened often,
had to pay a forfeit in the form of more liquor. The animals
ld die slowly and in agony. Finally the meat was carved up and
ed for winter use and the money that was obtained for
elping the hide", which meant stripping it of tallow before
ling the skin, was also spent in drink.

She turned from him and went up the stairs. They were
barians, all of them, cruel barbarians; not only the poor, but
rich. Mantraps, deer stalking, rabbit coursing, cock fighting,
l baiting . . . and bull killing, men holding an animal while
ther beat it to death. The world was a cruel place.

the Saturday night Mrs Loam reminded her son once again
t he was driving her to the chapel at Allenheads on the morrow,
ere a minister on a circuit was stopping to preach; and to this
d replied, "You don't let me forget. Every day this week
've been on about it. You rattle on as much as your loom."
nodded towards her where she was sitting in the corner of the
chen weaving a narrow strip of cloth on a small loom.

"But you still haven't washed the cart down," she said.

"I'll wash it down all it's gona get in the mornin'," he replied.
nd it's a useless task, as I see it, 'cos it'll be as bloody again
hin a few hours. . . ."

n bed that night Fred whispered, "Why won't you come along
us the morrow?" and she answered, "You know why; I

think you'll agree that I have enough of your mother's compa[ny]
as it is."

It said something for Fred's even temper and his understandi[ng]
of his mother, and his wife also, that he didn't press the point; n[or]
did he in any way rebuke her for her plain speaking, but what [he]
did say was, "Well, what will you do with yourself, it bei[ng]
Sunday?"

"I may go for a walk."

"Over the hills?"

"Yes, over the hills."

"Ah well" – there had come a solemn note into his voice no[w]
"you want to be careful, as I see it those hills spell trouble [for]
you."

And there he let the matter rest; and, pulling her into his arn[s]
he went about the business of claiming the rights of a husban[d].

The sky was low; it seemed as if the hills all about were trying [to]
pierce it and that soon one of them would break its skin and le[t the]
deluge fall. The air was heavy; it swelled her lungs and pres[sed]
hard against her ribs as she breathed it in.

She pulled off her bonnet that seemed to weigh on her head a[nd]
opened her cloak and wafted the bodice of her cotton frock ba[ck]
and forward from her breasts to give herself air. She was hot [and]
shivering, but the shivering was inside, in her chest, causin[g a]
sickly feeling. Suppose he were away, he would have no kno[w]-
ledge of her coming; and if he wasn't in, she would get drench[ed]
before she got back. But what did that matter, really?

As a streak of lightning flashed across the hills and the peals [of]
distant thunder vibrated about her, she started to run, and wh[en]
she had climbed the slope and reached the wall of the yard [she]
had to stop for a moment to get her breath.

She stood now looking across to the doors. They were sh[ut]
and there was no sign of life about. But she was only half-w[ay]
across the yard when she saw that the big lock was hanging on [its]
chain to the side.

She was about to open the door without knocking when [she]
thought better of it. What if that woman were there; being a [?]

214

f rest people took walks on Sundays. She tapped once; then wice; and when there was no answer she pushed the door slowly pen and went inside.

Owing to its size and the small windows the room always ooked dim, but now because of the lowering sky outside it was s if she had walked into the night, and she had to stand some ninutes before she could accustom herself to the darkness.

She heard the champing of the ponies in their stalls. Moving lowly forward, she came abreast of the platform to the right of er, and there on the straw he was lying, stretched out, sound sleep.

Softly now she walked towards him and stood looking down at im. He was flat on his back, his hands on his stomach. The first nger on his right hand was linked between the remaining finger nd thumb of his left, and the stump of the middle finger stuck up ust above the knuckles of his right hand. For the rest there was a igzag scar running up to the bone of his wrist, and the back of he hand looked twisted, as if it had been tortured.

When another flash of lightning illuminated the room and was mmediately followed by a deafening clap of thunder, the ponies eighed and stamped and Ned opened his eyes. His lids opening lowly, he looked up towards the cobwebbed beams for a moment, ut the next second he was sitting bolt upright, his feet over the dge of the platform, gaping at her.

"It . . . it was the thunder that . . . that woke you, that . . . hat. . . ." It was as if she were saying, "Don't blame me."

He wetted his lips, blinked, rubbed his hand tight round his hin, but said nothing.

"I . . . I saw Tessie yesterday. She . . . she gave me a message."

"What?"

She had noticed before that he always said "What?" even when e had heard aright; but she repeated, "Tessie. Tessie gave me a nessage; she said you wanted to see me."

Again he was staring at her in silence, and again he rubbed his and tightly over his skin; then getting to his feet, he walked way from her towards the middle of the room, saying, "Aye, aye. es I did. But 'twas some time ago I saw her."

Another clap of thunder caused her to hunch her shoulders up against it and she watched him go towards the line of stalls, saying "It's all right. It's all right. Calm yourselves." Then he turned towards her and spoke across the room, his voice loud, "They don't like storms, makes them uneasy. . . . Do you want a drop of something, a cup of tea?"

"Yes, yes, please."

Slowly she followed him into the back kitchen, and she was quick to note that everything looked tidy and so thought she detected a woman's hand here.

"Sit yourself down." He motioned towards a chair. "And we'd better have some lights on the subject or we'll have to put our fingers in our eyes and make starlights." He gave an embarrassed laugh, but she said nothing.

She sat by the table now and watched him light the lamp, then thrust the big black kettle into the heart of the fire, after which he took the teapot from the delf rack, spooned into it four spoonfuls of tea, which told her that it would be so strong she wouldn't be able to drink it. Then with one of his quick jerky movements he swung a chair round and was sitting opposite her; and they stared at each other for a moment or so before he said, "Well, how are things with you?"

She did not answer his question, but through the lantern light she stared him straight in the face and said, "Why did you want to see me?"

"Oh that." He was now rubbing the side of his face with the finger and thumb of his left hand. "Well, 'twas. . . . Oh" – he shook his head vigorously – "you always get me off on the wrong foot. An' that time you came upon me on the hillside, there you were goin', marching off leaving me high and dry. You have a habit of doing that, walkin' off. And I wanted to tell you it was all right, you needn't worry. I mean about this" – he now wagged his hand by the wrist in front of her – " 'cos 'tis funny, I've learned a lot through this, it's been like an education to me, proved the things you can do without. That's true you know, you can learn to do without most things. Well mind, if it had been the thumb" – he wagged his thumb – "I don't know how I would have felt then because that's the most important part of the hand. Did you know that?"

216

She stared at him wide-eyed without blinking.

"Well." He brought his hand down on to his knee and left it resting there and, looking down at it now, he went on more quietly. "That's it then, I just wanted you to know you needn't worry about me, 'cos from what I hear you've got enough on your plate. God!" – he shook his head now – "that you should have ended up like that, under a she-devil out of hell such as Daisy Loam. And to think she might have been my mother." He gave a short laugh. "She was after my dad years ago. By! if ever there was a bastard of a woman she's one. An' Fred. Well, he's gormless; but there's no badness in him, not like her, at least I shouldn't say so. But you'd be the best judge of that." He was looking at her sideways now.

Her eyes were still wide, still unblinking; she couldn't speak, not to utter one word. There was a great swelling inside her, it was rising upwards like a river in flood; she watched it mounting, knowing that in a moment it would drown her.

When it burst from her she let out a cry and fell forward over the table while her two hands, doubled into fists, beat the top of her head.

When his arms went about her and pulled her round and upwards to be pressed tightly against him, she still moaned, she still wailed, she still cried.

"There! There! Hannah. Hannah. It's all right. It's all right. Aw! for Christ's sake don't, don't make that noise, Hannah."

He was holding her from him now, shaking her by the shoulders, until, gasping and choking, the wailing subsided even while her tears still flowed.

When after a moment she fell against him, he gripped her so tightly that she could have cried out with the pain of it.

"Oh God! Oh God! Hannah, don't blame yourself. You're not to blame, you're not." He was talking into her hair now. "I should have told you; even before you were married I could have gone down and told you and given you a choice; him or me, I would have said; but I was too bloody stubborn, too bloody hurt. I blamed you for not knowing, not guessing. And what were you? A bit of a lass, brought up mostly in that school with the old she-women, like nuns. What did you know?

"Hannah!" He held her from him now and, pressing her down into a chair, he dropped on to his hunkers before her and, holding her hands in his, he said quietly. "You know what I'm saying to you, don't you? I love you. I love you, Hannah. I always have. An' I guess that's how it will go on. I've lived no saint's life, no good denyin' it, I've got a name. Well, you know that, don't you? But that isn't love, that isn't the thing that burns you up, gets atween you and your wits, makes you walk when you should be sleepin' and so damned tired that you sleep when you should be working . . . How do you feel about me, Hannah?"

"Oh, Ned! Ned!" she drew one hand from his and touched his cheek. "I . . . I didn't know what it was all about, I . . . I only knew that I've always needed you. I . . . I thought I loved John and then . . . then when she said I had to marry Fred I came rushing up to you. And you were away. And then when I tried to speak to you, you . . . you wouldn't have any of me."

He bowed his head, saying, "I know, I played the big fellow an' by God! haven't I suffered for it since." Then looking at her again, he said, "You care for me? Really care for me, I mean, not as a child or a young lass? . . . Well, you know what I mean."

"Yes, Ned, yes, I know what you mean." Her face was moving slowly towards him as she spoke, and when her lips touched his mouth he became totally still for a moment; then once again she was whipped up from the chair and into his arms, and he was kissing her in a way that she had never been kissed before, not even by Fred at the height of his rough passion. But this, this was a different kissing because she was responding to it, as she had never imagined herself responding to anyone in her life. She was holding him as tightly as he was holding her, she was sinking into him, becoming lost in him, her senses were reeling; then she was back on the chair again where he had pushed her, and now he was standing above her laughing, as she had seen him laugh years ago yet with a difference, because now there was joy in his laughter and, his voice thick, he said, "Do you want that tea?"

She stared back at him speechless, then watched him hurrying away from the kitchen, and when she heard the bolt being pushed into the main door she turned her head to the side and bit tight on her lip for a moment in an effort to stop the trembling of her body.

He was standing at the kitchen door now, his hand extended towards her, and she rose swiftly and placed hers in it; then he was leading her up the steps and into the room above. Still holding tight to her hand he drew her across it and into the bedroom and there, holding her at arm's length, he looked at her through the dim light and said softly, "You're sure?"

"Oh yes, Ned. Oh yes, I'm sure."

His hands now went to the collar of her dress and slowly he unloosened the top button, and the next, and the next, and she remained still all the while staring at him.

Finally he lifted her up in his arms and laid her on the bed, and she lay and watched him as he undressed. His movements were still slow, even leisurely, and when he lay down beside her he took her face between his hands and, his words so emotionally weighed that he seemed to growl them out, he said, "The times I've dreamed of this. Way back even before I first saw you, I dreamed of someone like you lying beside me like this. It's sad to think that I've lost part of that dream, through my own fault. Mind, I'm not blamin' you. No, no." He moved his head slowly. "But a fellow such as Fred could never have meant anything to you, stirred you, loved you. . . . Did he?"

She closed her eyes and whispered, "No, Ned, no. I've wanted to die. Then I learned to think of you and that helped."

"You did? You thought of me when you were with him?"

"Yes, Ned."

"Aw, Hannah! Hannah!"

He rose on his elbow and bent over her, but now it seemed as if a different man still was kissing her, for now his loving was gentle, slow, and her body seemed to expand with it until her happiness filled the room and spilled over on to the hills, and rose high into the air and sang like a chorus of larks.

Neither of them was aware of the time when the storm passed, but eventually the brightness of the room brought his gaze from her, and he laughed aloud as he said, "The sun's out."

"Oh yes, yes!" She turned on her back and looked towards the window. He was looking down on her again as he said, "Could you do with that cup of tea now?"

"Oh Ned! Ned!" She cupped his lean cheek.

"You happy, Hannah?" The question was quiet.

"Happy!" She moved her eyes from one side of the room to the other. "I only know I've never felt like this in my life and never expected to feel like it. I don't care what happens to me now."

"What do you mean, you don't care what happens to you now?"

"Just that. I could die and be happy."

"Don't talk so soft." He rolled off the bed, stood up, pulled on his small clothes, then his trousers, and lastly his shirt; and when he had tucked it in his trousers he stood tightening his belt as he looked towards her and said, "We're going on from here, Hannah. I don't know how yet, but this is only the beginning for us. Understand?"

She stared at him for a moment. Then pulling the patchwork quilt over her, she sat up, saying quietly, "It's . . . it's going to be difficult, Ned. If they once saw me coming up here. . . ."

"To hell with them!"

Now he was bending over her and grinning at her as he asked, "She goes to chapel on a Sunday I suppose, every Sunday?"

"Yes."

"Aye. Well, what does he do?"

"Goes to bed in the afternoon."

"And you?" The grin slid from his face.

"No. Never."

"Well, you could take a walk, couldn't you?"

"Yes, yes, I could take a walk." She smiled quietly.

"Then we'll take it one bit at a time, eh? Come on, get up out of that." He took her hand and pulled her across the bed, and when she went to grab at her things, he said, "Hold on; I took them off, and I'll put them on; an' from now on."

"Oh Ned! Ned!" She was in his arms again, and he was kissing her eyes, her nose, her ears and in this moment she realized that his love-making was the outcome of practice but that it didn't matter because she was special. She knew that, she believed that. If she were ever to believe anything in her life again she believed that.

When finally they went into the other room, he said, "Stay here; I'll bring the tea up," and she sat down in the wooden rocking chair to the side of the fireplace. There was no fire in this grate but she could imagine what it would be like of a winter evening with the flames roaring up the wide grate and a pan of broth on the hearth, and the table there set with a white cloth and those wooden bowls for their supper.

She looked at the set of wooden bowls on top of the oak rack. There were six of them, three large and three small. Like the rest of the furniture, they looked hand-made. She gazed about the room, so different from the one she had left an hour ago . . . two hours ago . . . three hours ago. What time was it? Close on six o'clock she would say. She must be soon getting back.

As she sat she noticed again that everything here, too, was tidy as had been the kitchen downstairs, and this fact brought a little niggling fear into her. That woman. Did she come here and tidy up for him? And not only tidy up for him?

She was standing by the dresser fingering the bowls when he came into the room carrying a tin tray on which was the brown earthenware teapot, a jug of milk, a bowl of sugar, and two mugs, and she lifted the largest bowl and turned it in her hand as she said, "Everything looks neat and tidy; have you someone come in?"

She heard him put the tray down on the table, and when he didn't answer she swung round and looked at him. His face was straight but his eyes were laughing at her. "Aye," he said; "Nell Dickinson. You met her. Twice a week she comes over. She lives over on The Bottoms." He jerked his head in the direction of the window and the belt of woodland.

"Oh." She turned and put the bowl back in its place.

"Aye; fine lass, Nell. . . . How much sugar?"

"Oh, just one spoonful, please."

He poured out the tea, then said, "Aye well, aren't you going to come and get it."

She turned from the delf rack, saying, "You have some nice pieces of china."

He let her sit down, then he pushed the mug towards her and, bringing his face close to hers until their noses were almost touching, he said, "She's got a husband, as big and strong as two bulls. He taught me all I know about boxing. He married her when she was fifteen; he's given her eleven bairns; she lost four at one go with the cholera; and she took me to school, that is when she could get me there; and I've never had her to bed, at least not yet." As he nodded his nose flicked hers and he ended, "But mind, she's of good heart, there's not a kinder, and if she thought I needed someone very badly that way I'm sure she would have obliged. Oh aye, I'm sure of it."

She had her arms about his neck; they were laughing loudly together; and once again he was on his hunkers before her and now, his mouth wide, his eyes twinkling, he said, "You're jealous."

"No, no; I just wondered." She was shaking her head.

"That for a tale." He gently slapped her cheek. "Own up and shame the devil, you're jealous. What would you have done if it had been as you were thinking?"

Her face became serious now and her voice equally so as she said, "Very hurt, but . . . but I wouldn't have blamed you, knowing of your need. And I would have wished that I could have been in her place because" – she paused – "I love you so, Ned. I love you so."

"Aw . . . aw, don't; don't, my dear one, don't cry."

"I'm not. I'm not."

"Come on, drink this tea. Funny, a day like this, a day to celebrate, and I haven't a drop of hard in the house. Do you know something?" He had dropped from his hunkers on to his knees now, and he put his arms around her waist and laid his head between her small breasts as he said, "This is the happiest day of me life."

5

During the following months a number of events happened which dominated the talk in the dale.

There was the band contest, an event never to be forgotten. The contestants were from Allendale Town, Acomb, Catton, Carrshield, Langley and Nenthead. Allendale Town, Acomb and Catton took first, second and third prizes in that order; the other bands didn't see eye to eye with this decision and they showed their displeasure by setting about the judge, a Mr Boosey, a well-known composer and adjudicator from London. So violent were they in their attitude towards him that the poor man had to be spirited away to Haydon Bridge and then to the nearest railway station. This fiasco created laughter, arguments and disgust according to the place where it came under discussion.

Then there was the weather, always a thing to be taken into consideration, especially by the farmers. It was such a dry summer that corn and hay crops were light and the grub got into the turnips and almost destroyed the whole crop.

Then the weather, still remaining contrary, produced one of the hardest and longest winters anyone could remember. The pity of it was that animals died by the score, mostly the sheep, and it was said that the entire flocks would have been wiped out had it not been for the importation of large quantities of hay from Holland.

The winter seemed long to everyone, but most of all to Hannah. There were weeks on end when she never saw Ned. Even when the snow was packed down hard and it would have been possible to walk she couldn't get out, for if her mother-in-law was housebound, then so was she.

She had made arrangements with Ned that should it be possible he would walk the ridge of the first hill in the direction of Allendale Town around noon on a Sunday just to let her know that all was well with him. Obviously, they would not signal to each other but she would see him plainly against the skyline, and he might see the darkened form of her against the window-pane.

During the summer and autumn she had been hard put at times to suppress her inward happiness. One day, thinking her mother-in-law was out in the yard and Fred in the back shop, she began to sing quietly to herself, only for her voice to be cut off by the little woman standing behind her demanding, "An' what have you got to sing about may I ask?"

She had been whitening the hearth and she remained for a moment on her hands and knees before swinging round, the wet cloth in her hand, and crying in no small voice, "Nothing that you have given me. But I'll sing in spite of you. Do you hear? Because nothing you do or say has any effect on me any more. So when you're going blue in the face with temper it would be to your benefit if you remembered you can't hurt me, only yourself."

"You cheeky young bugger, you!"

At this Hannah rose to her feet and, bending over the old woman, hissed at her, "And you bitter vicious old one!"

When she saw the little woman scurrying from the room down the stairs she stood with her back to the table and, her chin drooping on her chest, she chuckled to herself.

Then Fred appeared in the doorway, saying, "What's up now? She . . . she says you insulted her."

Hannah threw back her head and let out a high laugh, crying, "She said that? Well, if she thinks I've insulted her then I've achieved something. And you can tell her that from now on I'll go on insulting her."

"What's come over you lately?" he demanded. "'Twas a time when you didn't open your mouth."

"I've grown up since then." She bent and picked up the wet whitening cloth from the hearth, adding, "And I'm not standing for her bullying me any more; and you can go down and tell her if she shouts an order to me when I'm passing through the shop again I'll shout back at her, and let the neighbours see she's not getting it all her own way. And that'll please them, because she's

224

hated. Do you know that, Fred? Your mother is hated, almost as much, in fact more than Mrs Thornton is; it's a shame to waste two houses between them."

He stood staring at her slightly bewildered. This wasn't the refined, educated miss he had married; she was reacting in the same way as any lass in the village would have done. There was a time when he had wished she would stand up for herself a bit more and answer his mother back, but now she was overdoing it. Of course, he wasn't entirely displeased that she was tackling the old girl, he wished he himself had done it years ago; but it was too late now for him to start.

But he wasn't quite happy about the change in Hannah's attitude. Up till now it had been a source of pride to him that he had married someone from the Thornton house, even if as it turned out she was no connection with them, because she had been educated as a lady, but the way she was acting lately was far from ladylike. He turned from her, saying, "I'd go steady; she won't stand for too much."

And then she almost choked with laughter inside as she called after him, "All right, if she won't stand for too much she can sit down while I'm giving her three much."

It was an old silly saying of Bella's and she had to turn quickly about and make her way to the bedroom because the expression of amazement on her husband's face had almost made her burst again into loud, even raucous laughter this time.

In the bedroom with her back to the door and her hand over her mouth, she breathed deeply as she said to herself, "Really! fancy me reacting like that. But oh! thank God I can. Thank God I can."

She went to the window and, leaning her hands on the sill, looked out over the hills towards the Pele house. The joy she had experienced over the past Sundays was, she felt, intoxicating her. A moment ago in the kitchen she had acted like someone slightly drunk; and she was drunk, deeply, deeply drunk with love of the man over there, and he with her. Oh yes, he with her. She knew now what it felt like to be worshipped. The thought was blasphemous but she didn't care, she was worshipped . . . in a rough, natural way she was worshipped.

225

At their very last meeting he had said, "What are we going to do? We can't go on like this, not even seeing each other once some weeks." And she had answered, as if the matter was quite simple, "I'll leave him, I'll come up. Just say the word, Ned."

He had shaken his head slowly at her as he replied, "No, no; your life wouldn't be worth living. We'd have to go away, we'd have to sell the place and start up elsewhere."

"But you wouldn't want to sell the Pele, you love it." And to this he had answered, "I love you more."

Then before they knew it the winter had come upon them, the winter that became an eternity, snow, sleet, blizzards, packed ice; days, weeks, shut in these three rooms with the two of them. The evenings spent with her mother-in-law madly treadling the loom, Fred snoring by the fireside, and herself patching, turning sheets, ends to middle, darning socks, or on some nights silently sitting at one end of the frame while Mrs Loam sat at the other making hooky mats. Sticking the hook through the taut hessian, pulling the rag up into the required loop, on and on and on, row after row after row; and as she progged she would recall how Tessie and Bella had made similar mats for the kitchen, and she had looked upon it as their recreation. Recreation! At the end of the evening her fingertips were so sore that sometimes she imagined that they would burst.

But now it was a Friday towards the end of February and a thaw had set in, though there were still flurries of snow showers that could at any time turn to blizzards. If the thaw continued, by Sunday the roads would be passable, even if ankle or knee-deep in parts with sludge.

She knew that her mother-in-law was as anxious to leave the house as she was, and so she prayed that she would go to chapel on Sunday evening and that Fred would follow a custom he had taken up some months ago, to his mother's disgust, that of spending the evenings in the local inn, and not always staying in the local one, but sometimes going as far afield as Allendale Town or in the opposite direction to an inn on the road close to Allenheads. When he went to either of these it would be by the cart, and once or twice of late it was only the knowledgeable horse that had got him home.

226

Strangely, Hannah didn't mind Fred getting drunk, the drunker he better, for then he made no demands on her, all he did was chatter and talk until he fell into a snoring sleep.

Of course, Mrs Loam laid the blame on Hannah for her son taking to drink. Before his marriage, she insisted her son had been a sober, God-fearing individual. Whenever she put this version to customers they would listen with grave shakes of the head, then go out and laugh themselves silly.

The thaw lasted, but it was late on the Sunday afternoon before Hannah was able to fly over the hills. The twilight had set in and she knew she'd have to make her way back in the dark, she hadn't brought a lantern, but what did it matter? She was panting when she reached the door of the Pele house. Pushing it open, she hurried into the horse room, then stopped abruptly when the sound of voices came to her from the kitchen. As she moved slowly across the room Ned appeared in the doorway. For a moment he looked startled and, turning his head, said, "Won't be a minute, Peter," before coming towards her and grasping her hand and whispering, "I thought you couldn't get."

"Who have you got here?" She was staring into his eyes.

"A couple of bodgers."

She screwed up her face, and he explained in a whisper, "Bodgers, drovers you know."

"Oh, yes, yes."

"They just looked in; they're about to go."

"Will I . . . will I slip into the barn?"

He was about to answer when two men appeared in the kitchen doorway, one of them saying, "Well, Ned, we're for the road again".

"Oh yes. Aye." Ned turned and looked at the approaching figures, but they were looking past him towards the young woman with the mass of chestnut hair which was uncovered for she had thrown her hood back on her shoulders. They stared hard at her, and as they passed her they acknowledged her with a jerk of their chins; her head already half bowed, she returned their salute with the slightest of nods.

"Well, we'll be seeing you, then, Ned?"

"Aye, aye, Arty. An' I'll think on what you said. It sounds as if it could be profitable."

"Oh, it'll be profitable all right. Of course" – the man now laughed – "you'll have to keep awake to beat the Welshman, but trust you, Ned, you weren't born yesterday."

"Nor the day afore," added the other man, and at this Ned laughed and said, "Well, 'tis one fact that I was born on one day and a second fact that I'll die on another day, and that's about th only thing a man can be sure of in this life."

"Aye, aye; or how to break a horse in. You're sure of that, Ned nobody surer. So long, so long."

"So long, Peter. So long, Arty." He closed the door behind them, but waited a moment before placing the bar quietly across it. Then he was standing in front of her again, swearing now "Damn and blast them to hell's flames! Never seen them fo months and they would look in the day. But what does it matter what does it matter. . . . Hello, love."

She didn't answer, but fell into his arms, then lost herself fo a moment as his lips found hers.

They were in the kitchen now, she sitting in a chair by th side of the roaring fire, he in his favourite position on his hunker at her knees, and when he asked quietly, "How goes it?" sh answered, "Unbearable at times. And it's been so long. Oh Ned! She cupped her face in her hands. "What are we going to do I can't bear the thought of going on like this for ever."

"Well, you needn't, it's up to you. We'll up and go just lik that." He snapped his fingers.

"But . . . but this is your home. I wouldn't mind what th villagers said, what the town said, what anybody said, I'd com up and . . ."

He put his hand out now and his fingers pressed gently on he lips as he spoke. "You don't know what you're talking abou It'd be all right for a couple of weeks, a couple of months, the it would get you down. I've seen it happen. I've seen it com about in this very house."

She shook her head and lifted his hand from her lips and sai "Here?"

"Aye, here. After me ma died, me da got thick with a woma she was from the next village, an' she'd had a life of it with he man. He was a miner and never sober; he'd beg, borrow or ste

228

to get his drink, and so she left him and come here. But she also left behind her a fifteen-year-old son and a fourteen-year-old daughter, and when she dared to go into Allendale Town one market-day her own son picked up a stone and threw it at her. And that seemed to act like a signal. They tried to put her in the stocks; the stocks were still there then. I can see it plainly although I was only about six at the time. I can see me da fighting them off, and in the scuffle the pen that used to house the stray cattle an' sheep was broken down and the animals scattered like mad. The overseers came out and things quietened down, but she hardly ever put her nose outside these doors again until the day she died. And that wasn't long after."

Still on his hunkers, he turned from her, took up the poker and stirred the fire; then went on, "She was supposed to get caught in the swollen river when she was crossing by the stones, just below here, but me da knew what she had done because it was the first time she had gone further than the yard since that day in the market. So you see, Hannah" – he turned to her again – "I know what I'm talkin' about. And although that took place twenty-two years back folks haven't altered; they don't alter in these parts. Do you know, some of 'em, at least half of them in that village down there, have never been as far as Allenheads in their life. And there's others, believe it or not, who've not been into Hexham, ten miles away; you could walk to either place there and back on a fine day. No" – he shook his head slowly – "no, Hannah, when you come to me for good, it won't be in this house. But don't worry, it'll be sooner than you think. Those two that have just gone, they've put me on to a good thing. You know I collect me ponies from here and there but they're getting hard to come by, for the farmers are nipping them up and think they have priority in supplying the mines. But Peter, Peter Turnbull, the tall fellow, he's just come back from Gearstones, driven a big herd back from there. He said they walked on their bones they were so lean, poor beggars, but he brought them for the Batemans' farm. There's plenty of good pasture down there and come Christmas he says Bateman will make a packet on them, but that apart, what he told me is that the Welshman brings ponies as far as there, and a fine, sturdy wild lot they are, and they go cheap because not only have they to be

229

broken in but to be herded to the place where they're going to be broken in, and it isn't everyone who can handle a string of mettlesome ponies like meself, I'm pleased to say." He grinned at her. "So a couple of trips down there and a little bit of hard work this end and come the end of the summer I should be well set; added to what I've got here."

He now dug her gently in the waist with his fist as he said, "Do you remember one particular night when I bragged about all the money that was stacked away here? Well, like all braggarts I stretched it a bit. But mind, there should have been a nice little pile, but the old 'un had gone through it. On what, God only knows. You see it was a kind of unwritten law that the bag behind the bricks belonged to the eldest till he went, and it wasn't anybody's business to nosey into what was there, an' I, like a damn fool, felt that the old 'un had been adding his bit to the pile. I remember me da saying that all told there should be nigh on a hundred, an' that was in his time. Anyway, when I rolled the stones away, like they did in the Bible, what did I find? Well, like them, nowt behind two of them – they'd all had their own hidey holes you see – and about thirty pounds in the last one. An' that was the lot."

"Thirty pounds." She shook her head slowly. "Well, that seems quite a bit of money."

"Aw, lass" – he patted her knee – "not when you're starting from scratch. But the house. Now if I could sell this, it would bring nigh on a hundred because there's two and a half acres of signed and sealed land around it."

"Wouldn't it be worth more than that if it was mining land, as you said?"

"Aw, Hannah" – he hung his head deeply on his chest now – "you mean all that spouting I did the day you found me raking?" He raised his eyes to her and, his expression sheepish, he muttered, "I was raking for flints, arrow-heads as they call them. There's lots to be found hereabouts, but if you come across good ones in good shape there are men who are interested in them an' will buy them off you. But mind" – he now wagged his finger at her – "it could just be possible that someone like Beaumont would buy this house and the land, and that's exactly what they'd do, they'd open a mine here. . . . Oh yes, aye, they would. But as for yours truly starting one, well, as you so wisely remarked that day, it takes a lot of money to dig out a lead mine."

"Hannah." He rose and pulled her to her feet and, his face quite straight now, he said, "If you take me on for good it'll be as a horse-dealer, because that's all I can do. At one time I had another string to me bow, I could box. . . . Now, now, now" – he held up his hand in warning – "if this hadn't happened" – he wagged the finger and thumb at her – "me boxing days would still have been over. It's a young man's sport. Bare knuckles are not enough, you want fleet feet and the stamina of a horse. But . . . but you know something, love? We're wasting time. Come on."

As he pulled her up to him he whispered, "The bed's warm. You know something else? I always stick the oven shelf in every Sunday dinner-time after I've cooked me meat, hoping . . . hoping."

Their heads drooped together for a moment, then they went out and up the ladder to the rooms above.

6

In April she suspected she was pregnant, but she wasn't sure for her cycle had always been erratic – and painful. Moreover, she had no one with whom she could discuss her condition.

The weather had gone mad again and continued in much the same fashion until the middle of May, and for most of the month Mrs Loam had been house-bound with a chest cold. But when Hannah began to feel sick on rising she knew she was carrying a child.

She had managed to keep her condition to herself by making for the closet first thing in the morning; that was until a certain Monday morning in the wash-house when the news was broken to her husband, but not by her.

She had risen at six o'clock and lit the fire under the wash-house pot and had a boiling of coarse sheets rinsed and mangled when a wave of nausea attacked her. She had thought she was over this stage for she hadn't felt sick for some time. But now as she stood leaning on the splash board of the wooden mangle a voice to the side of her said, "Well, you've managed it at last, have you? What you tryin' to hide, are you ashamed of it? But this I'll say, you've taken your time over it."

She stared at the old woman while her stomach heaved.

"Why haven't you told him? He's got a right to know, hasn't he?"

"I'll . . . I'll tell him when I think fit."

"Oh you will, madam, will you? By God!" – the little woman shook her head – "I've never met anybody like you in me life afore. You're not human. Here he's been waitin' for this to happen for two years now, and when it does you keep it to versel. An' I'd like to bet if I hadn't caught you spewing you wouldn't have mentioned a word of it until your belly gave you away."

When Mrs Loam turned about and left the wash-house, Hannah gripped the splash board and closed her eyes, and as she lowered her head deeply on to her chest she swore to herself that no matter what happened she wouldn't be here when the child was born. . . .

"Is it true then?"

She turned and looked at Fred. His big red face was aglow. He looked so pleased with himself that for a moment she felt pity for him.

"Why didn't you let on?" He was standing close to her now. "Eeh! you're a funny lass. But by! I'm glad. God, I thought it would never happen. I was beginnin' to worry; I thought perhaps I was no use." He pressed his lips together and grinned while he wagged his head from side to side as at an absurd notion; then he kicked out at the poss tub, took hold of the poss stick and banged it twice up and down on to the wet clothes, saying as he did so, "They were beginnin' to chaff me down at the pub. Well now, I've let them see, haven't I?" He turned his head towards her and stared at her for a moment before asking, "Why don't you say something? Aren't you glad?"

She could look him fully in the face as she answered, "Yes, I'm glad."

"Well then" – again his head was wagging – "we go on from here, don't we?" . . .

But that night he found to his amazement that they didn't go on from there, for when he went to put his arms about her she actually sprang out of bed and through the darkness she hissed at him, "I won't be touched, do you hear me? I won't be touched again until . . . until it's born?"

"What d'you mean . . . you won't be touched?"

She knew he was sitting up in the bed.

"Just what I said."

"Why" – there was utter bewilderment in his tone – " 'tis better for the bairn to have it, every fool knows that, helps feed it, it does, makes it healthy an' keeps it from catching things. An' if by what you say you're well gone so you've been touched."

"Well, I won't be any more. And . . . and if you insist I'll lie in the kitchen."

"God Almighty! there's months to go. Now look here, Hannah, I'm havin' none o'this. What do you take me for, a bloody mug?"

When his hand came on her she actually cried out and he let go of her as quickly as he had caught her, saying, "Shut up for Christ's sake! You'll have her in here in a minute."

"Well, leave me alone. It's been night after night, night after night, I can't bear any more. Now . . . now you should be satisfied I'm . . . I'm carrying a child."

There was silence in the darkness now, it was as if he was pondering her last remark.

When she heard him getting back into the bed she waited, her body stiff but shivering with the cold; then he spoke. "Aye well, we'll see about this. Get back into bed."

She still waited a moment before she moved; then when she finally lay down it was on the edge of the bed with her back to him and she let the bedclothes fall around her so that she wouldn't come in contact with him.

On the following Sunday she almost thought she would go mad when her mother-in-law was unable to go to chapel because of another stomach upset, and how she got through the following week she didn't know. When Sunday came round again she had to warn herself not to get agitated in case she should give herself away and one or other of them would suspect something.

When at last Mrs Loam, still muttering implications of what would eventually happen to her for not turning to God, left the house, and Fred, surly now, made for the inn, she could hardly make herself wait the required minutes before she flew out of the back door. At least she was flying inside, for she always made herself saunter until she was out of sight of the village.

The twilight was deepening when she reached the Pele house. But tonight Ned had no visitors and he was waiting for her outside the wall.

After their first embrace in the stable-room he muttered into her hair, "Where've you been all these years?" Then pressing her from him, he asked, "Did you pass John and Annie Beckett on your way over?" and she shook her head, saying, "You mean from next door? No, no; I didn't see them."

"They must have turned down towards the cemetery then, I felt sure you'd run into them if you were on your way."

"I could have," she laughed, "because I had my head down and I was running most of the time. But" – her face straightened – "why do you ask?"

"Aw, nothing, nothing; only this is the third time I've seen them pass the wall there in the last month. The first time I thought it was just a Sunday jaunt, now I'm not so sure . . . Does she speak to you?"

"Hardly ever. She nods at me sometimes when I'm down at the midden emptying the slops."

"My God!" He ground his teeth now. "When I hear that I feel like a bull looking at a red rag. Down at the midden emptying the slops. Why the hell can't he do that? How does he pass his time away, anyway? He rarely kills more than one beast a week; a few sheep perhaps, an' a pig or two. But what's that?"

"Never mind; come in here." It was she now who was leading him by the hand into the kitchen, and when she was standing in front of him and he was unloosening the neck of her cloak she said, "I have something to tell you, Ned Ridley. Oh" – she shook her head – "I don't know how I haven't shouted it across the hills. I nearly died when I couldn't get across last Sunday."

"Just as well you didn't, I was away; but come on, Hannah Boyle." He had never called her by her married name. "Don't keep me in suspense."

"Guess what?"

He screwed up his face and looked up towards the ceiling as he said, "Dame Thornton has come down and begged you to go back home."

"Huh! that'll be the day I'll never live to see. And it's odd you know, but I've never seen her once since I left the house . . . the church that day. But be serious, look at me."

He looked at her and said, "Well?"

She waited for a number of seconds before she said slowly,

and with emphasis on one word, "I'm going to have . . . *your* child."

For almost a minute he stared at her. His expression did not alter; then he said briefly, "Mine?"

"Yes, yours."

She watched now as his lips spread wide and his teeth clamped together; and then with his eyes closed tightly his arms shot out and about her and they swayed as one, and their laughter joined for a moment. Then he was holding her by the shoulders and looking into her face, his expression once more blank as he asked her, "How can you be sure?"

"I am. I can. The time, in February, and . . . oh" – she shook her head and turned it from him – "and other things that I can't explain. I only know, Ned, it's yours, ours."

"February? February? My God! then you're well on. Why didn't you say?"

"I . . . I wasn't sure. To tell the truth, I didn't know much about it. I . . . oh, I can't explain."

"Aw, Hannah! Hannah!" He took her face in his hands and moved it gently from side to side. Then drawing her to a chair, he knelt by her, and he said now, "Well, that puts the lid on it. I'll have to get cracking; I will that. It's a good job I've something in the offing. You know what I told you about the Welsh ponies? Well, I've been over to Gearstones; it's a trek and a half. Peter Turnbull and Arty Heslop, you know the two fellows you met in here, they were droving sheep back and so I went along with them, so I would know the way meself. And it's a good job I did for I'd never been along that trek afore. Anyway, I saw the fella and he's promised me a string, and another if I want them afore the bad weather sets in. Between trips I should have me hands full at breaking them in, at least manageable in a way, for by the sound of it some of them are imps of Satan. But also, by the sound of it, I should have a nice little packet at the end of the job. And I'll tell you something else I'm doing, I'm going over into Hexham the morrow to a property dealer there to ask him to come out here and tell me what I'll get for this."

She sat looking at him, her throat too full to speak, and he said softly, "Come on, love, don't cry; it's not a time for cryin',

it's a time for celebratin', for a drink. And you know something?"
He stood up. "I haven't a drop of hard in the house. Can you
imagine it? This is happening too often now, me without a drop
of hard in the house. Anyway, we'll have a sup tea, strong enough
to stand up by itself."

"I'll make it."

"You'll do no such thing." He turned and swept up a number
of loose sheets of paper from the table and as he went to put
them on the delf rack he looked at them, then said, "I mapped
out me way. Look at that; not bad for somebody who couldn't
stand schooling, is it?"

She took the three sheets of paper from him and looked at the
contours of the hills and paths he had sketched on them; then
glancing up at him, she said, "You drew all this?"

"Yes, who else?" He tossed his head in mock pride. "And
mind, it's some distance." He was now bending over her.
"Seventy-five miles or more."

"Seventy-five miles!" Her tone was awe filled.

"Yes, look there. I go to Allenheads, and on to Wearhead – see
that mark, that means I stop there the night; then the next day
I make for Langdon Common, and like Peter and Arty did, I'm
following the river Tees towards Newbiggin. And there's the
mark again. I kip there the second night. The next day – that's
over the page, look there – I go over Lunedale and Baldersdale
and by God's Bridge, and then if I'm lucky I reach the inn at
Tan Hill."

"Now on this page" – he had taken the third piece of paper
from her – "I go down to Stonesdale Moor and on to Thwaite,
through Buttertubs Pass on to Hawes. And you see there's the
mark again, I stop for the night. I could at a pinch, that is if I
gallop, go up Widdale Beck and right to Gearstones, but that's
another seven to eight miles, so I'll likely stop as I've said at
Hawes. Now what do you think about that for a journey?"

"Tremendous! And you're going to bring the ponies back all
that way?"

"Well, I'm not just going for the walk, love."

They laughed together now; then he said soberly, "It's a real
bonny trek, some wonderful scenes from the hills and the valleys,

237

but oh, lonely mind. Oh aye, I used to think there was no lonelier place in the world than that stretch between Whitfield and Alston, but some of the places on that route are lonelier still."

At the mention of Alston, she asked quietly, "Couldn't you buy as good bargains at the Alston Horse Fair?"

"No; there's too many at the same game round here, too many farmers with side-lines. Gearstones is a bit too far for them to trek, although there's nothin' to stop them paying a drover to do the work for 'em, as some of the bigger farmers do with their cattle. But sooner them than me 'cos I wouldn't trust any drover as far as I could toss him."

He turned swiftly to her again and, bending, he kissed her on the lips before saying, "I'll be back afore you've known I've gone. I hate to cause you worry but at the same time I like to know you're worrying over me."

She put her arms around his neck as she asked, "Where will we go when we leave here?"

"Any place in the world, but I've got a fancy to see the countryside that lies beyond London. That's where we'll go, beyond London."

She knew the geography of the land much better than Ned did, but at this moment the country beyond London appeared to her further away than America where Robert had gone, further away than Australia that was right below her feet at the other side of the world. It was another planet and no one would find them there. They would start life anew; she'd be Mrs Ridley, and her child would be called Ridley, and that would be his rightful name.

7

The child was heavy in her when Ned made his second trip to Gearstones. He had been gone almost three weeks now. She hadn't worried so much on the second Sunday when she found the Pele house door still barred, but on the third Sunday when she had to take shelter in the shippon doorway she felt sick with worry.

It had rained almost all the time he had been away. Last summer had been known as one of the driest in memory, this, one of the wettest. The crops were soggy and the corn impossible to dry. The roads were like quagmires, the air continually chill, and the houses damp.

Although she felt better in herself, her spirits were at a low ebb. She was now nearing her eighth month of carrying the child. Her duties in the house were no lighter; her mother-in-law frequently informing her that she herself had had to work up till the last minute, scrubbing, washing, and baking, and there had been no one to pamper her. But yesterday she had dared to turn on her and retaliate by saying that if what she had to do came under the heading of being pampered, then she wasn't likely ever to experience cruelty. Whereupon Mrs Loam had almost screamed at her, "Cruelty! What do you think you're doin' to my lad? He's told me of your capers. You should be horsewhipped. You know what I'm gona do? I'm gona bring the minister to you, an' if he doesn't shame you into doin' your duty nobody will. You know something? I can sympathize with her at the far end of the village now, by! I can that. What she must have had to put up with from you! It's a wonder she didn't throw you out years ago."

As Hannah now stood in the shippon doorway she wondered just how much longer she could put up with the repeat of yesterday. Women, she thought, were much more cruel than men; men could be brutal, physically brutal, but women seemed to have the knack of torturing you mentally. Mrs Thornton had never spoken to her directly in her life, and that had been a special kind of torture, whereas her mother-in-law never stopped talking at her, and that was another kind of torture; she didn't know which was the worse; perhaps the silence was more unbearable than the talking because with the latter you could always answer back.

It was getting dark, it was no use waiting. She drew in a long breath, then let it slowly out and murmured to herself, Oh Ned. Ned.

She now walked from the shelter of the doorway and across the yard, out through the opening in the stone walls and on to the hillside again. As she turned her head against the driving rain she saw a dim figure in the distance and stopped for a moment, hope rising in her. But then the figure was lost to her as it moved away in the opposite direction. Anyway, if it had been Ned he would have bounded towards her.

She slipped quietly into the back shop, took off her cloak, shook it vigorously to get the wet off it, saw that her clogs were clean by wiping them with some rags – her fine leather shoes were worn out – then as she went up the stairs she wiped her face and the front of her hair with her handkerchief.

It was when she opened the stairhead door that she came to a stiff halt for there, standing in the middle of the kitchen, was Mrs Loam.

"Well, well! so you've got back then?"

"I . . . I went for a walk." She went past her now towards the bedroom.

"In the rain?"

"In the rain."

As she went to hang her cape in the cupboard she heard the pounding on the stairs, and the sound made her heart jump and her body tremble with a new kind of fear. It was as if she already knew what was about to happen. In a way she had been expecting it; and suddenly she was sorry for Fred for he wasn't really to blame for what had happened; they were both victims. To someone else he would have been a good husband. He would have been so to her if she had been able to love him; and perhaps without his mother that might have come about. . . . No! She glanced towards the bed, and the memory of the nights that seemed to stretch back into eternity echoed loudly, No! No! Never!

Shaking from head to foot, she turned about and went to face what was coming.

When she re-entered the kitchen he was standing near the table. His face had lost every hue of its ruddy complexion and looked livid. He kept his eyes fastened tight on her while he spoke to his mother. "You were right then, Ma. An' to think I nearly knocked Arty Heslop's teeth down his bloody neck. . . . That's what they've been sniggerin' at for weeks. 'Have a pint, Fred. How's your wife, Fred? . . . Hear you're goin' to be a dada, Fred. Well, better late than never. . . . Reckon you managed it on your own, Fred?' . . .

"By God! do you know what I could do to you?" He was advancing on her. "I could pull your entrails out, you dirty little whorin' bastard you!"

As his hand came up she heard her mother-in-law cry, "Them next door knew about it all the time. Soon as we were out of the house she skitted across, Sunday after Sunday. . . . Shameless bitch!"

When the flat of his hand landed full across the side of her face her feet left the floor and she seemed to remain horizontal for a moment before falling by the side of the steel fender.

If he had struck her with his doubled fist it would surely have killed her, because his hand that wielded the hammer on the beasts was like an iron club in itself.

"Oh my God! you've done for her." Daisy Loam straightened the prostrate form out; then, her fear-filled face turned up to her son, she said again, "You've done for her, and the bairn."

He stood above them trembling, his face working as if with ague; and now he started to mutter like someone demented: "She asked for it. They won't do anythin' to me, she asked for it. Unfaithful wife, that's what she was. I'll tell them. . . ."

"Shut up! Bring that dish of water." She thrust her arm out towards the side table.

Even when he brought the water and handed it down to her he was still muttering, "They can't do anything to me. She fell, that's what happened, she fell."

"Don't be so bloody gormless, her face 'll be black and blue in any case by mornin', and Arnison's only got to see that, then he'll have your neck. He's never had any time for either of us."

After having splashed handfuls of water on to Hannah's face with no response, she cried, "Get her up out of this!"

When he had lifted Hannah up and carried her into the bedroom and laid her on the bed, he turned to his mother, and like a child now said, "Do somethin', can't you?"

Pushing him aside she did something. She laid her ear to Hannah's breast, then stood up, and her small frame seemed to expand with relief, then as she let the air out of her body she muttered, "She's breathin'."

They stood looking at each other for a moment. But then, the colour rushing back into his face, he shouted at her, "You're to blame for this, you've driven her to it. An' you've always been at me to belt her." But before he could get any further she interrupted his tirade with equal fury, crying, "Get out of me sight, you great soft lout! It's a pity you hadn't finished her off; you might have died like a man at the end of a rope then." Whereupon, his whole body jangling as if on strings, he went towards the door, spluttering, "You! You! you're a bitch of a woman. That's what you are, Ma, a bitch of a woman, an' if anything happens me bairn. . . ."

"Whose bairn?"

"What?" He turned in the doorway, and she repeated slowly, "Whose bairn? That's what I said, whose bairn?"

8

～❧～

he was three days in bed. One side of her face was swollen to
almost twice its size and from her brow to her chin the skin was a
purplish blue; added to this, she had a pain in her side where it had
struck the end of the fender. She ate nothing for two days but she
drank the cups of tea that her mother-in-law brought in and
silently placed on the little table beside the bed.

Mrs Loam had spoken to her only once, and that was when she
had first come round. It was then she had said, "You've got
nobody to blame but yourself, you've asked for it."

For the three days she had been in bed she hadn't seen Fred – he
must have slept on the couch in the kitchen – but when at last she
got up he was waiting for her.

It was as if he had never moved from the spot where she had
last seen him standing, and he repeated almost word for word
what his mother had said. His head wagging, he muttered, "You
asked for it, you can't say you didn't. You've only yourself to
blame. Anyway, I'll say to you now, I'm willin' to let bygones be
bygones if you'll tell me you'll not go up there any more."

She stared at him, her eyes unblinking, her lips set tight.

"Well?"

She didn't speak.

"I've asked you a civil question an' I want a civil answer."

Still she didn't speak, and, his head wagging even more widely
now, he blustered, "Well, if that's your attitude 'tis all right with
me, but . . . but I'll see to it you take no more trips alone, by God!
I will, if I've got to chain you up." . . .

And in the days that followed Hannah felt that that's what he
had done, chained her up, because never for a moment was she
alone.

Then there came the Allendale Town market-day when she was forced to accompany him to the town.

It should happen that Mrs Loam was troubled with a loose bowel that made her so weak she had taken to her bed, and she had said to her son, "I can't see to her, you'll have to take her along of you." So that is what he did. Sitting beside him on the high seat of the wooden cart, she went into Allendale.

The journey wasn't made in complete silence for every now and again Fred would make a remark such as, "Nice bloody state of affairs." "Might as well be married to a deaf-and-dumb mute." "Don't think you can carry on like this 'cos I won't put up with it making a bloody fool out of me, that's what you're doin', laughing stock. Well, the next one that laughs at me he'll go home without any bloody teeth, an' I'm tellin' you."

Though the market square seemed to be full of people, it wasn't, as many remarked, so full as in other years. A newfangled railway was having an effect; people were now carrying their wares far and wide. Things were changing. Why, forty years ago there were a thousand people living in the town and now there was less than half that number. Yet the King's Head and the Golden Lion, the Temperance Hotel and the six inns still did a roaring trade on days such as these. Better, some of the hard cases laughed, than the Wesleyan and Primitive Methodist chapels did on a Sunday, not forgetting the Quakers.

But the town was too full for Fred; he couldn't see everybody at once, and he was on the look out for one particular man, yet at the same time hoping he didn't come across him, for Ned Ridley might have only one and a half hands but he would still know how to use them; he hadn't been a boxer for nothing. Not that he himself couldn't hold his own. No, by God! no, as anybody who had seen him fell a beast knew. And on this thought he pushed his shoulders back and thrust out his chest and looked about him; then put his hand quickly to his stomach.

Now what was he going to do? He had caught his mother's damn trouble. He had gone just before he came out, and now he'd have to go through one of the pubs and into the back. Since they had been stopped using the open middens it meant that a man had almost to pay for going to the netty.

"Hannah."

He turned quickly to see the speaker standing in the middle of he pathway.

"Oh, Margaret. Oh, Margaret. Oh, it is good to see you."

"And you. And you."

They were clasping hands tightly.

"What are you doing here, visiting?"

Margaret shook her head. "No; I've been to say good-bye to ohn. . . ."

Before Hannah could enquire further Fred was speaking. Look," he said; "I've got to go over there." He pointed to the n. "I won't be more than five or ten minutes." He stared at her. Not more mind. You can go in there till I come back." He ointed to the hotel behind them. "You can get some tea up in the eneral room, or something." He now turned to Margaret and dded, "You stay along of her, won't you, Miss Margaret?"

Margaret looked questioningly at Fred, then said, "Yes, yes, of ourse, Fred." But Fred had already turned and almost at a run vas making his way through the crowd towards the low-fronted n across the square, and now she turned to Hannah, saying, Shall we go into the coffee room?"

"I . . . I haven't any money, Margaret."

"Oh, well, I have enough."

They said no more until they were seated side by side on the vooden settle in the corner of the large room, and after Margaret ad given an order for coffee and had added, "No thank you, othing else," she looked hard at Hannah before saying, "You've ad a fall?"

"Yes, I had a fall, Margaret."

As their gaze held Margaret muttered, "Oh, I'm sorry, Iannah," and to this Hannah replied, "Well, I suppose some vould say he was within his rights. You see I've . . . I've been eeing Ned."

"Ned? You mean Ned Ridley?"

"Yes, Ned Ridley."

Margaret now shook her head slightly before going on, "You mean you've been seeing him for . . .?"

"Yes, Margaret, for other purposes than friendship. You see I

found out too late that I loved Ned; it's he I should have marrie
I think I would have if he had been there at the time your moth
made other arrangements for me."

"Oh, Hannah!" Margaret's hand came across the table an
clasped Hannah's wrist; then slowly and sadly she said, "What
mess she's made of our lives! More so in your case; in mine, I ha
a choice, but it was the wrong choice."

"What happened?"

"Oh." Margaret now brought her two hands together; he
fingers touching, she made as if to clap them. "I thought he wa
attracted to me, but apparently it was my supposed position. H
saw me as the daughter of a man who could afford to send me to
private school, and so, therefore, there must be money in th
family. And, of course, the house was another proof that we wer
if not wealthy, then very comfortably off, and that my fathe
would surely do something for his eldest daughter's husband. A
least that's how I reasoned it out. There was no other explanatio
for his polite note and his scampering from the town."

"Oh, I'm so sorry, Margaret."

When Margaret made no answer but continued to sip her coffe
Hannah asked, "What are you doing now?"

"The same as I did when I first went back to the school; but jus
as then I still receive no wage. I think sometimes I might as we
be in a convent; at least there I would be given a free habit." Sh
smiled wryly, and with a touch of bitterness she added, "It's . .
it's disquietening to say the least, how people can change toward
you when they know you are dependent on them."

"You mean Miss Barrington?"

"Yes, and Miss Rowntree. Miss Emily tries to remain the same
but she finds it difficult for she has to do the housekeeping. You
see I must eat, and also the room I occupy is depriving them o
another pupil; as you remember, the house wasn't large."

Hannah found her throat so full that she couldn't make an
comment. She had considered her own life hard, and even unbear
able, but at the back of it she had the love of Ned; apparentl
Margaret had no one.

"It's all right. It's all right." Margaret was holding her hand
again. "I'm on the look-out for a situation as a governess." Sh

gave a slight laugh now. "I went to an agency two months ago
thinking they would jump at me. Dear, dear!" She shook her
head. "I never realized there were so many emancipated young
women looking for employment. The agent's book was full of
young ladies offering themselves as governesses and companions,
even as lady-housekeepers. But something is bound to come along
soon. Anyway, let me tell you about John."

"Oh yes . . . John. You said you had come to say good-bye to
him?"

"Yes; he and Pansy are leaving on Monday for America; they
are joining Robert."

"No!"

"Yes." Margaret's head moved deeply up and down. "Now
would you believe that?"

"But why?"

"Oh, for many reasons, but mainly because, I think, Mrs
Everton is a replica of Mama; she still treats her daughter as if
she were a child and not a married woman, and Pansy is a very
high-spirited girl. Moreover, I think Mr Everton found John
rather slow. He considered he must have very little initiative or
he would have risen higher in the mining industry. Moreover,
John was expected to help on the farm . . . in a gentlemanly way
of course." She pulled a face now at Hannah. "But at every spare
moment. Anyway, apparently Robert sent glowing reports of his
life on this cattle ranch and I understand him to have said if a
man is willing to work and a woman willing to help there are
fortunes to be made; whether that be true or not, John grasped
at it as a chance to get away, and Pansy backed him, and so they
leave on Monday. John wrote and asked me to come for a few
days and, to be truthful, I was glad of the invitation, but after
only three days in the house I was equally glad to take my leave.
. . . It's odd" – she shook her head sadly now – "I shan't miss
John like I did Robert. Robert was the only one I really cared for.
And you, of course; and you, Hannah. Yes, I cared for you. And
I miss you. Oh, don't cry, dear, don't cry." But even as she
appealed to Hannah there were tears in her own voice. "I . . . I
suppose," she said now, "you know that Mama has sold the
house?"

Hannah's eyes widened as she shook her head.

"Oh, yes. Yes; and I understand they'll be moving any time now. They've taken a little place in Corbridge, very small by what John says, but Mama will be near her cousin. She is to act as companion to her. She lost her husband lately, I mean Mama's cousin did." She gave a short laugh now as she added, "I don't envy Mama her new position; Aunty Riverdale, as we called her, was a martinet at the best of times. I've only met her on three occasions. She never visited us, our station was much too lowly." Again she pulled a face.

"Tessie and Bella and . . . and Dandy, what are they going to do?"

"Oh, Dandy went a long time ago; and she was able to keep Bella and Tessie on only because of Aunty Riverdale. Now they will likely come to the hirings here" – she motioned her hand towards the window and the town square – "and be bonded to someone, a farmhouse likely . . . I hope they don't get separated. Bella looks upon Tessie as a daughter and Tessie sees Bella as her mother, they've been so long together. The trouble is Bella is getting on in years and won't be everybody's choice. It's a sad state of affairs. I'm glad to say Dandy found work on a farm." She again sipped from her cup, then said, "You haven't drunk your coffee, Hannah."

"Oh! Oh no." Hannah took two sips from the now almost cold liquid, then said, "Will you write to me, Margaret?"

"Yes, yes, of course."

"I . . . I don't mean just now and again but . . . but every week?"

"Yes; yes, I will. In future I'll write to you every week. I promise."

"I . . . I want to know what's happening to you."

"I'll let you know, dear, don't worry. Anyway, I don't want you to be concerned over me, you have enough to contend with by all accounts, and I feel guilty at times about my share in it."

They stared at each other hard for a moment, then simultaneously rose and went from the room.

Fred was outside waiting and, looking at Margaret, he said abruptly, "If you're going by carrier into Hexham you'd better look slippy, he's ready."

"Oh!" Margaret looked quickly across the square, then said, "Oh yes, yes. Well, good-bye, dear." She bent forward and kissed Hannah on the cheek, and Hannah held her tightly for a moment, then watched her hurrying towards the carrier cart, the hem of her serge skirt dusting the ground. She looked shabby, lost somehow, and no longer a girl, not even a young woman.

"Let's get a move on."

She turned and went with him, not by his side but by choice a step behind him; yet to those who saw them together it appeared that Fred Loam couldn't after all be all wind and watter for he had mastered his wife – as was evident by her face – and so much so that he had put her in her place and made her tail behind him.

They were about half-way home, just rounding the bend where the burn ran below a steep bank to the left side of them. Hannah had her head down. She was lost in thoughts of Margaret and John and Robert and herself and what had happened to them all in the past two years, when out of the bushes at the near side of the road a man stepped, grabbed the horse's bridle rein, and pulled the animal to a stop.

When Hannah saw who the intruder was, her heart seemed to stop within her breast. She put her hand over her mouth, and when the long stick came up towards her, its end like a shepherd's crook, and with an expert twist flicked her hood from her head she looked down into Ned's face and whimpered, "No! no! don't. Please, please Ned, go away."

"What the hell do you think you're up to?"

Ned looked at the blustering countenance on the far side of Hannah, then said quietly, "I heard you had marked her. Get down!" At this he walked round the back of the cart and to the other side, and Fred, who had made no move as yet, now yelled at him, "Aye, I'll get down, and you'll be sorry for it."

"No, no, please!" When Hannah grabbed with both hands at Fred's arm, he thrust her back with such force that he almost toppled her from the cart; and then he was facing Ned, in the stance of a boxer.

Ned was standing apparently at ease with his arms hanging by his sides and his voice sounded quite ordinary as he said, "Before I give it you, I want you to know she's mine, an' she always has been, and she'll continue to be."

It seemed that even before he finished the last word his right fist shot out and into Fred's stomach, and as the blow brought Fred bending forward he caught another blow under the chin, this time from the half hand, and although the second blow hadn't the force of the first it was still enough to bring Fred momentarily to his knees.

Ned looked down at Fred for a moment, dusted the palms of his hands together as if knocking dirt off them, then, turning his back on Fred he went to the cart and, swinging his arm up to the seat he said, "Come on, get down out of that, you're going home."

It was at the moment that she put her hand out towards him that she also let out a shrill cry, for Fred, his animal stamina coming to the fore, had risen drunkenly to his feet, and Ned although warned by Hannah's cry, turned swiftly but too late, and then it was he who was doubled up and in agony as the toe of Fred's heavy boot caught him full in the groin. Perhaps it was the sight of Ned writhing on the ground that turned Fred into a madman for the moment, because now he started to kick him all over his body and was only brought to a shuddering stop when Hannah threw herself on top of Ned, for the next blow from his foot would have contacted her.

Like an enraged giant he stood over them, his face crimson, the sweat running down it dripping from his chin, his saliva running from his mouth in long driblets. Then uttering unintelligible sounds, he bent over them and swung her upwards by one shoulder, before using his foot again to thrust the prostrate form off the road and down the bank towards the stream.

She struggled and screamed at him, "No! No! he'll die. You devil you! He'll die; you can't leave him there. I'll see you hang! Yes I will! I will! . . . Oh, don't leave him there. Oh!"

She was blinded now with her crying and weak from her struggling when, gripping her with both hands, he growled, "Get . . . up . . . there! An' you'll not live to see me hang. By God! I'll swear on that. No, you'll not live to see me hang."

Gripping the reins in one hand, he held on to her with the other; then yelling at the horse, he drove it forward, almost at a gallop.

Having no stable of their own, he rented space for the horse and cart from Ralph Buckman, the blacksmith, and it was his usual procedure, except when there was a dead beast in the cart, to drive straight to the stables behind the smithy, see to the horse, then carry his purchases home; or, if his mother was with him, send her on ahead. But today, as when he was carrying a beast, he drove the cart around the back lane that was thick with glar; then, pulling Hannah from the seat, he thrust her up the yard, through the back shop and to the foot of the stairs, and there he yelled, "Ma!"

After calling three times and receiving no response he pushed Hannah before him up the stairs and towards his mother's bedroom.

When he thrust her door open she was leaning on her elbow in bed and, her voice weak for her, she said, "What's up with you? I'm bad; I've never been off the pot since you left."

"Sick or no sick, keep your eye on her, and she'll tell you what's up. Anyway, I've put her fancy man out of action for a bit. I'm away to see to the horse."

He was about to close the door when he thrust his head in again and, looking at his mother, said fiercely, "Whatever you have, you've given it to me."

When the door banged closed, Mrs Loam lay back on her pillows in the big box bed and gasped, "What 've you caused now, girl? Trouble is your shadow. . . . Oh my God!" She now turned on her side, her body almost doubled, and Hannah, swaying on her feet, stood watching her, not moving either towards her or away from her. She herself was feeling sick and ill, her mind was in a turmoil, her only clear thought was she must get help for Ned. If he lay there in the stream he could be dead by morning; if he wasn't already gone.

"Get me a drink, girl. Get me a drink. . . . Don't stand there! Do you hear? Get me a drink."

As if in a nightmare, Hannah turned slowly about, went into the kitchen and to the pail that stood on a side table under the window and there ladled a tin mug full of water, then took it into the bedroom and handed it to her mother-in-law.

When Mrs Loam had drunk the water she lay back and, her head tossing from side to side on the pillow, she muttered, "He'll have to get me the doctor. I should have had him a week gone when it first started. I've caught a fever, I know I have."

As Hannah turned towards the door, Mrs Loam cried, "Don't go, girl. Don't go, I need you. The pot's full; empty it." Then in her next gasping breath, she said, "No, no, don't. Wait till he comes back. He's mad, I can see that, never seen him like that afore. Oh you! the things you bring on folk, girl."

Hannah sat slowly down on the wooden chair near the door. She was being called *Girl* again. She had been knocked into a woman, but it was strange, those who hated her never allowed her to lose her youth, it was always *The Girl* or merely *Girl*. At times she forgot she had a name, except when she was with Ned.

Ned. Ned. She must get to Ned, or get someone to go to him. Who? The doctor? Yes, the doctor. Her brain began to work. Mrs Tyler across the green, her baby was due. Ma Fletcher had gone over this morning, she had seen her; that meant it was near; and although Ma Fletcher would bring the baby, the doctor would look in once. Had he been today?

She heard herself speaking across the room to the hated woman on the bed. "Mrs Tyler's baby's due; the doctor may be calling on her."

It seemed a long moment before Mrs Loam answered her. Then she said, "You've said something useful at last."

After that there was silence between them until Fred entered the room; then without giving him the chance to speak, his mother cried, "Go across the way to Tyler's; she's due, the doctor mayn't have been yet. If not, tell them to tell him to come across. I'm poorly. Oh, I'm poorly."

"An' you're not the only one." Then as he turned to go, she cried after him, "She can't sit in here all day an' I want the pot emptied."

"Well, that'll have to wait till I get back; I'm lockin' the doors. An' you" – he stabbed his finger down at Hannah – "if you don't want murder done an' you know what's good for you, you'll stay put."

Silently she looked back at him, staring him out; then, his head wagging like that of a bull about to charge, he turned on his heel and went out.

The shop door banged and she rose from the chair, went out of the room, across the kitchen and into her own bedroom. There she took off her cloak and, sitting on the edge of the bed, her hands gripped tightly on her bulging stomach, she rocked herself as she planned what she would do if the doctor didn't call tonight. She'd open her mother-in-law's bedroom window that faced the square and scream out to anybody who was passing to go to the burn bend because Ned Ridley was lying there, perhaps dead; and somebody would go, if only out of curiosity.

What the result of her action would be she didn't care, she had gone through so much of late that of a sudden she wished for an end to it all. And if Ned died, as well he could, well, the sooner she went the better.

Doctor Arnison came at seven o'clock. When he examined Mrs Loam he found her stomach tender to pressure and rose-coloured spots on her abdomen, chest, and back; but it was her stools that confirmed his diagnosis. Mrs Loam had typhoid fever and she must have had it for a week or more.

The doctor coming out of the bedroom, put his black bag on the table, looked straight at Fred, who was standing with his back to the fire, and said abruptly, "How's your bowels, are you costive or the other way?"

"Costive? No, I wish to God I was, doctor; I've nearly been run off me legs this last few days, just like her."

"Well, I'm sorry to hear that. How you feeling otherwise?"

"Bit hot at times, headaches, a bit off me food an' all; but then I've had plenty to knock me off me food, doctor." He now glanced towards Hannah where she was standing at the far side of the table.

"Well, Fred, I'm sorry to hear this because I'm afraid you're in for what your mother's got."

"And what's that?"

There was a long pause before the doctor said, "Typhoid. Typhoid fever."

Hannah now looked from the doctor to Fred and she saw his high colour slowly seep from his face, and from the blustering figure of a man he seemed to change almost instantly into a frightened boy.

"Ty . . . typhoid? God! how . . . how did we get that? Is it about? I've never been further than the town. Never heard nobody's got it."

"Well, it isn't a thing that people notify the crier about, not in the beginning at any rate. But I've had three cases already this week, and for your information, Fred, I'll tell you you don't have to go any further than that." He now turned and pointed to the bucket standing on the table.

"The watter?"

"Aye, the water. . . . Where do you get it from?"

"She draws it mostly." He now jerked his head towards Hannah, then demanded, "Where did you get it from?"

Hannah looked at the doctor as she said quietly, "I always put the bucket under the ripple that comes out of the bank, never into the stream."

"Well, the ripple is usually clean, but it's the water or the milk."

"Milk?" Fred's face was screwed up now.

"Yes, milk. It's been discovered of late that that's how you catch typhoid. Dirty water and milk. The water is polluted, the cows drink the water, you drink the milk. There you have it. In future' – he now looked at Hannah – "boil every drop of water you bring into the house. The same with the milk." He pulled at his beard as he said musingly, "It's a pity about the milk, I like milk."

"God! what's going to happen to us?"

"Nothing much if you take care. Go to bed and stay there. I'll call in tomorrow. In the meantime I promise you you won't feel hungry. Sip the boiled water or the boiled milk, keep warm and quiet and you'll get through it."

Fred stared at the doctor as he went past him towards the door. For the moment he seemed to be bereft of speech, until Hannah said, "I'll see you out, doctor." Then coming to life, and his fear damped down for a moment, Fred said, "No, you won't! Oh no, you won't! I'll see the doctor out."

"Doctor!" The note in Hannah's voice brought the doctor around to her and he said quietly, "Yes? What is it, Hannah? You're all right?"

"I haven't got the fever, doctor, but I'm in great fear." She now cast a hard glance towards Fred, then rushed on, "I'm in fear for Ned, Ned Ridley. He's lying down by the burn bend, at least he was at four o'clock this afternoon. He may be still there for the grass is high near the water and you could pass by without seeing him. . . ."

The doctor now turned from her and looked at Fred, saying slowly, "You and Ned had a fight?"

"That's about it, doctor. He set on me, stopped the horse, and when I got down he set on me."

"He . . . he just hit you with his hands." Hannah was bending towards him now, her chin thrust out. "But you kicked him. You not only kicked him to the ground but you kicked and kicked and kicked him when he was lying there. Like a madman you were. And when he was lifeless you kicked him over the edge." Her voice and her whole body trembling, she now turned to the doctor, crying, "If he's dead, doctor, he's been murdered."

The doctor's face was very straight as he looked from one to the other; then his gaze resting on Fred, he said, "Well, I hope for your sake, Fred, that he's not dead, because if he is it would be senseless getting over the fever." And on this he turned, saying, "I can let myself out."

They were left alone in the kitchen staring at each other, and Fred put his hand to his neck cloth and pulled it loose, then loosened the top button of his striped shirt before saying, "You want to see me dead, don't you? Well, let me tell you I won't go alone. You can rely on that. I won't go alone because this I swear on, he'll never get you, you're me wife an' me wife you'll stay."

He went to move across the room towards his mother's bedroom but, with his hand going quickly to his stomach, he turned and ran down the stairs. . . .

Typhoid fever. People died with typhoid fever. Well, an old

woman like his mother might die but he wouldn't, he was too strong. He bragged about having a constitution like a horse and that constitution would see him through. But once they were both in bed, too sick to move, they'd be unable to stop her leaving. And if anything fatal happened to Ned, nothing would stop her from flying from this house. She wouldn't let either pity or compassion turn her, she would get away. Where she would go to she didn't know, and it wouldn't matter, but she'd go . . . run . . . fly. She had to put her hand over her mouth to stop herself from screaming.

The doctor came the next morning and, finding Fred standing stoically in the shop, he said to him, "All right, if you want to die, you stay there. And as for selling that meat that you're cutting up, I can't allow that. The very fact that you've handled it could contaminate the whole village."

"What am I to do with it then?"

"Burn it. Bury it. But what you've got to do with yourself is get upstairs and into bed. . . . Man, don't be so stupid!" He pushed him towards the stairway. "You're dropping on your feet."

"How long will I have to stay in bed?"

"That depends on you, and how quickly you let yourself get over it."

Up in the kitchen Fred turned to the doctor while he pointed backwards towards Hannah washing up crocks at the side table, and said bitterly, "If I take to me bed, she'll walk out."

"No, she won't; she's your wife and she's not inhuman, even if you are, so go on, get in there and get your things off, and let me have a look at you."

Fred now almost staggered towards the bedroom door, and when it closed behind him Hannah turned swiftly from the table and, coming to the doctor, she whispered, "Have . . . have you any news of Ned?"

"No." He shook his head. "I went down to the burn bend straightaway. There was no sign of him there. I even went back to the Pele house. That was all locked up. I then enquired in the town thinking he might have staggered back there. But don't worry" – he put his hand on her arm – "someone must have picked him up. I'll enquire on my rounds."

As she drooped her head forward on to her chest, he said, "Now look, Hannah, you've got enough to worry about here; they're two very sick people."

She was looking at him again and, her voice slow and bitter, she said, "I don't care how sick they are, doctor, I don't care if they die."

"Hannah!" He sounded shocked.

"I mean it, doctor. You don't know what I've gone through these past two years, no one does. That woman is a fiend."

"Well –" He turned and opened his bag and made a sound like a small laugh before he said, "I was well aware of that long before you, Hannah; but now you must show your Christian spirit. That's what the good book tells us we must do." He cast a quizzical glance at her. "But I'm going to tell you something in confidence." He pushed his head close to hers. "I myself find it very hard to follow it at times" – his head jerked upwards now – "we must make the effort, we must try, especially at times like this. Now, do your best, Hannah. Whatever you decide to do afterwards, when they're on their feet again, is up to you. But the first thing you must do now is to stick a notice on the door saying shop closed. Anyway, I don't suppose there'll be many customers come near here for some time; the fever scares them as bad as the cholera."

As he went towards the bedroom, he said, "Let everything slide except what is necessary, and you'll have your work cut out doing that. See the pots are emptied often and rinse your hands afterwards. Yes, see to that. Don't let any of the stools get on your hands because that way you can catch it. I mean it might infect your food, or the milk, or anything. Oh yes, and the milk and water. It's important that every drop be boiled. Now don't forget." . . .

As if she could forget. All day long she went silently between the two rooms, her face stiff. She emptied their chambers, she placed glasses of boiled water to their hands on the bedside tables and she even swabbed their sweating faces with cold water, while her whole body recoiled whenever she touched them.

She was exhausted long before the twilight set in and as she took the last pail of the day and emptied it into the stream the stench made her want to vomit; the smell inside the house was unbearable but there seemed to be no getting away from it outside either.

No one had been near her all day. The village seemed quiet, it was as if everyone had deserted it; and there had been no banging on the shop door, the reason for the notice being now well known.

During the last twenty-four hours the child seemed to have grown inside her, so heavy had her body become.

When she re-entered the back shop, the sight of the great collops of meat turned her stomach and she had to turn and run quickly into the yard and there, standing with her hand against the house wall, she retched.

After a few moments she straightened up and wiped her mouth. She couldn't go on, it was too much to expect of any human being, she just couldn't go on.

As she was going through the back shop again she was startled out of her weariness by a sharp rapping on the shop door, and when she opened it there stood the doctor.

She had hardly closed the door when she muttered, "You . . . you've found him?"

"Yes, yes; I've found him. Now it's all right. It's all right. Come and sit down." He looked round for a chair but there were none in the shop; and so he pushed her through into the back place, and she sat down on the box set against the wall. He looked round the room, saw another box, pulled it swiftly towards him, then sitting down opposite her, he said, "You look exhausted, but if it's any comfort I can tell you you're not the only one; this thing's spreading."

She was staring at him as she said quietly, "Ned?"

"He's at the Dickinsons'. They live quite some way out on The Bottoms."

"He's . . . he's all right?"

He paused a moment before he answered, "No, no; I'm afraid he's not all right, he's far from all right."

She went to rise from the box. "He's not going to . . .?" She couldn't bring herself to say the word, and as he pressed her down again, he said, "Now don't get hysterical. I don't know whether he's going to die or not, but if he doesn't it's because of two things: his strong constitution and Nell Dickinson." He shook his head slowly. "It's a long time since I've seen a man so badly handled, and as you so rightly said if he had been left out all night he certainly would have been found dead. It should happen that young Dickinson saw the whole thing. He was along in the brushwood hiding. He didn't say why he was hiding, and I didn't enquire because he's second to none at poaching, and that's taking account of his father Big Dick an' all. Anyway, the lad tells me he ran hell for leather over the hills and brought his mother and one of the other lads, and Nell Dickinson sent the lads post haste into the town to find his father; it being Friday and the day of the pays she knew exactly which inn he'd be drinking at. To cut a long story short, between them they carried Ned back over the hills to the house, and I'm telling you, Hannah, that must have taken some doing for it was all of two miles and no easy going, and although they're a big couple, Ned is no light weight. Anyway, the next thing they did was to send word for me and I got the message when I arrived home late last night. It just said would I call round at the Dickinsons', so I put them on my list for today. What with all the calls I didn't get there until late afternoon. I tell you, Hannah, I was shocked at the sight of Ned. And I must also tell you something else. It doesn't matter whether he lives or dies, the matter won't rest there, for Big Dick was so incensed he goes off into the town this morning and brings the constable. So it's now turned into a case, and the constable would have been here before now confronting Fred with what he's done but for the fact that it's known the two of them" – he jerked his head towards the ceiling – "are down with the fever. But come he will, and that's certain. And if anything should happen to Ned, well, it's going to be a poor look-out for Fred. Even if he survives, Fred could go along the line because if there was ever a case explained by the term 'assault and battery' Ned is it."

They were peering at each other in the dimness and the doctor, now putting his head on one side, said, "It's strange, Hannah, how you seem to court disaster wherever you go. . . . Unwittingly you seem to breed trouble wherever your feet tread. No, no" –

he put his hand on her knee – "don't take it to yourself, I'm not meaning it as a criticism, just trying to work out why beauty must always pay the price of beauty. 'Tis no fault of yours, my dear, you're just fated. From time to time there's women put into the world like you who have the power to drive men crazy. 'Tisn't only how you look." He shrugged now, his hands going out wide. "I don't know what it is. The gods must laugh anyway when they dole it out." He sighed, then ended, "I don't know where it's all going to end, my dear."

She swallowed deeply, pressed her lips together, blinked the tears back from her eyes and said soberly, "I do, doctor. When Ned gets better . . . and he must get better, we're going away. We had it all planned. He was to bring the second string of horses over from Yorkshire and then we'd have enough money to start somewhere else, even if he didn't sell the house."

He nodded at her as he rose from the box, saying quietly now, "Well, who's to blame you? Who's to blame you? But in the meantime" – he put out his hand and touched her shoulder – "do what you can for those two. They don't deserve it, neither of them, yet I must say if we all got our deserts many of us would be lying naked on the fells." He smiled wearily now as he ended, "I'll look in on them, then make for home; I've had a long, hard day."

"I'm sorry, doctor."

"Well then, we're both sorry for each other, and we're both very tired, so after I'm gone get yourself bedded down. By the way" – he turned in the doorway – "talking about bedding. The sheets you take off the bed you'll put straight into the pot and boil, won't you?"

She nodded slowly before she answered, "Yes, doctor, yes."

Alone in the room, she joined her hands together, then turned and pressed them against the rough stone wall, and leaning her brow on them she prayed, "Oh God, I'm sorry I bring trouble on people. I don't mean to, you know that, you know that. And don't punish me by taking Ned. Keep him safe, that's all I ask. That's all I'll ever ask, just keep him safe."

9

Hannah felt that her mind had ceased to function. For fourteen days now she had worked like a machine. She carried slops down the stairs, brought water up, boiled it, carried it into the bedrooms, took more slops down the stairs, brought more water up. In between times she changed the sheets on the beds. This she found to be the worst task of all because she had to touch their bodies. She'd take the linen downstairs, put it into the boiling wash pot, which she kept going day and night, rinse, and mangle the bedding, nightshirts, and nightgowns, dry them if it were possible outside, then hang them round the kitchen to air. Some days this process had to be gone through twice.

But for the fact that the doctor brought her daily news of Ned she would, she knew, going by the dictates of her body, have given up; she would not, however, have walked out, she was too weary for that now. She would have just lain down on the pallet of clean straw she had placed on top of the horsehair sofa and let sleep and the desire for death have their way. But there was Ned, there was still Ned, and he was recovering; at least the doctor said they could count him out of danger now, but it would be some time before he'd be on his feet.

It was on Wednesday, the twelfth day, that she noticed a change in Fred. Whereas she knew that all along he had been aware of her and her ministrations, now he began to be mentally confused and to take her for his mother or his Aunt Connie. She had met his Aunt Connie only three times. She lived on the far side of Allendale Town and ran a wayside inn. She was Mrs Loam's sister but appeared totally unlike her in temperament, being big-made and jolly.

Besides going into delirium, he had bled twice during the day from the nose and had brought himself up in bed groaning and holding his stomach as if he were experiencing intense pain.

Once when he called out, she was in Mrs Loam's room, and that lady asked querulously, "What's up with him?"

"He seems in pain."

"Well, I'm in pain an' all; he's not the only one. But what's he yelling like that for?"

"I think his fever has increased."

"Well, his constitution should be able to fight any fever. And he's young; his years should battle for him. . . . Give me a drink, girl, I'm parched."

When Hannah, who was at the window, didn't answer, Mrs Loam groaned at her, "Do you hear me, girl? Stop your star-gazing and get me a drink."

"I will in a minute." The tone of Hannah's voice silenced the woman and she stared from the bed in amazement as Hannah, thrusting up the window, shouted, "Bella! Tessie! stop a minute. Stop a minute! I want a word with you." When she thrust the window down, Mrs Loam brought herself up from her pillow and demanded, "What you at now? I told you to give me a drink."

Hannah almost thrust the glass into her hand, saying, "There you are then."

"Where you going? Who are you callin'? Was that Bella Monkton and young Tessie? What do you want with them?"

As if injected with new life, Hannah ran down the stairs. She knew what she wanted with Bella and Tessie. Pulling open the shop door, she looked at them where they were standing below the step in their outdoor clothes, each with a bundle on one arm and a bass bag held in the other hand.

"You're going to the market?"

. ."Aye, Miss Hannah, we're going to the hirings. An' I'm not sorry to leave there I can tell you that; she's mean to the core she is. There they are coming down the street in the trap now" – she jerked her head to the right – "and never offered us a lift."

Hannah looked to her right, and yes, there was the trap coming down the road, the missis driving, with Betsy to her side.

She turned her gaze back to Bella and Tessie and she asked quietly, "Would you be frightened to come in?"

"No, not me, Miss Hannah. Some folks are afraid of the death they'll never die, but as I said to Tessie here only last night, it's one thing you don't do twice, you die but once and after that the judgement."

"And you, Tessie?" Hannah was looking at Tessie, and Tessie gave a little grin as she replied, "Where Bella goes I go."

"Come in then." Her voice was eager, but as she pushed the door backwards and thrust out her other arm as if gathering them to her she stopped; in fact they all stopped and turned and looked towards the trap that was passing them on the roadway, for both Anne Thornton and her daughter were looking towards them, at least they were looking at Hannah; and Hannah stared back over the distance to the woman whose bane she had been, and who in turn had been hers. Then with a welcoming gesture her arms seemed to encircle both Bella and Tessie and she drew them over the step and banged the door. Then turning to them, she said, "That will give her something to think about, won't it?"

"Oh aye," Tessie laughed, "it certainly will, miss. It certainly will."

"You know they've both got the fever?" Hannah thrust her hand backwards.

"Aye, we know that." Bella nodded towards her.

"Well, I must tell you it's the bad kind, and it's getting worse with him, but I'm at my wit's end, I can't cope for much longer on my own." She put her hand on the raised dome of her stomach that was pushing out the apron from below her breasts. "I'm weary both inside and out. It's the washing and the running up and down stairs. Do you think you could stay for a few days? You'll miss the Allendale hirings but there'll be one next week-end in Hexham, and . . . and I'll see you get paid."

Bella remained silent for a moment, then she looked at Tessie as she said, "Well, speaking for meself I'm willin' enough, but it's Tessie here."

"Well, I'm willin' an' all. Don't worry about me, I'm not afraid of the death I'll never die."

"Oh, thank you. Thank you both." She put her arms out and her hands held each of them on the shoulders; and Tessie now laughed and said, "Eeh! isn't it funny how things turn out? I never did think I'd be workin' for you, miss, but I'm right glad I am, I am that. 'Twill be like a holiday."

"Oh." The word was a groan and Hannah drooped her head forward slowly as she said, "Oh, Tessie, it'll be no holiday."

"Well" – Tessie's voice was still bright – "it all depends how you look at things. You think things are bad till you meet something worse. Anyway, tell us what we've got to do, an' then we'll see."

"Well, it's mostly washing, and emptying slops. And then there's the meat outside; it's gone rotten and it has to be buried or burned. And the whole place" – she wrinkled her nose – "it needs a scrub down. All that and a thousand and one other things."

"Where will we put our bits an' pieces?" Bella's tone was brisk.

"Well now" – Hannah looked about her – "you could clear the back shop out and leave your things in there. And as for sleeping, well, you haven't much choice. I sleep on a straw pallet on the sofa; you can make similar ones and sleep upstairs or down here It'll be warmer upstairs. But then I'll leave it to you."

"First things first then, we'll clear this place up." As Bella bustled into the back shop Hannah said on the lightest note that had been in her voice for weeks, "I'll make you a pot of tea." And on this she went heavily upstairs.

As soon as she got up to the kitchen she was greeted by Mrs Loam's voice calling, "Girl! Girl!"

Standing at the bedroom door she looked across the room and said flatly, "Yes?"

"What you up to? You bring those two in?"

"Yes, I've brought them in, and they're going to stay in and help me."

"They're what!"

"You heard what I said."

A bout of harsh coughing almost choked the woman and she gasped, "You . . . you brought them into my . . . my house?"

"It's either I have help or I walk out; you can take your choice."

"By God! I'll deal with you when I'm better. Oh, by God! I will. See if I don't."

"And me with you."

As another fit of coughing attacked Mrs Loam, Hannah turned away and went about the business of making a pot of tea.

During the doctor's visit that afternoon he became greatly disturbed not only by the change in Fred but also by Hannah's condition.

Coming into the kitchen where she was waiting for him, he said, "This is serious, he's a very ill man. He's the last person I would have imagined would have succumbed like this. Now if it had been the old one" – he nodded towards the other door – "I wouldn't have been a bit surprised. But Fred, with a constitution like he has!"

"What has happened?"

"Oh, a number of complications have set in. I . . . I think he is bleeding from the bowel. There's a perforation there. The fact that he's in pain and that he has been vomiting bears this out. Yet I would have imagined his stamina would have weathered this. But I'm afraid, very much afraid, it's going to result in peritonitis."

"What is that?" Her voice was low, tired sounding.

"Oh, it is difficult to explain in a few words but it can lead to death."

She remained still and checked herself from the blasphemy of thinking that God was answering her prayers. Then of a sudden she was made to imagine that He was indeed chastising her for she was brought double by a grinding pain in her stomach.

"Hannah. Hannah. Oh! don't start that; not at this time."

"Oh! Oh! Doctor." The sweat was running off her as she gasped, "It's too early isn't it?"

"If we're sticking to the book, yes; but with a first it can come early or late. Is this the first pain you've had?"

"Yes. Yes, like this. Yet I haven't felt well for some days, but I put it down to the work and . . . and worry. . . . Ned. I . . . I wanted to ask you. . . . How is he?" Her words were brought out between gasps.

"Oh, going along slowly." He did not look at her as he spoke but attended to his bag and added, "I'm not worried about Ned at the moment."

"What is actually ... wrong with him, doctor? Tell me, please."

"Well now, if you were to ask me what isn't wrong with him I'd be able to answer that more simply. He's had bad concussion; he was bruised from head to foot; his groin was split open."

"Split open!" She mouthed the words twice before they made any sound.

"Yes, split open. He had to be stitched in various parts, but he's standing up to it." He turned and bent towards her now and whispered, "I shouldn't be carrying messages because I in no way represent a messenger of the gods, and after all you are still a married woman, but I'll tell you this, he was sufficiently himself yesterday to ask after you."

She took a long breath, then said, "Thank you, doctor.... Oh!" Her mouth opened wide; she groaned, and again she was bending forward and holding herself, tightly now.

"Goodness! Goodness me! This is bad. You're for it, my girl. Bella! Bella!" His voice rang through the house as he held her. "Talk about God working in a mysterious way; if those two hadn't come your way we'd be in a nice pickle at this moment, for I don't see any of the neighbours rushing about. It's funny how people will generally dash forward for most things, even dive into the ice cold river to save a dog, yet with typhoid or cholera they flee from the very name of it. As Bella just said to me, you've only got to die once. Good woman, Bella, very good woman. . . . Ah, there you are, Bella . . . see what we've got here, somebody struggling to be born, while back there – " He shook his head. "You and Tessie are going to have a night of it, I'm afraid."

"It won't be the first time, doctor. . . . Come on, my dear, come on."

As Bella led Hannah towards the couch the doctor said, "I've got to go, I've had an urgent call from the Burn farm, but I'll look in on my way back."

"Thank you . . . doctor. Thank you for, for everything."

"That's all right, Hannah . . . keep pressing, and who knows he may arrive before me." . . .

When he had gone Bella said, "There now, we'll get your

clothes off and make you comfortable . . . at least as comfortable as it's possible on a horsehair sofa."

"Oh! Bella." Hannah grasped Bella's hand. "What . . . what would I have done if you, you hadn't come?"

"Well, I did. God seems to know what He's about, at least sometimes, an' we're told He makes the back to bear the burden, and tempers the wind to the shorn lamb."

Hannah gave birth to a son at two o'clock the following morning. Bella delivered it as if she had been performing the function at regular intervals all her life. When Hannah gave one final heave and an agonized gasp, Bella brought the child forth, and she didn't need to hold it by its legs or slap it to make it breathe for it gave evidence of vital life almost immediately, and within seconds of its cry, another cry came from Mrs Loam's room demanding to know what it was.

"What is it? What is it?"

"Let her wait." Bella turned towards Tessie. "The old vixen. Here, take him, till I see to Miss Hannah."

"Oh, he's bonny. Oh, he is. He's bonny, Miss Hannah, he is." Tessie leant towards the couch where Hannah lay in complete exhaustion and when she made no response, Bella said, "Don't bother her; let me see to her; you wash him an' keep him warm. Listen to that old devil. Listen to her." She turned her head towards the door. "Go on, tell her or else we'll have her in here in a minute. . . . Lay him in the clothes basket there afore the fire. . . . Oh, my God! Listen to her. If I go in I'll give her a mouthful.". . .

When Tessie entered Mrs Loam's room the old woman was sitting on the edge of her bed, and when, her croak coming from high in her head, she demanded, "Well, what is it? You heard me calling, didn't you, you young scut!" Tessie compressed her lips tightly for a moment, then came out with the old senseless rhyme about birth: "A goat on a hayrick an' a three-legged poss stick, if you want to know."

"You! You!" It looked and sounded as if Mrs Loam was about to choke.

"It's a lad." And on this abrupt information, Tessie went out closing the door none too gently after her, muttering as she did so, "Wicked old witch!"

It was an hour later when Bella laid the baby in Hannah's arms, saying, "He's a fine lump of a lad."

Hannah turned her face slowly on the pillow and looked at the child. She was concerned not about the size of him but how he looked. Did he look like Fred, or Ned? He looked like neither. He hadn't Fred's square face, or Ned's long one; his face looked oval, heart-shaped like hers. If he didn't change too much as babies often did, he would grow to look like her. All the time she was carrying she had been sure it was Ned's child in her; now perhaps she'd never know; well, not until his character began to form.

Hannah started, as did Bella, when Mrs Loam's bedroom door was pulled open and, looking like the witch Tessie had called her, she came staggering across the room, supporting herself by gripping the backs of the chairs until she reached the head of the couch, and there, bending over it, she glared down on Hannah and the child.

" 'Tis not like him, not a feature. 'Tis not like him."

"Go back to bed, Mrs Loam." Bella had hold of her arm now, and the old woman turned to her. "You've got eyes. 'Tisn't like him. You can see for yourself."

"The child's like his mother."

"Bah! jiggery-pokery! Like his mother!"

"Go on back to bed."

Mrs Loam now put her hands to her stomach, drew in two sharp breaths, then turned about and stumbled back towards her room. But before she reached it the main bedroom door opened and Tessie came out carrying a bucket of slops.

"How is he?" Mrs Loam stood gripping the stanchion of her door now.

"I'd say he was right bad, that's what I'd say. An' he's smellin' like a poke of devils."

Whatever retort Mrs Loam was about to make she thought better of it, and with her remaining strength she stumbled back

268

into the room. But her weakness didn't prevent her from banging the door behind her.

Doctor Arnison was very pleased with Hannah, and he was equally pleased with Bella. "You did a fine job, Bella, I couldn't have done better myself. Afterbirth, the lot. Glad you had the sense to keep it for me. She's a good midwife, isn't she, Hannah?"

"She's wonderful. They both are." Hannah smiled weakly from one to the other where they stood behind the doctor. "And they must be so tired, they've had hardly any sleep."

"Well, they'll have to take it in turns, because there's going to be a lot of work before them." He nodded from one to the other. "There's a very sick man in there."

When the doctor jerked his head backwards Hannah lowered her gaze. She was weary in body and mind, she was feeling strangely apart from everything around her. At one point during the early hours of this morning she had thought she wouldn't mind if she were to die; neither her need of Ned, nor the child's need of her, seemed to have the power to hold her to life; and certainly not the need of the man who was her husband, the very sick man.

"I wish we could move you to some place more comfortable, Hannah."

"Oh, that's all right, doctor. I'll . . . I'll be up in a day or two."

"Oh no, you won't. You'll stay there for a week or more."

She didn't say "We'll see;" she didn't want to talk, not even at this moment to ask after Ned.

A groan coming from the main bedroom caused the doctor to turn and look towards the door before, picking up his black oblong, bulbous bag, he said to no one in particular, "I'll be along later in the day."

True to his word, Doctor Arnison came back that same evening and then on each of the next three days he called twice, because as he said, it was touch and go with Fred.

On the third day of Fred's delirium his mother staggered from her room and into his; then returning almost immediately into the kitchen she cried at Hannah who was propped up in the couch, "He's dying. God Almighty! he's dying. Do you know that, girl? He's dying."

Hannah made no reply, she just stared dully back at her mother-in-law; then watched her turn to Tessie and cry, "Bring me a paper an' pen, girl. Paper an' pen, quick! Off that shelf there!"

Tessie did as she was bid, and when she held out the pen and paper Mrs Loam grabbed at it, then slapped it on to the table and, her hand shaking visibly, she scrawled something on the paper. Then turning to Bella and Tessie she asked, "Can you write your names?"

They both looked at her without speaking, and so she demanded, "Tell me! can you write your names?"

"We make our crosses." Bella's reply was muttered.

"Well, come on in here and make your crosses."

As she went to move from the table, Bella and Tessie spoke almost simultaneously. "No. No."

"What!"

"We're not making our crosses on that" – Bella pointed to the piece of paper in Mrs Loam's hand – "'cos I know what it is, I know what you're up to."

The look that the old woman passed over them would, if it had been possible, have struck them dead; and now turning on Hannah, she ground out through her almost closed lips, "I'll see it burnt down afore you get it. And what's more, I'll have the bringing up of him." She now pointed to where the child lay in the basket before the fire. And visibly swaying now she made for her son's bedroom. And there, bending over Fred, she cried, "I'm here! I'm here, lad! Listen to me."

"Ma. Ma."

"Listen to me, Fred. Listen to me. Take this pen in your hand. . . ." The pen was suddenly knocked flying as the great arm began to thrash up and down on the quilt. Then his body became still for a moment, and he gasped and passed his swollen tongue round his swollen lips as he turned and looked at her in recognition, croaking now, "Ma. Ma."

"Fred, listen!"

"Ma . . . I'm bad . . . Ma."

"Yes, lad, I know, I know. But do this for me, will you? Do this for your ma. Sign your name on this paper here. I'll hold your hand. 'Tis about the house. . . ."

"'Tis done. 'Tis done . . . Got to get the meat . . . cut up." The paper and pen were again knocked out of her hand and fell at the foot of the bed.

Mrs Loam picked the paper up and, her head moving from side to side, she gazed down at the words she had written there: I leave everything I have to me mother. Then she turned one long look on to her son before stumbling from the room and into the kitchen again. But she stopped at her own bedroom door and, supporting herself against it, she cried at Hannah, "Whatever happens to him, I'll live, if it's only to see me day with you. I've said it afore an' I'll say it again, I'll see me day with you, me girl. By God! I will; I'll see you on the street beggin' your bread."

All three watched the figure in the long calico nightdress stumble the few steps into her room, and when her door was closed, Tessie whispered, "She is . . . she is like a witch, a wicked witch!"

But what Bella said was, "Can she do you out of the house an' all that if he dies, Miss Hannah?"

Hannah stared back at Bella before replying, "She'll try, Bella. I can't see how she'll do it but she'll try." And it was in this moment that there returned to her the urge to live, if only to beat that dreadful old woman.

10

⚜

On the fifth day Hannah got up from the couch, and two days later Fred died. He died at four o'clock on the Sunday morning. He was unconscious to the end; and when the breath left his body his face slowly changed and Hannah, looking down on him, saw for a moment the young fellow who was always pleasant to her when, as a schoolgirl, she went into the shop. But she felt no remorse, only a great, great intense relief, as if she herself had died and her body and mind were floating free in a new atmosphere, a new world.

Bella and Tessie laid him out, and when Bella said, "Shall we tell her?" Hannah replied, "No; don't waken her, we'll wait till daylight. But go now, both of you, and get some rest for you look worn out."

When reluctantly she entered her mother-in-law's room at seven o'clock that morning, she did not go near her bed; seeing she was awake she stood just within the doorway and said quietly, "He's gone."

The answer she received amazed her, for Mrs Loam, looking steadily back at her, said, "I could have told you that. He's been gone these last two days. So now once they've laid him away you'll be free to go, won't you? An' those two with you."

"Perhaps I will and perhaps I won't."

"What do you mean by that?"

"Just what I say. I was his wife, I have rights."

"What rights have you?" Mrs Loam pulled herself up in the bed. "You've got no rights in this house. You try an' claim them an' you'll see what'll happen to you."

"You forget I have a son."

"Huh! that! Whose son, eh? Wait till I open me mouth, you won't have a leg to stand on."

To this Hannah made no reply, she merely turned about and went out of the room.

Doctor Arnison said the normal period for the body to lie coffined in the house before burial must be waived; in this case the matter must be dealt with as soon as possible; and so on the third day after he had died Fred was buried, and it was said the grave-digger had a job to dig the grave, so frozen was the ground.

The following to the funeral was small. There was Ralph Buckman the blacksmith; Will Rickson the joiner; Walter Bynge the stonemason; Thomas Wheatley the grain chandler; backed by a few of the older male inhabitants of the village and three business men from Allendale Town . . . and the doctor.

Breaking with tradition, no one came back to the house of the deceased to indulge in a gargantuan meal except the doctor, and he didn't come to eat. Standing in the back shop facing Hannah, he said, "Well, now it's all over, Hannah, what are you going to do?"

"I don't know, doctor; I need some advice. How do I stand as regards what was his, the property, money from the business and such?"

"Oh" – the doctor let out a long breath – "I'm not in the legal profession but I think, as the law stands, if the child hadn't been born before Fred died then you and the old 'un would have shared the estate, or something like that. As it is now, I don't think she comes into the picture, unless there's a will."

"I don't think he left a will. She . . . she tried to force him to sign a paper that she had written one day last week but he was too ill to comply. She still thinks though that she can claim everything."

"Well then, if that's the case she's a stubborn old fool. Of course she always has been. Anyway, she should have the sense to know that when a man takes a wife it misplaces his mother, at least in part."

"Do . . . do you think I should see a solicitor, Doctor?"

"Yes. Yes, I do. Have you got Fred's papers, business papers and things?"

"No; they're in a box in her room."

"Well, I should just walk in and take them. Then go and see Mr Ransome in Allendale . . . you know, he has an office just off the square, he'll advise you as to what your rights are. As far as I can judge from my experience, there shouldn't be any hitch. That being so" – he smiled at her now – "the tables will be turned, she'll be relying on your charity. Oh, and Dame Loam won't like that a bit, will she?"

"No, doctor, she won't." Hannah didn't return the doctor's smile, but she said, "Thank you very much, not only for your advice but for everything you have done for me. . . . Will you be seeing Ned soon?"

"I'll be going that way tomorrow, that's if the snow doesn't start again and the road is passable, for it lies deep down on the bottoms."

"Does . . . does he know about Fred?"

"Yes, he knows."

"What . . . what did he say?"

"Well, since you ask, he quoted God's ways, which was unusual, at least coming from Ned because he's no churchman. What he said was, God doesn't take side tracks over the mountain when He's got a miracle to perform. His translation might be a bit free but his meaning was plain. Of course" – he smiled wryly now – "'tisn't everybody who would look upon Fred's death as a miracle. Yet for you and Ned it must appear so. As for me, well, from where I stand I view it as a most unexpected happening, because with a constitution like his I would have bet my last shilling he would have battled through; at the same time I would have gambled a hundred to one against his mother surviving. Yet she will survive. . . . But where she survives, well, that seems to be up to you, Hannah, doesn't it?"

"There is one thing I can assure you of, doctor, and you can gamble on it too, and you'll win, and that is she won't survive alongside me."

"No? Well, that's something you'll have to work out for yourself."

"And I'll do that, doctor."

"Good-bye, Hannah."

"Good-bye, doctor. Doctor."

"Yes, Hannah?" He turned from the door.

"Do . . . do you think I could go across and see Ned if . . . if he weather holds?"

"No, no, I definitely don't. That's one thing you shouldn't think of doing, Hannah, because in his present low state he could pick up anything." His heavy eyebrows strained upwards towards his receding hairline as he went on, "Who knows but you could be a carrier; carriers never seem to catch the disease themselves but they spread it. I'm not saying you are, but you've been here in the thick of it, and in a very low state of health yourself, and you haven't picked it up. No, no; don't expose him to that risk. Have patience a little longer; you'll see enough of each other likely before you're finished." He went out muttering something that sounded like "if nothing else happens".

Mrs Loam's recovery was slow; it seemed as if she were making the most of Tessie's ministrations, as rough as they were. When either Bella or Tessie was in the room she would always remain tight-lipped, but some days later, following the funeral, she spoke to them both, and what she said was, "If you two think you're gona be paid you've got a surprise comin' to you."

"Is that so?" put in Tessie quickly. "Well, I'm gona tell you something. We won't be the only ones."

"What do you mean by that?"

"Just what I said. Miss Hannah's gone into the solicitor's and it'll be up to him to decide who runs things from now on."

"*Me box. Me box.*"

Mrs Loam was sitting upright in the bed now looking towards the corner of the room, where on a small table had stood a wooden box, its top inlaid with mother-of-pearl. In it her husband had kept the deeds of the house, their marriage certificate, the baptism certificate of their son, together with his savings bank book. Now the box was no longer there.

The piercing scream the little woman let out of her almost

lifted both Bella and Tessie from the ground, and Tessie, putting her hands over her ears, shouted back, "Stop that!"

"She's a thief! She's a thief!"

Taking the woman by the shoulders, Bella pushed her none too gently back into the pillows and, bending over her, she said, "She's no thief; she's left your marriage lines and your son's birth certificate there, the rest she's taken into the solicitor. If he's not holding any kind of a will then she says, and rightly, that the place and all in it is hers . . . and the child's."

"And" – put in Tessie now – "the money that's in the bank an' all; so if I was you, Mrs Loam, I'd keep a civil tongue in me head . . . to all concerned, that is."

Both Bella and Tessie glanced at each other apprehensively as they watched the woman on the bed gasping for breath, for they thought she was about to choke.

"Have a drink of water." Tessie was now holding the glass out to Mrs Loam. But she made no movement to take it, and Tessie, putting it back on the table, said, "Well, please yersel."

They were both about to leave the room when there came the sound of pebbles being thrown against the window-pane, and again they looked at each other in surprise; then hurrying to the window, Bella pushed it open and looked out and down into the large face of a large woman.

"Do you want something?"

The woman in the street below now called up, "Just to know how she's farin'."

"Oh, she's getting on nicely, I would say."

"Tell her I won't come in; 'twouldn't be wise."

"I'll tell her. What's your name?"

"I'm her sister Connie."

"Oh, her sister?"

"Connie! Connie!" Now Mrs Loam was sitting up in bed again and, waving her hand towards Bella, she cried, "Tell her to come up. I want her, I want to see her."

"She says will you come up, she wants to see you?"

"No, no. As I said, 'twouldn't be wise, but tell her as soon as she's over it to come along to me an' we'll settle what's to be done about the business and such like, you know."

"I'll tell her." Bella closed the window and looked towards the bed, then said, "Well, you heard that, didn't you? She says as soon as you're well you've got to go over to her, and you can arrange about the business and such like."

Mrs Loam swallowed deeply, then brought out slowly, "When I get out of this bed God help you two, I'm tellin' you."

"You're still sure of yersel." Tessie's head was wagging at her now. "I wouldn't count me chickens afore they're hatched, if I was you."

It again appeared to Bella that Mrs Loam was about to have a seizure so she pushed Tessie before her out of the room, and as she did so Mrs Loam's croak followed them, spluttering, "An' God'll strike her down dead. Blasphemy . . . going across the doors afore she's churched!"

In the kitchen, Bella whispered, "If Miss Hannah can get the better of that one, then she'll be able to tackle anybody. But she's right about one thing . . . she did go out afore she was churched, an' she's church, not chapel."

They stared at each other. Then Tessie said, "Aw, what matter. It's the solicitor man that matters; it'll all depend on what he says."

"Yes. Aye," Bella repeated; "aye, it'll all depend on what he says." . . .

About this time the solicitor man was treating Hannah with great courtesy. On his desk before him he had the documents she had brought with her, and he moved them here and there with his forefinger as if he were playing cards as he said, "It would seem, Mrs Loam, by what you tell me with regard to your mother-in-law trying to get your husband to put his name to a paper that there was no will made. It's very odd about wills." He now put his elbows on the arms of the chair and joined his fingertips together. "Men have to be persuaded to make wills. They have the idea that once they sign their name to a will it is as it were the signature to their death sentence; the smaller the business the greater their reluctance to sign it away, because that is what they feel they are doing, signing it away. If a man has children, then he knows that without a will his wife will inherit a third of the estate, and the children the rest; and should his own mother be alive he would expect them to look after her. But to get some of them to put in writing just how they wish their mother to be taken care of i considered to be nothing less than an insult to their integrity, and that of their offspring. And so, in this case as there appears to be no will then the law will say that your son and you are the rightful inheritors, he will come into two-thirds and you one-third, and i will be up to you what provision you make for your mother-in-law out of the whole. It will be merely a matter of your charity." He paused here, then added, "I did not do business for either M Loam Senior or Junior, but from what you have told me you husband inherited everything from his father, so things should be plain sailing as to your claim, and naturally that of your son; and would be pleased to act for you in this matter, if you so wish."

"I'd be very grateful if you would, Mr Ransome. . . . How . . how long do you think it would take to settle?"

"Oh" – he shook his head – "the law is slow in these cases o probate, yet there is no one to contest your claim, as I see it."

"I . . . I think my mother-in-law might."

"How can she" – he brought his head forward, his chin thrus out – "if there is no written word to the effect that she is in any way a beneficiary? You, as I see it, have a double claim. You are not only the deceased's wife, but you are the mother of his child . . . There is one thing that puzzles me though, it is the bank book It states here that the amount is four hundred and thirty-five pounds, but the last entry was made in June 1856. Now your husband's business was small compared with some butcher businesses, but in some years there was deposited in the bank" – he tapped the book on the table – "as much as sixty pounds; bu nothing since June 1856, which makes me think that there must be money stored somewhere else. There was no other place in th house where deeds or bank books could be kept?"

"No; only in the box as I explained. It was always kept in m mother-in-law's bedroom, and it was always locked; but recentl when cleaning the room I happened to find where she kept th key."

Again the solicitor put his elbows on the arms of the chair, an now his fingertips drummed against each other and his face move slowly into a smile while his lips remained tightly closed, until he said in low amused tones, "I think I can give a good guess where the money is, that is the profits since '56. Does your mother-in-law lie on a box bed?"

"Yes; yes, she does." Hannah's eyes stretched wide now. "Of course. Of course, that's why she would never let me turn the bed tick."

"It happens all the time, Mrs Loam. A man suddenly decides that the bank or outsiders know too much about his business; if they think he's got money someone might want to borrow from him. He cannot believe that bankers or solicitors can keep secrets, in fact must keep secrets, as well as doctors or priests. So they put around they've had a bad year, and the profits go into the box bed or behind a brick in the wall."

As he continued to smile at her, she thought of Ned and the loose bricks in the Pele house.

"Can you get access to the bed?"

"Pardon?" She blinked and he repeated, "Is it possible for you to strip the bed and find out if there's any money hidden there?"

"Not at present; she's convalescing from the fever."

"Could she be moved?"

"Yes, yes, in a day or so, I suppose she could." She returned his smile and nodded, adding, "Yes, she could be moved, with a little persuasion, that is."

"Well then, you must use a little persuasion. And I'll be interested to know your findings. In the meantime, I shall get in touch with the bank and you will likely have to come in to town again in a day or two for the account to be transferred to your name. You'll then be able to meet such debts as are outstanding, such as the funeral expenses. . . . And then, of course, you must live. Now do you want to take the deeds of the house back with you or leave them with me?"

"I'd prefer to leave them with you; and also the bank book, if I may."

"Certainly, certainly, Mrs Loam."

When she rose to her feet he rose too.

"Good-bye, Mr Ransome, and thank you."

"Good-bye, Mrs Loam. It's been a pleasure meeting you."

He preceded her through the outer office and opened the door for her himself while his clerk, who had risen to his feet, stood to the side. Again she inclined her head towards him, then went out into the square, conscious that through the clear upper half of the window both men were watching her progress.

She wasn't wearing her cloak today but a thick grey Melton cloth long-coated costume with a fur collar. It was the last outfit the mister had bought her and she had not worn it since she was married.

The last time she had walked across this square she had kept her head down in order to cover her bruised face; now she held it high and she made her step jaunty although she was feeling far from jaunty inside. Not only was she still feeling weak, but also the stench of body excrement remained in her nostrils and so strong was it she felt it would be years before she was rid of it.

What would have happened, she asked herself now, if she hadn't looked out of the window and seen Bella and Tessie that day? She'd likely be dead herself. She would never forget them and she would repay them a thousandfold for what they had done for her. Oh yes, she had plans for Bella and Tessie . . . and Margaret.

Yes, she could now send the letter off to Margaret. She had hesitated to do so until her position had been confirmed by the solicitor. It was still early in the day and it would catch the mail van and be in Hexham by this evening and Margaret would receive it at the latest by tomorrow morning; then perhaps by the following day she would be with her. It would be wonderful to be all together again, Margaret, Bella, Tessie. . . . Strange how things were turning out. . . . Very strange.

As Hannah waited for the carrier cart she was the subject of covert glances from the people who passed back and forth across the square, for she was a figure of interest. Was she not the cause of hell being let loose between Ned Ridley and Fred Loam? Now one was dead and the other in such a state it was said he'd be lucky if he ever got over it. And many of them, as they glanced at her, remembered back to the story of her being dumped on the Thornton household by a woman of the Newcastle streets who claimed that Matthew Thornton was her father. And it had been the cause of misery in that household, and all for nothing because hadn't she found out on her wedding-day that she had no claim on Matthew Thornton. And what had she done then? Run helter-skelter to the mine to the young fellow who was supposed to be her half-brother, she had, and her not married an hour gone to Fred Loam. Then from him on to Ned Ridley. Aye, and what happened then? To save her from the man-trap he loses half his hand. But if all tales were true he had already lost more than half his heart to her, and that was saying something for Ned Ridley whose heart had been spread around the hills since he was a chip of a lad. But they were saying that it was because of her he hadn't married Lena Wright.

Then after all that caffuffle what does she go and do but take secret trips up to the Pele house; and as is often the case the whole village knew about it, except the man most concerned; and when he does, what happens? He swipes her one. Well, who's to blame him? No man is going to stand being made a monkey out of. Then big Dickinson's lad finds Ned battered almost to a pulp and big Dickinson goes and gets the polis. Now that was surprising, wasn't it? Big Dick going for the polis and the polis hoping to catch him out for years! 'Twas a laugh, that one. Then them all waiting for Fred to get over the fever so they can lock him up; and what does he do? He goes and kicks the bucket.

Who says, they asked of one another, that nothing happens in the country?

And there she was standing now as straight as a die, and after just giving birth an' all. And when you took a good dekko at her you could see what all the trouble was about, for there was no doubt she had grown into a fine lump of a woman, a beautiful woman. And she had something about her. What, they couldn't exactly put a name to: something to do with her eyes, or her hair? Now that alone could fetch a man.

Not that her looks would have any effect on her mother-in-law. By God! no. There was a little vixen if ever there was one. Indomitable she was, harder to get through than the Roman Wall. It would be something to look forward to seeing how the young matron intended to stand up to her.

Hannah was not completely oblivious of the trend that the

conversation would take that evening in the inns and hotels of the small town, but it didn't disturb her. There was a disdain in her for most of them and it showed in the tilt of her chin. Not even Mrs Thornton could have called her *The Girl* any more.

Apart from the doctor, Mr and Mrs Wheatley and Mr and Mrs Buckman and their sons Bill and Stan, hardly anyone else had given her a pleasant word during the last two years, and the way she felt now she could do without their good opinion.

When she returned to the house Bella had a meal ready for her, and although she wasn't at all hungry she ate it because Bella would have been upset if she hadn't, and as she sat at the table Mrs Loam's voice came at her from the bedroom every now and again, crying loudly first of all, "You're back then!"

Then: "You daren't show your face in here."

"Where's me box?"

"I'll have the polis on you, you thieving skit you!"

"You'll go out neck and crop, an' them two along of you as soon as I'm on me feet proper. By God! you will."

As she sopped up the last of the gravy with a piece of new bread, Hannah looked from Bella to Tessie, who sat one on each side of her, and said quietly, "I'd better get it over."

And on this she rose and went into the bedroom, and her tone even, she said, "You wanted to see me?"

"Wanted to see you! You thievin' bitch! I tell you I'll have the polis on you, I'll take you to court."

"No, you won't take me to court. And if you continue to be uncivil I'll take you to court . . . for abuse." She now walked nearer to the bed and continued, "I've been to see a solicitor; I've put the whole case before him. He says that my son and myself are the rightful owners of this house, all it contains, and the money in the bank." She refrained from adding, "And what lies under you."

"You can't!" Mrs Loam was now sitting upright in the bed, her hands opening and shutting over handfuls of quilt. "They won't allow it. I won't allow it. It's mine. All this." She now flung one arm wide over her head. "I've worked for it all me life."

"Your husband worked for it, Mrs Loam; and you led him, as everyone knows, a hell of a life. Your husband left you nothing, he left it all to his son. I married your son. Now he has gone. What was his is mine and his son's. The solicitor tells me that how you fare in the future relies entirely on my discretion." As she talked there was part of her feeling gratitude for the education she had received for otherwise she would not have been able to state her case in this fashion. And she continued to talk in the same manner: "And if you are amenable then I may see my way clear to making some provision for you; but I must inform you straightaway, Mrs Loam, it won't be in this house. Your sister seems a very pleasant woman, and has some concern for you, because I should imagine she has not suffered at your hands, so I would suggest that you take up your abode with her. What sum I shall provide you with I have yet to consider but I shall discuss it with my solicitor. So as soon as you're fit to travel, arrangements will be made to take you wherever you wish to go." . . .

She stopped abruptly because she really thought that her mother-in-law was about to have a fit. She was now lying back on the pillows, her whole face working while her two thumbs and forefingers continuously plucked at the counterpane as if she were stripping a fowl. Her mouth opening and shutting like a fish landed on a bank, she lay glaring at Hannah. Then after some time, her voice cracking in her throat, she said, "You can't do this to me."

"I can, Mrs Loam, and I shall. During the time I have been in this house you have treated me inhumanly; never one civil word, let alone a kind word, have you given me. You have tormented me on every possible occasion. If I were to put you out in the street nobody would blame me, but I won't do that, I shall see that you are provided for by giving you a sum of money on the condition that you leave this house quietly. If you don't agree to this then I shall make no allowance for you whatever; but I shall still insist that you leave this house, and if you end up in the Workhouse then it will be no one's fault but your own. I'll leave you now to consider my proposition."

She was trembling and feeling a little sick herself as she turned from the woman, and when she entered the kitchen she had to sit down hastily, and Bella, bending over her, said, "You're upset. You're bound to be. But you've told her, an' you were right. That woman would drive a saint mad. She's getting me down, miss, I'll tell you that, she's getting me down; how you've stuck her all this time God in heaven only knows. The missis, she was bad enough, but she was a different kettle of fish altogether to that 'un in there. She's a demon she is, a demon. Don't worry yourself about her; but the quicker she's gone the better."

It was odd, Hannah thought, but all her life she had been subjected to demons of women.

It was four days later when Margaret arrived. Her face bright, her eyes wide, she stood in the shop and embraced Hannah, murmuring, "Oh, Hannah! Hannah! When I got your letter I . . . I couldn't believe it. It . . . it renewed my faith in God. For weeks, months, I have prayed that something like this would happen, yet never believing that it would eventually come about. Your . . . your idea is marvellous." She looked around the shop; then nodded and said, "Yes, yes; I can see it all."

"Oh! Tessie." She was now holding out her hands to Tessie, and Tessie was exclaiming, "Eeh! Miss Margaret. Oh! Miss Margaret. Isn't it lovely to see you! Bella! Bella!" She simply bawled out the name, and Bella came stumbling down the stairs; and now she too was exclaiming, but slowly and in a tearful voice: "Aye, Miss Margaret, I never believed I'd live to see the day we'd all be together again. I mean we lot that mattered most to each other."

"Oh! Bella, I'm so happy to see you. I was just saying to Hannah, God has answered my prayers. And it's strange how He answers prayers. But" – she turned to Hannah again, adding softly, "you had to suffer very much before all this could come about. . . . How is the baby?"

"Oh, he's fine. You'll see him in a minute."

"He's the spit of her, Miss Margaret." Tessie poked her head forward, and Margaret, the tears in her eyes, looked again at

Hannah, and Hannah said hastily, "It's all over, it's all past, there's just the days ahead, the future. Come on, give me your things."

As Hannah took Margaret's handbag from her, Tessie relieved her of her coat and hat, while Bella lifted up the bass hamper, shaking her head over it and saying, "Miss Margaret, fancy you havin' to travel the country with a bass hamper." Then turning to Hannah, she asked, "Where am I to put her things, Miss Hannah?"

"Well" – Hannah looked at Margaret – "that's a problem at present, it's something we'll have to sort out. But come in here, Margaret. This was the back shop, you remember, where the meat used to be hung, but Bella and Tessie have scrubbed it from ceiling to floor. And look, they've unblocked the old fireplace. It was the original kitchen I suppose, and I'm sure there's a good oven behind that wall. Anyway, we'll see." She turned quickly to Tessie, now saying, "Make some coffee Tessie and bring down the scones Bella baked this morning." . . .

Ten minutes later they were all seated round what had once been the butcher's block, drinking the coffee and eating scones and listening to Hannah talking.

"What gave me the idea," Hannah said with excitement in her voice, "was when I remembered back to the summer and the people passing the house on their way to the hills, women wearing quite short skirts and wielding walking sticks. One day I counted all of eight women, four pairs, and two more accompanied by men. These stopped at the inn door. The men went in but the ladies had to stay outside, and it was then I thought what they needed was a cup of tea or coffee, not ale. Once I did see a lady standing outside Mrs Robson's drinking a mug of water. Well, it was recalling that memory that set me thinking again."

She glanced from one bright face to the other. "I thought, this was a butcher's shop, why not make it into a bakery shop, a cake shop. Bella used to excel at cakes." When she nodded towards Bella, Bella flapped her hand at her. "And there's nobody waits on people better than Tessie. And so I thought, added to the cake shop could be a little rest room, with say three or four tables and the requisite number of chairs. The villagers mightn't take to it at first, I mean buying fancy bread and cakes, but I'm sure they'll come to it in time. You remember, Margaret, the little shop near the market place in Hexham?"

"Oh yes, yes. Some days you couldn't get near the door; people coming to the market always took cakes back home with them."

"Well, in a much lesser way it could be the same here. But it doesn't matter so much about making a big trade, just as long as it supported the three of you."

"Just the three of us?" Margaret stared hard at Hannah now, her face straight, and Hannah said, "Yes, just the three of you, because as soon as Ned comes for me I am leaving to go and live at the Pele."

"Oh. . . . And you're willing to let us stay here and . . . and work a business?"

"More than that, Margaret, more than that; but I'll have to talk it over with the solicitor. What I can tell you now is, so far there's four hundred and thirty-five pounds in the bank, and a third of it will be mine. When all the bills are paid I should come into well over a hundred pounds. There may be more to add to it, I don't know yet but I have worked it out like this. If the bank will advance me my money until the estate is settled by law I'll leave you twenty-five shillings a week for the time being: fifteen shillings to cover your food; five shillings for your personal needs, Margaret; three shillings for you, Bella, and two shillings for you, Tessie. Will that be satisfactory to you?" She was looking at Bella and Tessie now, and Bella said, "Oh! miss. Satisfactory! Why I'd be willin' to work for nowt but me grub and a good home. Oh! miss."

"Me an' all, Miss Hannah." Tessie swallowed deeply.

Margaret said nothing, but she bowed her head and Hannah went on rapidly now, "Once I have the assurance from the solicitor I'm going to contact both Mr Rickson and Mr Bynge. I'll get Mr Bynge to take that wall down" – she pointed towards the fireplace – "and if there isn't an oven in there he'll install one. Then I'm going to get Mr Rickson to put up a partition to form another corridor from the shop to the back yard and have installed there a water closet, a real water closet with a pipe running from it to the ditch. It'll make this" – she spread her arms wide – "a little narrower but there'll be a separate door to enter the corridor next to that one there." She pointed. "And upstairs, you, Bella and Tessie, will have what is my room and Miss Margaret the front room. And we'll have some new pieces of furniture, comfortable pieces for the kitchen upstairs which will be turned into a sitting-room."

"Now, I don't know what this will all cost" – she looked around them – "but I should imagine that the alterations will run to nigh on thirty pounds. Oh, of course" – she laughed gently now – "there will be a new shop counter and the tables to buy, and wooden shelves for display in the window. Oh yes, it will be all of thirty pounds. But as long as eventually you take in as much as will pay and feed you, then all will be well. Even if you don't there'll still be enough money for some time to keep things going; but I'm sure, I'm positive it will be a success. . . . Oh, Margaret, please don't, don't cry."

"Aw, Miss Margaret, aw, don't." They were all standing round Margaret now for she had lowered her head on to her arms and was sobbing bitterly.

After a few moments Hannah silently shooed Bella and Tessie away; then with Margaret to herself, she looked at her and said with a little hesitation, "You . . . you won't be ashamed to go into business like this?"

"Oh" – Margaret now jerked her whole body upwards and, putting her hand to her brow, she said, "Hannah! Hannah! Ashamed? After my drudgery and humiliation at the school it's like having an honour bestowed on one. That was something I didn't tell you. Whenever I met some of our late friends in the town, or they came with their parents to visit their younger sisters, they would nearly all ignore the fact that we had once been bosom companions. I think that was the hardest cross to bear. . . . Oh! Hannah. Ashamed of going into business? You really, really don't know, nor never will know what you have given me, what you are doing for me; and never, never will I be able to repay you. I shall try. Oh I shall try, but I can't see myself ever being able to do anything for you that will compare with your kindness to me. And while we're on the subject, Hannah, I must tell you that you've weighed heavily on my conscience. You see I blame myself for being the cause of your suffering over the past two years,

287

because it was I who persuaded you to go ahead and marry Fred.
The only thing I can say in my defence is that I really thought he'd
be kind to you, and that his mother must surely come to love you.
Oh, I've. . . ."

"Now, now!" Hannah took her hand. "Look at it this way,
Margaret. If you hadn't persuaded me we wouldn't be here
together now. But as for Fred being kind to me, give him his due,
if I could have loved him in the smallest degree he would have
been kind, but my open dislike of him brought out the worst in
him. I can see now that he had some good qualities which under
other circumstances I might have fostered. As for his mother" –
she shook her head widely now – "his mother is a woman so
insensitive that to compare her with an animal I would consider
an insult to the animal. But come, see for yourself. You remember
one side of Mrs Loam, well, during the next few days you will
definitely see and hear another."

A further addition to the family seemed to stun Mrs Loam, and
contrary to Hannah's warning Margaret found the present Mrs
Loam much quieter than the one she remembered behind the
counter in the butcher's shop; that was until the day Hannah gave
the order that the patient must become convalescent and sit up for
an hour in the kitchen while Bella and Tessie thoroughly cleaned
the room.

Mrs Loam didn't object to sitting up but she wished to stay in
her room. "They can work round me," she said.

"No, they can't," Hannah said and, looking fully at Mrs Loam,
went on quietly, "I wish you to sit in the kitchen for a while. If
you don't feel strong enough to manage it Bella and Tessie will
carry you out."

After a long silence during which the old woman glared with
open ferocity at Hannah, she walked slowly and unaided into the
kitchen. As soon as she was seated comfortably before the fire,
Hannah, with a movement of her head indicated to Bella and
Tessie that they were to begin their task.

During this time Margaret had been making a pot of tea which
she placed on a tray, together with a plate of small fancy cakes, and,

setting it on a side table to Mrs Loam's hand, she drew up a chair opposite her and, much to the amazement of Mrs Loam, began to dispense tea and cakes as if she were at an afternoon's party. And she bemused her because she talked all the while about the baby and how well it looked, and how like Hannah it was; and wasn't she, Mrs Loam, lucky to have Hannah to look after her during her awful illness. She talked so sweetly and so fast that Mrs Loam didn't notice Hannah go into the bedroom.

Once in the room Hannah tiptoed quickly towards the bed which Bella and Tessie had stripped down to the base, and Tessie, looking at Hannah, whispered, "There's nothing hidden under here, miss."

"Wait." Hannah inserted her fingers into the small opening between the end of the box bed and the base and, lifting it up, held it for a moment as she turned her head slowly and looked from one to the other; then swiftly she lifted out from the bottom of the box a number of small bags, six in all. Five were full and tied at the top with string, the sixth was open and lay flat in her hand. Quickly now, she lifted her skirt and transferred the bags to the pocket of her petticoat. Lastly she bent again and swished her hand as far up underneath the bed boards as it would go but she found nothing further.

Nodding at Bella and Tessie, whose faces both showed their glee, she signalled to them to remake the bed; then, having straightened her back, she walked quietly from the room and into the kitchen, to be met by a hard enquiring stare from Mrs Loam, and a question from Margaret: "Would you like a cup of tea, Hannah?"

"No, thanks, Margaret; I've got a touch of indigestion. It's Bella's good cooking I think." She paused to let this sink in before adding, "I don't want to give Matthew wind."

"Matthew! Who said he's going to be called Matthew?"

"I did."

Before the old woman could retort, Hannah had turned away and gone down the stairs.

Hurrying through the back shop and into the wash-house, she knelt down by the side of the wash-house pot where she removed a loose stone from near the bottom of the wall; then taking the bags from her petticoat, she thrust them one by one down into the cavity, and replaced the stone.

Many of the stones of the wash-house walls were loose; she had tested a number of them yesterday at the time she was pondering on what she would do with the money, should she find it, until she had time to take it into Allendale and the solicitor's.

Standing up, she now dusted her hands whilst nodding down to the stones and saying, "And so much for you, Mrs Loam. May your heart stand the shock of the discovery you're about to make." Then of a sudden, her mood changing, she sat heavily down on the upturned rinsing tub and whispered to herself, "Oh! Ned. Ned."

She'd had a strange feeling about Ned for some days now, and she had put it down to weakness. Yet it seemed that something other than his illness was keeping them apart. It was more than six weeks since she had seen him being kicked into the stream and it seemed like six years. She must see him soon; it was becoming more imperative that she see him soon. Doctor Arnison appeared reluctant to talk about him. "All in good time," was the only answer he gave her when she asked how long it would be before she was able to go to him. She was sure the doctor was keeping something from her.

It was as if her thinking had conjured up the doctor for when she returned through the back shop Tessie was letting him in the front door.

"Oh, there you are, Hannah," he said. "How are you feeling?"

"Oh, quite well, doctor. Quite well."

"Good. Good. And how is the patient?"

"Oh, I think I'll leave you to be the judge of that."

The doctor laughed, then went before her up the stairs.

As soon as he entered the kitchen and saw Mrs Loam, he exclaimed, "Good! Good! I'm glad to see you on your feet." And at this Mrs Loam got to her feet and went into her room.

As he followed her, Doctor Arnison looked towards Margaret and said, "Nice to see you settled, Margaret. Nice to see you settled," and she replied briefly as she smiled at him, "Thank you, Doctor."

In the bedroom, Doctor Arnison let out a long breath before he commented, "Ah well, now you'll soon be making for your sister's. . . ."

"Who said anything about me goin' to me sister's?"

"Oh, I've been given to understand that you agreed to that proposal."

He watched her sitting champing on her lip before she ground out, "I've been swindled, robbed."

"Well, if you think that then you must go and see your solicitor, but if he takes the matter up it'll cost you something. Whether you win or lose it'll cost you something. And to win you've got to have proof, and proof, in this case, as I understand it, means being able to produce a will entirely in your favour. But if you lose, again as I understand it, you won't have much choice about where you'll live, will you, because I don't suppose even your sister will welcome you empty-handed? People don't, you know." He let out another long breath. "I think if you're wise you'll accept your daughter-in-law's proposal."

"And what does she propose?"

"Well, what she tells me she proposes to give you is to my mind a very generous offer under the circumstances." He turned his head now and cast a hard sidelong glance on to her. "You know, many in her position would see you further before giving you a penny. Anyway, as I understand it, when the matter has gone through probate she proposes to give you a hundred pounds. And she can, I understand, do this because she'll be trustee for her son until he comes of age."

"A hundred pounds! It won't keep me for life, will it?"

"I don't see why not. You'll shortly be able enough to take up light work. You could buy yourself a little cottage, grow your own vegetables, keep your own hens, and still have a good bit over. You can do a lot with a hundred pounds."

"This is my house."

He didn't answer until he reached towards the door, and then he said, "Not any more it isn't, Daisy. That's what you've got to face up to, not any more it isn't." And then he went out.

Hannah was waiting for him at the foot of the stairs, and he patted her on the shoulder and smiled as he said, "I don't think you'll have any trouble with her; I know her, she's ready to go.

And I think she was quite bowled over by the offer of the hundred pounds. It was a generous gesture. And you did right, for you won't have her on your conscience."

"Thank you, doctor."

As he went towards the shop door he looked about him and, his face moving into an appreciative smile, he nodded back at her and said, "It's a very good idea of yours; I can see it working. It needs something like this in the village. . . . And it's nice to see Margaret back. Strange how things have turned out for that family, strange, very strange. Well, let's hope all is peace from now on. Good-bye then. Good-bye."

"Good-bye, doctor. And thank you so much."

Margaret and Hannah were lying side by side in bed, and the wash-basket holding the baby was on the floor to the side of the bed. Bella was on the sofa and Tessie on a straw tick in front of the fireplace but out of range of sparks; and they were all asleep, or dropping off to sleep, when the scream brought them bolt upright.

Margaret reached the kitchen first. Hannah didn't hurry, for she knew what had happened and knew what to expect, and as she came out of the bedroom Mrs Loam's door was pulled open and the enraged woman stood for a moment gripping the front of her calico nightgown in both hands as if she were about to tear it from her body; then the gown seemed to swell as she opened her mouth wide, drew in a long breath and screamed, "You thieving bugger you! You've taken me money."

"Your money?" Hannah stepped in front of Margaret and Bella and Tessie who were now standing together in the middle of the room, and advancing towards Mrs Loam and endeavouring to keep her own voice low, she said, "I wasn't aware you had any money, Mrs Loam. You accused me only a day or two ago of turning you out penniless."

"Th . . . that money ba . . . back in there" – she was now thrusting her arm in the direction of the bed – "that was my hard-earned savin's of years."

"No, Mrs Loam. Going on the solicitor's reckoning, I should

say the forty pounds in each bag was the profit for each of the last five years. Since your husband died there has been no money put into the bank, and no one but a fool would be convinced that this business has been run without a profit."

Mrs Loam now clutched at the stanchion of the door with two hands. It was evident she was under great emotional strain, and Hannah said, "I'd advise you to go back to bed, Mrs Loam, and we'll discuss the matter further in the morning, but before . . . before you leave for your sister's."

The look Mrs Loam levelled at Hannah should have at least paralysed her with fear, if not killed her outright, and now she ground out through clenched teeth, "You'll come to a bad end. I'll pray every night of me life to God that He'll give you your just deserts and bring you to a tortured end."

There was a concerted gasp from behind her, and although Hannah knew the words were merely the mouthings of a bitter, cruel natured woman, she nevertheless shuddered. But she didn't take her eyes from those of her mother-in-law, and she didn't move until the woman had turned about and banged the door after her with such force that the house shuddered; then she moved slowly round and looked at the others.

Margaret, coming towards her, took her by the arm, saying softly, "Come. Come away; it'll be all over by this time tomorrow."

Hannah returned to bed but not to sleep. After Margaret, holding her gently, had said, "Think nothing of it, go to sleep now. She's a wicked woman! you did the right thing;" she lay still until Margaret, under the impression that she had fallen asleep, released her hold and turned away on to her side. But the dawn was showing its light through the small window before she finally closed her eyes, and then not before she had given the child its feed from her swollen breast.

Her mother-in-law's curse was lying heavily on her, filling her with dread, recalling the doctor's words, "Unwittingly you seem to breed trouble wherever your feet tread." . . . Was she fated? Was there something about her that always led to tragedy? Would she in the end be the cause of bringing final tragedy to Ned? Through her he had lost half his hand, through her he had almost lost his life, and she had yet to find out exactly what scars Fred's boots had left on him. Was she bad? Was there some deep badness in her inherited from her mother?

No! No! The protest against this self-accusation was loud in her head. She had never wished people ill, not even the missis, and God knew she'd had every cause to pray that something bad would befall that woman. But she hadn't. And she hadn't up to the last wished any evil on her husband, although she had grown to hate him. . . . Had she on his mother? Perhaps, for she'd wished her dead, but now all she wished was to put distance between them. . . .

When she finally awoke the weak rays of sun were lying across the counterpane. She could hear a murmured conversation from the kitchen. She lay for a moment recalling the incident of last night, then told herself she must get up and face the day and the last battle with that woman. But when she went to rise, her head swam and she fell back on the pillow. She felt sick. What was wrong with her? She put up her hands to her head. She wasn't going to have the fever? . . . No. No. It was the long night lying thinking of that woman and her curses. She couldn't face her. She couldn't.

She called out, "Margaret! Margaret!"

A moment later Margaret was standing by her side saying, "What is it, dear?"

"I don't feel well, Margaret. I have a headache, and I feel sick."

"It's all the worry. You stay in bed this morning. You need rest anyway. It's a wonder you've stood up to it this long with what you've been through." She tucked the clothes around her.

"Margaret. I . . . I want her to go today."

"Yes, I know you do, dear. Leave it to me. I've been thinking about it. I'll make the arrangements. She certainly can't go by carrier cart so I thought of sending Tessie down and asking Mr Buckman if he would allow Bill or Stan to bring your cart and drive her over to her sister's."

"Yes, yes, Margaret, that's a good idea. And" – she put her hand out – "tell her . . . tell her that when she gets settled in a cottage of her own – " She drew in a deep breath and paused before she went on, "Tell her she can have her own bed and

294

bedding and some cutlery, and the easy chair and the small table from the kitchen, and a mat or two, and . . . and her ornaments and any trinkets she wants. Tell her . . . tell her that."

Margaret now squeezed her hand and smiled as she said, "Yes, I will, dear; I'll tell her."

"And . . . and Margaret, tell her to go to Mr Ransome, the solicitor in Allendale and . . . and he'll give her the sum of money I promised as soon as it's possible. She'll have to sign for it there. If . . . if I was giving it to her in sovereigns there would be no proof but that I had turned her out penniless. But anyway the money must be put in the care of the bank first."

"Yes, I'll tell her. Now don't worry, just lie still. Would you like some breakfast?"

"No, thanks, dear. A cup of tea perhaps." . . .

Hannah lay all morning listening to the bustle in the kitchen and every now and again the deep ominous tones of her mother-in-law's voice. It was strange, she thought, that a woman so small should have such a deep, booming voice.

It was towards noon when the commotion in the kitchen seemed to intensify, and Hannah actually jumped in the bed when there came three loud bangs on the bedroom door and Mrs Loam's voice followed, crying, "You'll regret this day, me girl. I'll turn the whole countryside against you; you won't be able to lift up your head in the town. An' I'll curse you till the day I die."

"Mrs Loam! Mrs Loam! please. Come, the cart is waiting."

The voices died away. She lay taut on the bed listening to the footsteps going down the stairs, then the shop door opening.

She didn't hear the door close for some time and in the interval she seemed to hold her breath; then when finally she heard the distant click she sank back into the bed. She was sweating profusely. It was over. It was over. Dear God, could she believe it. That woman had gone . . . that creature had gone.

She now turned her head slowly to the side and her tears swamped her face and rained into the pillow. . . .

She was in bed for a week. Doctor Arnison said it was reaction and all she needed was rest and care.

And she was getting the latter in abundance for Margaret seemed to take pleasure in fussing over her. She had just tucked the clothes about her and had straightened the top sheet over the quilt; and now, sprinkling some eau-de-cologne on to a lawn handkerchief, she pressed it into the cuff of Hannah's nightgown as she said, "We've had three callers already today asking how you are. And Mrs Ramsey left a jar of pickles."

"Mrs Ramsey?" Hannah's eyes opened wide. "You mean the Mrs Ramsey from the other end of the street?"

"Yes, yes, that Mrs Ramsey."

"And one of the Nicholson boys from the pit cottages called and left a cabbage." Margaret laughed outright here. "He was very funny. He said his ma had told his da to cut the biggest in the plot, and he said his ma sent a message to say she wished you well. Then Mrs Buckman called and left a pie. She wanted to come up and see you but I said you weren't quite well enough yet, but in a day or two you'd be very pleased to have a visit from her."

"She wanted to come up and see me?" Hannah's eyes stretched wide.

"Yes, yes, she did. Of course, the gift of the pie didn't please Bella because she considers Mrs Buckman a very poor cook."

Her mother-in-law had prophesied that she would turn the village and the whole countryside against her. Well, the curse didn't seem to be working, it was comforting in a way, but only in a way, a small way. . . .

It was about two o'clock in the afternoon when she heard the knocking on the front door, and then the sound of voices below in the shop followed by the tread of heavy feet on the stairs. It wasn't the doctor, he had called earlier. Margaret was bringing someone up.

When the bedroom door opened Margaret stood there, her face smiling gently as she said, "Here's a visitor for you, Hannah."

She raised her head from the pillows and waited. The visitor seemed a long time putting in an appearance; then, walking with the aid of a stick, there came through the doorway a man she hardly recognized.

"N . . . ed!" The name was drawn in a thin whisper through her lips as she pulled herself into a sitting position and stared up into the face now hanging over her. It was his face, Ned's face, but not as she had ever seen it before. She found her mind playing strange tricks with her. It was working out his age. He was twenty-nine years old, at least he should be, but the face that was looking at her seemed to be that of a man twice that age because there was no flesh left on it, the cheeks looked hollow, the skin drawn tight over the bones was pale, almost like that of a woman's. Ned's skin had been brown and ruddy, hard looking, like hide.

"Well, have you nothin' to say to me?"

She closed her eyes tightly, gulped in her throat, drooped her head for a moment, then took a deep breath. It was Ned's voice; that hadn't changed. This was Ned . . . *Ned*. She thrust up her arms and when she flung them round his neck he stumbled and had to support himself on the bed as he said, "Now hie up! Hie up! You want me in there with you?"

When Margaret pushed a chair behind him, he turned and, groping for it, sat down and, looking up at Margaret, he said, "Thanks."

"Would you like a cup of tea, Ned?"

"That would be very nice, very nice, thanks."

When the door closed on Margaret they looked at each other; then, their hands linked tightly, they continued to stare until Ned said, "I . . . I didn't know till this mornin' you were bad. He kept saying you were all right . . . Doctor Arnison. An' not to worry, you'd be along to see me shortly now that the fever scare was over. I . . . I wondered what was keeping you. . . . Where is he?"

"Other side of the bed." She pointed; and now he rose stiffly to his feet and went round the foot of the bed, and there, bending over the basket, he stared down on the child for some time before slanting his eyes in Hannah's direction saying, "Can't see any resemblance to me in him."

"It's inside; outside I'm told he takes after his mother."

"That's good enough for me."

Again he looked down on the child before turning away and coming back to her side again.

"Oh Ned! Ned!" She hitched herself nearer the edge of the bed and him. Again her arms went up; and now his went around her, and he held her tightly but didn't kiss her.

After a moment he pulled away, straightened up, and said

297

thickly, "I've been kept well informed of all you've been up to."

"Doctor Arnison?"

"Aye. But he only told me what he thought was good for me. The real news I got through Big Dick. He tells me that there were some wanted to hang flags out for you the way you've handled the old girl. Funny, isn't it, that you've had to have dealings with the two most hated women in the district. You know something?" He bent towards her. "Daisy Loam was really feared by half the villagers, and not a few in the town either. Some were afraid of her tongue, others thought she had an evil eye an' that nothing could down her. But . . . but apparently – " He moved his head slowly and there was the old grin on his taut features as he ended, "They hadn't reckoned with Hannah Boyle."

She didn't answer the smile on his face but said sadly, "I could never have downed her, Ned. It was just the simple fact that Fred left no will, and that the child was born before he died, otherwise I doubt if I'd be here this minute."

"Well, in that case you would have been some place else, wouldn't you?"

He had been smiling, but now his whole expression changed and he was silent for a moment before he said, "We've got to talk, Hannah. That's what I've come about really. Things have changed all round. By! they have that. And, well, you're a woman of property now and not short of a bob or two, and as I understand it with ideas an' all of what you're going to turn this place into. Now me." He spread his good hand wide. "Well, to put it plainly, Hannah, I'm not the man I was. His boots didn't only kick the daylights out of me, they kicked something else. What it is, well, I don't know, I can't put a name to it, but it's as if he's dampened down the fires in me an' all."

"Oh! Ned. Ned." She was gripping his hands and pulling him to her breast.

"No, no; listen to me, Hannah. Listen me out." He pressed her from him. "It'll be some time afore I can sit a horse again. Sitting a horse is me business, so as I see it, although I'll likely get along on me own, I cannot see meself providing for a wife an' family for some time to come an' . . . an' – " He held up his hand quickly now and, his voice harsh, he went on, "Hear me out, I say." Then

298

after a pause he went on, "There's one thing I don't feel inclined to do, an' that's live on Fred Loam's earnin's. You, yourself, you've got a right to them; as I see it you've worked for them, suffered for them; but in my case, well, it's different. If I have a wife an' bairns I want to support them."

"Ned. Ned, listen to me." She was shaking his hand. "I don't want the money, the house, or anything in it, all I want is you. All I want is to be near you, to live in the Pele house. Oh yes, to live in the Pele house. That is my home, the Pele house. The only time I ever felt at home as a child was in that house. And another thing, Ned. You'll grow well and strong again; it'll be impossible not to, being you. But you know something? If you had come in that door without arms or legs, well, to me you'd still be a better man, a bigger man, than any I've ever met in my life."

She looked at his bowed head. Even his black hair had lost its lustre. She bent forward and buried her face in it. Then their arms were again entwined. And now their lips were close, clinging hungrily. But after a moment he pulled himself away from her, twisted round in the chair and, turning his head still further from her, he bowed it.

She had never thought in her life to see Ned cry. She could well imagine him being deeply moved, sad, and if his sadness should be caused through injustice then it would show in anger. But she had never imagined him being reduced to tears. She reached out and brought him gently around to her again; and now she soothed him, saying, "Don't. Don't, my dear, don't. Oh, dearest Ned, don't be upset." . . . Strange, she hadn't used that term to him before. She had told him she loved him, but she had never used such an endearment on him. Now she poured endearments over him, murmuring and stroking his hair, and he remained still in her arms until the sound of laughter coming from the kitchen brought him upwards, and after rubbing his face with his red handkerchief he blew his nose and muttered, "You see, you see what the great Ned, the big fella Ridley has been reduced to? Bubbling."

Softly now she said, "I'll . . . I'll be with you in a day or two."

"No, no." He shook his head. "There's . . . there's a lot of talking to be done." He paused now as he glanced sideways at her, and again making reference to the child, he said, "And you've got to look after him."

"I'll look after both of you."

"Well, we'll see later on."

"Don't talk like that, Ned. Look, if you keep on so you'll make me believe in that woman's curses. Do you know she cursed me before she left and said she would pray each day for me to be brought low? Oh, and much more."

"Well, you can laugh at that."

"I hope I can, Ned, I hope I can. But it will depend upon you in the end. In the end it will all depend upon you."

He took out his watch now and said, "I'll have to be on me way. Dick said half an hour. He dropped me off at the end of the village; he was taking a load of wood to Paterson's."

"Oh, won't you stay and have a meal? Oh" – she put her hands out towards him, her disappointment showing in her face and voice – "I'm sure they're getting something ready."

"Another time, Hannah, another time." He pulled himself to his feet, and now he seemed to back from her, and she leaned further forward in the bed, beseeching, "Don't go like this, Ned, please. You'll leave me distraught. Come here."

He now leant over and, taking her face gently in one hand, he kissed her on the lips; then picking up his stick that was leaning against the bed, he turned away.

"Ned! Ned, wait." There was anguish in her plea. "Are you still with the Dickinsons? I must know."

He half turned towards her but didn't look at her as he replied quietly, "No, I'm back in the house and managing fine. Nell has seen to everything for me." And on this he went slowly from the room.

When the door closed on him she fell back in the bed and covered her face with her hands and whimpered through her fingers, "Oh Ned! Ned! I've lost you. I've lost you. What is the matter with me? There is a curse on me. There must be. They're right. They're right."

The next minute she was sitting bolt upright in the bed. No! no! She wouldn't let this happen, not this thing that was a matter of life and death to her, because without Ned she really wouldn't want to go on living, she would finish it and take the child with her. And Mrs Loam would have triumphed.

"Margaret! Margaret!" She found herself yelling at the top of her voice.

"Yes, dear? What is it?"

"Close the door."

Margaret closed the door and came hastily to the bed.

"Sit down."

Margaret sat down and listened wide-eyed and open-mouthed as Hannah gabbled at her, "He won't have me; he's pushing me off because . . . because I've got the house and Fred's money. He won't live on Fred's money, and he thinks he'll never be well enough to earn enough to keep us. Margaret – " She wagged her head frantically now and gathered spittle into her mouth, then almost choked on her words as she went on, "Margaret, I don't give a damn about the money, the house, anything, all I want is to be near Ned. Do you understand? Do you understand?"

"Yes, dear, yes, dear; but please don't get so excited."

"Excited! Margaret. I'm going after him, today . . . now!"

"Oh, my dear. . . . No! no! That would be madness."

"Madness or not I'm going. . . . Listen. Go now, right now, and tell Tessie to go down to Mr Buckman's again and ask him if he'll do me the service of letting Stan or Bill take me and the child up to the Pele house."

"Hannah . . . Hannah, you mustn't get so excited."

"I'm not excited, Margaret. I know what I'm doing, it's now or never. This is important to me. It means life to me. Yes, just that, because if I don't have Ned I'll want nothing from life, and it won't be worth going on with. I've gone through too much to let this chance of happiness slide through my fingers for the matter of pride. Will you tell Tessie, or shall I call her?"

Margaret rose from the bed, went out and gave the order to Tessie; then coming back, she resumed her seat and Hannah, now taking hold of her hand, said, "This is what I'm going to do, Margaret. Now listen carefully and don't interrupt. I'm going straight up to the Pele house and I'm going to stay there, but when I'm gone I want you to go to the Reverend Crewe and ask him if he will call on us at his convenience with regard to putting up the banns. Don't look like that, Margaret. I know Fred's hardly cold, but that doesn't matter to me. I know there'll be talk, but that doesn't matter to me either; nothing matters, only that I shall be legally married to Ned, that I know he'll be mine and I his. Now for another important part, and don't say a word. Now I'm telling you, don't say one word while I'm speaking. I'm going into Allendale to the solicitor's as soon as possible and I'm going to transfer what money is coming to me to you." She now shook Margaret's hands that were jerking between her palms and she repeated, "What money is coming to me . . . to you, and it won't be all that much if they don't take the hundred pounds that I promised to that she devil out of Matthew's inheritance. But there will be a condition. I shall ask you to make a will that should you die, which God prevent you don't until you are a very, very old woman, but should it happen, then the monies and what has been made out of the business shall revert to me or my husband, or children. It's funny." She shook her head now from side to side. "It's as if I'd been planning this in my mind for weeks, it's all so very clear. Anyway, it will all be stated in writing – done legally. Oh, and also provision for Bella and Tessie in their old age. But we'll have to go into all this with Mr Ransome. I'm just giving you a rough idea. . . . Open your eyes, Margaret, and look at me."

Margaret opened her eyes and said quietly, "I cannot accept this amazing offer, Hannah; it will be quite impossible for me to accept it."

"If you love me and want my happiness you'll do as I ask."

"I can't, because it's too much. And you may live to be sorry for your generosity. Ned feels like this now but he'll change, and when he's stronger he'll see sense."

"Not Ned. No; I know Ned, he's all men rolled into one in that he must be master; when it comes to his pride being touched, the pride of the breadwinner to support a wife and family, he must be master. No, I know Ned."

"What can I say?"

"Nothing, only do as I ask. You are my friend, my very, very dear friend, my sister . . . yes, my sister. No one else could do this for me but you."

"But . . . but there must be some provision made for you, a safeguard, like a share in the business or something. I couldn't take it wholesalely."

"Well, we'll go into that, dear, only let me be able to go up there and say that I'm passing it on to you."

"And he will call you a fool."

"Not him. Oh, not him, Margaret. He'll look at me steadily; he'll take me in his arms and he'll say, 'Hannah. Hannah Boyle.' "

"Help me now to get dressed, then pack up a couple of bundles for me, and the child. Some warm clothing and night attire; we'll see to the rest later."

"Will . . . will the place be aired?"

"Yes, yes; Mrs Dickinson's seen to everything. He's back there living on his own." . . .

It was just half an hour later when Hannah went back into the bedroom and closed the door behind her. She wanted, she told herself, to look round this room for the last time, this room that had represented nights of purgatory and hell to her; this room that had witnessed her entry into womanhood, a slow painful awakening, that had flung romance away as a thing of dreams and brought her face to face with the realities of life.

She looked towards the side table whereon lay her mother-in-law's Bible. She had forgotten to take that with her. At one stage of Fred's illness she had brought it in and read a passage from it and left it there.

That a woman so vicious could imagine that God was on her side would always remain a great puzzle to her. She walked towards the table now and picked up the book. It fell open at a page wherein lay a piece of folded newspaper, one of the hundreds of squares that she herself had cut for Fred's use after using the chamber. She lifted the paper out with her finger and thumb as if it were already soiled. Then she noticed something different about it; it had writing scrawled across it, but it was almost illegible against the close black print. She put her head to one side and narrowed her eyes as she endeavoured to read the writing. Then going to the window, she held it at an angle to enable her to make out the pencilled words, and after a few moments this is what she read:

"I'm feeling very bad. If I am to go I want me mother to have everything. And it's up to her what she does for the other one.
Fred Loam."

Hannah turned her eyes from the scrawled writing, and looked out of the window, and not until she drew a sharp breath into her lungs did she realize that her mouth was wide open. Like a stone now she sat down on the edge of the bed. This was a will, but there were no witnesses to it. Would it stand up in court? Maybe. And if it did it would make the way plain for her, she could go to Ned without any fuss. She'd be penniless, thrown out on to the world because Mrs Loam would not of her charity give her a hundred pounds. Nor would she support the child. Oh no, not Mrs Loam unless it was under her care. . . .

But then what would happen to Margaret, Bella, and Tessie? That woman would throw them out on to the street and praise the Lord while she was doing it. Bella and Tessie would be bonded again and used as drudges for a pittance. . . . And Margaret. What would become of Margaret? Her lot would be even worse than theirs; the mere fact of her being refined would make her suffering more intense.

She turned her head in the direction of the chatter coming from the kitchen. They were all so happy together; they were a family.

The door opened and Margaret said, "Well, dear?"

She stared at Margaret, not speaking, and Margaret came towards her, saying, "What is it? What's wrong?"

"Oh. Oh" – she shook her head and blinked – "nothing. Nothing. I . . . I was just looking at that." She pointed towards the Bible on the table. "Mrs Loam forgot to take it with her; she'll likely want it when she comes for the things."

"Well, she'll certainly have it, my dear, and I hope it will do her some good. What is that?" She pointed to the piece of paper Hannah was holding, and Hannah, screwing the square tightly up into her fist, said, "Oh, nothing, nothing; only one of the hundreds of squares I had to cut up." She walked swiftly from the room and into the kitchen and, standing before the fire, she hesitated a moment before stretching her hand out and dropping the paper into the flames; then turning towards the three faces looking at her, she held out her arms, and they all came into them and entwined her in their embraces.

Her laughter was a little hysterical as she said, "You'd think I was going miles away. I'll be down here every day. Don't you forget that, Bella. I'll be down for my buns and I want plenty of currants in them."

"There's the cart."

Bella and Tessie, picking up the bundles and Margaret's bass hamper, ran on ahead down the stairs, while Hannah and Margaret stood looking at each other for a moment before Margaret picked up the basket with the child in it, and Hannah said quietly, "Don't worry if I'm not down for a day or two. But if you shouldn't see me for three or four days bring me up some nice things to eat."

"Oh! my dear."

"Now, now, stop it, Margaret."

Hannah turned from her and went down the stairs, through the shop and into the street, and there Stan Buckman looked at her from under his brows, touched his cap and said, "Nice to see you out again, missis."

She paused a moment and smiled at him. He hadn't called her Mrs Loam or Hannah, but he had given her the title of missis, and so she said, "Thank you, Stan. It's nice to be out."

He now almost lifted her up into the front seat of the cart, tucked an old rug round her, then took the basket from Margaret and put it on the floor at Hannah's feet before taking his place behind the horse and shouting, "Gee up there!"

As the horse trotted off, Hannah turned and waved to the three standing by the door.

But they weren't the only ones standing by their doors. It was as if the word had gone round the village that *she* was off some place; and they knew this some place, for not a couple of hours ago hadn't Ned Ridley been to visit her? Well, well! some people were laws unto themselves. And when all was said and done it really was indecent for she was hardly out of childbed, and her man hardly cold.

Those who thought along these lines didn't wave to her, they just stared, but a few others called a greeting from their doors.

And towards these she inclined her head, but gave them no reply.

Twenty minutes later the cart went through the opening in the wall and drew up opposite the open door of the stable-room, and when Stan had lifted her to the ground and handed down to her the basket, she said, "Just drop the bundles to the side of the door, Stan."

After Stan had done this, she put down the basket again and from her purse brought out a half sovereign and said, "I would like you and Bill and your father to have a drink on me in return for your kindness to the horse." She smiled as she nodded towards the animal, and Stan looked at the golden piece in his hand for a moment; then, a broad grin on his face, he said, "And we'll do that certainly. Aye, we will, missis. And what's more" – he leant towards her – "we'll drink to your future. And may it be bright for a change."

"I'm sure it will, Stan. Thank you."

"Good-bye, missis. Be seein' you down yonder."

"Good-bye, Stan."

She watched the horse turn the cart around and go towards the opening before she picked up the basket again and went through the door.

She knew that Ned must have heard the cart but he had made no effort to come out. He was standing just in front of the opening to the kitchen. It was as if nothing had happened. She was a young girl of fourteen, fifteen, sixteen, seventeen, coming into the Pele house to see Ned Ridley, and he was always either coming down the ladder or coming out of the kitchen, except, of course, when he was tight and lying on the platform sleeping it off.

He made no move towards her and she walked over the stone floor, but stopped a few arm lengths from him and, laying down the basket once again but on a bale of straw now, she said quietly, "Well! here I am. I haven't any money and my possessions are outside the door. I've given all that Fred left to Margaret. We're going into the solicitor's in a day or two to have it signed and sealed. She's agreed, so what do you say?"

She watched his face lengthen, she saw his jaw drop, she saw it snap closed and his lips press tight together; then his head hung down for a moment deep on his breast before he walked towards her. And his head was still down when his arms went about her and, his voice thick, his words choked, he muttered, "Oh Hannah! Hannah Boyle!"

He was kissing her, kissing her as he had done on that particular day when they came together for the first time; he was kissing her as if he were drawing strength from her body; he was kissing her as if he never meant to stop; and although she was feeling faint and weak on her legs she didn't beg him to stop. This was Ned Ridley, alive and vital still behind his scarred body, so vital was his love for her that it was like a smelting mill that would reduce to ashes her mother-in-law's curses and evil wishes for her, and at the same time dredge the dross and the dirt from their lives and leave only the worthwhile lead and a sprinkling of silver.

He sealed her happiness when, pushing her bonnet back, his lips went into her hair and he muttered, "Oh! Woman. Woman. There's not another like you in the wide world."

Woman, he had called her. *The Girl* was gone, buried in the past. She never wanted to hear that name again. She was a woman for better for worse. Whatever the future might bring she could face it as a woman, Ned Ridley's woman.

CM